W9-AJU-405

Major publications by Theodore Dreiser

Novels

Sister Carrie (1900)
Jennie Gerhardt (1911)
The Financier (1912)
The Titan (1914)
The "Genius" (1915)
An American Tragedy (1925)
The Bulwark (1946)

Stories

Free and Other Stories (1918)
Twelve Men (1919)
Chains (1927)
A Gallery of Women (1929)

Autobiography

A Book About Myself (1923)
Dawn (1931)
American Diaries 1902–1926 (1982)
An Amateur Laborer (1983)
Newspaper Days (1991)

Miscellaneous

A Traveler at Forty (1913)
A Hoosier Holiday (1916)
Plays of the Natural and Supernatural (1916)
The Hand of the Potter (1918)
Hey Rub A Dub Dub (1920)
The Color of a Great City (1923)
Moods, Cadenced and Declaimed (1926)
Dreiser Looks at Russia (1928)
Tragic America (1931)
America Is Worth Saving (1941)
"Heard in the Corridors" Articles and Related Writings by
        Theodore Dreiser (1988)
Theodore Dreiser Journalism, Vol. 1: Newspaper Writings
        1892–1895 (1988)

THEODORE DREISER

FULFILMENT AND OTHER TALES OF WOMEN AND MEN

COLLECTED AND EDITED
BY T.D. NOSTWICH

BLACK SPARROW PRESS
SANTA ROSA · 1992

LIBRARY OF CONGRESS CATALOGING-IN-PUBLICATION DATA

Dreiser, Theodore, 1871-1945.
    Fulfilment & other tales of women & men / Theodore Dreiser ;
collected and edited by T. D. Nostwich.
        p.   cm.
    Includes bibliographical references (p. 385).
    ISBN 0-87685-882-5 (cloth) : — ISBN 0-87685-883-3 (deluxe cloth) :
— ISBN 0-87685-881-7 (pbk.) :
    I. Nostwich, T. D., 1925-   . II. Title. III. Title: Fulfilment and other tales
of women and men.
PS3507.R55A6   1992
813'.52—dc20   92-25060
                                                                   CIP

Table of Contents

Introduction

*A*PART FROM THE FACT that he was a genius, the most important thing to know about Theodore Dreiser is that he was born poor, on the wrong side of the tracks, and early learned that middleclass Americans looked upon him and his family as outsiders; and that, because of this painful recognition, he felt compelled—at least till the late 1920s when he had become famous and wealthy—to prove that he was as good as society's "insiders." The need for self-vindication explains in large part what drove him to create out of the experience of living in America a fiction marked by a compassionate understanding of life's rejects and failures, and a sympathy for those who burn with desire for more love, wealth, and power than life can ever provide—a fiction that stands with the greatest of the twentieth century.

Dreiser was born in 1871 in Terre Haute, Indiana, the next to youngest in a brood of five boys and five girls. His father, an emigrant from the Rhineland, a weaver by trade, an obviously intelligent though rigidly pious man, was the victim of a run of bad business luck, beginning soon after Theodore's birth, that broke his spirit and left him virtually destitute for the rest of his life. Dreiser's mother, the uneducated daughter of an Ohio farmer, naturally warm-hearted, sympathetic and loving, was the impoverished family's emotional center, the one to whom the children always turned for solace and encouragement. In his writings Dreiser never mentions her with anything but adoration.

Dreiser's boyhood, spent mostly in rural or small-town Indiana, was a period he remembered in his autobiography *Dawn* as one of mingled privation and pleasure, sadness and joy. Often there was not enough food for the family or money for household expenses, but the boy found excitement and fascination in exploring the world of nature at his doorstep and the world of literature in such books as came his way.

The family was bilingual. Young Dreiser grew up hearing German spoken by his parents, and his earliest education was obtained in parochial schools where the heavily doctrinaire instruction was in that language, a fact which some critics speculate was a formative influence on his literary style. In 1884 when the need to take employment wherever it could be found caused a temporary breakup of the family, the mother moved with her three youngest children—Theodore, his younger brother Ed, and his older sister Claire—to Warsaw, Indiana. Here for the first time he was enrolled in a public school, a great mind-opening experience that not only introduced him to areas of learning previously unknown, but that also began his liberation from the strictures of religious dogma that had dominated his view of himself and the world—a liberation which in time led him to scornfully reject his father's Catholicism and to regard all theological theories of life with skepticism.

At the same time he began to experience the powerful upwelling of sexual hunger that was to endure, for good or ill, through the remainder of his long life. Later, of course, Dreiser would become a pioneering advocate for the honest recognition in American writing of the importance of the sex drive, and he would champion the right and need to treat it explicitly in fiction. For young Dreiser in early puberty, however, this newly awakened yearning simply added to his personal sense of awkwardness and social inadequacy. His family had a bad name, was sometimes disgraced by the drunken public behavior of an older brother and the loose conduct of several older sisters. He himself was homely, clumsy, and ill-schooled in the social graces. In such circumstances some boys might have resigned themselves to being born-to-lose outsiders, fated never to amount to anything. But Dreiser burned with secret pride and was determined that life should serve him better. He felt superior to his circumstances, more so than anyone in Warsaw might guess, although he had little more to encourage him than the faith of his mother and a few teachers who perceived his sensitivity and intelligence.

In the summer of 1887, most of the Dreiser family reunited to try to make of a go of it in Chicago. Here Theodore worked at whatever jobs an untrained youth might then find available—as dishwasher in a Greek restaurant and as stockboy in a wholesale hardware house—until in 1889 he was sought out by Mildred Fielding, a former Warsaw teacher, mindful of the promise she had seen in him, who generously offered to send him to Indiana University for a year. Dreiser eagerly grasped this opportunity and spent the school year 1889-90 sampling the wares of that institution. But here again, despite a fair degree of academic success, he was oppressed by his poverty and sense of social inferiority, made all the more intense when he compared himself to sophisticated, well-to-do classmates—young collegians who excelled in athletics and were accomplished wooers of the breathtakingly beautiful girls Dreiser himself ached to possess. Concluding sadly that he must make his way in some other kind of world, he declined Mildred Fielding's offer of support for a second year and returned to Chicago in June of 1890. What followed was another round of dead-end jobs—as driver of a laundry pickup-and-delivery wagon, as harum-scarum real estate agent, as collector of installment payments for a household furnishings firm.

In November the sudden death of his mother shattered the family. For about a year afterwards the little group tried to keep together, but rivalries between the older sisters and rancorous disagreements over household duties inevitably led to a breakup. Dreiser, his sister Claire and brother Ed tried to live together on a share-the-expense basis for a while, but the experiment soon failed and Dreiser was left to make his own way.

Stimulated by an admiration for the daily columns of the famous Chicago journalist Eugene Field, Dreiser began to eye the career of a reporter, attracted by its apparent glamor and the possibility it seemed to offer of opening doors to higher worlds. After trying repeatedly to get a berth on the city's leading newspapers and being routinely turned down for utter lack of experience, he landed a temporary job on a third-rate daily, the *Globe*. Here through the summer of 1892 he showed enough skill at newsgathering and writing feature articles to attract the attention of the prestigious St. Louis *Globe-Democrat*—then one of the best newspapers in the Midwest—which offered him a permanent job. After six months of good work done here, he moved on to a rival newspaper, the *Republic,* where he became a star reporter. From there in early spring of 1894 he set out for the

East, hoping to find a job on a paper in New York, the Mecca of all ambitious newsmen in the 1890s. And, indeed, following brief hitches on papers in Toledo, Cleveland, and Pittsburgh, he was at last taken on as a lowly space-rate reporter by Joseph Pulitzer's New York *World,* reputedly the greatest paper of the day. But here in the bitter winter of 1895 his reportorial career came to a permanent end when he recognized that his talents were little valued at this dynamic daily, and that, anyway, they were not really suited for this kind of work out of which he was just barely scraping a living.

He next gave some thought to becoming a writer of magazine fiction. But a cursory examination of stories in the day's leading publications left him in despair because the life they pictured in no way resembled that which his destitute childhood and his newspaper experiences had exposed him to.

> Love was almost invariably rewarded in these tales. . . . Almost invariably dreams came true—in the magazines. Most of these bits of fiction, delicately phrased and colorfully spun, flowed so easily, with such an air of assurance . . . that I was quite put out by my own lacks and defects. . . . in the main they seemed to deal with phases of sweetness and beauty and success and goodness such as I rarely if ever encountered anywhere.
>
> (*Newspaper Days,* p. 657)

Convinced that he simply did not have it in him to cook up such trite happy-ending confections, he turned to the writing of non-fiction. Over the next five years—which included a two-year stint as editor of a magazine put out by the music-publishing house of his older brother Paul, a successful songwriter—he supported himself as a freelance writer of feature articles.

In December 1898, following a prolonged engagement, he married Sara White, a Missouri schoolteacher whom he had met while a reporter for the St. Louis *Republic.* In 1914, however, their union ended in a permanent separation (though not a divorce) owing to irreconcilable differences in temperament and to Dreiser's chronic inability to remain faithful to one woman.

In the summer of 1899, at the persistent urging of Arthur Henry, a close friend, Dreiser made a stab at writing some

10

fiction. A few short stories were the result, and then in a burst of creativity he wrote his first novel, *Sister Carrie* (published in 1900), a work which has come to be regarded as a great classic of realistic fiction. In it, Dreiser drew on the troubled life of one of his own sisters, who in her youth ran away with an older married man to New York where she endured nearly a decade of unhappiness before finally parting from him. In his novel Dreiser transmutes his sister's experiences into a compelling tale about a pretty, naive, young country girl who becomes a popular Broadway actress after having been spirited away to New York by her lover, Hurstwood. What gives *Sister Carrie* its powerful dramatic impact and tragic validity is Dreiser's totally convincing account of Hurstwood's steady descent from prosperous middleclass respectability to the miserable lot of a skid row panhandler and finally to suicide in a Bowery flophouse.

While in this first novel Dreiser's genius is clearly and unmistakably manifested, the book's publication was attended by great difficulties. How it met with opposition and critical hostility is one of the more familiar episodes of American literary history and need not be gone over in detail here. Suffice it to say that after accepting the novel, Dreiser's publisher, Doubleday, Page, sought to get out of its contract, having developed misgivings about issuing such an unvarnished story that failed to condemn its characters for immoral conduct. When Dreiser refused to acquiesce, Doubleday, Page went ahead and met the letter of its contractual obligation. It published the book but did not advertise it or send it out to reviewers. As a result the first edition of *Sister Carrie* sold fewer than five hundred copies, and Dreiser, who had by now invested all his hopes in its success, fell into a state of depression that endured for some two years, so deep at times that he even contemplated suicide. Despite this cruel setback, the writing of *Sister Carrie* had once and for all settled for him the question of what his calling was to be. Though in the next dozen or so years he had to support himself by various editorial jobs, he could never have doubted that his true vocation was to write novels.

Fewer than ten years after its first publication *Sister Carrie* was re-issued by another publisher, this time to comparative critical acclaim. It began to find an audience of perceptive readers who could appreciate a novelist with the courage to write truthfully about the unpleasant sides of life. In 1911 appeared Dreiser's second novel, *Jennie Gerhardt*. Suggested in part by the experiences of another sister, this is a touching story about the daughter of a poor emigrant German family who sacrifices her respectability for the love of a wealthy man whose mistress she becomes and whom she eventually gives up so that he can claim his inheritance and marry a woman of his own class. Not as harrowing as *Sister Carrie,* this novel still is memorable for its convincing characterization and compelling plot. Though some readers have objected to touches of sentimentality in it, after more than eighty years its factual honesty and emotional truth still have the power to convince and move.

In 1912 and 1914 Dreiser published *The Financier* and *The Titan,* two novels of a projected "Trilogy of Desire" detailing the life history of a representative nineteenth-century American capitalist and empire builder. Using the personality and career of Chicago traction magnate Charles T. Yerkes as a model, Dreiser forged in his hero, Frank A. Cowperwood, an amalgam of the obsession with wealth and power of a typical "Gilded Age" tycoon and of his own personal hunger for the beautiful, both feminine and artistic. These two novels carry Cowperwood from childhood through mid-life to the crest of his powers. Together they constitute probably the most definitive fictional portrait of the big businessman in American literature. (Unfortunately Dreiser was never able to bring his full genius to bear on the concluding volume of this trilogy. The story of Cowperwood's decline and death is told in skeletal summary in *The Stoic,* posthumously published in 1947 after being patched together in Dreiser's last years when, regrettably, his inspiration and creative energy were nearly exhausted.)

Dreiser's next published novel, *The "Genius,"* appeared in 1915. Like most of his fiction, this long work hews to historic fact, in this case that of his own life. Its protagonist, Eugene Witla, is a gifted realistic painter. Hailing from the Midwest, he achieves a measure of recognition in New York, gains wealth and prestige as a magazine editor, but sees his marriage turn sour when he falls deliriously in love with a much younger woman. As thinly concealed autobiography *The "Genius"* is a most interesting work.

It seems obviously to have been written out of Dreiser's personal need to examine, explain, and justify the circumstances of his failed marriage.

The *"Genius"* occupies a significant place in American literary history, for in 1916 the New York Society for the Suppression of Vice declared the book obscene because of what it deemed to be sexually suggestive passages, and it forced the skittish publisher to withdraw the book from sale. In a sense, respectable society once again was telling Dreiser that he was not fit company. What followed was a long campaign against the interdiction mounted by his good friend H. L. Mencken, who rallied for support many leading American and British writers. In the early 1920s a compromise was worked out that permitted the book to be sold once again with minimal textual changes. Dreiser suffered anguish and financial loss in this protracted controversy, but the general health of American letters was improved by it through the weakening of the prudish censor's power to dictate what a writer could say.

In 1925, ten years after the first publication of *The "Genius,"* appeared *An American Tragedy*, the novel considered by many to be Dreiser's masterpiece. Based again on an actual case history, it tells the story of a poor but ambitious young man who, just on the verge of gaining entry into upper-class society, finds himself threatened by his lower-class sweetheart whom he has made pregnant and who insists that he marry her. Fearing that his social aspirations are about to be thwarted, he plots to murder her. When she dies by accidental drowning, he is indicted for what appears to have been a crime, is found guilty, and is electrocuted. Dreiser's belief was that cases of this sort were characteristic of American society. He had noted quite a few examples of them over the years, and he concluded that they occurred inevitably as the consequence of society's inculcating young men with selfish materialistic values that stimulate a desire for a luxurious life while that same society imposes on them unnaturally restrictive rules of sexual conduct. Such a theme, given the nature of Dreiser's own youth and temperament, must inevitably have had a strong personal significance for him. In unfolding the events and developing the characters of *An American Tragedy*, he employs all the skills of characterization, plotting, and making a story lifelike by amassing details that he had acquired in writing his earlier books. What he succeeds in creating is a novel that for all its length moves steadily with an almost fated inevitability to its tragic conclusion. Told with profound compassion and understanding, *An American Tragedy* is surely one of the saddest but most believable of stories.

Immediately upon its publication it was recognized throughout the world as a masterpiece. Doubts about Dreiser's reputation and the worth of his work that had hung over him from *The "Genius"* scandal were forgotten, and he was now hailed by critics as America's greatest living novelist. *An American Tragedy* became a best seller, and with the royalties from its sale and with the fat check Hollywood paid for its screen rights, he became modestly wealthy. The boy born on the wrong side of the tracks, once dismissed by polite society as a person of no consequence, had come in his mid-fifties to be a figure of international prominence whose reputation preceded him wherever he went and whose opinion on timely questions was sought out and seriously listened to.

On the road to ultimate recognition Dreiser had been a very productive writer. In addition to the major novels that have been mentioned, he wrote and published philosophic essays (many of them gathered in *Hey Rub-a-Dub-Dub*), more than half a dozen plays (most notably *The Hand of the Potter*), two books about travel experiences (*A Traveler at Forty* and *A Hoosier Holiday*), two volumes portraying interesting men and women whose lives had touched his own (*Twelve Men* and *A Gallery of Women*), enough short stories to make two collections (*Free* and *Chains*), a multitude of poems, and two hefty autobiographies (*Dawn* and *Newspaper Days*—deemed by Dreiser's most recent biographer, Richard Lingemann, to be among the most truthful ever written).

Once *An American Tragedy* had secured Dreiser's fame and fortune, however, his creative urge markedly diminished. In the 1930s instead of producing stories he preferred to devote his energies to various socio-political causes to which he felt intense commitment. For example, he supported the striking miners of Harlan County, Kentucky, and those seeking justice for the Scottsboro Boys and for Tom Mooney; he sought relief for the victims of the Spanish Civil War; he urged non-involvement of the United States in the Second World War, and then just as strongly urged involvement in it after Germany's attack on the Soviet Union. Such matters required much energy and time, often

14

involved pamphleteering and lecturing across the country. Little time was left for concentration on imaginative writing. However, the bulk of Dreiser's output stands solid and substantial today. Most of his fiction up to and including *An American Tragedy*— nearly all of it good, much of it incontestably great—is as alive and pertinent as it ever was.

Theodore Dreiser was a born story teller. Though he is remembered primarily for his massive novels, the complete inventory of his writing includes a profusion of short stories. Indeed, his earliest fiction took the form of brief anecdotes written for newspapers, and the short story often seemed to him best suited for the plot ideas his observations of life provided. Despite his frequently quoted statement that to tell his kind of story he needed the novel's vast canvas, the brief tale served him well too.

At their best Dreiser's short stories can move us as his greatest novels do. They have the same capacity to invest commonplace lives with interest and significance. Admittedly they lack the sophisticated innovations of modernist fiction—making little or no use of symbolism, ambiguity, unconventional thematics, flawed points of view—yet their uncomplicated true-to-life plots and their convincing characterization give them great validity. Engagingly direct in narration and feeling, they stand out distinctly from the common run of fiction of their time. How few American short stories of the multitude published in the first three decades of this century have today the vitality of Dreiser's; how few, indeed, retain any life at all. But what his stories have to say about the human situation is as relevant as ever. Nor was their effectiveness achieved by chance. Joseph Griffen, the critic who has commented most perceptively on Dreiser's short fiction, asserts that while his talents were certainly best suited for the long, detailed novel, he still regarded the brief narrative as worthy of his most serious thought and effort, and that he always shaped and reworked his material until he had achieved the effect he desired.

Gathered here are some of Dreiser's best pieces of short fiction and semi-fiction. Most of them are drawn from books long out of print and not found in currently available collections. The term *tales* has been chosen to describe them since it embraces both semi-fiction (the proper classification for those narratives about real individuals drawn from *Twelve Men* and *A Gallery of Women*) and fiction. For a writer like Dreiser the coupling of semi-fiction

15

and fiction is not inappropriate since in all his tales the line between the real and the imagined is always a very thin one. With Dreiser the origin of a story seems usually to have been some actual case history. (In fact, of the pieces included here only for the protagonists of "Fulfilment" and "Sanctuary" have real-life counterparts not yet been identified.)

In choosing items for this volume no criteria other than interest and artistic merit were used. Nevertheless, while consistency of theme was not deliberately sought, at least one skein of meaning runs through and unites nearly all of them. Sad though their stories are, these characters (even, surely, the brilliant, despairing aesthete Mathewson at an earlier time in his life) have in common an intense hunger for life and a desire for the fulfillment of the promises, however humble, life seems to hold out. But one of the great truths Dreiser absorbed from experience and that he asserts over and over again here is that these promises are as often as not only illusions, never to be realized fully. His constant if unvoiced refrain is that the capacity of people to dream always exceeds the willingness of life to deliver. Most of his characters have to learn this lesson. Shirley in "The Second Choice" is a good case in point. Heartbroken over the loss of her dashing lover Arthur, the man of her dreams, she has to choose between marriage to faithful, stolid Bart, the railroad clerk who adores her, or the mediocre life of an old maid—a choice as unappetizing to her as the choice of steak or liver her mother offers her for supper.

Compassionately and pityingly, for a variety of characters in a variety of situations, Dreiser shows us the undeniable truth life had taught him, that (as he says in "The 'Mercy' of God") "circumstances are stronger than personalities, and the impotence of individuals is the tragedy of everyday life." What we hear in these tales, assuredly, is the voice of a man who, as James T. Farrell put it, "spoke with awe and respect of traveling that road of life which is so short, so accompanied with pain."

T. D. Nostwich
Iowa State University
July 1992

16

ACKNOWLEDGMENTS

Acknowledgment is due to Harold J. Dies of the Dreiser Trust who kindly made this book possible.

The editor would like to thank Daniel Traister and Lee Ann Draud of the Dreiser Collection in the Van Pelt-Dietrich Library Center at the University of Pennsylvania for their assistance and courtesy.

For funding that helped make research travel possible, he is indebted to Frank Haggard, former Executive Officer of the Iowa State University English Department.

He would like to express special thanks to his wife Ann Nostwich for her characteristic patience and practical support without which this project could not have been completed.

TEXTUAL NOTES

The copy-texts for the stories reprinted in this edition are as follows:

For "Rella," "Reina," "Ida Hauchawout," and "Bridget Mullanphy," *A Gallery of Women,* published by Horace Liveright in 1929.

For "Peter," " 'Vanity, Vanity' Saith the Preacher," and "Muldoon, the Solid Man," *Twelve Men,* published by Boni & Liveright in 1919. More specifically, the text of the fourth printing of February 1920 has been followed since it incorporates Dreiser's corrections of some of the errors in the first printing.

For "The Second Choice," *Free and Other Stories* published by Boni & Liveright in 1918.

For "Fulfilment," "The 'Mercy' of God," "Chains," and "Sanctuary," *Chains: Lesser Novels and Stories* published by Boni & Liveright in 1927.

For "Mathewson," *Esquire,* May and June 1934.

The texts of "Chains" and "Mathewson" are supplemented
with hitherto unpublished passages drawn from typescripts in the
Dreiser Collection of the University of Pennsylvania, reprinted
courtesy of the Van Pelt-Dietrich Library Center.

● ● ●

Without editorial comment, grammatical and typographical
errors have been corrected, and punctuation and sentence construction have occasionally been revised to prevent misreading.
The few editorial changes of wording made to clarify puzzling
or incoherent passages are recorded in the notes.

● ● ●

Notes begin on page 387.

Fulfilment
&

Other Tales

of Women & Men

Foreword

THIS STORY, "RELLA," INNATELY TRUTHFUL and self-revealing, was outlined to me one evening in Greenwich Village many years ago by an American poet who has since died; and before him by his wife and the girl to whom he referred. Since no names appear, and his quondam fame, as well as name, has dimmed with time, there can be, to me, no conceivable reason why the sketchy transcript I made of it then should not now be enlarged upon according to the mood in which he related it to me.

—The Author

Rella

WHENEVER I THINK of Rella I think of a backwoods state such as Arkansas. Those round knobs and tumbled earthen breakers called the Ozarks; the great fields of wheat and corn and oats amid which her young life was laid; the tumbling, sparkling rill of a stream which ran diagonally across a corner of the large farm owned by her father; and the fine upstanding trees and tumultuous spread of wild flowers all about. Great argosies of woolly clouds sailed the heavens in summer and gave rise to dreams of blue seas and white sails. From the fields came the whirr of the reaper, the call of many farmhands employed for the harvesting, the lowing of cattle and the bleat of sheep.

"Her father, Samuel Howdershell, was a successful farmer as well as a politician of sorts. At least he had contrived to secure from the leaders of his party the position of United States marshal which occupied but a small portion of his time. When he was not able to look after his farm in person, the shrewd and talkative little woman who was his wife, and who obviously liked the world in which she found herself, was there to do it for him. And she did it with a will and with skill, assisted by her two ruddy and vigorous sons, who seemed to look upon her as their guide and mentor. In winter they were away at school, as was the girl about whom I am writing.

"But the air of smartness that went with their apparel in that far-away region—the something of city manners and city tastes! Automobiles were few in those days, but each of the Howdershell children had a riding horse. And the large barn sheltered several polished conveyances as well as the farming machinery which equipped so large a farm; also the immense crops of hay and corn which were reaped from the fields. Indeed, Howdershell had an office in the barn, in which he kept his papers and books, also a typewriter which either his wife or one of the children operated when necessary. Then there were parties and regional affairs of considerable importance to which the ordinary run of native farmers and their folk were not invited but of which the family of a United States marshal was an integral and respected part. In short, these people moved in a busy, genial, sociable world, which at that far-from-happy period in my own life impressed me as particularly blessed and fortunate.

"I was married at the time—presumably happily married. And yet, the truth was that at thirty, and only two years married, I had begun to realize that for me marriage was a mistake. Either mine was not a temperament which lent itself to marriage, or I had erred in selecting the mate with whom it might have proved a success. Being young and far this side of an adequate conception of the mysteries of life and the harsh compulsions of society and the state, which invariably seek to preserve themselves at the expense of the individual, I was at a loss to understand my predicament. Perhaps I was suffering for my early ignorance and folly. But the laws of society were immutable, of course. Once married, always married . . . 'Whom God hath joined together, let no man put asunder.' . . . These and similar decrees and ordinances and injunctions of our derived society haunted me like the voice of fate. From every tree and bush, to say nothing of the ordinary palaver of the home and the street, came voices to say that even the dark whisperings within me were wrong, very wrong; and yet about me, gay with temptation, were youth and love at play. Who would take me by the hand and lead me forth from that slough of despond? Whither—whither—from the great urge within that gave me no rest? Those who know nothing of the love of beauty that walks hand in hand with passion will never understand. To them the mysteries remain the mysteries.

"However, being young, I could not but hope against hope. I had just had a play accepted and was writing poems and stories and getting them published—finding myself, as it were. My wife, as I could plainly see, was pluming herself on the fact that I had a future and that she was to share in it in an interesting way. But, as I often thought, she was entitled, certainly, to all the joy that life might bring her. On the other hand, here was this union which for me could only end in beclouding my life, however much sunshine it might result in for her. Was I to work, work, work,

22

nd share all with one who could only be an annoyance and a weariness to me? And yet, this very thought, at that time, seemed to me the very substance of evil. Ought one not, rather, crucify oneself upon the cross of duty, charity, sympathy? Ought one not? I went about brooding over my lot, wondering almost hourly what was to become of me. And in so doing I could only marvel at this mystery of love. For here was a girl—my wife—as attractive physically as any of those about me—and yet, after two years and for, to me, some almost inexplicable reason, meaning less to me than almost any other. Her ways! I knew them all. Most of her moods and views, apart from her ultra-conventional ones, interested me, but she did not. And this was the same girl who only a year or two before had seemed to me to be the all-desirable. Let him explain who can!

"And yet, because of sympathy for her and self-condemnation for what I considered an unconscionable vagary in myself to which no well-constructed individual would think of giving way, I had in no way indicated my change of mood. And in so far as I could judge, she had no inkling of it. Yet, in spite of this, let any one of her friends—women, the attractive ones, especially—conduct themselves in any but the most formal way about me, and she was off upon a lecture which concerned the compulsions and moral safeguards of the married state. Her chief social desire, apparently, was to know whether the men and women of her circle were morally, and hence socially, sound and pure. And however dull and uninteresting the sound ones might be, they were infinitely to be preferred to those who were not. At least they were good people. To the end of establishing this fact, therefore, she studied all and sundry, with a view to weeding out the unfit.

"And yet, when it came to the world at large, realizing that there were degrees of talent and that by some queer twist of life the morally unsatisfactory too often provided whatever flare and color the visible social scene might have, she was inclined to study the successful and the beautiful, unmoral or what you will, and from them to copy such nuances of style and manner, and thought, even—where it did not conflict with her own convictions—as would serve to heighten her own charm. And by the same token, those who were decidedly moral, but at the same time not smart and not so well-placed socially or financially as some others, were not, apart from certain safe contacts she was inclined to court, likely to attract her interest. This self-protective cleverness, however admirable it might appear to some, did little more than puzzle and at times irritate me. Her idea, as I was beginning to see—or thought I was—was to strengthen herself by such arts as these evil ones might suggest without at the same time contaminating herself or her blissful married state.

"But all the while I was miserably restless and unhappy, and daily becoming more so, constantly contemplating in my mind's eye what I considered to be the happier love states of others. And envying them their bliss. Oh, youth, youth, youth! Beauty! The scorching lure of it! Without the favor of some gloriously beautiful girl, as I reasoned, I might as well be dead! But at the same time I was convinced that being married, no woman, young or old, good, bad or indifferent, would have anything to do with me! Least of all one such as at this time could have filled the frame of my fancy. Had I been more assured—less convinced of my own conclusion—some rather obvious indications or proofs to the contrary might have swayed me—but I was not.

"It was June of a lovely summer that found us visiting my wife's relatives in D———, a town situated in one of those great states which adjoin Arkansas and the region pictured. Previous to this I had met nearly all my wife's people, and had liked them—as I still do. They were a pleasant, home-loving, if very conventional, company, all rather respected for their honesty, industry, and all those other admirable virtues which constitute in society its most sustaining and binding threads. Nearly all of them were well-to-do, interested in trade, banking, or farming, and all intensely interested in each other, at least to the extent of wishing to see that none fell below the ideals or standards of the group or class to which all belonged. As for ourselves, we were welcomed as peculiarly worthy examples of the social code they represented and the success for which they all strove.

"The region in which they lived was not unappealing to me, even at first glance, although it was of that dead levelness that characterizes so much of the land west and east of the Mississippi. At longish intervals were those small grayish-white, humdrum, wooden towns, with their Main Street, their one or two church steeples, their few stores, and their straggly and not too often tree-shaded residence streets so characteristic of the then only partially formed America. The town, a part of which they were, numbered about fifteen hundred people, all of the same workaday, small-town type. The particular house which my wife's parents occupied was a simple, low, eight- or ten-room affair, standing at the extreme end of a street, the last house but one. (This other home, by the way, was occupied by another son-in-law, of some prominence in the local political world.) No pretense of show or luxury was there. The automobile had already arrived in some places, to be sure, but not here. In its stead were horses, buggies, wagons and the dreadful dirt roads that went with them. Cows, pigs, chickens, and geese were the usual equipment of all sturdy homes, even the most successful. To west and east and south stretched the level prairie with here and there a house, or a tree, or a barn, but mainly a flat, unobstructed sunbaked world. Behold the fields! They were either deep and green with swaying, rustling corn, or faintly yellowing with wheat. Such trees as there were stood out ragged and lorn against a wealth of sky. A single-track railroad carried the trains of a great trunk line, but few of the trains stopped here. Farmers and strangers trailed in and out of town in buggies, wagons, or on horseback, always offering a genial 'Howdy?'

"I confess that in this seemly world—being an aspirant at letters, not trade—I at first felt a little out of place. Later, due to my real liking for these people, I felt much at home. Perhaps because I offered a sharp contrast to most of the other sons-in-law—being a writer, or 'artist,' maybe—a somewhat mysterious being, in short, who could afford, for some strange reason, to loaf or walk or sit before a desk at his ease and scribble upon paper with a pen—I was rather looked up to and made much of. Then, too, ordinarily I—weekday in and out—dressed in what here passed for Sunday and holiday best, whereas quite all these others—banker, grocer, politician, minister—wore during the weekdays, at least, carefully designed, albeit more picturesque and durable, garments. (And they possessed more material wealth than I at that time ever hoped to have!) So for weeks, or the length of our stay, there was a kind of holiday atmosphere among these same. We were different—hence interesting. Other sons and daughters, married and unmarried, came and went. They were a teasing, amusing lot, full of the silly quips and jests of the countryside and most loyal and affectionate where others of their group were concerned. And yet it was easy to see that their envies and rivalries underneath were in some cases very keen. They interested me as types, and I made common lot with them, giving and taking with their humors as best I might.

"My object during this holiday season was to write, and this I did when the holiday-making would permit. After a few days I was quite in love with the country—its broad, hot fields, the silent streets, the long, dusty roads, the farmers and the citizens and their simple, homely ways. Near at hand was a graveyard, with a record of some sixty years of village life, and here I studied the tombstones. A mile or two away a creek trailed along between muddy, tree-shaded banks, and here I sat and fished. Over the way was the winter home of a well-to-do farmer and cattleman, a close neighbor of this family, which had been turned over to my parents-in-law for the summer. It was in this house, in a large, cool, and stiff 'parlor' such as most farmhouses boast, that I had my work-table and books and papers.

"However, in spite of a long procession of golden, sunshiny days, with the bees that hummed, cows that tinkled distant bells, flower scents, bird calls and flashes, trains that whistled mournfully in the distance, I was unhappy. There was a void which no beauty of life, no social efforts to please or entertain, could quite fill. By day, by night, under the clear stars, I dreamed of love and beauty, and wished. For only see, see, life, the lovetime, all beauty, were slipping away! My best years! And these people, however much I might like them, were still small-town souls, and would remain so. No fault of theirs. They could not think the thoughts I was thinking or gather the import of my dreams. The church, as I could see, meant everything to them spiritually. It eased the lacks in their lives in this world by promising them bliss in the next. Of books there were none, pictures none, music none, aspirations . . . well, here and there, perhaps an aspiring soul, but . . . In consequence, between reading Keats, Shelley, Hardy, Omar, and watching the procession of the days, I was by turns sad and gay. My wife, of course, offered me at least mental or spiritual companionship, but I was tired of her, preferring to be alone and work, or read, or walk and think.

"And then one day, to greet the new 'in-law' and to see what he was like, of course—came an additional brother-in-law, whom, as yet, I had not seen, that same aforementioned Howdershell, with wife and daughter, the latter a girl between seventeen and eighteen years of age and as pink and laughing and vivacious as one would wish to see. How truly simple and lovely youth can be at times—shapely, graceful, rhythmic, ruddy, with—in her case—a wealth of corn-colored hair, large, melting, gray-blue eyes, and small hands and feet. In short, on first glance and with a romantic and emotional ache because of my lorn state, I decided that she was exactly the type of physical loveliness of which I had been dreaming. Yet with no least knowledge of life or books, as anyone could see; on the contrary—as she conveyed to me, at least—a gaiety of spirit based on inexperience and illusion. Those innocent, non-coquettish smiles! That ringing laugh! That almost deranging sense of health in abundance! Those quick, easy, graceful movements! 'Heavens!' I fairly gasped, 'how utterly delicious and natural.' For there was about her an innocent pertness, without a trace of brassy sophistication, that held me spellbound. Indeed, as I said to myself and at once, here was the natural geniality of one who knows all too little of life and assumes the world to be rather better than it is.

"But her father! That tall, lank, weather-indurated soul! Positively, he looked to have the tensile strength of whipcord and the ignorance of ten. He was lynx-eyed, self-opinionated, recessive, and suspicious, as becomes a United States marshal, I presume. Thus far in his career, as I now learned, he had captured one or two criminals of serious import, and, if I recall aright, had 'justifiably' slain two. Vain, courageous, opinionated, and yet reserved of speech, he stalked about in a long-tailed frock coat, his head adorned with one of those wide-brimmed sombreros so treasured of all American rurals—his hips carrying a pistol or two, I am sure. Yet, among relatives and friends he was the soul of geniality and, no doubt, clannish affection. Woe to anyone who should chance to injure any of his, I thought, and worse, had a feeling that a Kentucky feudist would have done no more. His wife, as I have said, was small, talkative, cricketlike, and bounced here and there in a jumpy way. She was constantly relating anecdotes and incidents portraying the humors and eccentricities of her husband and others of this rural world. They lived, as I now learned, twenty-five miles to the south of this, in Arkansas and in a region of hills and picturesque river scenes, very different from this flat world in which we were.

"But it was this girl Rella who alone of all these now held my attention. Once having seen her I could scarcely turn my eyes from her as she moved here and there, running errands to the store or from one to another of her relatives, and finally, and gaily, setting the evening table for her grandmother. Truly, I thought, here is one who is startlingly beautiful. And so unusual—and so wholly uninformed. And yet the pull of her for me—the beauty, beauty, beauty of her! And to complete my enslavement, I was at once identified by her, and in the most innocent and affectionate of manners, as one of the family. For forthwith she addressed me as Uncle Dan, and apparently listed me among those most fortunate males of this family who were to be looked after by her and all of the women. Oh, what beauty, I thought! What eyes! What lips! What hair! How trim and lissome a figure! Indeed, observing her now, I proceeded to meditate upon how two such homely persons as her parents could possibly have produced such a paragon!

"But, as always in those days, I decided forthwith that she was not for me, and prepared in a dreary way to make the best of it. Incidentally, I was conscious of the eyes of my wife, watchful and jealous. No least show of interest on my part, however innocent, could escape her, as I knew, and it would at once be interpreted as evidence of potential, if not plotted, unfaithfulness. Her manner at such times was most disturbing to me, and fiercely and instantly now I resented this espionage. To be sure, from her point of view she was right, or at least within her rights, in trying to defend her interests or forfend against a destructive affection of any kind. But what about myself? My dreams? And to preserve this present and only seeming stability of our relationship required a great deal more than watchfulness, I thought—a reflection which made me sad. That love should fade! That one's happiness should end! Anyone's! And only love, as I knew, could preserve one's dreams. Not self-interest. I registered a sorrowful, and yet useless, sympathy for her. For of what value is sympathy to one who has no power to compel a real affection?

"The first night passed, and by morning I was doubly conscious of an irritated mood in regard to all this—my marriage, my contracted and controlled actions, and, so, life itself. God! To be cribbed, cabined, confined! Why had I so early in life handicapped myself in the race for happiness? What a fool, to tie myself down in this way! Would I never be free again? Here was this laughing, happy, beautiful creature who but for this early mistake might now be mine. But . . . was I sure of that? Could she be made to care for me? No, no, no! Married or unmarried, how should I . . . being as unattractive as I was . . . attract her? Nevertheless, it was some satisfaction to me to find that after the first day she was still here. She had not flown, and love or no love, I would still have the delight of looking at her. And to my intense delight, on the second day I discovered that they were to remain a week.

"Yet that very morning, just the same, I went sorrowfully to my desk, thinking that it were best, perhaps, if I were to shut myself away from all this. I could not ever have her, anyhow—so why brood? Yet that afternoon, idling because idleness seemed in the air, I sat in a hammock and watched this girl and her cousin, the daughter of the politican over the way, race about, mock quarreling over the possession of a trinket. Later, because of a friendly laugh from me, they came to the hammock and sat with me, each taking an arm and proceeding to examine the book I had been reading. But this proving of no interest, they soon turned to the playful labor of swinging me in spite of a pretended wish on my part not to be swung. But by this time the mere proximity of this girl was proving toxic. I was made faint, as well as hungry, by the fullness of her beauty. A feeling of languor alternated with one of intense depression over the brevity of so great a joy as well as the inadequacy of any act or qualification of mine to interest such beauty, youth, innocence. A deadly drug could not have acted with greater power. In vain I told myself that if by so much as a look I should betray even a trace of what I was feeling I would be thereafter most carefully avoided, not only by herself but by her relatives. . . . In vain! I could not help yearning over her. And how intensely. And yet, also—for the nonce, at least—I played the tolerant young uncle, fourteen years her senior and very circumspect and emotionally if not amusedly unconcerned. She was not for me! Not for me. And then, heartsick because of the seeming remoteness of this youthful world which never again could know me as a citizen, I was ready to give over and return to my writing room over the way.

"Yet now—miracle of miracles!—it seemed to me that she was more than ordinarily playful, springing into the hammock with me and once there attempting to push me out or upset me. And the feel of her arms, body—her glorious young strength tugging at me! And later she took my book from me and began to read in a mock solemn voice, her pretty head pushed close to mine. But when of a sudden, as I also noted, she saw my wife approaching, she straightened and assumed a more distant air. Now, thought I, what does that mean?

"That same afternoon I, having gone back to my desk and returned, one of my cousins-in-law volunteering to root plantain weeds out of the lawn with a dibble, I joined her, working with a table knife and fork for want of anything better. And the day being so fine, my thoughts soon wandered off to her whom above all earthly things I now so suddenly craved. How magical now the sunlight on the grass—the shade of the trees in the sunlight and this simple dooryard and lawn! Had I not seen her tripping over it but an hour before? Four trees spaced evenly beyond the street walk threw a grateful shade. If one could sit here with her! But the hammock was now occupied by the marshal, who proceeded to make sport of us workers.

" 'Better come down to my farm,' he jibed. 'We've got lots nicer weeds down there.'

" 'Let's see the weeds!' I called, hopefully.

" 'Dare you to come down and even look at 'em,' he returned, mockingly.

"I was tempted to accept, but just then the paragon herself appeared, returning from the village post office with letters. And quickly, laughing over the great work, finding a fork and joining us. She had donned a slate-blue apron, which caused her yellow hair to take on an added luster. Seating herself nearby, she too dug and jested.

" 'Oh, here's one with a whopper of a root! I'm afraid I'll never be able to get this one out without help!'

30

"Needless to say, I went to her aid.

"And then, because of her gay spirits, I had an intense long-ing to play with her. To further this desire I suggested a game of mumblety-peg, and she agreed, asserting at the same time that she could beat me or anyone any day. A pocket knife was pro-duced, and we sat on the grass facing each other. Her gestures seemed to take on an innocent artfulness. She cocked her head, parted her lips in an interested and expectant manner before each throw, and pouted so demurely when she failed. I could scarce-ly play for watching her. The wisps of damp hair about her forehead! The mock intenseness of her eyes! The sweet rhythmic value of her gestures! Once, as she was holding the knife to her chin preparatory to tossing it, she looked straight into my eyes. My senses reeled. That dreamy, tremulous glance—that faraway something that was like an inner sea of blue dotted with romanc-ing sails—what could it mean? Then she spoke softly, almost in a whisper: 'I'll miss if you look at me like that.'

" 'Miss, then.'

"I continued to gaze, confused by her brazen coquetry and my limitations in the field of gallantry and courage and charm. Another relative, unconscious of this tête-à-tête, joining us, we made it a three- and later a four-handed game. Soon after I retired to brood over the meaning of her words and the splendor of her beauty. For hours I could do nothing but sit and dream of her, confused and all but numb with joy. I could not, and would not, believe that she was becoming interested in me. That could not be. And yet . . . that playful and yet seeking look; that excited and enticing laugh when we were alone. I went to my desk in the house across the street, dubious of the import of it all and yet tremulously elate. Just before six, to my immense surprise and delight she came, bearing a bowl of nasturtiums and a pitcher of water, which she handed through the window before my desk.

" 'Aunt V——— said I might bring these,' and with this came a warm friendly glance. And: 'You must begin to get ready for dinner now. I'm making biscuit. Do you like biscuit?'

" 'If you're making them, I'll like them,' I said, moved beyond the meaning of my words by her charm and the joyous manner in which she did everything. 'But how well you do your hair!' I added, for want of another thought.

31

" 'Oh, if you tell me things like that, I'll make you lots of nice things!'

" 'You are all the nice things. You needn't make me anything. May I tell you that?' I looked at her pleadingly.

"She began to move away, but without any suggestion of fear or reproach—rather as though it were quite all right, only not best for her to answer. I sensed her wisdom and said no more. But as she crossed the yellow, dusty road, still warm though the cool of the evening was at hand, I studied her. Her figure suggested that of one who might dance divinely. I was beside myself with delight. Could it really be that there was springing up between myelf and this girl, my aged self and this bud, an understanding which, were I but free, could profit me so gloriously?

"But as I was thinking, my wife came to fetch me, and behold—weariness of soul! What could be the end of this? How could there be anything other than a hopeless, fruitless infatuation, ending in negation and enforced regulation? None the less, I was caught in the grip of an affection that was tumbling me pellmell whithersoever it would. And all about me the warmth of this wonderful summer—a land bucolic and fecund. That great red ball in the west that was only now sinking beneath the level of the grass there. And this air, heavy with odors, floral and moving. The lowing of cattle only a little distance away. The twittering evensong of birds. The spreading shadows, soon to be begemmed with stars . . . I stood in a side door facing the west and sighed over my lot, viewing this painter's dream before me.

"The next morning, on pretext of bringing me a pitcher of water and more flowers—services which I could not understand my wife permitting—Rella came inside the room where I worked. She stood beside my chair and looked over my shoulder at a half-written page.

" 'Oh, what a small straight hand! You almost write backwards, don't you? You ought to see my scrawl!' She was leaning over me, her face near mine—her cheek. And giggling infectiously. She affected me like fire.

" 'No flattery, now!' I half choked. 'I write badly, and I know it. But let me see how you do. I'll bet you write beautifully.'

" 'Oh, gee!' (A gurgle.) 'I used to get such scoldings at school. Once my teacher hit me over the knuckles with her

32

ruler. And she always said my I's looked like J's. See!'

" 'They look like stars now,' I said. I was looking into them as I said this. More, I had placed an arm about her and was holding her, which caused her to flush and exclaim, 'Oh!' All at once I drew her to me, bringing her yellow hair close to my mouth. I put a hand to her chin and pulled her face close to mine. There was color in her cheeks, a weak, yielding look in her eyes. Our lips met. Suddenly she straightened up.

" 'I'd better be going now,' she said, a little flustered.

" 'No, I have you now.'

" 'I must! I can't stay.'

"She permitted me to kiss her again. Her lips flamed against mine. I let her go and she ran out, stopping to lean over a bed of nasturtiums in order to recover herself. I sat and meditated. Could only a dreary separation be the end of this? For three days more we met in hallways and corners, among flower bushes and trees, and in the old house across the way when an errand could be contrived. Once she said: 'Would you like me to come to New York when I've finished school?'

" 'Would I!' was all I could say. She danced away, adding as she went: 'Maybe I will, if I can.' A wild dream anent the possibilities of this filled my mind for days.

"By some irony of chance at this time, her father now began to display a sudden and affectionate interest in me. He began to linger in my presence, discussing the area in which he was an officer, the politics and social friendships and biases which governed the execution of his orders. Like so many others at that time, he was curious as to the charm of New York and desirous of visiting there. Agreeably I asked him to visit us, and thereafter nothing would do but that we must visit him at his ranch, some twenty-five miles distant. He would rig up a working chamber for me in the house or the barn. If I liked, I could work in an old sheep-shearer's hut on a hill not far from the house, and one of the children could see that I was called in time for dinner, or would bring it to me there. (Rella, said my mind.) More, we could return with them now. Later he would send one of his sons over for our trunks. I might stay the winter and see the character of life in the Ozarks.

"Where but an hour before I was facing pitch gloom at the

thought of certain and impending separation, I was now at once beside myself with happy anticipation. But, in order to misdirect suspicion, I pretended to doubt the wisdom of imposing upon such liberality. It was too kind of him. It could not be. I really could not. But this merely sharpened his insistence, as I hoped it would. And to make doubly sure that I should be swayed, he set about coaxing my wife, who, to my surprise and delight, was rather in favor of the journey. So, she had noticed nothing, I decided. And at last and to my sardonic pleasure it was she who persuaded me to go.

"At dusk then one evening a day or two later, we set forth to drive the twenty-five miles. It has been a number of years now, but to this hour I can scent the odor of grasses and blooms and vines and bushes, wet with the dews of night. Through rocky valleys and along clear streams, which rippled and murmured over pebbly beds, the light three-seated vehicle, drawn by two spirited mares, rolled and careened. On either hand immense fields of corn and wheat and hay new-mown glinted dimly and spectrally under a full moon. Here and there bats and owls winged their lumbering ways, and beetles in full flight bumbled and thumped against us. In distant cottages winked yellow lights, and overhead was the bright moon, all but blotting out the stars. Because Mrs. Howdershell wished to talk about New York and my work there, I was squeezed in between her and Rella. I recall my joy now when a furtive little hand was laid in mine under the blanket. The exchange of glances in the moonlight! Her gay laughter and comments! The shine of the moonlight in her eyes!

"Life at moments verges upon sheer magic. The astonishing impulse to generation and decay which we call living so richly orchestrates itself at times, so sensitively responds to exterior tones, odors, shadows, as to achieve witchery. The blending is so moving. So profoundly we dream; so eagerly we seek.

"It seemed to me, as we rode at first between level fields, then over low hills, and through dreamy, misty valleys, that life, try as it might, could never attain anything more wonderful than this. Indeed, so intense was my mood, so great was the pull between myself and this girl, that I was all but translated to a less tangible realm, where life seemed to be dream rather than a reality. And yet, sadly, too—oh, how sadly and mournfully—I

34

speculated as to whether anything permanent could come of this. How might I seize her? How, in all her bright beauty, keep her? Strangely, and without immediate cause, I was jealous of everyone—her parents and the future. Should I win her, or might not some other take her from me? The bitterness of that! I was riddled with pain by speculations as to loss, not victory. My wife! My wife! Married, married! The words were as the notes of a tolled bell. And yet, in truth, I was not interested (even in her case), in a long-enduring marriage or the usual formal procedures in relation to love. Had I not secured this girl who was my wife, and did I now desire her permanently? But why not? Darkly I speculated as to why love should necessarily pass into this more formalistic and irksome relationship, only later to end in death. I questioned (and reasonably enough, I think), whether all women wished to be married permanently. It seemed to me that many— the more beautiful ones, at least—scorned marriage. Yet I personally was at a loss as to how to provide a saner method of procedure. Tragedy or dissatisfaction or ennui seemed to lurk at every corner and down every path; danger, death, and extremes of all kinds to provide the very necessary fillip whereby love found its zest and continuance.

"At the same time, the attitude of this girl puzzled me. For her parents, strict and dogmatic people both, had, no doubt, emphasized to her all the social virtues as they understood them. And yet here she was now, playing at love with one whom she knew to be married. My wife, her aunt, before her in the seat beside Howdershell—and so jealous and suspicious, as Rella already sensed I was sure. But did that in any way affect her? It did not. Could youth, strongly shaken by life's primal and driving impulse, be so affected? I knew well it could not. All the solemn lessons inculcated thus far were plainly as nothing to her. She too was in love. The misery which might ensue to her aunt counted as nothing. She either could not understand or would not consider.

"As the night wore on we finally descended into a valley surrounded by great hills. Through this valley ran a stream, its waters tumbling over white stones, and sparkling and rippling in the moonlight. A single light far to the right was hailed as home. And, as we drew nearer, I made out a great barn near the stream.

And then came the house, shadowed by several great trees. I helped Rella and her mother down and followed them toward the house, where, as we neared it, we met two young, strong, sleepy sons coming to greet us.

" 'I'll tell you what you do, Rella,' called the mother, enthusiastically. 'Take a candle and go down to the cellar and bring up some apples and cider.'

"Forthwith I was invited to carry the candle and a basket, while she carried the pitcher. Lighted by one feeble, yellow flame, we kissed in the shadows under the beamed floor, and then gathered a few apples and drew a pitcher of amber juice. I recall the thrill and bubble of Rella's manner, the magic of her young face vaguely illuminated, the sense of danger in her eyes.

" 'You'd better let me go now. Aunt V——— might come down.'

"Thinly experienced in life and its vagaries at the time, I was full of wonder that one so young and seemingly inexperienced could so practically and tactfully relinquish what she so obviously desired in favor of what might later be. Yet events were to demonstrate to me that caution, a sense of balance and self-protection, were as much a part of Rella's make-up as her gayety and affection. Only no undue emphasis was placed on caution; as a matter of fact, she seemed to me unconscious of danger; and yet the quickness with which she was ready to seize a favorable opportunity, or to relinquish a dangerous moment, showed all too clearly how innate and secure was her sense of intrigue and the fitness or unfitness of the deeds and moments that compounded it. After one such moment as this, she could return— as I now saw—to the others, and with the air of one whom love has never touched.

"(Bright bird! Beautiful butterfly! Let me hold you, your wings untarnished!)

"The cider, cookies and apples disposed of, all confessed to weariness, and retired, while I once more wandered forth into the night. It was all too beautiful and exciting, and I could not sleep. Instead I walked, sitting finally upon the slope of one of the hills that rose directly behind the house, and meditating under the stars. Oh, love, love, I thought! Youth, youth! The fever, the agony of this infection! How could it have flown so quickly in the one case only to burst so quickly into flame in another? Were we, after all, but vials of fluid, compounded by another than ourselves and reacting to laws or stimuli which had little or nothing in common with our own social theories and procedures? Or it seemed so—as though the very electrons of one's being in conclave assembled, or as by revolution voted or decided or swayed one, and that in the face of the staid polity of the world without. But whatever it was, the fever was exquisite. I burned. I ached. God, I thought, her exquisite young face, her graceful young body, her motions, smile, eyes. That they should do this to me . . . and to her, maybe! Or could it, in her case? Was it so doing? Did she really love me—respond as I was responding? The thought was so painful that I could not longer endure it and so arose and returned to the silent house.

"But the next morning I was up early, eager to see her first. The slightest glimpse of her was fire. And beside this delicious country land in July time, its smooth, green hills, its wide yellowing fields of wheat, and the still green fields of corn. The stream, an adjacent wood, a white ribbon of road leading out in two directions, all interested me. Within the barnyard were pigs and chickens, and about the eaves of the barn strutted a flock of pigeons. A cultivated field of vines, heavy with raspberries and still half-grown blackberries, adjoined the house lot. In the fields beyond the men were already reaping, my host and his sons among them.

"After an hour or two spent in idling about, I returned to the house, to find upon a shaded kitchen veranda commanding a wide panorama, a table spread with berries and cream, coffee, bacon and eggs, and fresh biscuit, as well as milk and buttermilk—and all offered with apologies! My wife, wishing to help her sister, had already eaten, thus leaving me to make the best of a meal supervised by Rella. Yet I could scarcely eat for looking into her fresh young face—her eyes, her mouth, her hair!

"At the same time I was writing for several magazines, but I found myself scarcely able to work for thinking of her—the hope of seeing her, hearing her voice, looking into her eyes, touching her hand, all but deranging me mentally. And to increase the fever, she was here and there throughout the day, laughing, encountering me, at times, seemingly on purpose, at others avoiding me.

There were calves and chickens to feed, a cake to make, furniture to dust. Gaily, as one who makes a pleasure of such tasks, she went about them, smiling or singing as she worked. Once, her hair down about her shoulders, she waved to me from an upper window. Another time she came to me where I wrote, presumably to bring water, but really for a kiss—yet how slyly, and with a cautioning finger to her lips.

"Beyond the barn was a great corn field—a huge lake of corn—and beyond this the hut of an old fisher and trapper, who had come to the house on our first day and in whose life I had expressed a keen interest, thereby winning an invitation to call. When I spoke of going to visit him, I was told by Rella how easily I might go by a path which followed a fence and then cut through the field. 'And if you come back along the eighth row,' she whispered, 'I might meet you.'

"At any other time I would have found this man interesting. In his hut were silver and red fox skins from this very region. He knew the art of fishing and hunting and had traveled as far west as the coast of California. But all the afternoon my heart and mind were elsewhere. I wanted the sun to sink, the evening perfumes to rise, to meet Rella among the rustling corn.

"And at last I took my leave, eager—feverish, even—and yet dawdling along the path between rows of corn that whispered and chaffered of life, and myself reciting scraps of a dozen poems. The perfume of the ground, the wind among the stalks and the distant trees, the calls of the birds—how they tortured now with their sweetness! Indeed, they thrilled and fevered me as might great verse, having the lilt and ring of great lines. Of a sudden life seemed young, unbelievably glorious. For I saw her afar tripping between the sworded corn, her head bare, an apron holding something and yet tied so as to take care of itself. She looked behind her from time to time as she came, and then drew near and put up her arms. I held her close and poured into her ear the fascination she exercised for me. She did not speak at first, merely holding her lips to mine, then prattled of the weariness of the day without me. But soon she declared, as always: 'But I can't stay. I must run. They think I'm in the barn.' She left me, and misery settled upon me again.

"There was another day. I went to a small stream to fish,

hoping that she would visit me there. And where I stopped, vines and overhanging branches contrived a dell in which was a pool, a sandy beach, and fish visible in the clear water. Arcady. Wondering where she was and what she was doing, I turned, and there she was, peeping out from behind some greenery a dozen yards away. Dinner was only an hour off and yet she had brought me cake and a glass of milk in a small basket. 'I suggested it to Aunt V———,' she laughed, 'and she told me to bring them.' She laughed again. I took her in my arms.

"The ground beneath the trees was mottled with sunshine. The small strand was of golden sand, as yellow as her hair. Beyond the stream was a solid, lichen-covered wall of gray granite, rising all of thirty feet, and behind us a thicket of bushes, making of this leafy place an almost secret chamber. Alone with her here I felt freest of all, yet always in danger. For could we know whether we had been or were being observed? Howdershell, her mother, brothers, my wife. And yet, regardless, I ventured to hold her here—and she to submit—pulling her to a stone and sealing her mouth with mine. At last she ran away, picking up her basket as she went. Fifty feet away she put her head through some leaves and smiled back at me. 'You're not catching many fish, are you?' And she was gone.

"The next morning, before sunrise, I was up and out, seeking some dewberries I had seen growing near the wall of wood at the south end of the berry field. The wood-perfumed air and wet grass underfoot gave me a sense of living, breathing poetry, of life dreamily and beautifully lived. A surging sense of the newness and perpetual youth of the world was upon me. Here, I said, in the face of all individual age and death, in such fevers as these, in such moments as these, life contemptuously shows how forever young and new it is. I may age, or another. I may die, or another. But life and youth go on. Sunrises come and go, and they are new to those who are newly come. The birds also, and the trees. New springs, new summers, new autumns, new winters, new springs again. New blood is being created to continue the whole thing forever. But what of my love? What of my unhappy marriage? Soon this must end. I must end. And then what? How much, if any, of this eternal newness for me?

"And, as though to punish me for my gloomy philosophy,

from that day on things seemed to take a turn for the worse. I had expected Rella to follow me into this glorious dawn to pick berries with me, but she did not. Instead, as she told me later, she could not—her mother had remarked that she might be annoying me. Later in the day I told her I was going to the stream to fish, but she did not come. Her mother had filled her moments with tasks. So that day passed, and with glances only, and those darkly veiled. The next day was almost as bad. I was beginning to feel that the shadow of suspicion was darkening the scene and making my stay untenable. Yet late that afternoon, having been for a walk and coming down the hill at the back of the house, I found her picking berries. She had on an old sunbonnet of her mother's, and looked the fresh and innocent schoolgirl that she was, a fit companion for the summer and the fields. I felt sick at the thought of losing her.

" 'Want to help me?' she began, with a safeguarding glance in the direction of the house.

" 'Oh, do I?' I replied, drawing near.

" 'But I don't know,' she began at once. 'I believe mamma suspects. You'd better not stand so close,' and she pointed to a bush a few feet away.

" 'Rella,' I said, bending over the more distant bush and yet talking to her, 'you don't know—I can't tell you how it is with me. I want you so. I can scarcely sleep. What will come of this, do you suppose? Could you come to New York ever? Would you run away with me if I wanted you to?'

" 'Oh,' she paused meditatively. 'I don't know. I hadn't thought of that, you know. I don't think I could now—not yet, anyhow—but I might come sometime if Aunt V——— would let me.' She looked at me earnestly, dubiously, then laughed amusedly at this last thought.

"I felt a sinking sensation at the pit of my stomach. This optimism. This laughter here and now. Could she really feel as I felt—sense any of my great want? I feared not—almost *knew* not—and my heart was heavy, my spirit prone on the earth. I stared helplessly.

" 'I don't know how I'm going to get along without you, Rella,' I sighed.

" 'Oh, I'll miss you terribly, too,' she said, but not as I

had said what I had said. It was all too tragic to me.

" 'Oh, Rella!' I went on, feverishly. 'Do you really love me?'

" 'Yes.' She bent over the bush.

" 'Do you?'

" 'Yes. Yes. But you'd better look out, Uncle Dan. They might see you from the house.'

"I moved away. 'How can I go away and leave you?'

" 'Oh, how I wish I could go with you! I do! I do!' was all she said. We talked but little more then, for her mother called to her for something.

"The next afternoon, working in the shade of an east porch which ran along the side of the house, I was made well aware that Rella was making as much of my presence as conditions would permit. She passed almost too often for one alive to the need of distracting attention, and finally, in order to be near me, as I guessed, decided to wash her hair so that she might come out and sun it near me, and perhaps—the vanity and coquetry of girlhood!—parade its golden glory to my view. Only, as she said—whispering it to me at first—she could not stay long. The atmosphere of suspicion in connection with us was plainly too great. But she could, and did, manage to pass and repass on one errand and another between the sunny veranda where I was and the inner room in which she was, touching me each time with either her hand or her skirt. And the glory of her bright hair now loose, haloing her wonderfully vivid and youthful face—the water-clarity of her eyes—the exquisite form and fullness of her lips! How mad it was, I said to myself over and over now, for me to even look at her, let alone wish. For was not, as I now noticed for the first time, my wife observing us from a window? Yet Rella again, passing me, stopped and asked me to *feel* her hair, how soft and fine it was. And as she did so the look she bent on me was one of sick repression—a look which greatly reassured me as to her own feeling for me, at the same time that it reduced me the more because of the immanence of loss. To think of her eyes speaking this longing! In spite of my wife, who was not visible at the moment, I took the mass of it in my hands and pulled her face toward me. She looked swiftly about, then gave me an eager, swift kiss, and went on. Scarcely had she done so though than my wife appeared in the doorway. There was in her eyes, as I saw at once, a hard, brilliant light which showed only when she was very angry. She went into the house again, only to return and just as Rella had ventured to come out once more. And now she said: 'Rella! Your mother wants you.'

"From that moment I realized that the worst impended. Black looks and secret persistent spying were in store for me. And a series of veiled, if not open, comments. For she would not, as I now knew, stay here any longer. And without her, how could I? What excuse would there be? Sadly, if dourly, I proceeded to face realities. Apart from going with her if she decided now to go, there was but one thing—and that radical and incautious—an elopement with Rella. But, supposing the plan were put to her, would she say yes? If not, then what? Defeat and misery, of course. And yet, should she consent . . . then what? The hard and savage Howdershell, once he knew; the whispered and open comments in this region. Rella's repute. Mine. The vengeful ire of my loving but jealous wife. For needless to say, one such move on my part and she would seek redress of Howdershell himself; effect, if possible, the return of Rella at any cost. And as for myself, once away with Rella, then what? The battle; the pursuit; the expense and social and mental disruption of flight. I was ensnared, yes—and oh, how much! The agony of it! But this . . . to Rella . . . to me . . . to all. Slowly, but surely, sadly and grimly—being neither radical nor incautious—I faced the inevitable.

"And from that hour, as I feared, I was met with suggestions from my wife as to the unwisdom of a longer visit here. A message from the home of her parents—or so she said—had already urged us to return there—for some event of no importance—a street fair, I think. Also the valuelessness of a longer stay in the West was emphasized. Was I not becoming weary of this country life? But when I pretended not to understand the meaning of this sudden change from pleasure in all this to a desire to leave, there were at first looks, then a fit of dark depression, and finally tears. I knew what was wrong. Did I dare pretend that I did not? I . . . I . . . who had done this . . . that . . . And so, in a flood, a flashing picture of my evil heart. Ah, what was I not? Had I no shame, no decency? Were innocent young school girls not safe even in their own homes? Was I not

42

astounded at myself, my scandalous temerity in attempting a flirtation with a girl fourteen years my junior, a mere girl in her teens,
and who, by the way, ought to be ashamed of herself, too? It
was high time we were getting out of here. We would go, and
we would go at once—now—tomorrow!

"But, no—we would not go tomorrow—we wouldn't go
before the following Monday, if then—and it was I who said so!
Let her rage! Let her tell the family, but I would not go unless
ordered by them, if she wished that. I was resting. Why should
I leave? To avoid a possibly more trying scene for herself, she
finally yielded to this. But with stormy words and in a
tempestuous mood. And so it was, with this situation in mind,
that I was now compelled to face Rella—to tell her softly and
with suggestions as to caution for herself, how matters stood.
It was she who was being blamed, as well as myself—she, as well
as myself, who had a problem to face—the first and greatest she
had ever faced—and a dangerous one for her as well as myself.
And now, how would she do? Elope with me, for instance, or
stay here and lose me? And how did she feel? Was she at all
frightened? Could she, and would she, think and act for herself?

"But now, to my surprise and satisfaction, instead of exhibiting any trace of fear or tremulousness, she merely faced me,
cool, even pale. It was too bad, wasn't it? Dreadful. If only she
were a little older. She had hoped we would not be found out,
but since we had been . . . perhaps . . . perhaps . . . well . . .
Perhaps the best thing was to wait. And her father and mother
might cause trouble right now because of Aunt V———, and what
she might do. But later . . . listen . . . next winter she would be
going to school over at Fayetteville, a hundred miles away. How
about coming over there? We could see each other there. The
fifteen hundred miles that would lie between us at that time were,
as it seemed to me then, all but meaningless to her. I could do
anything, very likely. And yet, I knew so well that I could not—
that she did not understand. I was poor, not rich; married, not
free; shackled by the forces of life as much as she was, if not more,
and yet dreaming of freedom and love, wishing to fly.

"And so it was that late that night, walking up the hill that
lay to the south of the house, I was prey to the gloomiest of
thoughts. Despite a certain respect for convention and order which

43

was still strong within me, the rude and haphazard compulsion which I now saw operative in all nature about me suggested another and less orderly course. For was I to be thrown to and fro like a ball by this intense desire; derive no reward? No, no, no! Never, never, never! For this girl cared for me, and if pleaded with would yield, would she not? From where I sat even now I could see a light in Rella's room, and if I were to whistle or signal in some way, I knew she would come. But on the other hand, there was this respect—to a degree at least—for the feelings of these, her parents. And not only that but the fear of consequences to Rella and myself. Did she really know her own mind as yet? Could she? Was she really, truly, in love? Ah . . . the light in that window! Her unloosened hair . . . her face! I meditated a further extension of time here . . . beyond Monday . . . beyond the following week, even. But there was the battle that would have to be fought between myself and my wife. And betimes could she not, and would she not, whisper to her sister, the mother of this girl? And then what? The departure of Rella, of course.

"Beyond where I sat, the light poured like filtered silver over the fields of corn and wheat, and the patches of meadow bordered by squares of dark wood. Here and there in a small house still winked a yellow lamp. Dogs barked, hounds bayed, an owl or two 'woo-hooed.' And yet, for upwards of an hour, I sat thus, my head in my hands, meditating on beauty, and love, and change, and death. Life was too bitter and too sweet, I sighed, begrudging every fleeing moment of it here. For soon, in spite of all I might do now, this visit would be over. And I would return to D———, and then to New York. And when, if ever again, would I see Rella? When? Her tall, cold, thin-minded father, how I wearied of him now! And her mother, what of her? Could, or would, Rella ever really wish to escape the corded meshes of their goodness, their virtues? So, brooding, I sighed, and in heaviness of soul finally arose and started down the hill. Yet, halfway down, in the shadow of the wood alongside which ran the path, I was startled by a hooded figure hurrying toward me. Nearing me, the shawl was thrown back, the head lifted, and—it was Rella, perfect but pale in the sheen of the moon!

" 'Darling!' I exclaimed.

" 'I had to come,' she gasped. 'I couldn't stay away any

longer. I know it's late, but I slipped out. I hope no one heard. I was afraid I might not get to talk to you again. Mother suspects, I think. And Aunt V——— has talked to her. But I had to come! I had to!' She was short of breath from running.

" 'But, honey, dearest! Your mother! Your father! If they should see you!'

"I paused, for I was thinking of something else now. For here she was with me at last, had come of her own accord. Therefore, now . . . since . . . was I not justified in . . . ? I paused, holding her, a strong, possessive, almost ruthless, fever driving me. And yet, so philosophic and reflective was my mind that even now I could not help asking myself in what unsophistication, unworldly innocence, was it that she had really come here—one too young, truly, to know the full import of her own actions or desires. But holding close to me and babbling of her love.

" 'I know papa's over at Walter's, and mamma's in bed. So is Aunt V———. I went up to my room and then slipped down. They won't know. I sometimes come out this way. But I had to see you! I had to! But, oh, I can't stay! You know I can't! It would be terrible for you if I were seen here. You don't know my father.'

" 'I know, I know, dear,' I whispered. 'You little innocent, you sweetheart,' and I drew her head against my shoulder and kissed her and smoothed her hair. 'But how did you know I was here, and how shall I do without you now? Will you be mine? Will you go with me now—tomorrow—next day?'

"She looked up at me nervously and seemingly comprehendingly, thoughts of many things apparently scampering through her mind, then hid her face in my coat.

" 'Oh, no, no, not now!' she said. 'I can't. I know . . . I know what you mean . . . but I can't. Not this way. Not now. You don't know my father, or my mother, either. He would kill you. Yes, he would. Oh, dear! I mustn't stay. I mustn't. I knew you were going, and I had to come. I couldn't stay away. Maybe next winter . . . if you would come for me. . . .' And she drew nervously away.

" 'Yes,' I replied, wearily, sensing the impossibility of it all. And thinking: If Howdershell should know—if he should even guess! And yet you coming this way, just when I want you most—when it is hardest to resist. And not even understanding clearly.

God! And in a storm of pain I held her, saying: 'Next winter, maybe, if I can arrange it. So go now. And write me. I will slip you an address tomorrow. And I will write you here, or anywhere, anywhere you say!'

" 'Oh, yes, yes, at Fayetteville. That's sure, is it?' she gasped, hurriedly. 'But I must go. I'll write you, sure.'

"She hurried down the hill in the shadow, and I gazed after her. The end—the end—I thought. There was blood on the thought. I heard a collie bark, then saw the kitchen door open and someone look out. I could only hope that she had safely reached her room.

"Coming out by the woodpile below the house some ten minutes later I stood gazing at the scene which the house presented. It was so simple, so rural—a strong, beamed affair, with rambling rooms, angles, small verandas and windows. But now no light. And inside Rella, safe, I hoped, not having been seen. But thinking what, now that she was alone? As I was? Or was she? But I loving her so. And beaten! Beaten by circumstances —life, parents, marriage, I know not what. I cursed, and hated even, for I was sick of love—poisoned by it even.

"And then, of a sudden, as I stood there—and from nowhere, as it were, out of the dark or mist but without a sound—directly before me Howdershell! And cool and still in the moonlight, not a word issuing from his lips, his steady, green-blue eyes fixed upon me. Aha, I thought! Trapped! He has seen, heard! Now then, what? The worst, I suppose. The storm. I braced myself, my blood chilling. I was unarmed and I knew he was always armed.

" 'A fine night, isn't it?' he began, calmly and, as I thought, coldly pretending a friendship he did not feel. (The instinct of the trapper, I added to myself. It is so he begins. How should I have hoped to defeat him?) My veins were running ice water. 'Been out for a walk?' His words had, to me, a mocking sound.

" 'Yes,' I replied, as calmly as I could.

"To my immense relief, almost my amazement, he now began drawling concerning a horse that had been, and still was, sick, and that had needed his attention. Also of a neighbor who had come to assist him with his wheat. And damp with perspiration, I listened, concluding after a time that after all he had seen nothing, suspected nothing. Then this secret approach was without significance, a country gesture, the sly quip of one who liked to surprise and frighten another? But with what consequences, really, had he come upon Rella and myself!

"And then Monday—the day set by my wife for our departure but with us staying over for a day or two just the same. Yet, because of this shock—the dubious mood evoked in me by this moonlight meeting—no further attempt on my part to persuade Rella against her will. Rather only a dark, oppressive realization of the futility of all this. Yet, love and desire, an enthralling and devastating sense of her beauty—of what union, even free companionship, with her must mean. And so the pain of restraint and loss.

"Deep amid the tall, whispering corn, only one day before I left, a last meeting with her, to say goodbye. And it was she who, watchful, elusive, contrived it. She would write . . . she would come, even. I need not fear. And then, kisses, kisses. And after that, what glances! And almost before the eyes of her parents and her aunt. The lovelight that beckoned! At breakfast on that last morning she even sighed as she handed me something. I was wondering if she was really feeling as I was.

" 'Don't you want me to send her poisoned candy?' she whispered, jestingly. This was apropos of a celebrated poisoning case then in the papers.

" 'Rella!' I reproved. The thought startled me.

" 'Oh, I wouldn't, but I feel like it,' she said, sadly.

"The stark, merciless, unheeding nature of love was being brought home to me then with a greater force than ever before. For here was youth, innocence, beauty—a paragon in form, really—and yet what was the defeat of this other woman to her? Nothing. A blood relation, and yet an enemy to be defeated. And as for life and law? What were they to this eager, seeking girl? Either not understood or only dimly, perhaps, and scoffed at. Yet even I in my fever could not help thinking of the ruthlessness of life. And yet, such was my own infatuation that now in nowise could I be displeased with her for her fierce thought. Rather I was inflamed by it—made more desirous—perceiving as I did through this the depths of nature in this girl.

"And then, at parting, to see her boldly and proudly put her

lips to mine (and that in the very face of her aunt), and then turn
and offer those same lips to her, which offer was icily accepted.
And all this before her mother (who must have known, yet for
diplomatic reasons did not wish to indicate her knowledge), and
her father, and the other members of the family. Even now I recall
my wife's eyes, clouded with hate and suppressed rage. And Rella
smiling and defiant, proud in her young beauty. And then myself,
riding back over the hills and through the valleys to D———,
and despite the mood of the woman beside me, lost in reflections that were immensely depressing—to her as well as to myself.

"For here I was, for all my fever and tossing, defeated. And
my wife, for all her defeat, still, after a fashion, victorious. Yet
both unhappy. And Rella, too. And so, further reflections as to
the essential helplessness, and even slavery, of man—and this
despite all his formulae and in the face of his compelling passions. And so sickening because of the anachronisms of life. For
here was I, wishing most intensely to be doing one thing and yet
being shunted along this wretched path of custom and duty
against my will. And afraid, or unable, to break the chains which
held me. And behind me, Rella, who for all her strong desire
and daring, was helpless. And beside me a woman, fuming and
brooding about a force she could not possibly control, yet resolved
never to resign what was 'rightfully' hers, and so clinging to the
ashes of a long-since burnt-out love. And the parents of Rella
and my wife's parents assuming that happiness and order reigned
where instead were molten and explosive opposition and
dissatisfaction. And law and custom approving heartily.

"What a thin veneer is the seeming of anything, I thought!
How indifferent, and therefore merciless, are the forces that
despite our notions and moods and dreams drive us all!

"In New York later I received some letters and a complaint
from Rella to the effect that not only against her will was she
being sent to a higher school but also being urged to marry a
doctor whom she did not like; also a faint hint that if I would
provide the means she might run away. But means at the time
were not mine. More, for me at the moment life was wearing
a face which made even love seem almost worthless. In fact, I
was all but destroyed at the time, not only financially but
physically—and so, not able to do anything. True, I wrote her

48

in explanation but later ceased, knowing that only trouble could follow her through me.

"And later, of course, other women took Rella's place. As other men mine in her life. The unhappy union of which I was then half was finally broken up. Rella, sent to a relative in Texas, eventually married an oil speculator, whom I trust she loved. The last news I had of her was that after a visitation of some disease she had been left with a partially paralyzed eyelid, which completely marred her beauty. Also, that much of her wonderful hair had fallen out. And this before thirty."

•   •   •

Verily, "what is man that thou art mindful of him? He cometh up as a flower, and is cut down. He fleeth as a shadow, and continueth not."

Peter

*I*N ANY GROUP OF MEN I have ever known, speaking from the point of view of character and not that of physical appearance, Peter would stand out as deliciously and irrefutably different. In the great waste of American intellectual dreariness he was an oasis, a veritable spring in the desert. He understood life. He knew men. He was free—spiritually, morally, in a thousand ways, it seemed to me.

As one drags along through this inexplicable existence one realizes how such qualities stand out; not the pseudo freedom of strong men, financially or physically, but the real, internal, spiritual freedom, where the mind, as it were, stands up and looks at itself, faces Nature unafraid, is aware of its own weaknesses, its strengths; examines its own and the creative impulses of the universe and of men with a kindly and non-dogmatic eye, in fact kicks dogma out of doors, and yet deliberately and of choice holds fast to many, many simple and human things, and rounds out life, or would, in a natural, normal, courageous, healthy way.

The first time I ever saw Peter was in St. Louis in 1892; I had come down from Chicago to work on the St. Louis *Globe-Democrat,* and he was a part of the art department force of that paper. At that time—and he never seemed to change later even so much as a hair's worth until he died in 1908—he was short, stocky and yet quick and even jerky in his manner, with a bushy, tramp-like "get-up" of hair and beard, most swiftly and astonishingly disposed of at times only to be regrown at others, and always, and intentionally, I am sure, most amusing to contemplate. In addition to all this he had an air of well-being, force and alertness which belied the other surface characteristics as anything more than a genial pose or bit of idle gaiety.

Plainly he took himself seriously and yet lightly, usually with an air of suppressed gaiety, as though saying, "This whole business of living is a great joke." He always wore good and yet exceedingly mussy clothes, at times bespattered with ink or, worse yet, even soup—an amazing grotesquery that was the dismay of all who knew him, friends and relatives especially. In addition he was nearly always liberally besprinkled with tobacco dust, the source of which he used in all forms: in pipe, cigar and plug, even cigarettes when he could obtain nothing more substantial. One of the things about him which most impressed me at that time and later was this love of the ridiculous or the grotesque, in himself or others, which would not let him take anything in a dull or conventional mood, would not even permit him to appear normal at times but urged him on to all sorts of nonsense, in an effort, I suppose, to entertain himself and make life seem less commonplace.

And yet he loved life, in all its multiform and multiplex aspects and with no desire or tendency to sniff, reform or improve anything. It was good just as he found it, excellent. Life to Peter was indeed so splendid that he was always very much wrought up about it, eager to live, to study, to do a thousand things. For him it was a workshop for the artist, the thinker, as well as the mere grubber, and without really criticizing anyone he was "for" the individual who is able to understand, to portray or to create life, either feelingly and artistically or with accuracy and discrimination. To him, as I saw then and see even more clearly now, there was no high and no low. All things were only relatively so. A thief was a thief, but he had his place. Ditto the murderer. Ditto the saint. Not man but Nature was planning, or at least doing, something which man could not understand, of which very likely he was a mere tool. Peter was as much thrilled and entendered by the brawling strumpet in the street or the bagnio as by the virgin with her starry crown. The rich were rich and the poor poor, but all were in the grip of imperial forces whose ruthless purposes or lack of them made all men ridiculous, pathetic or magnificent, as you choose. He pitied ignorance and necessity, and despised vanity and cruelty for cruelty's sake, and the miserly hoarding of anything. He was liberal, material, sensual, and yet spiritual; and although he never had more than a little money, out of the richness and fullness of his own temperament he seemed able to generate a kind of atmosphere and texture in his daily life which was rich and warm, splendid really in thought (the true reality) if not in fact, and most grateful to all. Yet also, as I have said, always he wished to *seem* the clown, the scapegrace, the wanton and the loon even, mouthing idle impossibilities at times and declaring his profoundest faith in the most fantastic things.

Do I seem to rave? I am dealing with a most significant person.

In so far as I knew he was born into a Midwestern family of Irish extraction whose habitat was southwest Missouri. In the town in which he was reared there was not even a railroad until he was fairly well grown—a fact which amused but never impressed him very much. Apropos of this he once told me of a yokel who, never having seen a railroad, entered the station with his wife and children long before train time, bought his ticket and waited a while, looking out of the various windows, then finally returned to the ticketseller and asked, "When does this thing start?" He meant the station building itself. At the time Peter had entered upon art work he had scarcely prosecuted his studies beyond, if so far as, the conventional high or grammar school, and yet he was most amazingly informed and but little interested in what any school or college had to offer. His father, curiously enough, was an educated Irish-American, a lawyer by profession, and a Catholic. His mother was an American Catholic, rather strict and narrow. His brothers and sisters, of whom there were four, were, as I learned later, astonishingly virile and interesting Americans of a rather wild, unsettled type. They were all, in so far as I could judge from chance meetings, agnostic, tense, quick-moving—so vital that they weighed on one a little, as very intense temperaments are apt to do. One of the brothers, K———, who seemed to seek me out ever so often for Peter's sake, was so intense, nervous, rapid-talking, rapid-living, that he frightened me a little. He loved noisy, garish places. He liked to play the piano, stay up very late; he was a high liver, a "good dresser," as the denizens of the Tenderloin would say, an excellent example of the flashy, clever promoter. He was always representing a new company, introducing something—a table or laxative water, a shaving soap, a chewing gum, a safety razor, a bicycle, an automobile tire or the machine itself. He was here, there, everywhere—in Waukesha, Wisconsin; San Francisco; New York; New Orleans. "My, my! This is certainly interesting!" he would exclaim, with an air which would have done credit to a comedian and extending both hands. "Peter's pet friend, Dreiser! Well, well, well! Let's have a drink. Let's have something to eat. I'm only in town for a day. Maybe you'd like to go to a show—or hit the high places? Would you? Well, well, well! Let's make a night of it! What do you say?" and he would fix me with a glistening, nervous and what was intended no doubt to be a reasoning eye, but which unsettled me as thoroughly as the imminence of an earthquake. But I was talking of Peter.

The day I first saw him he was bent over a drawing board illustrating a snake story for one of the Sunday issues of the *Globe-Democrat,* which apparently delighted in regaling its readers with most astounding concoctions of this kind, and the snake he was drawing was most disturbingly vital and reptilian, beady-eyed, with distended jaws, extended tongue, most fatefully coiled.

"My," I commented in passing, for I was in to see him about another matter, "what a glorious snake!"

"Yes, you can't make 'em too snaky for the snake-editor up front," he returned, rising and dusting tobacco from his lap and shirtfront, for he was in his shirt sleeves. Then he expectorated not in but to one side of a handsome polished brass cuspidor which contained not the least evidence of use, the rubber mat upon which it stood being instead most disturbingly "decorated." I was most impressed by this latter fact although at the time I said nothing, being too new. Later, I may as well say here, I discovered why. This was a bit of his clowning humor, a purely manufactured and as it were mechanical joke or ebullience of soul. If anyone inadvertently or through unfamiliarity attempted to expectorate in his "golden cuspidor," as he described it, he was always quick to rise and interpose in the most solemn, almost sepulchral manner, at the same time raising a hand. "Hold! Out—not in—to one side, on the mat! That cost me seven dollars!" Then he would solemnly seat himself and begin to draw again. I saw him do this to all but the chiefest of the authorities of the paper. And all, even the dullest, seemed to be amused, quite fascinated by the utter trumpery folly of it.

But I am getting ahead of my tale. In so far as the snake

was concerned, he was referring to the assistant who had these snake stories in charge. "The fatter and more venomous and more scaly they are," he went on, "the better. I'd like it if we could use a little color in this paper—red for eyes and tongue, and blue and green for scales. The farmers upstate would love that. They like good but poisonous snakes." Then he grinned, stood back and, cocking his head to one side in a most examining and yet approving manner, ran his hand through his hair and beard and added, "A snake can't be too vital, you know, for this paper. We have to draw 'em strong, plenty of vitality, plenty of go." He grinned most engagingly.

I could not help laughing, of course. The impertinent air! The grand, almost condescending manner!

We soon became fast friends.

In the same office in close contact with him was another person, one Dick Wood, also a newspaper artist, who, while being exceedingly interesting and special in himself, still as a character never seems to have served any greater purpose in my own mind than to have illustrated how emphatic and important Peter was. He had a thin, pale, Dantesque face, coal black, almost Indian-like hair most carefully parted in the middle and oiled and slicked down at the sides and back until it looked as though it had been glued. His eyes were small and black and querulous but not mean—petted eyes they were—and the mouth had little lines at each corner which seemed to say he had endured much, much pain, which of course he had not, but which nevertheless seemed to ask for, and I suppose earned him some, sympathy. Dick in his way was an actor, a tragedian of sorts, but with an element of humor, cynicism and insight which saved him from being utterly ridiculous. Like most actors, he was a great poseur. He invariably affected the long, loose flowing tie with a soft white or blue or green or brown linen shirt (would any American imitation of the "Quartier Latin" denizen have been without one at that date?), yellow or black gloves, a round, soft crush hat, very soft and limp and very *different,* patent leather pumps, betimes a capecoat, a slender cane, a boutonnière—all this in hard, smoky, noisy, commercial St. Louis, full of Middle West businessmen and farmers!

I would not mention this particular person save that for a

time he, Peter and myself were most intimately associated. We temporarily constituted in our way a "soldiers three" of the newspaper world. For some years after, we were more or less definitely in touch as a group, although later Peter and myself, having drifted eastward and hobnobbing as a pair, had been finding more and more in common and had more and more come to view Dick for what he was: a character of Dickensian, or perhaps still better, Cruikshankian, proportions and qualities. But in those days the three of us were all but inseparable; eating, working, playing, all but sleeping together. I had a studio of sorts in a more or less dilapidated factory section of St. Louis (Tenth near Market; now I suppose briskly commercial), Dick had one at Broadway and Locust, directly opposite the then famous Southern Hotel. Peter lived with his family on the South Side, a most respectable and homey-home neighborhood.

It has been one of my commonest experiences, and one of the most interesting to me, to note that nearly all of my keenest experiences intellectually, my most gorgeous *rapprochements* and swiftest developments mentally, have been by, to, and through men, not women, although there have been several exceptions to this. Nearly every turning point in my career has been signalized by my meeting some man of great force, to whom I owe some of the most ecstatic intellectual hours of my life, hours in which life seemed to bloom forth into new aspects, glowed as with the radiance of a gorgeous tropic day.

Peter was one such. About my own age at this time, he was blessed with a natural understanding which was simply Godlike. Although, like myself, he was raised a Catholic and still pretending in a boisterous, Rabelaisian way to have some reverence for that faith, he was amusingly sympathetic to everything good, bad, indifferent—"in case there might be something in it; you never can tell." Still he hadn't the least interest in conforming to the tenets of the church and laughed at its pretensions, preferring his own theories to any other. Apparently nothing amused him so much as the thought of confession and communion, of being shrived by some stout, healthy priest as worldly as himself, and preferably Irish, like himself. At the same time he had a hearty admiration for the Germans, all their ways, conservatisms, their

56

breweries, food and such things, and finally wound up by marrying a German girl.

As far as I could make out, Peter had no faith in anything except Nature itself, and very little in that except in those aspects of beauty and accident and reward and terrors with which it is filled and for which he had an awe if not a reverence and in every manifestation of which he took the greatest delight. Life was a delicious, brilliant mystery to him, horrible in some respects, beautiful in others; a great adventure. Unlike myself at the time, he had not the slightest trace of any lingering puritanism, and wished to live in a lush, vigorous, healthy, free, at times almost barbaric, way. The negroes, the ancient Romans, the Egyptians, tales of the Orient and the grotesque Dark Ages, our own vile slums and evil quarters—how he reveled in these! He was for nights of wandering, endless investigation, reading, singing, dancing, playing!

Apropos of this I should like to relate here that one of his seemingly gross but really innocent diversions was occasionally visiting a certain black house of prostitution, of which there were many in St. Louis. Here while he played a flute and someone else a tambourine or small drum, he would have two or three of the inmates dance in some weird savage way that took one instanter to the wilds of Central Africa. There was, so far as I know, no payment of any kind made in connection with this. He was a friend, in some crude, artistic or barbaric way. He satisfied, I am positive, some love of color, sound and the dance in these queer revels.

Nor do I know how he achieved these friendships, such as they were. I was never with him when he did. But aside from the satiation they afforded his taste for the strange and picturesque, I am sure they reflected no gross or sensual appetite. But I wish to attest in passing that the mere witnessing of these free scenes had a tonic as well as toxic effect on me. As I view myself now, I was a poor, spindling, prying fish, anxious to know life, and yet because of my very narrow training very fearsome of it, of what it might do to me, what dreadful contagion of thought or deed it might open me to! Peter was not so. To him all, positively *all*, life was good. It was a fascinating spectacle, to be studied or observed and rejoiced in as a spectacle. When I look back now on the shabby, poorly-lighted, low-ceiled room to which he led me "for fun," the absolutely black or brown girls with their white teeth and shiny eyes, the unexplainable, unintelligible love of rhythm and the dance displayed, the beating of a drum, the sinuous, winding motions of the body, I am grateful to him. He released my mind, broadened my view, lengthened my perspective. For as I sat with him, watching him beat his drum or play his flute, noted the gayety, his love of color and effect, and feeling myself *low,* a criminal, disgraced, the while I was staring with all my sight and enjoying it intensely. I realized that I was dealing with a man who was "bigger" than I was in many respects, saner, really more wholesome. I was a moral coward, and he was not losing his life and desires through fear—which the majority of us do. He was strong, vital, unafraid, and he made me so.

But, lest I seem to make him low or impossible to those who instinctively cannot accept life beyond the range of their own little routine world, let me hasten to his other aspects. He was not low but simple, brilliant and varied in his tastes. America and its point of view, religious and otherwise, were simply amusing to him, not to be taken seriously. He loved to contemplate man at his mysteries, rituals, secret schools. He loved better yet ancient history, medieval inanities and atrocities—a most singular, curious and wonderful mind. Already at this age he knew many historians and scientists (their work), a most astonishing and illuminating list to me—Maspero, Froude, Huxley, Darwin, Wallace, Rawlinson, Froissart, Hallam, Taine, Avebury! The list of painters, sculptors and architects with whose work he was familiar and books about whom or illustrated by whom he knew, is too long to be given here. His chief interest, in so far as I could make out in these opening days, was Egyptology and the study of things natural and primeval—all the wonders of a natural, groping, savage world.

"Dreiser," he exclaimed once with gusto, his bright beady eyes gleaming with an immense human warmth, "you haven't the slightest idea of the fascination of some of the old beliefs. Do you know the significance of a scarab in Egyptian religious worship, for instance?"

"A scarab? What's a scarab? I never heard of one," I answered.

"A beetle, of course. An Egyptian beetle. You know what a beetle is, don't you? Well, those things burrowed in the earth, the mud of the Nile, at a certain period of their season to lay their eggs, and the next spring, or whenever it was, the eggs would hatch and the beetles would come up. Then the Egyptians imagined that the beetle hadn't died at all, or if it had that it also had the power of restoring itself to life, possessed immortality. So they thought it must be a god and began to worship it," and he would pause and survey me with those amazing eyes, bright as glass beads, to see if I were properly impressed.

"You don't say!"

"Sure. That's where the worship came from," and then he might go on and add a bit about monkey-worship, the Zoroastrians and the Parsees, the sacred bull of Egypt, its sex power as a reason for its religious elevation, and of sex worship in general; the fantastic orgies at Sidon and Tyre, where enormous images of the male and female sex organs were carried aloft before the multitude.

Being totally ignorant of these matters at the time, not a rumor of them having reached me as yet in my meager reading, I knew that it must be so. It fired me with a keen desire to read—not the old orthodox emasculated histories of the schools but those other books and pamphlets to which I fancied he must have access. Eagerly I inquired of him where, how. He told me that in some cases they were outlawed, banned or not translated wholly or fully, owing to the puritanism and religiosity of the day, but he gave me titles and authors to whom I might have access, and the address of an old-book dealer or two who could get them for me.

In addition he was interested in ethnology and geology, as well as astronomy (the outstanding phases at least), and many, many phases of applied art: pottery, rugs, pictures, engraving, wood-carving, jewel-cutting and designing, and I know not what else, yet there was always room even in his most serious studies for humor of the bizarre and eccentric type, amounting to all but an obsession. He wanted to laugh, and he found occasion for doing so under the most serious, or at least semi-serious, circumstances. Thus I recall that one of the butts of his extreme humor was this same Dick, whom he studied with the greatest

59

care for points worthy his humorous appreciation. Dick, in addition to his genuinely lively mental interests, was a most romantic person on one side, a most puling and complaining soul on the other. As a newspaper artist I believe he was only a fairly respectable craftsman, if so much, whereas Peter was much better, although he deferred to Dick in the most persuasive manner and seemed to believe at times, though I knew he did not, that Dick represented all there was to know in matters artistic.

Among other things at this time, the latter was, or pretended to be, immensely interested in all things pertaining to the Chinese and to know not only something of their language, which he had studied a little somewhere, but also their history—a vague matter, as we all know—and the spirit and significance of their art and customs. He sometimes condescended to take us about with him to one or two Chinese restaurants of the most beggarly description, and—as he wished to believe because of the romantic titillation involved—the hangouts of crooks and thieves and disreputable Tenderloin characters generally. (Of such was the beginning of the Chinese restaurant in America.) He would introduce us to a few of his Celestial friends, whose acquaintance apparently he had been most assiduously cultivating for some time past and with whom he was now on the best of terms. He had, as Peter pointed out to me, the happy knack of persuading himself that there was something vastly mysterious and superior about the whole Chinese race, that there was some Chinese organization known as the Six Companies, which, so far as I could make out from him, was ruling very nearly (and secretly, of course) the entire habitable globe. For one thing it had some governing connection with great constructive ventures of one kind or another in all parts of the world, supplying, as he said, thousands of Chinese laborers to anyone who desired them, anywhere, and although they were employed by others, ruling them with a rod of iron, cutting their throats when they failed to perform their bounden duties and burying them head down in a basket of rice, then transferring their remains quietly to China in coffins made in China and brought for that purpose to the country in which they were. The Chinese who had worked for the builders of the Union Pacific had been supplied by this company, as I understood from Dick. In regard to all this Peter used to analyze and dispose of Dick's self-generated romance with the greatest gusto, laughing the while and yet pretending to accept it all.

But there was one phase of all this which interested Peter immensely. Were there on sale in St. Louis any bits of jade, silks, needlework, porcelains, basketry or figurines of true Chinese origin? He was far more interested in this than in the social and economic sides of the lives of the Chinese, and was constantly urging Dick to take him here, there and everywhere in order that he might see for himself what of these amazing wonders were locally extant, leading Dick in the process a merry chase and a dog's life. Dick was compelled to persuade nearly all of his boasted friends to produce all they had to show. Once, I recall, a collection of rare Chinese porcelains being shown at the local museum of art, there was nothing for it but that Dick must get one or more of his Oriental friends to interpret this, that and the other symbol in connection with this, that and the other vase—things which put him to no end of trouble and which led to nothing, for among all the local Chinese there was not one who knew anything about it, although they, Dick included, were not honest enough to admit it.

"You know, Dreiser," Peter said to me one day with the most delicious gleam of semi-malicious, semi-tender humor, "I am really doing all this just to torture Dick. He doesn't know a damned thing about it and neither do these Chinese, but it's fun to haul 'em out there and make 'em sweat. The museum sells an illustrated monograph covering all this, you know, with pictures of the genuinely historic pieces and explanations of the various symbols in so far as they are known, but Dick doesn't know that, and he's lying awake nights trying to find out what they're all about. I like to see his expression and that of those chinks when they examine those things." He subsided with a low chuckle all the more disturbing because it was so obviously the product of well-grounded knowledge.

Another phase of this same humor related to the grand artistic, social and other forms of life to which Dick was hoping to ascend via marriage and which led him, because of a kind of anticipatory eagerness, into all sorts of exaggerations of dress, manners, speech, style in writing or drawing, and I know not

61

what else. He had, as I have said, a "studio" in Broadway, an ordinary large, square upper chamber of an old residence turned commercial but which Dick had decorated in the most, to him, recherché or *different* manner possible. In Dick's gilding imagination it was packed with the rarest and most carefully selected things, odd bits of furniture, objects of art, pictures, books— things which the ordinary antique shop provides in plenty but which to Dick, having been reared in Bloomington, Illinois, were of the utmost artistic import. He had vaulting ambitions and pretensions, literary and otherwise, having by now composed various rondeaus, triolets, quatrains, sonnets, in addition to a number of short stories over which he had literally slaved and which, being rejected by many editors, were kept lying idly and inconsequentially and seemingly inconspicuously about his place—the more to astonish the poor unsophisticated "outsider." Besides it gave him the opportunity of posing as misunderstood, neglected, depressed, as becomes all great artists, poets, and thinkers.

His great scheme or dream, however, was that of marriage to an heiress, one of those very material and bovine daughters of the new rich in the West End, and to this end he was bending all his artistic thought, writing, dressing, dreaming the thing he wished. I myself had a marked tendency in this direction, although from another point of view, and speaking from mine purely, there was this difference between us: Dick being an artist, rather remote and disdainful in manner and decidedly handsome as well as poetic and better positioned than I, as I fancied, was certain to achieve this gilded and crystal state, whereas I, not being handsome nor an artist nor sufficiently poetic perhaps, could scarcely aspire to so gorgeous a goal. Often, as around dinner-time he ambled from the office arrayed in the latest mode—dark blue suit, patent leather boots, a dark, round soft felt hat, loose tie blowing idly about his neck, a thin cane in his hand—I was already almost convinced that the anticipated end was at hand, this very evening perhaps, and that I should never see him more except as the husband of a very rich girl, never be permitted even to speak to him save as an almost forgotten friend, and in passing! Even now perhaps he was on his way to her, whereas I, poor oaf that I was, was moiling here over some trucky work. Would my ship never come in? my great day never arrive? my turn? Unkind heaven!

As for Peter he was the sort of person who could swiftly detect, understand and even sympathize with a point of view of this kind the while he must laugh at it and his mind be busy with some plan of making a folderol use of it. One day he came into the city-room where I was working and bending over my desk fairly bursting with suppressed humor announced, "Gee, Dreiser, I've just thought of a delicious trick to play on Dick! Oh, Lord!" and he stopped and surveyed me with beady eyes the while his round little body seemed to fairly swell with pent-up laughter. "It's too rich! Oh, if it just works out Dick'll be sore! Wait'll I tell you," he went on. "You know how crazy he is about rich young heiresses? You know how he's always 'dressing up' and talking and writing about marrying one of those girls in the West End?" (Dick was forever composing a short story in whch some lorn but perfect and great artist was thus being received via love, the story being read to us nights in his studio.) "That's all bluff, that talk of his of visiting in those big houses out there. All he does is to dress up every night as though he were going to a ball, and walk out that way and moon around. Well, listen. Here's the idea. We'll go over to Mermod & Jaccard's tomorrow and get a few sheets of their best mono-grammed paper, sample sheets. Then we'll get up a lcttcr and sign it with the most romantic name we can think of—Juanita or Cyrene or Doris—and explain who she is, the daughter of a millionaire living out there, and that she's been strictly brought up but that in spite of all that she's seen his name in the paper at the bottom of his pictures and wants to meet him, see? Then we'll have her suggest that he come out to the west gate of, say, Portland Place at seven o'clock and meet her. We'll have her describe herself, see, young and beautiful, and some attractive costume she's to wcar, and we'll kill him. He'll fall hard. Then we'll happen by there at the exact time when he's waiting, and detain him, urge him to come into the park with us or to dinner. We'll look our worst so he'll be ashamed of us. He'll squirm and get wild, but we'll hang on and spoil the date for him, see? We'll insist in the letter that he must be alone, see, because she's timid and afraid of being recognized. My God, he'll be crazy! He'll think we've ruined his life—oh, ho, ho!" and he fairly writhed with inward joy.

The thing worked. It was cruel in its way, but when has man ever grieved over the humorous ills of others? The paper was secured, the letter written by a friend of Peter's in a nearby real estate office, after the most careful deliberation as to wording on our part. Extreme youth, beauty and a great mansion were all hinted at. The fascination of Dick as a romantic figure was touched upon. He would know her by a green silk scarf about her waist, for it was spring, the ideal season. Seven o'clock was the hour. She could give him only a moment or two then—but later—and she gave no address!

The letter was mailed in the West End, as was meet and proper, and in due season arrived at the office. Peter, working at the next easel, observed him, as he told me, out of the corner of his eye.

"You should have seen him, Dreiser," he exclaimed, hunting me up about an hour after the letter arrived. "Oh, ho! Say, you know I believe he thinks it's the real thing. It seemed to make him a little sick. He tried to appear nonchalant, but a little later he got his hat and went out, over to Deck's," a nearby saloon, "for a drink, for I followed him. He's all fussed up. Wait'll we heave into view that night! I'm going to get myself up like a joke, a hobo. I'll disgrace him. Oh, Lord, he'll be crazy! He'll think we've ruined his life, scared her off. There's no address. He can't do a thing. Oh, ho, ho, ho!"

On the appointed day—and it was a delicious afternoon and evening aflame with sun and in May, Dick left off his work at three p.m., as Peter came and told me, and departed, and then we went to make our toilets. At six we met, took a car and stepped down not more than a short block from the point of meeting. I shall never forget the sweetness of the air, the something of sadness in the thought of love, even in this form. The sun was singing its evensong, as were the birds. But Peter—blessings or curses upon him!—was arrayed as only he could array himself when he wished to look absolutely disconcerting—more like an unwashed, uncombed tramp who had been sleeping out for weeks, than anything else. His hair was over his eyes and ears, his face and hands dirty, his shoes ditto. He had even blackened one tooth slightly. He had on a collarless shirt, and yet he was jaunty withal and carried a cane, if you please, assuming, as he always could and in the most aggravating way, to be totally unconscious of the figure he cut. At one angle of his multiplex character the man must have been a born actor.

We waited a block away, concealed by a few trees, and at the exact hour Dick appeared, hopeful and eager no doubt, and walking and looking almost all that he hoped—delicate, pale, artistic. The new straw hat! The pale green "artist's" shirt! His black, wide-buckled belt! The cane! The dark-brown low shoes! The boutonnière! He was plainly ready for any fate, his great moment.

And then, before he could get the feeling that his admirer might not be coming, we descended upon him in all our wretched nonchalance and unworthiness—out of hell, as it were. We were most brisk, familiar, affectionate. It was so fortunate to meet him so, so accidentally and peradventure. The night was so fine. We were out for a stroll in the park, to eat afterward. He must come along.

I saw him look at Peter in that hat and no collar, and wilt. It was too much. Such a friend—such friends (for on Peter's advice I was looking as ill as I might, an easy matter)! No, he couldn't come. He was waiting for some friends. We must excuse him.

But Peter was not to be so easily shaken off. He launched into the most brisk and serious conversation. He began his badger game by asking about some work upon which Dick had been engaged before he left the office, some order, how he was getting along with it, when it would be done; and, when Dick evaded and then attempted to dismiss the subject, took up another and began to expatiate on it, some work he himself was doing, something that had developed in connection with it. He asked inane questions, complimented Dick on his looks, began to tease him about some girl. And poor Dick—his nervousness, his despair almost, the sense of the waning of his opportunity! It was cruel. He was becoming more and more restless, looking about more and more wearily and anxiously and wishing to go or for us to go. He was horribly unhappy. Finally, after ten or fifteen minutes had gone and various girls had crossed the plaza in various directions, as well as carriages and saddle horses—each one carrying his heiress, no doubt!—he seemed to summon all his courage and did his best to dispose of us. "You two'll have to excuse me," he exclaimed almost wildly. "I can't wait." Those golden moments! She could not approach! "My people aren't coming, I guess. I'll have to be going on."

He smiled weakly and made off, Peter half following and urging him to come back. Then, since he would not, we stood there on the exact spot of the rendezvous gazing smirkily after him. Then we went into the park a few paces and sat on a bench in full view, talking—or Peter was—most volubly. He was really choking with laughter. A little later, at seven-thirty, we went cackling into the park, only to return in five minutes as though we had changed our minds and were coming out—and saw Dick bustling off at our approach. It was sad really. There was an element of the tragic in it. But not to Peter. He was all laughter, all but apoplectic gayety. "Oh, by George!" he choked. "This is too much! Oh, ho! This is great! his poor heiress! And he came back! Har! Har! Har!"

"Peter, you dog," I said, "aren't you ashamed of yourself, to rub it in this way?"

"Not a bit, not a bit!" he insisted most enthusiastically. "Do him good. Why shouldn't he suffer? He'll get over it. He's always bluffing about his heiresses. Now he's lost a real one. Har! Har! Har!" and he fairly choked, and for days and weeks and months he laughed, but he never told. He merely chortled at his desk, and if anyone asked him what he was laughing about, even Dick, he would reply, "Oh, something—a joke I played on a fellow once."

If Dick ever guessed he never indicated as much. But that lost romance! That faded dream!

Not so long after this, the following winter, I left St. Louis and did not see Peter for several years, during which time I drifted through various cities to New York. We kept up a more or less desultory correspondence which resulted eventually in his contributing to a paper of which I had charge in New York, and later, in part at least I am sure, in his coming there. I noticed one thing, that although Peter had no fixed idea as to what he wished to be—being able to draw, write, engrave, carve and what not—he was in no way troubled about it. "I don't see just what it is that I am to do best," he said to me once. "It may be that I will wind up as a painter or writer or collector—I can't tell yet. I want to study, and meantime I'm making a living—that's all I want now. I want to live, and I am living, in my way."

Some men are masters of cities, or perhaps better, of all the elements which enter into the making of them, and Peter was one. I think sometimes that he was born a writer of great force and charm, only as yet he had not found himself. I have known many writers, many geniuses even, but not one his superior in intellect and romantic response to life. He was a poet, thinker, artist, philosopher and master of prose, as a posthumous volume (*Wolf, the Memoirs of a Cave-Dweller*) amply proves, but he was not ready then to fully express himself, and it troubled him not at all. He loved life's every facet, was gay and helpful to himself and others, and yet always with an eye for the undercurrent of human misery, error and tragedy as well as comedy. Immediately upon coming to New York he began to examine and grasp it in a large way, its museums, public buildings, geography, politics, but after a very little while decided suddenly that he did not belong there and without a by-your-leave, although once more we had fallen into each other's ways, he departed without a word, and I did not hear from him for months. Temporarily at least he felt that he had to obtain more experience in a lesser field, and lost no time in so doing. The next I knew he was connected, at a comfortable salary, with the then dominant paper of Philadelphia.

It was after he had established himself very firmly in Philadelphia that we two finally began to understand each other fully, to sympathize really with each other's point of view as opposed to the more or less gay and casual nature of our earlier friendship. Also here perhaps, more than before, we felt the binding influence of having worked together in the West. It was here that I first noticed the ease with which he took hold of a city, the many-sidedness of his peculiar character which led him to reflect so many angles of it, which a less varied temperament would never have touched upon. For, first of all, wherever he happened to be, he was intensely interested in the age and history of his city, its buildings and graveyards and tombstones which pointed to its past life, then its present physical appearance, the chief characteristics of the region in which it lay, its rivers, lakes, parks and adjacent places and spots of interest (what rambles we took!), as well as its newest and finest things architecturally. Nor did anyone ever take a keener interest in the current intellectual resources of a city—any city in which he happened to be—its museums, libraries, old bookstores, newspapers, magazines, and I know not what else. It was he who first took me into Leary's bookstore in Philadelphia, descanting with his usual gusto on its merits. Then and lastly he was keenly and wisely interested in various currents of local politics, society and finance, although he always considered the first a low mess, an arrangement or adjustment of many necessary things among the lower orders. He seemed to know or sense in some occult way everything that was going on in those various realms. His mind was so full and rich that merely to be with him was a delight. He gushed like a fountain, and yet not polemically, of all he knew, heard, felt, suspected. His thoughts were so rich at times that to me they were more like a mosaic of variegated and richly colored stones and jewels. I felt always as though I were in the presence of a great personage, not one who was reserved or pompous but a loose bubbling temperament, wise beyond his years or day, and so truly great that perhaps because of the intensity and immense variety of his interests he would never shine in a world in which the most intensive specialization, and that of a purely commercial character, was the grand role.

And yet I always felt that perhaps he might. He attracted people of all grades so easily and warmly. His mind leaped from one interest to another almost too swiftly, and yet the average man understood and liked him. While in a way he contemned their mental states as limited or bigoted, he enjoyed the conditions under which they lived, seemed to wish to immerse himself in them. And yet nearly all his thoughts were, from their point of view perhaps, dangerous. Among his friends he was always talking freely, honestly, of things which the average man could not or would not discuss, dismissing as trash illusion, lies, or the cunning work of self-seeking propagandists, most of the things currently accepted as true.

He was constantly commenting on the amazing dullness of man, his prejudices, the astonishing manner in which he seized

68

upon and clung savagely or pathetically to the most ridiculous interpretations of life. He was also forever noting that crass chance which wrecks so many of our dreams and lives—its fierce brutalities, its seemingly inane indifference to wondrous things—but never in a depressed or morbid spirit; merely as a matter of the curious, as it were. But if anyone chanced to contradict him he was likely to prove liquid fire. At the same time he was forever reading, reading, reading—history, archeology, ethnology, geology, travel, medicine, biography, and descanting on the wonders and idiosyncrasies of man and nature which they revealed. He was never tired of talking of the intellectual and social conditions that ruled in Greece and Rome from 600 B.C. on, the philosophies, the travels, the art, the simple, natural pagan view of things, and regretting that they were no more. He grieved at times, I think, that he had not been of that world, might not have seen it, or, failing that, might not see all the shards of those extinct civilizations. There was something loving and sad in the manner in which at times, in one museum and another, he would examine ancient art designs, those of the Egyptians, Greeks and Romans, their public and private house plans, their statues, book rolls, inscriptions, flambeaux, boats, swords, chariots. Carthage, Rome, Greece, Phoenicia—their colonies, art and trade stuffs, their foods, pleasures and worships—how he raved! A book like *Thaïs, Salammbô, Sónnica, Quo Vadis?* touched him to the quick.

At the same time, and odd as it may seem, he was seemingly in intimate contact with a circle of friends that rather astonished me by its catholicity. It included, for instance, and quite naively, real estate dealers, clerks, a bank cashier or two, some man who had a leather shop or cigar factory in the downtown section, a drummer, a printer, two or three newspaper artists and reporters —a list too long to catalogue here and seemingly not interesting, at least not inspiring to look at or live in contact with. Yet his relations with all of these were of a warm, genial, helpful, homely character, quite intimate. He used them as one might a mulch in which to grow things, or in other words he took them on their own ground; a thing which I could never quite understand, being more or less aloof myself and yet wishing always to be able so to do, to take life, as he did.

For he desired, and secured, their good will and drew them to him. He took a simple, natural pleasure in the kinds of things they were able to do, as well as the kinds of things he could do. With these, then, and a type of girl who might not be classed above the clerk or manicure class, he and they managed to eke out a social life, the outstanding phases of which were dances, "parties," dinners at one simple home and another, flirting, boating, and fishing expeditions in season, evenings out at restaurants or the theater, and I know not what else. He could sing (a very fair baritone), play the piano, cornet, flute, banjo, mandolin and guitar, but always insisted that his favorite instruments were the jews'-harp, the French harp (mouth organ) and a comb with a piece of paper over it, against which he would blow with fierce energy, making the most outrageous sounds, until stopped. At any "party" he was always talking, jumping about, dancing, cooking something—fudge, taffy, a rarebit, and insisting in the most mock-serious manner that all the details be left strictly to him. "Now just cut out of this, all of you, and leave this to your Uncle Dudley. Who's doing this? All I want is sugar, chocolate, a pot, a big spoon, and I'll show you the best fudge you ever ate." Then he would don an apron or towel and go to work in a manner which would rob any gathering of a sense of stiffness and induce a naturalness most intriguing, calculated to enhance the general pleasure an hundredfold.

Yes, Peter woke people up. He could convey or spread a sense of ease and good nature and give and take among all. Wise as he was and not so good-looking, he was still attractive to girls, very much so, and by no means unconscious of their beauty. He could always, and easily, break down their reserve, and was soon apparently on terms of absolute friendship, exchanging all sorts of small gossip and news with them about this, that and the other person about whom they knew. Indeed, he was such a general favorite and so seemingly impartial that it was hard to say how he came close to any, and yet he did. At odd tête-à-tête moments he was always making confessions as to "nights" or "afternoons." "My God, Dreiser, I've found a peach! I can't tell you—but oh, wonderful! Just what I need. This world's a healthy old place, eh? Let's have another drink, what?" and he would order a stein or a half-schoppen of light German beer and pour it down, grinning like a gargoyle.

It was while he was in Philadelphia that he told me the beginnings of the love affair which eventually ended in his marrying and settling down into the homiest of home men I have ever seen and which for sheer naivete and charm is one of the best love stories I know anything about. It appears that he was walking in some out-of-the-way factory realm of North Philadelphia one Saturday afternoon about the first or second year of his stay there, when, playing in the street with some other children, he saw a girl of not more than thirteen or fourteen who, as he expressed it to me, "came damned near being the prettiest thing I ever saw. She had yellow hair and a short blue dress and pink bows in her hair—and say, Dreiser, when I saw her I stopped flat and said 'me for that!' if I have to wait fifteen years! Dutchy—you never saw the beat! And poor! Her shoes were clogs. She couldn't even talk English yet. Neither could the other kids. They were all sausage—a regular German neighborhood.

"But, say, I watched her a while and then I went over and said, 'Come here, kid. Where do you live?' She didn't understand, and one of the other kids translated for her, and then she said, 'Ich sprech nicht English,' " and he mocked her. "That fixed her for me. One of the others finally told me who she was and where she lived—and, say, I went right home and began studying German. In three months I could make myself understood, but before that, in two weeks, I hunted up her old man and made him understand that I wanted to be friends with the family, to learn German. I went out Sundays when they were all at home. There are six children and I made friends with 'em all. For a long time I couldn't make Mädchen (that's what they call her) understand what it was all about, but finally I did, and she knows now all right. And I'm crazy about her and I'm going to marry her as soon as she's old enough."

"How do you know that she'll have you?" I inquired.

"Oh, she'll have me. I always tell her I'm going to marry her when she's eighteen, and she says all right. And I really believe she does like me. I'm crazy about her."

Five years later, if I may anticipate a bit, after he had moved to Newark and placed himself rather well in the journalistic field and was able to carry out his plans in regard to himself, he suddenly returned to Philadelphia and married, preparing beforehand an apartment which he fancied would please her. It was a fortunate marriage in so far as love and home pleasures were concerned. I never encountered a more delightful atmosphere.

All along in writing this I feel as though I were giving but the thinnest portrait of Peter; he was so full and varied in his moods and interests. To me he illustrated the joy that exists, on the one hand, in the common, the so-called homely and what some might think ugly side of life, certainly the very simple and ordinarily human aspect of things; on the other, in the sheer comfort and satisfaction that might be taken in things truly intellectual and artistic, but to which no great expense attached—old books, prints, things connected with history and science in their various forms, skill in matters relating to the applied arts and what not, such as the coloring and firing of pottery and glass, the making of baskets, hammocks and rugs, the carving of wood, the collection and imitation of Japanese and Chinese prints, the art of embalming as applied by the Egyptians (which, in connection with an undertaker to whom he had attached himself, he attempted to revive or at least play with, testing his skill for instance by embalming a dead cat or two after the Egyptian manner). In all of these lines he trained himself after a fashion and worked with skill, although invariably he insisted that he was little more than a bungler, a poor follower after the art of someone else. But most of all, at this time and later, he was interested in collecting things Japanese and Chinese: netsukes, inros, censers, images of jade and porcelain, teajars, vases, prints; and it was while he was in Philadelphia and seemingly trifling about with the group I have mentioned and making love to his little German girl that he was running here and there to this museum and that and laying the foundations of some of those interesting collections which later he was fond of showing his friends or interested collectors. By the time he had reached Newark, as chief cartoonist of the leading paper there, he was in possession of a complete Tokaido (the fifty-five views on the road between Tokyo and Kyoto), various prints by Hokusai, Sesshiu, Sojo; a collection of one hundred inros, all of fifty netsukes, all of thirty censers, lacquered boxes and teajars, and various other exceedingly

72

beautiful and valuable things—Mandarin skirts and coats, among other things—which subsequently he sold or traded around among one collector friend and another for things which they had. I recall his selling his completed Tokaido, a labor which had extended over four years, for over a thousand dollars. Just before he died he was trading netsukes for inros and getting ready to sell all these latter to a man, who in turn was going to sell his collection to a museum.

But in between was this other, this ultra-human side, which ran to such commonplaces as bowling, tennis-playing, golf, billiards, cards and gambling with the dice—a thing which always struck me as having an odd turn to it in connection with Peter, since he could be interested in so many other things, and yet he pursued these commonplaces with as much gusto at times as one possessed of a mania. At others he seemed not to miss or think of them. Indeed, you could be sure of him and all his interests, whatever they were, feeling that he had himself well in hand, knew exactly how far he was going, and that when the time came he could and would stop. Yet during the process of his momentary relaxation or satiation, in whatever field it might be, he would give you a sense of abandon, even ungovernable appetite, which to one who had not known him long might have indicated a mania.

Thus I remember once running over to Philadelphia to spend a Saturday and Sunday with him, visits of this kind, in either direction, being of the commonest occurrence. At that time he was living in some quiet-looking boardinghouse in South Fourth Street, but in which dwelt or visited the group above-mentioned, and whenever I came there, at least, there was always an atmosphere of intense gaming or playing in some form, which conveyed to me nothing so much as a glorious sense of life and pleasure. A dozen or more men might be seated about a poker or dice table, in summer (often in winter) with their coats off, their sleeves rolled up, Peter always conspicuous among them. On the table or to one side would be money, a pitcher or a tin pail of beer, boxes of cigarettes or cigars, and there would be Peter among the players, flushed with excitement, his collar off, his hair awry, his little figure stirring about here and there or gesticulating or lighting a cigar or pouring down a glass of beer, shouting at the top of his voice, his eyes aglow, "That's mine!" "I say it's not!" "Two on the sixes!" "Three!" "Four!" "Ah, roll the bones! Roll the bones!" "Get off! Get off! Come on now, Spikes—cough up! You've got the money now. Pay back. No more loans if you don't." "Once on the fours—the fives—the aces!" "Roll the bones! Roll the bones! Come on!" Or, if he saw me, softening and saying, "Gee, Dreiser, I'm ahead twenty-eight so far!" or "I've lost thirty all told. I'll stick this out, though, to win or lose five more, and then I'll quit. I give notice, you fellows, five more, one way or the other, and then I'm through. See? Say, these damned sharks are always trying to turn a trick. And when they lose they don't want to pay. I'm offa this for life unless I get a better deal."

In the room there might be three or four girls—sisters, sweethearts, pals of one or other of the players—some dancing, some playing the piano or singing, and in addition the landlord and his wife, a slattern pair usually, about whose past and present lives Peter seemed always to know much. He had seduced them all apparently into a kind of rakish camaraderie which was literally amazing to behold. It thrilled, fascinated, at times frightened me, so thin and inadequate and inefficient seemed my own point of view and appetite for life. He was vigorous, charitable, pagan, gay, full of health and strength. He would play at something, anything, indoors or out as occasion offered, until he was fairly perspiring, when, throwing down whatever implement he had in hand—be it cards, a tennis racket, a golf club—would declare, "That's enough! That's enough! I'm done now. I've licked-cha," or "I'm licked. No more. Not another round. Come on, Dreiser, I know just the place for us—" and then descanting on a steak or fish planked, or some new method of serving corn or sweet potatoes or tomatoes, he would lead the way somewhere to a favorite "rat's killer," as he used to say, or grill or Chinese den, and order enough for four or five, unless stopped. As he walked, and he always preferred to walk, the latest political row or scandal, the latest discovery, tragedy or art topic would get his keen attention. In his presence the whole world used to look different to me, more colorful, more hopeful, more gay. Doors seemed to open; in imagination I saw the interiors of a thousand realms—homes, factories, laboratories, dens, reserts of pleasure. During his day such figures as McKinley, Roosevelt, Hanna, Rockefeller, Rogers, Morgan, Peary, Harriman were abroad and active, and their mental states and points of view and interests—and sincerities and insincerities—were the subject of his wholly brilliant analysis. He rather admired the clever opportunist, I think, so long as he was not mean in view or petty, yet he scorned and even despised the commercial viewpoint or trade reactions of a man like McKinley. Rulers ought to be above mere commercialism. Once when I asked him why he disliked McKinley so much he replied laconically, "The voice is the voice of McKinley, but the hands—are the hands of Hanna." Roosevelt seemed to amuse him always, to be a delightful if ridiculous and self-interested "grandstander," as he always said, "always looking out for Teddy, you bet," but good for the country, inspiring it with visions. Rockefeller was wholly admirable as a force driving the country on to autocracy, oligarchy, possibly revolution. Ditto Hanna, ditto Morgan, ditto Harriman, ditto Rogers, unless checked. Peary might have, and again might not have, discovered the North Pole. He refused to judge. Old "Doc" Cook, the pseudo discoverer, who appeared very shortly before he died, only drew forth chuckles of delight. "My God, the gall, the nerve! And that wreath of roses the Danes put around his neck! It's colossal, Dreiser. It's grand. Munchausen, Cook, Gulliver, Marco Polo—they'll live forever, or ought to!"

Some Saturday afternoons or Sundays, if he came to me or I to him in time, we indulged in long idle rambles, anywhere, either going first by streetcar, boat or train somewhere and then walking, or, if the mood was not so, just walking on and on somewhere and talking. On such occasions Peter was at his best and I could have listened forever, quite as the disciples of Plato and Aristotle must have to them, to his discourses on life, his broad and broadening conceptions of Nature—her cruelty, beauty, mystery. Once, far out somewhere beyond Camden, we were idling about an inlet where were boats and some fishermen and a trestle which crossed it. Just as we were crossing it some men in a boat below discovered the body of a possible suicide, in the water, days old and discolored, but still intact and with the clothes of a man of at least middle-class means. I was for leaving, being made a little sick by the mere sight. Not so Peter. He was for

75

joining in the effort which brought the body to shore, and in a moment was back with the small group of watermen, speculating and arguing as to the condition and character of the dead man, making himself really one of the group. Finally he was urging the men to search the pockets while someone went for the police. But more than anything, with a hard and yet in its way humane realism which put any courage of mine in that direction to the blush, he was all for meditating on the state and nature of man, his chemical components—chlorine, sulphuric acid, phosphoric acid, potassium, sodium, calcium, magnesium, oxygen—and speculating as to which particular chemicals in combination gave the strange metallic blues, greens, yellows and browns to the decaying flesh! He had a great stomach for life. The fact that insects were at work shocked him not at all. He speculated as to *these*, their duties and functions! He asserted boldly that man was merely a chemical formula at best, that something much wiser than he had prepared him, for some not very brilliant purpose of his or its own perhaps, and that he or it, whoever or whatever he or it was, was neither good nor bad, as we imagined such things, but both. He at once went off into the mysteries—where, when with me at least, he seemed to prefer to dwell—talked of the divinations of the Chaldeans, how they studied the positions of the stars and the entrails of dead animals before going to war, talked of the horrible fetishes of the Africans, the tricks and speculations of the priests of Greek and Roman temples, finally telling me the story of the ambitious eel-seller who anchored the dead horse in the stream in order to have plenty of eels every morning for market. I revolted. I declared he was sickening.

"My boy," he assured me, "you are too thin-skinned. You can't take life that way. It's all good to me, whatever happens. We're here. We're not running it. Why be afraid to look at it? The chemistry of a man's body isn't any worse than the chemistry of anything else, and we're eating the dead things we've killed all the time. A little more or a little less in any direction—what difference?"

Apropos of this same a little later—to shock me, of course, as he well knew he could—he assured me that in eating a dish of chop suey in a Chinese restaurant, a very low one, he had found and eaten a part of the little finger of a child, and that "it was very good—very good, indeed."

"Dog!" I protested. "Swine! Thou ghoula!" but he merely chuckled heartily and stuck to his tale!

But if I paint this side of him it is to round out his wonderful, to me almost incredible, figure. Insisting on such things, he was still and always warm and human, sympathetic, diplomatic and cautious, according to his company, so that he was really acceptable anywhere. Peter would never shock those who did not want to be shocked. A minute or two or five after such a discourse as the above he might be describing some marvelously beautiful process of pollination among the flowers, the history of some medieval trade guild or gazing at a beautiful scene and conveying to one by his very attitude his unspoken emotion.

After spending about two or three years in Philadelphia— which city came to reflect for me the color of Peter's interests and mood—he suddenly removed to Newark, having been nursing an arrangement with its principal paper for some time. Some quarrel or dissatisfaction with the director of his department caused him, without other notice, to paste some crisp quotation from one of the poets on his desk and depart! In Newark, a city to which before this I had paid not the slightest attention, he found himself most happy; and I, living in New York close at hand, felt that I possessed in it and him an earthly paradise. Although it contained no more than 300,000 people and seemed, or had, a drear factory realm only, he soon revealed it to me in quite another light, because he was there. Very swiftly he found a wondrous canal running right through it, under its market even, and we went walking along its banks, out into the woods and fields. He found or created out of an existing boardinghouse in a back street so colorful and gay a thing that after a time it seemed to me to outdo that one of Philadelphia. He joined a country club near Passaic, on the river of that name, on the veranda of which we often dined. He found a Chinese quarter with a restaurant or two; an amazing Italian section with a restaurant; a man who had a $40,000 collection of rare Japanese and Chinese curios, all in his rooms at the Essex County Insane Asylum, for he was the chemist there; a man who was a playwright and manager in New York; another who owned a newspaper syndicate; another who directed a singing society; another who was president of a gun club; another who owned and made or rather fired pottery for others. Peter was so restless and vital that he was always branching out in a new direction. To my astonishment he now took up the making and firing of pottery himself, being interested in reproducing various Chinese dishes and vases of great beauty, the originals of which were in the Metropolitan Museum of Art. His plan was first to copy the design, then buy, shape or bake the clay at some pottery, then paint or decorate it with liquid porcelain at his own home, and fire it. In the course of six or eight months, working in his rooms Saturdays and Sundays and some mornings before going to the office, he managed to produce three or four which satisfied him and which he kept, plates of real beauty. The others he gave away.

A little later, if you please, it was Turkish rug-making on a small scale, the frame and materials for which he slowly accumulated, and then providing himself with a pillow, Turkish-fashion, he crossed his legs before it and began slowly but surely to produce a rug, the colors and design of which were entirely satisfactory to me. As may be imagined, it was slow and tedious work, undertaken at odd moments and when there was nothing else for him to do, always when the light was good and never at night, for he maintained that the coloring required the best of light. Before this odd, homely, wooden machine, a combination of unpainted rods and cords, he would sit, cross-legged or on a bench at times, and pound and pick and tie and unravel—a most wearisome-looking task to me.

"For heaven's sake," I once observed, "couldn't you think of anything more interestingly insane to do than this? It's the slowest, most painstaking work I ever saw."

"That's just it, and that's just why I like it," he replied, never looking at me but proceeding with his weaving in the most industrious fashion. "You have just one outstanding fault, Dreiser. You don't know how to make anything out of the little things of life. You want to remember that this is an art, not a job. I'm discovering whether I can make a Turkish carpet or not, and it gives me pleasure. If I can get so much as one good spot of color worked out, one small portion of the design, I'll be satisfied. I'll know then that I can do it, the whole thing, don't you see? Some of these things have been the work of a lifetime of one man. You call that a small thing? I don't. The pleasure is in doing it, proving that you can, not in the rug itself." He clacked and tied, congratulating himself vastly. In due course of time three or four inches were finished, a soft and yet firm silky fabric, and he was in great glee over it, showing it to all and insisting that in time (how long? I often wondered) he would complete it and would then own a splendid carpet.

It was at this time that he built about him in Newark a structure of friendships and interests which, it seemed to me, promised to be for life. He interested himself intensely in the paper with which he was connected and although he was only the cartoonist, still it was not long before various departments and elements in connection with it seemed to reflect his presence and to be alive with his own good will and enthusiasm. Publisher, editor, art director, managing editor and business manager, were all in friendly contact with him. He took out life insurance for the benefit of the wife and children he was later to have! With the manager of the engraving department he was working out problems in connection with copper-plate engraving and printing; with the official photographer, art photography; with the art director, some scheme for enlarging the local museum in some way. With his enduring love of the fantastic and ridiculous it was not long before he had successfully planned and executed a hoax of the most ridiculous character, a piece of idle drollery almost too foolish to think of, and yet which eventually succeeded in exciting the natives of at least four States and was telegraphed to and talked about in a Sunday feature way, by newspapers all over the country, and finally involved Peter as an actor and stage manager of the most vivid type imaginable. And yet it was all done really to amuse himself, to see if he could do it, as he often told me.

This particular hoax related to that silly old bugaboo of our boyhood days, the escaped and wandering wild man, ferocious, blood-loving, terrible. I knew nothing of it until Peter, one Sunday afternoon when we were off for a walk a year or two after he had arrived in Newark, suddenly announced apropos of nothing at all, "Dreiser, I've just hit upon a great idea which I am working out with some of the boys down on our paper. It's a dusty old fake, but it will do as well as any other, better than if it were a really decent idea. I'm inventing a wild man. You know how crazy the average dub is over anything strange, different, 'terrible.' Barnum was right, you know. There's one born every minute. Well, I'm just getting this thing up now. It's as good as the sacred white elephant or the blood-sweating hippopotamus. And what's more, I'm going to stage it right here in little old Newark—and they'll all fall for it, and don't you think they won't," and he chuckled most ecstatically.

"For heaven's sake, what's coming now?" I sighed.

"Oh, very well. But I have it all worked out just the same. We're beginning to run the preliminary telegrams every three or four days—one from Ramblersville, South Jersey, let us say, another from Hohokus, twenty-five miles farther on, four or five days later. By degrees as spring comes on I'll bring him north—right up here into Essex County—a genuine wild man, see, something fierce and terrible. We're giving him long hair like a bison, red eyes, fangs, big hands and feet. He's entirely naked—or will be when he gets here. He's eight feet tall. He kills and eats horses, dogs, cattle, pigs, chickens. He frightens men and women and children. I'm having him bound across lonely roads, look in windows at night, stampede cattle and drive tramps and peddlers out of the country. But say, wait and see. As summer comes on we'll make a regular headliner of it. We'll give it pages on Sunday. We'll get the rubes to looking for him in posses, offer rewards. Maybe someone will actually capture and bring in some poor lunatic, a real wild man. You can do anything if you just stir up the natives enough."

I laughed. "You're crazy," I said. "What a low comedian you really are, Peter!"

Well, the weeks passed, and to mark progress he occasionally sent me clippings of telegrams, cut not from his pages, if you please, but from such austere journals as the *Sun* and *World* of New York, the *North American* of Philadelphia, the *Courant* of Hartford, recording the antics of his imaginary thing of the woods. Longish articles actually began to appear here and there, in Eastern papers especially, describing the exploits of this very elusive and moving demon. He had been seen in a dozen fairly widely distributed places within the month, but always coming northward. In one place he had killed three cows at once, in another two, and eaten portions of them raw! Old Mrs. Gorswitch of Dutchers Run, Pennsylvania, returning from a visit to her daughter-in-law, Annie A. Gorswitch, and ambling along a lonely road in Osgoroola County, was suddenly descended upon by a most horrific figure, half man, half beast, very tall and with long hair and red, all but bloody eyes who, looking at her with avid glance, made as if to seize her, but a wagon approaching along the road from another direction, he had desisted and fled, leaving old Mrs. Gorswitch in a faint upon the ground. Barns and haystacks had been fired here and there, lonely widows in distant cotes been made to abandon their homes through fear . . . I marveled at the assiduity and patience of the man.

One day in June or July following, being in Newark and asking Peter quite idly about his wild man, he replied, "Oh, it's great, great! Couldn't be better! He'll soon be here now. We've got the whole thing arranged now for next Sunday or Saturday—depends on which day I can get off. We're going to photograph him. Wanto come over?"

"What rot!" I said. "Who's going to pose? Where?"

"Well," he chuckled, "come along and see. You'll find out fast enough. We've got an actual wild man. I got him. I'll have him out here in the woods. If you don't believe it, come over. You wouldn't believe me when I said I could get the natives worked up. Well, they are. Look at these," and he produced clippings from rival papers. The wild man was actually being seen in Essex County, not twenty-five miles from Newark. He had ravaged the property of people in five different States. It was assumed that he was a lunatic turned savage, or that he had escaped from a circus or trading ship wrecked on the Jersey coast (suggestions made by Peter himself). His depredations, all told, had by now run into thousands, speaking financially. Staid residents were excited. Rewards for his capture were being offered in different places. Posses of irate citizens were, and would continue to be, after him, armed to the teeth, until he was captured. Quite remarkable developments might be expected at any time. . . . I stared. It seemed too ridiculous, and it was, and back of it all was smirking, chuckling Peter, the center and fountain of it!

"You dog!" I protested. "You clown!" He merely grinned.

Not to miss so interesting a dénouement as the actual capture of this prodigy of the wilds, I was up early and off the following Sunday to Newark, where in Peter's apartment in due time I found him, his rooms in a turmoil, he himself busy stuffing things into a bag, outside an automobile waiting and within it the staff photographer as well as several others, all grinning, and all of whom, as he informed me, were to assist in the great work of tracking, ambushing and, if possible, photographing the dread peril.

"Yes, well, who's going to be him?" I insisted.

"Never mind! Never mind! Don't be so inquisitive," chortled Peter. "A wild man has his rights and privileges, as well as any other. Remember, I caution all of you to be respectful in his presence. He's very sensitive, and he doesn't like newspapermen anyhow. He'll be photographed, and he'll be wild. That's all you need to know."

In due time we arrived at as comfortable an abode for a wild man as well might be. It was near the old Essex and Morris Canal, not far from Boonton. A charming clump of brush and rock was selected, and here a snapshot of a posse hunting, men peering cautiously from behind trees in groups and looking as though they were most eager to discover something, was made. Then Peter, slipping away—I suddenly saw him ambling toward us, hair upstanding, body smeared with black muck, daubs of white about the eyes, little tufts of wool about wrists and ankles and loins—as good a figure of a wild man as one might wish, only not eight feet tall.

"Peter!" I said. "How ridiculous! You loon!"

"Have a care how you address me," he replied with solemn dignity. "A wild man is a wild man. Our punctilio is not to be trifled with. I am of the oldest, the most famous line of wild men extant. Touch me not." He strode the grass with the air of a popular movie star, while he discussed with the art director and photographer the most terrifying and convincing attitudes of a wild man seen by accident and unconscious of his pursuers.

"But you're not eight feet tall!" I interjected at one point.

"A small matter. A small matter," he replied airily. "I will be in the picture. Nothing easier. We wild men, you know—"

Some of the views were excellent, most striking. He leered most terribly from arras of leaves or indicated fright or cunning. The man was a good actor. For years I retained and may still have somewhere a full set of the pictures as well as the double-page spread which followed the next week.

Well, the thing was appropriately discussed, as it should have been, but the wild man got away, as was feared. He went into the nearby canal and washed away all his terror, or rather he vanished into the dim recesses of Peter's memory. He was only heard of a few times more in the papers, his supposed body being found in some town in northeast Pennsylvania—or in the small item that was "telegraphed" from there. As for Peter, he emerged from the canal, or from its banks, a cleaner if not a better man. He was grinning, combing his hair, adjusting his tie.

"What a scamp!" I insisted lovingly. "What an incorrigible trickster!"

"Dreiser, Dreiser," he chortled, "there's nothing like it. You should not scoff. I am a public benefactor. I am really a creator. I have created a being as distinct as any that ever lived. He is in many minds—mine, yours. You know that you believe in him really. There he was peeking out from between those bushes only fifteen minutes ago. And he has made, and will make, thousands of people happy, thrill them, give them a new interest. If Stevenson can create a Jekyll and Hyde, why can't I create a wild man? I have. We have his picture to prove it. What more do you wish?"

I acquiesced. All told, it was a delightful bit of foolery and art, and Peter was what he was first and foremost, an artist in the grotesque and the ridiculous.

For some time thereafter peace seemed to reign in his mind, only now it was that the marriage and home and children idea began to grow. From much of the foregoing it may have been assumed that Peter was out of sympathy with the ordinary routine of life, despised the commonplace, the purely practical. As a matter of fact it was just the other way about. I never knew a man so radical in some of his viewpoints, so versatile and yet so wholly, intentionally and cravingly, immersed in the usual as Peter. He was all for creating, developing, brightening life along simple rather than outré lines, in so far as he himself was concerned.

Nearly all of his arts and pleasures were decorative and homey. A good grocer, a good barber, a good saloonkeeper, a good tailor, a shoemaker, was just as interesting in his way to Peter as anyone or anything else, if not a little more so. He respected their lines, their arts, their professions, and above all, where they had it, their industry, sobriety and desire for fair dealing. He believed that millions of men, especially those about him, were doing the best they could under the very severe conditions which life offered. He objected to the idle, the too dull, the swindlers and thieves as well as the officiously puritanic or dogmatic. He resented, for himself at least, solemn pomp and show. Little houses, little gardens, little porches, simple cleanly neighborhoods with their air of routine, industry, convention and order, fascinated him as apparently nothing else could. He insisted that they were enough. A man did not need a great house unless he was a public character with official duties.

"Dreiser," he would say in Philadelphia and Newark, if not before, "it's in just such a neighborhood as this that some day I'm going to live. I'm going to have my little *frau,* my seven children, my chickens, dog, cat, canary, best German style, my garden, my birdbox, my pipe; and Sundays, by God, I'll march 'em all off to church, wife and seven kids, as regular as clockwork, shined shoes, pigtails and all, and I'll lead the procession."

"Yes, yes," I said. "You talk."

"Well, wait and see. Nothing in this world means so much to me as the good old orderly home stuff. One ought to live and die in a family. It's the right way. I'm cutting up now, sowing my wild oats, but that's nothing. I'm just getting ready to eventually settle down and live, just as I tell you, and be an ideal orderly citizen. It's the only way. It's the way nature intends us to do. All this early kid stuff is passing, a sorting-out process. We get over it. Every fellow does, or ought to be able to, if he's worth anything, find some one woman that he can live with and stick by her. That makes the world that you and I like to live in, and you know it. There's a psychic call in all of us to it, I think. It's the genius of our civilization, to marry one woman and settle down. And when I do, no more of this all-night stuff with this, that and the other lady. I'll be a model husband and father, sure as you're standing there. Don't you think I won't. Smile if you want to—it's so. I'll have my garden. I'll be friendly with my neighbors. You can come over then and help us put the kids to bed."

"Oh, Lord! This is a new bug now! We'll have the vine-covered cot idea for a while, anyhow."

"Oh, all right. Scoff if you want to. You'll see."

Time went by. He was doing all the things I have indicated, living in a kind of whirl of life. At the same time, from time to time, he would come back to this thought. Once, it is true, I thought it was all over with the little yellow-haired girl in Philadelphia. He talked of her occasionally, but less and less. Out on the golf links near Passaic he met another girl, one of a group that flourished there. I met her. She was not unpleasing, a bit sensuous, rather attractive in dress and manners, not very well informed, but gay, clever, up-to-date; such a girl as would pass among other women as fairly satisfactory.

For a time Peter seemed greatly attracted to her. She danced, played a little, was fair at golf and tennis, and she was, or pretended to be, interested in him. He confessed at last that he believed he was in love with her.

"So it's all day with Philadelphia, is it?" I asked.

"It's a shame," he replied, "but I'm afraid so. I'm having a hell of a time with myself, my alleged conscience, I tell you."

I heard little more about it. He had a fad for collecting rings at this time, a whole casket full, like a Hindu prince, and he told me once he was giving her her choice of them.

Suddenly he announced that it was "all off" and that he was going to marry the maid of Philadelphia. He had thrown the solitaire engagement ring he had given her down a sewer! At first he would confess nothing as to the reason or the details, but being so close to me it eventually came out. Apparently, to the others as to myself, he had talked much of his simple home plans, his future children—the good citizen idea. He had talked it to his new love also, and she had sympathized and agreed. Yet one day, after he had endowed her with the engagement ring, someone, a member of the golf club, came and revealed a tale. The girl was not "straight." She had been, mayhap was even then, "intimate" with other men—one anyhow. She was in love with Peter well enough, as she insisted afterward, and willing to undertake

85

the life he suggested, but she had not broken with the old atmosphere completely, or if she had it was still not believed that she had. There were those who could not only charge, but prove. A compromising note of some kind sent to someone was involved, turned over to Peter.

"Dreiser," he growled as he related the case to me, "it serves me right. I ought to know better. I know the kind of woman I need. This one has handed me a damned good wallop, and I deserve it. I might have guessed that she wasn't suited to me. She was really too free—a life-lover more than a wife. That home stuff! She was just stringing me because she liked me. She isn't really my sort, not simple enough."

"But you loved her, I thought?"

"I did, or thought I did. Still, I used to wonder too. There were many ways about her that troubled me. You think I'm kidding about this home and family idea, but I'm not. It suits me, however flat it looks to you. I want to do that, live that way, go through the normal routine experience, and I'm going to do it."

"But how did you break it off with her so swiftly?" I asked curiously.

"Well, when I heard this I went direct to her and put it up to her. If you'll believe me she never even denied it. Said it was all true, but that she was in love with me all right, and would change and be all that I wanted her to be."

"Well, that's fair enough," I said. "if she loves you. You're no saint yourself, you know. If you'd encourage her, maybe she'd make good."

"Well, maybe, but I don't think so really," he returned, shaking his head. "She likes me, but not enough, I'm afraid. She wouldn't run straight, now that she's had this other. She'd mean to maybe, but she wouldn't. I feel it about her. And anyhow I don't want to take any chances. I like her—I'm crazy about her really, but I'm through. I'm going to marry little Dutchy if she'll have me, and cut out this old-line stuff. You'll have to stand up with me when I do."

In three months more the new arrangement was consummated and little Dutchy—or Zuleika, as he subsequently named her—was duly brought to Newark and installed, at first in a charming apartment in a conventionally respectable and cleanly neighborhood, later in a small house with a "yard," lawn front and back, in one of the homiest of home neighborhoods in Newark. It was positively entertaining to observe Peter not only attempting to assume but assuming the role of the conventional husband, and exactly nine months after he had been married, to the hour, a father in this humble and yet, in so far as his particular home was concerned, comfortable world. I have no space here for more than the barest outline. I have already indicated his views, most emphatically expressed and forecasted. He fulfilled them all to the letter, up to the day of his death. In so far as I could make out, he made about as satisfactory a husband and father and citizen as I have ever seen. He did it deliberately, in cold reason, and yet with a warmth and flair which puzzled me all the more since it *was* based on reason and forethought. I misdoubted. I was not quite willing to believe that it would work out, and yet if ever a home was delightful, with a charming and genuinely "happy" atmosphere, it was Peter's.

"Here she is," he observed the day he married her, "me *frau*—Zuleika. Isn't she a peach? Ever see any nicer hair than that? And these here, now, pink cheeks? What? Look at 'em! And her little Dutchy nose! Isn't it cute? Oh, Dutchy! And right here in me vest pocket is the golden band wherewith I am to be chained to the floor, the domestic hearth. And right there on her finger is my badge of prospective serfdom." Then, in a loud aside to me, "In six months I'll be beating her. Come now, Zuleika. We have to go through with this. You have to swear to be my slave."

And so they were married.

And in the home afterward he was as busy and helpful and noisy as any man about the house could ever hope to be. He was always fussing about after hours, "putting up" something or arranging his collections or helping Zuleika wash and dry the dishes, or showing her how to cook something if she didn't know how. He was running to the store or bringing home things from the downtown market. Months before the first child was born he was declaring most shamelessly, "In a few months now, Dreiser, Zuleika and I are going to have our first calf. The bones roll for a boy, but you never can tell. I'm offering up prayers and oblations—both of us are. I make Zuleika pray every night. And say, when it comes, no spoiling-the-kid stuff. No bawling or rocking it to sleep nights permitted. Here's one kid that's going to be raised right. I've worked out all the rules. No trashy baby foods. Good old specially brewed Culmbacher for the mother, and the kid afterwards if it wants it. This is one family in which law and order are going to prevail—good old 'dichtig, wichtig' law and order."

I used to chuckle the while I verbally denounced him for his coarse, plebeian point of view and tastes.

In a little while the child came, and to his immense satisfaction it was a boy. I never saw a man "carry on" so, make over it, take such a whole-souled interest in all those little things which supposedly made for its health and well-being. For the first few weeks he still talked of not having it petted or spoiled, but at the same time he was surely and swiftly changing, and by the end of that time had become the most doting, almost ridiculously fond papa that I ever saw. Always the child must be in his lap at the most unseemly hours, when his wife would permit it. When he went anywhere, or they, although they kept a maid the child must be carried along by him on his shoulder. He liked nothing better than to sit and hold it close, rocking in a rocking chair American style and singing, or come tramping into my home in New York, the child looking like a woolen ball. At night if it stirred or whimpered he was up and looking. And the baby clothes!—and the cradle!—and the toys!—colored rubber balls and soldiers the first or second or third week!

"What about that stern discipline that was to be put in force here—no rocking, no getting up at night to coddle a weeping infant?"

"Yes, I know. That's all good stuff before you get one. I've got one of my own now, and I've got a new light on this. Say, Dreiser, take my advice. Go through the routine. Don't try to escape. Have a kid or two or three. There's a psychic punch to it you can't get any other way. It's nature's way. It's a great scheme. You and your girl and your kid."

As he talked he rocked, holding the baby boy to his breast. It was wonderful.

And Mrs. Peter—how happy she seemed. There was light in that house, flowers, laughter, good fellowship. As in his old rooms so in this new home he gathered a few of his old friends around him and some new ones, friends of this region. In the course of a year or two he was on the very best terms of friendship with his barber around the corner, his grocer, some man who had a saloon and bowling alley in the neighborhood, his tailor, and then just neighbors. The milkman, the coal man, the druggist and cigar man at the next corner—all could tell you where Peter lived. His little front "yard" had two beds of flowers all summer long, his lot in the back was a garden—lettuce, onions, peas, beans. Peter was always happiest when he could be home working, playing with the baby, pushing him about in a go-cart, working in his garden, or lying on the floor making something— an engraving or print or a box which he was carving, the infant in some simple gingham romper crawling about. He was always busy, but never too much so for a glance or a mock-threatening, "Now say, not so much industry there. You leave my things alone," to the child. Of a Sunday he sat out on the front porch smoking, reading the Sunday paper, congratulating himself on his happy married life, and most of the time holding the infant. Afternoons he would carry it somewhere, anywhere, in his arms to his friends, the park, New York, to see me. At breakfast, dinner, supper the heir presumptive was in a high chair beside him.

"Ah, now, here's a rubber spoon. Beat with that. It's less destructive and less painful physically."

"How about a nice prust" (crust) "dipped in bravery" (gravy) "—heh? Do you suppose that would cut any of your teeth?"

"Zuleika, this son of yours seems to think a spoonful of beer or two might not hurt him. What do you say?"

Occasionally, especially of a Saturday evening, he wanted to go bowling and yet he wanted his heir. The problem was solved by fitting the latter into a tight little sweater and cap and carrying him along on his shoulder, into the bar for a beer, thence to the bowling alley, where young hopeful was fastened into a chair on the sidelines while Peter and myself or some of his friends bowled. At ten or ten-thirty or eleven, as the case might be, he was ready to leave, but before that hour les ongfong might be sound asleep, hanging against Peter's scarf, his interest in his toes or thumbs having given out.

"Peter, look at that," I observed once. "Don't you think we'd better take him home?"

"Home nothing! Let him sleep. He can sleep here as well as anywhere, and besides I like to look at him." And in the room would be a great crowd, cigars, beers, laughter, and Peter's various friends as used to the child's presence and as charmed by it as he was. He was just the man who could do such things. His manner and point of view carried conviction. He believed in doing all that he wanted to do simply and naturally, and more and more as he went along people not only respected, I think they adored him, especially the simple homely souls among whom he chose to move and have his being.

About this time there developed among those in his immediate neighborhood a desire to elect him to some political position, that of councilman, or State assemblyman, in the hope or thought that he would rise to something higher. But he would none of it—not then anyhow. Instead, about this time or a very little later, after the birth of his second child (a girl), he devoted himself to the composition of a brilliant piece of prose poetry (*Wolf*), which, coming from him, did not surprise me in the least. If he had designed or constructed a great building, painted a great picture, entered politics and been elected governor or senator, I would have taken it all as a matter of course. He could have. The material from which anything may rise was there. I asked him to let me offer it to the publishing house with which I was connected, and I recall with interest the comment of the oldest and most experienced of the bookmen and salesmen among us. "You'll never make much, if anything, on this book. It's too good, too poetic. But whether it pays or not, I vote yes. I'd rather lose money on something like this than make it on some of the trash we do make it on."

Amen. I agreed then, and I agree now.

The last phase of Peter was as interesting and dramatic as any of the others. His married life was going forward about as he had planned. His devotion to his home and children, his loving wife, his multiplex interests, his various friends, was always a curiosity to me, especially in view of his olden days. One day he was over in New York visiting one of his favorite Chinese importing companies, through which he had secured and was still securing occasional objects of art. He had come down to me in my office at the Butterick Building to see if I would not come

90

over the following Saturday as usual and stay until Monday. He had secured something, was planning something. I should see. At the elevator he waved me a gay "so long—see you Saturday!"

But on Friday, as I was talking with someone at my desk, a telegram was handed me. It was from Mrs. Peter and read: "Peter died today at two of pneumonia. Please come."

I could scarcely believe it. I did not know that he had even been sick. His little yellow-haired wife! The two children! His future! His interests! I dropped everything and hurried to the nearest station. En route I speculated on the mysteries on which he had so often speculated—death, dissolution, uncertainty, the crude indifference or cruelty of Nature. What would become of Mrs. Peter? His children?

I arrived only to find a home atmosphere destroyed as by a wind that puts out a light. There was Peter, stiff and cold, and in the other rooms his babies, quite unconscious of what had happened, prattling as usual, and Mrs. Peter practically numb and speechless. It had come so suddenly, so out of a clear sky, that she could not realize, could not even tell me at first. The doctor was there—also a friend of his, the nearest barber! Also two or three representatives from his paper, the owner of the bowling alley, the man who had the $40,000 collection of curios. All were stunned, as I was. As his closest friend, I took charge: wired his relatives, went to an undertaker who knew him to arrange for his burial, in Newark or Philadelphia, as his wife should wish, she having no connection with Newark other than Peter.

It was most distressing, the sense of dull despair and unwarranted disaster which hung over the place. It was as though impish and pagan forces, or malign ones outside life, had committed a crime of the ugliest character. On Monday, the day he saw me, he was well. On Tuesday morning he had a slight cold but insisted on running out somewhere without his overcoat, against which his wife protested. Tuesday night he had a fever and took quinine and aspirin and a hot whiskey. Wednesday morning he was worse and a doctor was called, but it was not deemed serious. Wednesday night he was still worse and pneumonia had set in. Thursday he was lower still, and by noon a metal syphon of oxygen was sent for, to relieve the sense of suffocation setting in. Thursday night he was weak and sinking, but expected to come round—and still, so unexpected was the attack, so uncertain the probability of anything fatal, that no word was sent, even to me. Friday morning he was no worse and no better. "If he was no worse by night he might pull through." At noon he was seized with a sudden sinking spell. Oxygen was applied by his wife and a nurse, and the doctor sent for. By one-thirty he was lower still, very low. "His face was blue, his lips ashen," his wife told me. "We put the oxygen tube to his mouth and I said 'Can you speak, Peter?' I was so nervous and frightened. He moved his head a little to indicate 'no.' 'Peter,' I said, 'you mustn't let go! You must fight! Think of me! Think of the babies!' I was a little crazy, I think, with fear. He looked at me very fixedly. He stiffened and gritted his teeth in a great effort. Then suddenly he collapsed and lay still. He was dead."

I could not help thinking of the force and energy—able at the last minute, when he could not speak—to "grit his teeth" and "fight," a minute before his death. What is the human spirit, or mind, that it can fight so, to the very last? I felt as though someone, something, had ruthlessly killed him, committed plain, unpunished murder—nothing more and nothing less.

And there were his cases of curios, his rug, his prints, his dishes, his many, many schemes, his book to come out soon. I gazed and marveled. I looked at his wife and babies, but could say nothing. It spelled, what such things always spell, in the face of all our dreams, crass chance or the willful, brutal indifference of Nature to all that relates to man. If he is to prosper he must do so without her aid.

That same night, sleeping in the room adjoining that in which was the body, a pale candle burning near it, I felt as though Peter were walking to and fro, to and fro, past me and into the room of his wife beyond, thinking and grieving. His imagined wraith seemed horribly depressed and distressed. Once he came over and moved his hand (something) over my face. I felt him walking into the room where were his wife and kiddies, but he could make no one see, hear, understand. I got up and looked at his *cadaver* a long time, then went to bed again.

The next day and the next and the next were filled with many things. His mother and sister came on from the West as well as the mother and brother of his wife. I had to look after his affairs, adjusting the matter of insurance which he left, his art objects, the burial of his body "in consecrated ground" in Philadelphia, with the consent and aid of the local Catholic parish rector, else no burial. His mother desired it, but he had never been a good Catholic and there was trouble. The local parish assistant refused me, even the rector. Finally I threatened the good father with an appeal to the diocesan bishop on the ground of plain common sense and courtesy to a Catholic family, if not charity to a tortured mother and wife—and obtained consent. All along I felt as if a great crime had been committed by someone, foul murder. I could not get it out of my mind, and it made me angry, not sad.

Two, three, five, seven years later, I visited the little family in Philadelphia. The wife was with her mother and father in a simple little home street in a factory district, secretary and stenographer to an architect. She was little changed—a little stouter, not so carefree, industrious, patient. His boy, the petted F———, could not even recall his father, the girl not at all of course. And in the place were a few of his prints, two or three Chinese dishes pottered by himself, his loom with the unfinished rug. I remained for dinner and dreamed old dreams, but I was uncomfortable and left early. And Mrs. Peter, accompanying me to the steps, looked after me as though I, alone, was all that was left of the old life.

Reina

THE HOME FROM WHICH she came was a makeshift affair at best, with a mother who was soft and placative and sentimental and with no least grasp of life, and a semi-neurotic father of Dutch extraction who was little more than a leftover sprout of a decayed branch of a family tree that somewhere and at some time may have been something. Here (meaning a small town in our American Northwest) he was a locksmith, and from all accounts an erratic one. He curled his mustachios upward and donned a dress suit once or twice a year. He thought he could play the violin. He told vile stories and seemed to like to shock his own children. He was described to me as a physical coward, a man who browbeat his wife (where he was afraid of other men). Being the irresponsible that he was, he shifted most of the burden of life to her, who made a large percentage of the living by running a rooming house.

First impressions are keenest. When I first saw Reina I thought she was a silly, and yet not quite. That little lavender hat pulled down over her bobbed tow-colored hair (bleached to that shade, of course) and the lavender throw that accompanied it seemed to suggest a keen sense of harmony, as did the very light gray suit reaching to but an inch or two below the knees. She had a habit of standing as a boy will, legs far apart, head thrown back and gray-blue eyes dancing with an irresistible zest for life. At least, I said, she is alive—very much so. And then the really funny stories, always vulgar but laugh-provoking in spite of anything one might think, and leaving one wondering how she could have the effrontery to tell them so calmly. It seemed to imply disrespect and at times even a low estimate of oneself. And yet there was no least trace of pruriency in her stories; rather, it was a coarse and yet healthy sense of the ridiculous which prompted her. Let us say that she was unconsciously and at times even charmingly vulgar, which may seem to be a paradox but is not.

Rhoda, the elder half-sister, was a really beautiful girl, intelligent and very clever. Beautiful enough to be a figure of sorts in the movies, she was still sweet enough to retain the natural charms of a temperament that was as yet vague but beauty bent. She had not become hard or bold and pushing. Hers was a nature that craved the perpetuation of all home-ties and connections if possible. You are to remember that Rhoda had not seen Reina for nearly five years, herself having married and removed from her native city five years before. Since then Reina had married.

For months before meeting her I had been hearing of the interesting if not wonderful Reina. She was young, pretty, bubbling with life, a good horsewoman. She was affectionate and sisterly, and was now married to a young managing lumberman. They had had a little home in some interior lumber district in Washington, but Reina, accustomed as she was to the metropolitan delights of Spokane and Seattle, soon grew tired of this backwoods life and fled, riding on a caboose to a main-line station some forty miles away. The husband, seemingly unable to live without her, had thrown up his connection with the lumber business, which was earning him four thousand a year, and had followed her. Twice in a married life of not more than three years she had left him in this way because the conditions surrounding the thing he chanced to be doing were not to her taste. And in both instances he had dropped everything and followed her, hoping to induce her to come back to him. Temperamentally, apparently, he needed her. After knowing her for some time and realizing what a fool she was in some ways and what a pest she might prove to some men in almost every way, and knowing him too, as I did then, I could still see how he might like and even need her. She had health, energy, humor and youthfulness, at least, and probably represented those qualities to him. When things were going against them, though, instead of being an aid or a comfort, she could be very dour, nasty, really.

When I met Sven he was not more than twenty-five, good-looking and ambitious. More, he was tactful and approachable, but without the advantages of an education. His father, a Swedish farmer and dairyman, had apparently not

96

believed in giving his children even a common school education. On the contrary, so I heard, he did his best to handicap them in this respect and in consequence Sven, who had run away from the farm at fifteen, used such English as he had heard spoken about him. Unless cautioned he would use *done* for *did, learned* for *taught, seen* for *saw,* and some other of those amusing Americanisms beloved by those who constitute the rank and file. Once he learned that he was using incorrect English, however, he preferred to remain silent or to imitate those who were speaking correctly, which was much more than could be said for Reina. Professionally he was a good lumberman, with a practical knowledge of woods and skilled in their preparation for the market. He was also, as I know, an excellent garage man, having mastered the mysteries of the automobile and being able to manage a garage when necessary. And he was the type of youth who was willing to do almost anything in order to get along.

But if Sven used bad grammar Reina used worse. Mrs. Malaprop at her worst wasn't a patch. "Say, ya know what I done yesterday? Gee, I wish ya coulda seen! I sure come near ballin' things up, all right, all right. It was this way, see. Me an' Sven was walkin' along Seventh Street when who should come chasin' but—well, give a guess. Monty! Sure. The same old Monty. An' in a nobby coat, too. Gee, you oughta seen! That guy musta come into some money since I saw him last. An' it didn't make no difference to him that Sven an' me was married. He didn't get it, I guess. Ya can't learn that guy nothin'. Just grabbed me by the arm like he used to. 'Where ya goin'? Who's your friend?' Then I introduced him, an' Sven lookin' at me an' him all the time like he could swalla us. Can ya feature that? An' me always tellin' Sven there wasn't nobody could get fresh with me! Well, I come pretty near cashin' in then, but I had to laugh afterwards. But I got away with it. 'Here,' I says, 'do ya wanta get hurt? This ain't school days no more. Meet my husband, Sven, see?' Then he savvies an' gets awful polite an' nice like. An' Sven he softens a little because I ring in that Monty's father has money an' that Monty might be lookin' fer sompin to invest in, an' in a little bit they gets to talkin'. But can ya feature that stuff? An' Sven as jealous as he is? Well, when Sven wasn't lookin' ya bet I give Monty one look. 'Watcha doin'? Where ya goin'?' Ya bet

I got it over to him that he'd better cut that stuff. Los Angeles ain't Spokane by a lot. But fer a minute there I thought there might be sompin rough. I sure did. Ya know Sven when he gets hot. Gee! I sure was curled up there for a second or two. But he thinks Monty went to school with me, so it's all right now, see?"

That was typical of much that I listened to for months and months, and in spite of anything and everything done to make her see the error of her ways. Grammar was not to be impressed upon Reina, via correction, example or a stick. She could sit in upon the most perfect English spoken by as many as seventeen masters of the art and of a sudden burst in with "Whoja think me an' Sven seen?" or "Sven an' me was thinkin' . . ." And her sister, who because of her beauty had been able to marry an Easterner from upper New York State of no little position and social training, although she had since left him and had managed to place herself in a more interesting walk of life, was made restless and unhappy by the sharp realization that since leaving home she had encountered conditions which had taught her much that her sister did not know.

But what a bubbling, enthusiastic temperament! It was easy to understand why a man, if he were not too well informed about grammar himself, might become very much attracted to Reina. She had the pertness and inquisitiveness of a collie or a crow. And she was famishing for want of pleasures and luxuries such as others possessed but of which she had scarcely tasted as yet. Hence sister Rhoda's quaint little apartment in Hollywood, with its balconies, its flowers, its French windows, its Persian cat and chow dog, seemed to affect her as might strong drink a devotee of the demon rum. Gee!—her favorite expression. Everything was either "classy" or "swell" or "nobby" or, occasionally, "the cat's whiskers," or even—I blush to repeat a tithe of all the amazing expressions she used—"the cat's pajamas." A reproduction of *The Pot of Basil* which ornamented one wall was "swell," but "Gee, she's kinda long-legged, ain't she?" and "A dress like that wouldn't go now. She musta lived somewhere where they wore them things." The nude figure of a woman draped about one side of a glass fishbowl brought forth "Didja ever see a goldfish bowl like that before? Classy, eh? But she ain't got so much of a figure. Ya can see better'n that at Pantages any day."

98

"The trouble is, Reina," I suggested, "the artist lacked a suitable model. He should have had a graceful girl like you."

"Well, he oughta come with me. I could show him some that would make him leave his mother."

That Rhoda resented this brash and brassy line of comment, even while it amused her, was obvious from the first. She had been talking so much of the interesting Reina, thinking of her as she had been a few years before, whereas Reina had never been all or maybe any of the things she thought her. Most likely then she had judged her with scarcely any standards of comparison, whereas by now she had come upon many standards that had served to change her greatly. In consequence she scarcely knew what to think of Reina now, but was still too fond of her—the blood tie and old memories affecting her too much—to be severely critical. At the same time she was greatly troubled lest I conceive all sorts of queer notions concerning her and her parents, which were only partly true.

One of the things that interested me from the first was why so sober and industrious a man as Sven should have become so interested in Reina as to want to marry her and follow her about in this way. He was practical and quiet, determined to get along and provide Reina with all she desired, while Reina had no least sense of order or responsibility. Before and for some time after marrying Sven she had been the boon companion of a girl named Bertha, who appears to have been a combination of meal ticket and attendant. This girl possessed the double advantage of looks and charm for men, two qualities which Reina admired intensely in any woman. Plus some means—Bertha, by the way, was the daughter of a well-to-do laundryman, from whom she could always get money and a goodly portion of which Reina could get from her, as well as some little from her own mother. With these several sums at their command, and because the home town from which they derived was small and Spokane and Seattle and Tacoma within easy striking distance, they were accustomed to race back and forth between these places, where relatives were supposed to reside. I judged that Reina supplied the initiative and daring and inspired these same in her companion. But why their parents should have permitted all this is more than I could understand. Careful questioning of Reina from time to time (her prospective historiographer, you see) elicited the information that her mother thought that when they went to Seattle or Spokane or Tacoma she stayed with Bertha's relatives, whereas Bertha, in dealing with her own parents merely reversed this fabrication.

For something like a year and a half, which covered Reina's pre-nuptial contact with Sven, Bertha and Reina were almost always together. They went about with men, but according to Reina and in so far as she was concerned, not to do wrong but to get automobile rides, free dinners, trinkets and entertainment generally. For Bertha she made no claims. Often they were placed in perilous positions from which it took the greatest tact and craft to extricate themselves. The perils of Pauline were as nothing. The principal of these perils had arisen, as I soon saw, from the penchant of both for entering cars of youths who would then proceed to drive to some lone if not exactly forsaken spot where they would proceed to make advances which at least Reina, if one could believe her, was not willing to accept. Thus one night during a ride from Tacoma to Seattle in a taxi, a distance of thirty miles, they were attacked at a lonely point on the road by the chauffeur and a friend who had been brought along. The ruse by which they managed to escape would not bear publication, but the genuine perils of the situation would interest anyone. Once out of the car they ran through the darkness into the woods, where in the depths they were guided to a cottage by a lighted window. The chauffeur and his friend in search of them, once passed within a foot of the place where they were crouching but did not actually stumble over them. Once having gained the cottage the girls remained there until morning and then proceeded to Seattle.

Because of Bertha's generosity and worship of her, as well as what she gained in entertainment and trinkets by the adventures, there was set up in Reina's mind, I think, the thought that life was an easy game, or should be, and that somebody, somewhere, would always provide her with the comforts of existence as she conceived the same. Her interest in Sven, therefore, when he came upon the scene, was in part based on this philosophy. But so attractive was he to her that eventually he succeeded in interrupting and finally partially destroying this friendship with Bertha. Just the same and even when I knew Reina some three years later whenever things were not going to her taste

100

it was to Bertha and the old gay days that she was always reverting or thinking of returning to. And it was Bertha whom Sven disliked and feared most of all, I think.

But as a study in *dolce far niente,* when she was about and planning though not as yet executing some new mischief, Reina was all that the picture required. When left alone she might sit for hours in a comfortable chair or before her sister's three-panel mirror, twiddling her thumbs or rearranging or clipping or tinting her hair, rouging her lips and cheeks, touching up her eyebrows and eyelids, and perfecting her facial toilet generally. Sometimes she would spend hours in trying on her sister's hats or dresses and looking at herself in a tall mirror and call to me or anyone to see. "Swell, eh?" or "Classy, what?" She would lie abed of a morning, regardless of what any or all others might be doing, but by late afternoon or night she would be up and ready for some form of entertainment, to be provided by Rhoda, Sven or myself. And sometimes, though not often, she would help Rhoda prepare dinner if she could find no easy way of getting out of it, but always making herself more of a hindrance than a help so as to warn against future requests.

As a rule, however, there were no dinners prepared here. The restaurants were far more interesting to Reina, as they were to Rhoda, for that matter; but it was always Reina who would suggest a restaurant whether she had a dime or not. What about so and so's? Didn't they have dancing there? And wasn't it considered "swell" or "chick"? Well, so oriented or directed by hints, I might take both. Whereupon dinner over, and although at the time neither she nor Sven had any money for such things, he having come to this new city solely because she had broken up his connection elsewhere, she would still suggest the theater or a swimming pool or a concert, and apparently with never a thought that expense might be a factor. Somebody had to pay, so why should she think? More, what were men for if not to pay? They had to have girls like her, didn't they? "Betcha life." In consequence, she would usually do her best to heighten the expense, although, to do her justice, she certainly added to my entertainment, thus embarrassing Sven, if not me, greatly, because he was unwilling to accept invitations unless he could at least pay his share. But that had nothing to do with Reina's calculations.

101

She wanted to be entertained, and she was prepared to blink the sources of the supply as long as the entertainment was forthcoming.

All this by way of introduction. Once they were settled in Los Angeles—and, by the way, Rhoda's charming apartment caused Reina instanter to become openly dissatisfied with anything Sven could offer, and he had very little to offer just then—she made herself all but a permanent guest in her sister's home, and with scarcely so much as an invitation or a by-your-leave. For was not Rhoda her sister? And what are sisters for, pray? And Rhoda being one who attached almost much too much to blood kinship there was very little need of an invitation. Reina came and was lovingly and generously treated always, which was a mistake, as I saw it. For there was Sven, his difficulties and needs. And certainly Reina owed him something. Yet in spite of his needs and wishes and Reina's obligations as well as her own obvious lack of that perfection of beauty which made her sister so acceptable to the moving picture grandees about the various studios, still it was she, not Rhoda, who at once decided that she also was cut out for that work and her sister who generously suppoted her in her aspirations. And why not? Didn't men like her? Wasn't she as clever as anyone? Of course. Rhoda was earning from two to three hundred a week when she worked, sometimes more. Why couldn't she, Reina, also tap this golden dribble? The only things that stood between her and her goal were (1) Sven— her marital or household duties to him which she never fulfilled anyhow and (2) the various difficulties which Rhoda in her time had met and conquered. In short, like Rhoda, she would have to begin at the bottom as an extra, and that at seven-and-a-half a day—not forty and fifty, as Rhoda now received. She would have to get up as early as six or seven and be at the studio, made up, not later than eight-thirty. She would have to provide her own clothes and makeup and show considerable interest in and enthusiasm for the work—all of which threw a heavy wet blanket over the original fires of her ambition.

For Reina was one for whom there was never any real, constructive effort. She was a parasite by nature, and for that affliction there seems to be no cure. Her mind was not constructive; there was apparently not a trace of anything in it anywhere which related to building anything, for herself or others. Things happened; they were not brought about by the efforts of anyone. Luck was the great thing, luck and gifts. Never was it to be expected that one seek to make anything come to pass via the humdrum process of labor. Never! Bunk! All was to be sunshine, blue seas, waving awnings, ice cream, balcony dinners, automobile rides, clothes in the newest mode, dancing and cheerful friends. Anything less than this was an imposition on the part of either man or nature, but principally man. A man, if one is so gracious as to marry him, should provide all these things forthwith; otherwise he is a bonehead and worthless, solid ivory. If one has relatives of any means they should do as much; otherwise, why relatives? Such relatives owe it to all their kith and kin, but more especially to the one holding the above views, to provide him or her with joy and plenty. Reina held such views and was just like this, albeit she could be most agreeable so long as things were provided in sufficient quantity and to her taste.

Nevertheless and notwithstanding these traits, the moment she expressed the thought that she would like to enter upon this work her sister offered to take her about and introduce her to such directors and assistants as she knew, albeit she did talk to Reina of Sven, and how, unless she paid more attention to him, all this was most likely to end in marital destruction for both. Only Reina would never hear of Sven as an obstacle to anything. Not only that but now, as Rhoda also pointed out, such introductions to anyone really earnest to enter upon this film work should most certainly prove of the greatest help and Reina must be sure to take advantage of them—make them count. Just the same, and apart from going with Rhoda on one or two mornings when she did not have to get up too early, this proffer was neglected. These extremely early hours were too much for her. Not only that, but and although she was previously instructed that she must be prepared to endure the slights and snubs and insults and rank overtures even of nearly all connected with the great film industry in any official capacity, from the sixth assistant doorman up, still the information did not take. She was told, for instance, that if any of the directors or actors or what not were really interested, she might reasonably expect that they would attempt to ingratiate themselves by all sorts of unmeant promises, only Reina was not to listen. Rather she was to go on about her work—kidding them as much as possible, and if that failed and she really could not get rid of them or endure it, well . . . quit. Yet two visits made in this manner, and with but one or two side ventures of her own, and Reina was cured.

"What! Me fall fer them guys? And them makin' me wait around all day before they'll even letcha see anybody. Ya bet them guys ain't goin' to pull any of that raw stuff on me. An' I told 'em who I was, too, an' who sent me. Did that get me in? It did not. That little snit over at the Metro Studio gate just looked at me an' wouldn't even take my name. Said Mr. ——— was busy. An' the same with that smark aleck over at Lasky. I never seen such freshies in all my life, anyhow." And then came a long and pyrotechnic picture of what she would do to any of them if they really "got fresh" with her. They needn't think that because they had some squeak connection with the movies they could put anything over on her. Far from it. Of course, now, if a man was a regular fella and conducted himself as such, coming up to a girl with respect and ingratiating himself maybe by an invitation to dinner or an automobile ride—well, if he looked all right, that might be different. Sometimes a guy like that might turn out to be all right. . . . I often sat and laughed and egged her on, just to be permitted to enjoy this ebullience; for that was what it was, sheer animal spirits and a crazy kind of imagination and zest for life running wild.

But one thing she did decide upon, and that the most unreasonable, of course. Sven must get a place in Hollywood, where rents for small apartments furnished ranged from seventy-five for the poorest and smallest to two and three hundred and up for the better and more spacious ones. None the less, one of these for Sven, who, as I had gathered, had been rather hard-pressed by her vagaries in the past, and at this very moment, was for taking a smaller place downtown where rents were less and so shaping their lives to match his salary, which was then only forty a week or thereabouts. He was working as night man in a garage until he could get something better. "You wanta remember, Reina," I heard him caution her within twenty-four hours after their arrival, "that we haven't any too much money now and we'll just have to go slow. We can't live in Hollywood on nothing." And so the place they were compelled to take was not to her taste. At the other extreme, really. Yet why couldn't Sven do better? Wasn't he a man, and hadn't she married him? She had caught a glimpse of Hollywood now, and regardless of means an immediate way must be found to stay there or there would be few sweet smiles for him.

Sven not being able to do better at the time, and she being in no way concerned to add to the exchequer, she took out her pique in loafing about her sister's place in Hollywood, while the latter worked and worked hard. Also nightly, while Reina slept, Sven cleaned and repaired cars and looked after the garage, which was never closed. This meant that he had to sleep by day. But instead of that arousing a proper sympathy for one so industrious it seemed to irritate Reina because of what she considered either his dullness or his stubbornness. Why couldn't he get a day job, anyhow? What was the use of any man working at night when there was day work to be had somewhere? He needn't work in a garage; he understood other things. Besides, if he didn't, he ought to. In vain did the industrious and really handsome Sven point out that because of the low state of their finances he had to take what he could get at the moment. She did not like that. Time was the essence of her contract with him. He must hurry and do better by her. Debarred from such comfort as Rhoda enjoyed, she felt outraged. Besides, at night, just when they might go out for a little fun, Sven had to go to work. And in the morning when she wanted to sleep late, in he came fresh from his work and waking her up. The fact that he was considerate enough to breakfast before he came home was nothing to the point. He chose to work at night instead of during the day, and for little enough at that. He should look about and get something that paid more. One thing he pointed out to Rhoda not long after they arrived was the fact that it was because of Reina that he had to take the work and small salary they were now living upon. She would not stay where he had been able to make big money, not even long enough for him to get a real start and go into business for himself, which was his great hope.

The upshot of this was that Rhoda, sympathizing with Reina on the ground that she was young and hungry for life and had never really had anything, and yet sympathizing with Sven quite as much, was anxious to see them comfortable and hence was full of helpful suggestions. Reina ought to be more considerate of Sven. Sven ought to get day work if he could. It wasn't right to leave her all alone at night. To make things a little easier for them she first gave Reina a hundred dollars or so for her own use and then offered to lend Sven something to go on in case he would drop what he was doing and look for day work or find an interest in some lumber concern, which same he was fully competent to manage. Also she suggested that he get better rooms, even if she had to make up the difference. And if he found the right sort of company in which to invest she would lend him the money to make the investment. When he got on his feet he was to get a car so that they could see something of the world in which they had so summarily injected themselves.

Sven, being the sort of youth he was, was all honest gratitude and anxious to make the most of this windfall. Forthwith he proceeded to spend most of his daytime sleeping hours in looking up one and another of the many advertised opportunities. Eventually he uncovered one in which, for the sum of one thousand cash invested and the sale of certain number of shares that must be sold and the taking over of a number for himself, to be paid for piecemeal, he was to receive the title and assume the duties of secretary of a lumber company. He was to have a polished oak desk with his name on it, as well as his name on the door. Also a salary of sixty-five dollars, to begin at once. Rhoda approving when all this was duly laid before her, he proceeded to close the deal and to carry out the details of his part of the contract. Needless to say, Sven being cautious and careful and rather clever when it came to things of this sort, he was soon well along on the path toward a moderate competence. At once he began planning the construction of a number of small houses, to be sold for three thousand and which were to net him or his company nearly one thousand. He and Rhoda were to make real money in the future. She would never regret having aided him. And I am sure that he meant all he said.

But I wish you might have seen Reina once these plans had passed the tentative stage and bid fair to come about, or after Sven had actually assumed his duties as secretary and they had moved to three rooms farther out, where there were flowers and a lawn and a better view. The airs! The assurance and swelling superiority! Sven was now the secretary and part owner of a lumber company. And they were living in a three-room apartment with a balcony on the borders of Hollywood. And they had a small car, a secondhand something, but not bad-looking, for Sven was a judge of bargains in that field. Yet instead of interesting herself in Sven and what he was doing, she was now most interested to know what they could do in order to entertain themselves. At once, of course, they must motor to Santa Barbara, ditto to Big Bear, ditto to Riverside, ditto to San Francisco, ditto to Bakersfield. And wouldn't it be fine if they had a piano—or a new victrola, anyhow—and Rhoda would come and bring some of her friends and they could dance, etc., etc., etc. Everything, as you see, for Reina; very little for Sven. And yet I doubt if I ever saw a happier young man, for a while, anyhow. By Reina's own admission he was up early and back late, following closely the possibilities that were now before him. Within the space of a very few weeks he had been able to dispose of a large number of shares of stock. Also he was able to handle quite all the details of shipment and delivery, while others sold the lumber ordered from Northern firms. His one mistake, if it was a mistake, was his desire to clear off too quickly the cost price of the shares allotted him so that by the next year he and Reina might have plenty to live on. His mistake, if any, was in thinking that Reina might be persuaded or prompted to wholeheartedly help him do this.

Most assuredly that dream was not well-founded. I never saw a young wife do less for an ambitious husband and expect more. The garish moving picture atmosphere of Hollywood, as well as the summery sweet-to-do-nothing mood of Los Angeles as a whole, seemed to get into her veins and make her absolutely intolerant of anything save idleness and pleasure. Her main interest was to parade the smart shops, near which she lived, or to linger at her sister's in Hollywood, where, when she was not meditating or planning outings or decorating her face before a mirror, she would sit at the piano and in an ultra and hence amusingly romantic voice give vent to exaggerations of the sentiment in "Dear Old Pal of Mine," "Old Pal, Why Don't You Answer Me?," "Avalon," "Macushla," and such other romanticisms. And from here, with her sister and occasionally myself as pilots, and while her husband worked, she would joyously set forth to a swimming pool, a horseback ride, a beach restaurant or an automobile ride, yet without a thought of including her young husband, and even at times resenting, by a gesture or a mouth, the mere mention of him, as though he were nothing at all in her young life. When taxed with this, as well as her whole attitude toward Sven and marriage, she denied it. At first she denied being indifferent to him, then later charged him with being unnecessarily grouchy wherever she was concerned; too set on a humdrum existence. He wanted to work all the time and never play. Why, instead, couldn't he work, and give her all she wanted and play, too? Finally she admitted that she might be changing or that he had changed. He wasn't as lighthearted as he used to be. He seemed to think there was nothing in the world to do except work. He was stingy and didn't seem to think she needed to do anything but wait for him. When I pointed out that he seemed to be making a gallant fight for a place, and under trying conditions, she paid a genuine tribute to his industry and rather blamed herself. She "guessed" she wasn't cut out for marriage, anyhow, that she just couldn't stand humdrum things. Sometimes she did like Sven very much, was even crazy about him; at other times she felt as though she hated him. He could be so nasty. Once they had quarreled and he had threatened to strike her, or had struck her, and she had flung something at him and had cut his eye. Another time he had struck her after they had quarreled about her having gone to a place she had promised not to go to. Just now he wanted her to live just so until he got on his feet, and she didn't want to live that way.

The pointlessness of the outsider mingling in the affectional affairs of those unhappily mated is too obvious to need comment here. I ventured no advice and made no pleas, and I was not greatly surprised when, one morning, Reina arrived at her sister's apartment with the announcement that she and Sven were "through"— that she wasn't going to stay with that old grouch any longer. Rather she would pawn her rings and return to Spokane where her mother now lived and where, in company with Bertha, she was certain to find something to do. Her underlying thought, as I suspected at the time, was that Rhoda would not let her go.

And she was right. Rhoda suggested that she come there first for a few days, or go to a hotel and pretend that she had left for the North and see what Sven would do. Reina was to write a letter and have it mailed in San Francisco, saying she was on her way north. A little money was given her to stay at a nearby hotel. In the meantime Sven had returned home and found a letter such as only Reina could write, a most amazing affair, concocted in Rhoda's presence, which told him that she had gone and would not return. She had taken all her things. He need not bother Rhoda, for she was not going to Rhoda. But it seemed to me that Sven was very much put upon and that Reina did not know what she wanted.

Nevertheless, Sven did bother Rhoda, and at once. He was in many ways a simple and confiding person and did not at all understand the woman he had married. Yet in spite of her fantastic notions and her marked indifference to his well-being, he still cared for her as anyone could see—that silly, notional girl. It was enough to cause one to wag one's head in desperation.

Sven called that evening to see if Rhoda knew where Reina was. His hope, written in his eyes, was that she was there. In a straightforward way he proceeded to place before Rhoda the sum and substance of his wrongs. He loved Reina and always had and always would, he thought, but she knew the state of his finances. She knew how hard he had tried before coming to Los Angeles and why he hadn't got along better than he had. Every time he was just getting a start somewhere she would get dissatisfied and leave him, and here was the same thing again. He was just getting a new start, and now she had left him again. The big thing now was to get his stock paid for so that the interest it yielded should be paid him instead of being charged off against his debts. The trouble was that he had been trying to make his salary of sixty-five dollars pay all expenses, but that wasn't enough, it seemed. Reina was for spending all he made the moment he made it, and even more, while he was for saving it in case anything happened.

Personally I felt sorry for him. More, I respected him, and so did Rhoda, and to my intense satisfaction she saw the point and sympathized with him. Although the blood tie pulled strongly she wanted Sven to be helped and she wanted Reina to help him.

She was for a compromise in some form and so she and Sven, and she and Reina, entered upon long and tautological discussions. The substance of all this was that Sven should not throw up his place. Also that with her aid he might do just a little better by Reina in the matter of living, assuming that she came back. She had never had anything in her life and he knew how that was to a girl. And she was here in Hollywood, where there were many things to make her envious and unhappy. Couldn't he afford to get a still better place? Sven was fond of Rhoda and admired her common sense as well as her beauty, besides being very grateful to her. He promised that if Reina would come back and be nicer to him he would do better too. He would get a larger place and a better car. He had seen one, a Buick, which he could get on time for two thousand dollars, and then he and Reina could go about more. Perhaps he hadn't done as well as he should, but he had been trying to get a start so that both of them could have a better time later on. Sven left, full of hope for the future, though Rhoda still maintained that she did not know where Reina was.

He was scarcely gone, however, when in walked Reina, anxious to know what he had proposed to do. She was full of bravado until she saw how Rhoda felt about it. Her one thought seemed to be that so long as Sven was amenable she could use him about as one would a doormat. "I'll show him he can't treat me any old way," she began. "He needn't think he can treat me as though I wasn't deserving of nothing—" ("Anything, Reina!") "—Well, then, anything. Nasty old rooms down there! An' eating in cafeterias! I won't do it. He's makin' money now, an' he can just spend a little of it. He needn't think I'm goin' to live on nothin' all my life."

But since Rhoda inclined toward Sven in this argument and Reina really depended on her, a compromise had to be reached; otherwise Reina would have had to carry out her threat to leave Hollywood, which was exactly what she did not want to do. After some bluff and bluster, in which she sought to make it appear that she had really gone to San Francisco but owing to the plea of Rhoda had returned to Los Angeles, she did return to Sven, who proceeded to do his best to make things more agreeable for her. They then celebrated their reunion by a dinner to Rhoda, at which they made quite a picture of loving domesticity.

But once the interest of the new place had subsided a bit Reina was to be found most of the time in the apartment in Hollywood, dreaming as before. While Rhoda worked and schemed hourly as to how to advance herself, haunting the studios and practicing dancing, Delsarte, elocution, makeup and characterization, Reina was dreaming or playing the piano or waiting for her to return so that they might go somewhere. I often wondered what Sven was thinking of it all. To be sure, Rhoda, anxious for the welfare of the twain, did her best to iron out the rough places. Whenever possible she was for having Sven to the apartment for dinner and for a drive in her car, or to distant resorts over the weekends, even though Sven objected most definitely to accepting that for which he could make no adequate return.

It was plain that in spite of what Reina thought Sven ought to do for her, and what he lacked in the way of ability to provide, and what she was entitled to as his wife, she still made no great effort to fulfill her part of the marital relation. She was much interested by the admiration of other men and what wealth in the hands of another male might do for her, in case she chose to command the same. There were nights when Sven was detained at the office and on such occasions, if Rhoda was free from her work, Reina was for persuading her to go somewhere, usually to a swimming pool, where by reason of the large crowds that attended and the attractive bathing suit she wore it was possible to attract no little attention. Once there it would not be long before she could be seen flirting with some good-looking youth or man, making the most of her golden opportunities and her figure, which was far from unattractive. And unless Rhoda protested she might even disappear for an hour or two, to loaf in some nearby restaurant or ice cream parlor, while her sister waited. Rhoda was not inclined to quarrel with her on this account; she had the feeling that Reina might be deciding that she had made a mistake and was looking for an easy way out. But, as time proved, it did make a difference in her estimate of Reina. I think she felt that Reina was temperamentally unfitted for marriage with anyone.

Nevertheless, because of Rhoda more than anything else, I believe, her charming surroundings and possessions, her standing in the film world, and the fact that she had helped him make his latest beginning, Sven stood his ground for a time, or, rather, endured the slights that were so persistently put upon him. But after a time and when the worm had endured all it could, it turned. Late one Saturday night there was a terrific storm in the Bergstrom household, and that very night Reina appeared at her sister's abode, much the worse nervously for the argument. "Whadaya know?" Sven had quarreled with her for coming in late, even when he was working late himself, and had told her— well, needless to say what he had told her. But among other things he had said that unless there was a change, and a drastic one, he was through. She could go where she chose, and he would go his way. He was tired of being made a fool of. He would get a divorce, or she could get it. He wouldn't contest it. But unless she there and then made definite promises of reform which she intended to keep, she must leave or he would. . . . With all her memories of past victories fresh upon her, flights and reunions, there was but one thing that Reina could do: flee, of course, to let him see once more whether he could do without her. She had learned that he could not. He would follow and bring her back.

But this time there was no agitated and nervous Sven telephoning to know whether she was there. Complete silence in that quarter; and on the part of Rhoda dissatisfaction and a growing contempt; and on the part of Reina, for the time being anyhow, excited cackling. Sven had said this, and Sven had said that, and he had done or had not done thus and so. I marveled that anyone could have so poor a grasp of the human amenities as to think and act as she was thinking and acting and then blame another person. Fortunately the attitude of Rhoda was different now. Blood ties or no blood ties, she had come to see that there was something to Sven's side of the story.

Rhoda did not press this conclusion just then, but after a few days, in which Reina lay about waiting for the surrender of Sven, she began to take up the matter of her future with her. Either she must think of something she would like to do and be about the business of doing it, or she must return to her mother. Everybody worked; why not she? "You mustn't think that because I'm your sister," went on Rhoda, "and because I'm fond of you I can take care of you always. I can't, and I wouldn't if I could.

I don't think it would be a good thing for you. You're old enough now to decide what it is you want to do. If you don't want to live with Sven you ought to decide what kind of work you can do and make a try for it. I am willing to help you get work, but I do feel that you ought to do something and not expect to idle about and do nothing while you wait to see what Sven is going to do."

Reina declared vehemently that she was not waiting for Sven and that nothing would induce her to return. She was going north. She had written to Bertha and to her mother. Nevertheless she sat about, and still no Sven. And still Rhoda bore with her as patiently as one person could with another. She waited almost a week before she again pointed out the folly of waiting for a man who was evidently not interested to pursue. She had not treated him well and could not expect him to run after her. She must find work or arrange in some way that he do something for her, which she assumed he might do, at least until Reina could do something for herself.

But then, to my astonishment, after this conduct and her indifference in the past and her various threats, the moment Rhoda had gone I heard her calling up the North and South Lumber Company and asking if she might speak with one Sven Bergstrom. He was not in, but without caring what I might be thinking, since I was within earshot, she tried and tried, until finally she did catch him in. The burden of her message, once she had him, was that she wanted to see him, but by no means was this so directly conveyed. On the contrary, and apparently in the face of small encouragement from him, after endless roundabout hints, she was compelled to say that she was going to be downtown about six o'clock and that if he happened to be near where she was going to be she would be glad to see him. After this telephone conversation was over I began to rally her concerning her previous determination and all the things she had seemed to think were wrong with him. Her calm reply was that she still thought as she had but that she needed some money and he must supply it. He wasn't going to get off so easy, you bet. The very least he could do was to give her enough to live on until she found something to do.

If I were to devote one hundred pages to verbatim transcripts of subsequent conversations held between her and Sven, and which same she invariably forced upon him and all of which he appeared to wish to avoid, you would gather but faintly the strangely illusive and illogical and almost pointless processes of her reasoning. Her persistent statement was that at bottom she did not care for Sven and that she did not want to live with him, but that she did want some money and proposed to get it if she had to sue him for divorce. But her conversations with him would have convinced anyone that at bottom she really did care for him and that she was lying roundly when she said she did not. Her voice and even her manner over the telephone, as I now noted with astonishment, had a cooing, coaxing, pleading quality, which she seemed to think would have some effect on Sven. Yet even then or immediately afterwards she would assure me that she hated him. Also she would openly flirt with men who appeared to be drawn to her and who would follow her in their cars and solicit her company from time to time. And betimes, and much to her sister's chagrin, she would be let off at her sister's door by some individual in a most impressive turnout, and with whom she chose to linger and talk. The quarrels between her and Rhoda which followed some of these adventures were quite sharp enough to indicate a change in Rhoda. Finally, after she had gone to her husband's office one evening and stayed away the entire night, she was ordered out by Rhoda who did not understand until Reina herself explained that it was with Sven she had been and that Rhoda could call up and find out, which was done. After that she was readmitted but only after stating that she cared for Sven and was going back.

And she did return to him—because it was the easiest thing to do, I presume. And he, if you will believe it, seemed delighted to have her back. Yes—so it was. And soon there was a new and still better apartment and a better automobile. Indeed, there was something helplessly compulsory about many things that both of them did, as though in spite of his best or worst sense and hers each found it impossible to break with the other, the matter of a little support not really being at the bottom of it. She wanted to rule him, I think, and found it hard to believe that she could not. And he was getting to the place where he did not want to be ruled, yet could not quite break with her.

114

But then of a sudden came the end of all this. For one day, about a week before their final separation, there was an accident. The new car in which Reina had posed, calling at least once or twice a day to show off, was crashed into by a street car and put out of commission. It was so badly damaged that not less than four hundred dollars was required to restore it, and about four weeks must elapse before they could have it again. Worse, a smaller and cheaper car had now to be used, Sven having sunk all his spare cash in this larger one. Not only that but a legal contest would also have to be entered upon before any claim would be awarded, because the accident, as it turned out, was as much Sven's fault as the motorman's. This Sven himself admitted but gave as his excuse that he was worried and brooding at the time. Worse still, the car had been only partly insured, Sven having been too busy to have that matter properly attended to. And so Reina, much to her dissatisfaction, was reduced once more to a very commonplace car.

Whether this had anything to do with the final catastrophe I have often wondered. One thing is sure: Reina became most irritable in her manner toward Sven, claiming that he had not managed things right or the accident would not have happened. Also that she would not ride or live as she was now being compelled to. Yet Sven, as I noticed, was courteous and considerate and even apologetic at times. To me he seemed a little sad as he explained how it had all come about. He was thinking of something and had absentmindedly swung in front of a car which was coming too fast to stop. That frank admission, even among friends, infuriated Reina. It seemed "crazy" to her. She wanted him to deny all responsibility and sue the company, as well as to play injured and exact damages on that score. But Sven would do none of that, and went about his business as before.

And then one day he telephoned her that he would not be home before eleven or twelve that night. Curiously enough, instead of running to Rhoda's as usual, she decided to retire and read. But midnight came, and no Sven. In the morning, surprised and concerned at his absence, she called up the office and learned that he was not there, that he had left at five-thirty the day before. Further waiting and searching revealing nothing, she ran to Rhoda. But Sven was really gone. His business affairs appeared to be in good order, except that as time went on it developed that he had recently contracted a number of debts via loans and expenditures for things bought on time—the car, furniture, dresses and jewelry for Reina. The loans were against his salary and the stock in his possession but not yet paid for. Also certain cash sales of stock had not been accounted for. But, strangely enough, the other officers of the company did not seem much concerned, wishing only, as they said to Rhoda who went to see them, that he would come back. He was too good a man to lose. They explained that Sven had seemed troubled recently. Also that they feared that it might be about a woman. A woman had been seen entering his office at night. This sent Reina off on a wild goose chase, but the mysterious woman of whom she was instantly insanely jealous proved to be herself.

Followed such mental vagaries and variations on the part of Reina as set one casual observer, myself, no less, to whirling mentally like a pinwheel. Realizing, as time went on, that by her follies and indifference she had driven from her a man who was of some commercial ability and that she was now left high and dry without a penny, Reina appeared to be shuttled between fear and rage, a desire to weep, I think, and a desire for revenge; between the thought that Sven had not considered her worth even a goodbye, and the thought that she had miscalculated her hold over him. Another irritating and enraging thought appeared to be that Rhoda and I—and perhaps particularly I—looked upon her as fairly paid out for her airs and indifferences. At first she was inclined to think that an accident might have happened to Sven. But opposed to this was the fact that he had called her up so soon before disappearing. Also that on the day of his disappearance he had reassigned to the rightful owner not only the damaged car, which was partially paid for, but the smaller car that had been loaned to him. Also his small bank account had been canceled, which proved that he had really left her. His indifference to her last departure might have warned her that a change was impending if not actually at hand.

Came now a period of brooding and mooding, coupled with such curious developments as would tax an alienist to display, the sort of thing that happens in real life and seldom if ever creeps into romance. In connection with an hysterical after-search there

116

appeared upon the scene a detective who fell in love with her, a queer, showy, self-opinionated dandy connected with the office of the district attorney. His chief desire seemed to be to prove Sven a criminal, not that he should be punished but that he should not venture to return to Reina. And Reina, being in need of money, was inclined to make use of this sleuth, not to the extent of favoring him in any way but in order to have the use of his car, some cash, luncheons and dinners, while she followed up clues. But all the while she was amusingly critical of him, declaring that she would throw him over when she was through with him and expose him to his superiors if he proved obstreperous. Betimes she would play doleful melodies on the piano and seem lost in sad thoughts. Again, she would break forth into loud denunciations of her absent spouse. But she also must have realized that her attitude and her extravagance had driven him away and that she was the cause of his petty defalcations, if defalcations they might be called. The company, when appealed to by the detective, refused to make any charge.

Following the day when she finally abandoned Mr. Morello, the detective, bidding him begone and not annoy her any more, she was at a loss what next to do, for some form of employment was looming straight ahead, as troublesome a promontory as she ever wished to see, you may be sure. But while she meditated, her sister was working, and this now began to weigh upon her. All at once and in spite of various kindly overtures on the part of Rhoda she decided to transfer herself and effects to a room in the very heart of the city, where henceforth, as she said, she would live. Also she was going to get something to do, "You bet," the very first thing that came to hand. She wasn't going to hang around trying to get into the movies. It was too uncertain. So one day, in spite of an invitation to stay longer, she left and thereafter was seen only at such times as Rhoda besought her, which was often. But she did take the first work that offered, that of elevator starter in an office building.

And then soon and much to my amusement we began to hear of new friendships with girls who were so far below the walk to which her sister aspired as to be disturbing, but who were no doubt suited to the mind and mood of Reina at the time. These same were of that ignorant if not inexperienced flapper type which looks upon sex and the conquest of men as the end and beginning of all earthly interest. Yet I was never fully convinced that Reina was very much fascinated by them or their lives. Living among these girls now, however, and in order, possibly, to avoid boredom, she busied herself with them and their affairs for a time and seemed to be more at peace than before. Returning to her sister, betimes, she was constantly describing them as a sex-crazy "bunch" and their male friends as snipes with tin Lizzies, bootleg whisky and a little money. But sometimes even they appeared to bore her and she would appear at Rhoda's apartment with the thought written all over her that she would prefer to stay there, and yet refusing when she was asked. Yet as time wore on she seemed less determined to show Rhoda that she could make her own way in the world, and more determined to be friends with her; also her rage against her late husband subsided and there were times when she would speak of him and admit that she had made mistakes. "The trouble with me was," she once said simply and forcefully to me as she sat in Rhoda's boudoir and made a facial toilet with her sister's cosmetics, "I didn't know when I was well off. Sven wasn't such a bad fella. There's lots worse'n him, ya bet, an' I see it now."

"Oh," I laughed, "you see Sven in a new light now, do you?"

"Ya bet I do," was her frank admission. "Sven wasn't so bad. He was a little stingy but he was a hustler, all right, an' he woulda made money up there in Washington if I'd only helped him. An' it was the same with that garage business he had up there in Seattle. But I guess I musta been a fool then. Nothing ever seemed to satisfy me. I just couldn't bear the idea of stayin' in one place long. When I heard that Rhoda was doin' so well down here I just made up my mind to get Sven to come down here. An' of course I did."

"So you think you could get along with him now, do you?"

"Sure. I thought a whole lotta Sven. I was crazy about him once up there in Seattle, sometimes even after we got down here. But I got to wantin' too much, I guess, an' he was too easy with me. He'd never stand up an' fight. He'd rather go an' get me things when he couldn't afford 'em."

I looked at her, too pleased by this frank confession to wish to add anything. At last, as I said to myself at the time, she did see the point even if too late. But Sven had disappeared by then, and so far as I ever learned he never returned.

But in spite of this resurrected affection she went on in her ragbag way, seeking to make the most of her possibilities. One day she confessed to me that if she ever met another "fella" as sober and industrious and ambitious as Sven she would "nab" him, you bet. "An' ya bet I'll know how to act the next time. I've learned sompin." The thought that she ought to sober down somewhat as well as marry again had apparently taken root in her decidedly flighty brain, or at least that she ought to attach herself in some way to some man with money or the ability to make it. And so she now began to hint to her sister that she be introduced to someone of character and standing, which same was not to be thought of, of course. A few *we was's* and *he done's* would most certainly have frightened off the most tolerant of possibilities. When she saw that Rhoda would have none of her commonplace friends and that she was in no haste to introduce her to the personalities with whom she was in contact, Reina began to set her cap on her own account for such as she thought might prove of the right caliber.

"Say," she appealed to me once, "tell me the name of a book that a fella that knows sompin would think was all right, will ya? I wanta carry sompin that'll make 'em think I know more'n I do. How's that, eh?" and she laughed. She could muster a grin that would melt ice, and it was that and her honest frankness about everything which attracted so many to her, myself among them.

"You're on," I said, reaching for *The Way of All Flesh,* the best on my shelf at the time.

"D'ya think this would make a fella that knows a lot think that I was up on good books?" she queried.

"Well, if that won't do it, nothing will. It depends on how you talk about it, Reina. Unless you understand it you'd better not say too much, see?"

"Leave it to me to put over the wise stuff. I ain't givin' myself away. I'll read it first, see, an' what I don't understand I'll ask about." Once more that toothy grin. It was at such times that she became worth knowing, really charming.

For about a year thereafter, in which she worked first as an elevator starter, next as a telephone girl in charge of a switchboard (because "Startin' elevators is kinda common, dontcha think?") and finally as a clerk in a photographer's studio, because that was higher still, she was alive with stories of her adventures. For some reason—because of Rhoda, perhaps—she was determined to interest a man above the average, someone more interesting than Sven even, with whom she could be seen without having her friends think she was belittling herself; rather, with the thought that she was doing exceedingly well. Now it would be: "Gee, ya oughta seen the swell fella I met goin' over to Catalina last Saturday, me an' Marie. Oh, a swell guy! None of yer little snipes with their tin cars an' their talk of bootleg an' all that stuff. This was a real guy—big gray overcoat an' horn glasses an' a Paige turin' car with a California top. I saw him leave it at the garage before he come on. An' he was readin' a book—not then, ya know—he was just tellin' me about it. Didja ever hear of a book called *Divine Comedy*, or sompin like that? It's a novel, ain't it?"

"That's right, Reina. It's a novel."

"What's the name of the guy that wrote it—Danty?"

"Right again, Reina. He's a well-known writer. Henry A. Danty. You'll find his books in every library. He's one of our most popular authors. Everybody reads him. Why, they've done a lot of his stuff in the movies."

"Is that right? Ye're not kiddin' me, are ya?"

"Not for worlds. Ask any librarian. Henry A. Danty, author of *The Divine Comedy*."

"That's it—that's the one. He was tellin' me about that one. People dead an' in hell, see, an' devils torturin' 'em. Gee, it was interestin'. He was tellin' me about a fella that was dead an' was—" and here followed her version of the agonies of Francesca and Paolo, because of their illicit earthly love forever whirled in their Stygian tempest.

Yet again, it was another worthy citizen in tweed and raglan riding to his office of a rainy morning—"Oh, a swell fella. An' whadaya know, he's the general freight agent for one of these big steamship lines that runs between here an' South America. An' he was awful nice to me, too, ya bet. Wanted to know where I lived an' what I did—gee, an awful nice man. An' me an'

120

him—" ("He and I, Reina") "—well, he an' I, then, got to talking about the boats an' what they carry—coffee an' hides an' wool an' sugar—oh, lotsa things. An' he was tellin' me how they bring coffee an' hides an' wool down over the mountains there in little packtrains made up of them there—ah—burros. An' how little them Indians get. Gee, it was interestin', I wanta tell ya."

"I haven't a doubt of it. I wish I could meet him myself."

"Well, anyhow, I had that last book ya gimme, see? That was the way it started. He kep' lookin' at that, an' I kep' twistin' it around so as to be sure he seen what it was—" ("Saw, Reina") "—well, saw, then. An' when we got downtown he ast me if he could come around an' see me some time an' take me out to dinner. Said he thought I was a nice girl, see, an' all that bunk. But I liked him, all right. A nice, big, serious fella he was—big nice eyes. Them kind's different from the little snipes that are always chasin' after ya an' haven't got a bean. I'm offa that bunch fer life. A guy like that can learn ya sompin—" ("Teach, Reina") "—well, teach, then."

But I might present as many as thirty such casual encounters that came to nothing apparently, and still not exhaust the roster. Reina was "nuts," as she said, to find some man who really amounted to something. And at last she did find a man of at least some ability, as I judged, "a—now—one of these here—now—efficiency experts—is that it?" According to Reina, he was fifty years of age and connected with an organization which sought to make over or improve technically and financially such firms as were not doing as well in the matter of economy and waste prevention as might be. I saw him but once, and that in passing, a solid, contentious-looking person whose self-centered and defiant mien impressed me as more likely to drive off rather than encourage intimacies of a social or affectional nature. Yet Reina became friendly with him and in the course of time was to be seen seated at the wheel of the very elaborate car which she said was his. Beside her at times sat the master himself, in gray summer suit and cap, looking quite commercial and prosperous. Later this friendship appeared to have been cemented by a number of very solid and substantial gifts—a pair of jade earrings, a genuine gray squirrel coat, several throws with caps to match, shoes, lingerie, gloves and—but my memory fails me. At any rate, she

121

was suddenly most fulsomely and yet not too loudly outfitted with many of the things she had been craving this long while.

And then one day, reclining in this same car and looking the picture of grandeur, she came to Hollywood to announce that she was all but ready to depart on a tour of the Selkirks in southwestern Canada—Lake Louise, Banff, the totem-villages, etc. "An' not only that," she went on, "but looka here," and she proceeded to fell me by bringing forth a very fat purse from which she extracted a small thin roll of fifty and one hundred dollar bills. "An' what's more, he's crazy about me. He says if I'll go to school an' polish up my grammar I'll be just as smart as anybody. An' I'm a-goin' to, too. I'm not always goin' to stick around here and be a dub, ya bet. I know sompin already, an' ya just give me a year or two more an' I'll know a lot more. Anyhow, I got this much—pretty good, eh?"

"You said it, Reina. You're the candy girl, all right. They can't keep a good man down, can they?"

"Ya betcha life they can't. An' I'm a-goin' to save my money from now on an' behave myself an' marry a real man, an' maybe in a few years I'll be somebody."

"That's the way to talk. But it looks to me as though you were somebody already. It isn't everybody that can go to Banff and Lake Louise in July."

"I'll tell the world!"

There was little that Rhoda could say or do. Her attitude toward Reina is best expressed by a speech often despairingly made after some such scene as this: "Well, I can't help it, can I? I've done all I can do. She's my sister and I can't help being fond of her, but I'm not responsible for her. She won't listen to me, and she never gets any of the points I try to make. She'll just have to live her own life, that's all. I'm sorry for her, but neither Sven nor mamma could do anything, either."

But to return to this scene. Rhoda had remained silent while Reina swaggered and talked, and now Reina turned to her:

"What's the matter? Don't ya think it's pretty good—all these nice clothes an' this trip an' everything?"

"Why, yes, I suppose so, if you want to go and really like him," commented Rhoda rather heavily. "And I hope he really likes you and that it won't be just another of these silly adventures that you'll be sorry for afterwards. You might meet someone some day that you'll really care for, you know."

"Oh, I know. But I like him, all right. An' he said he never knew anybody that interested him as much as me. An' he's going to send me to school, too, to a seminary somewhere, see? Won't that be pretty good?"

"Cemetery, Reina, cemetery," I put in.

"Oh, now, ya hush. Guess I know, don't I?" Then with a burst of pent-up emotion and affection, genuine and unchanging for all her ragbag thoughts, she stepped forward and throwing her arms about Rhoda, kissed her goodbye. Even tears—a short shower. "An' I owe it all to you, Rhoda. Don't say I don't, 'cause I do. You've always been good to me. If it hadn't been fer you I never woulda come down here at all, an' I wouldn'ta got what I've got now." A few more tears. Then one last funny story. A burst of laughter. And then departure, with Rhoda gazing after her more astonished than ever. And myself, wondering where, in the long catalogue of the exceptions, she belonged. And at last deciding: on the Orpheum Circuit. Or in a farce.

But Rhoda . . . I turned to her. She was crying.

"Forget it," was all I could advise. "You can't help it, can you? She is as she is, isn't she? And if you're going to begin to cry over life you'll be crying all the time. Besides, you'll ruin your makeup." But it was already ruined.

To return to Reina. One day about six weeks before her departure she and a friend had appeared at Rhoda's apartment in search of something she had left behind. Rummaging in a box which contained some letters written by Sven to her and her to Sven she came upon one and stopped to expatiate to her friend about the quarrels she and Sven had had and how she had left him three or four times and he had always followed. Then and in my presence she had asked her friend to read a particular letter, which she had written to Sven during one of their separations. The friend reporting that she thought it "swell," Reina volunteered: "Well, I thought it was, myself. But I didn't send it, because afterwards I thought maybe I didn't mean it. But I coulda. Sven always fell for anything like that. That's why I wrote it."

Interested in this palaver and seeing her toss the letter back in the box, I said: "Aren't you going to take it along, Reina?"

"Sure not. It ain't no good to me now."

"But I thought you said you cared for Sven?"

"Well, I did—a little. Still I didn't send it. Read it an' throw it in the wastebasket when ye're through with it. It'll make ya laugh, but I thought I meant it when I wrote it."

Thinking later of its possibly illuminating character, I recovered it from the waste box where she had thrown it, and here it is:

Dear Sven:

As this has been such a wonderful night and I have stayed up late enjoying it I thought of you. Sven, it seems as though our 2 years of married life is a compleet failure. Its to bad but you have tried and I have tried but its gone, what our real love for each other, and no living person can be happy if love aint there can they. I know many times you think I was all to blame but Sven you can understand why I was cross and eritabel.

The last time we went back together was because I wasnt real sure I dident care for you and my longing to be with you I couldent understand, it was miserabel I had to have you. But now I know what I was lonesome for the Happy you use to be but I couldent find him and I was sorry and couldent live without you.

I know I am a dissapointment in your life and Sven its for the best even if a married duty calls one he or she cant respond if there true self wont let them.

At one time in our life together no woman could have been happier than me. I simply was wild with your love and never could such a thing as this happen. I feel sure you was the same but life acts queer sometimes. I never doubted you Sven in my life till you begun to hide things from me and lye once inawhile. But its one thing or another you have developed a different plain in life than I. or its that we are dissatisfied in one another neather of us have had a chance and now that yours has come I am still looking for mine.

Why can a person make another suffer so unless its hate or thoughtlessness. I always have tryed to make myself nasty when I was aking inside for you to be near me and for the kisses Ill never forget. Still I would rather live alone and cherish the love I had once than ever go back again and be dissapointed like we always have

124

been. I know its hard on you too dont think Sven I have no heart at all altho it looks that way sometimes I feel for you and would help you gladly if I could I understand you better than you really know and one must be helpful to you to be appreshiated still thats alright every one expects that even me.

Im so glad your work is helping you make a big success and there is no reason why you shouldent be way up in this world other men have made it self made and honest thats what I am hoping for you.

And now that your free of a married life and no its for the best theres no reason why you aint bound for the top. we are young yet and you may find some one would mean all the world to you then its time to think back we was right to quit and let our love find its mate.

So Sven please look at this thing the way I do and we will go on thru life just the same as we did before we met feeling there is someone who will care for everything we do.

Tell your folks Sven when you go home just how it was and that I always thought of them as my mother and father and wish them sinseer regards I am sure they wont condemn me at least I always feel they wont.

So I am sure Sven all the unhappy hours you put in with me will be forgot and Ill do the same starting a new sheet from today on. A divorce will be got as soon as I can save up the money we will erace the 2 years off our life and start at the beginning again.

I had to write and get this problem off my mind its been hard but solved.

So good Bye Sven its my last to you. please forgive and forget knowing and feeling its the only way we can offer one another I will close with my sinserest wish of your bright future and loyalship in one respect as my husband.

May god forgive us both as ever

Reina.

And about five months after Reina's departure from Los Angeles, the following note arrived from Sven to Rhoda. The letter was posted from Calgary, Canada, but contained no address.

Dear Rhoda:

You'll think it's funny to hear from me but I owe you one thousand and here it is. Please don't tell Reina. I know you won't anyhow but I couldn't stand it with her. I couldn't make a go of it. After the automobile accident I got discouraged. It looked like things was against me and so I quit. But I have been doing fine lately. That's why I'm sending this. But before I had it pretty hard for a year there. I wish I could see your pretty little place again and talk with you. I could make you see how I feel. Don't think too hard of me. Reina didn't care for me any more and when I found that out I couldn't see any use in sticking. But I wish you all the luck in the world and I hope Reina gets along too. She will though. And I hope I do too.

Sven

"Vanity, Vanity," Saith the Preacher

SOMETIMES A SINGLE LIFE will clearly and effectively illustrate a period. Hence, to me, the importance of this one.

I first met Robin at a time when American financial methods and American finances were at their apex of daring and splendor, and when the world was in a more or less tolerant mood toward their grandiose manners and achievements. It was the golden day of Mr. Morgan, Senior, Mr. Belmont, Mr. Harriman, Mr. Sage, Mr. Gates, Mr. Brady, and many, many others who were still extant and ruling distinctly and drastically, as was proved by the panic of 1907. In opposition to them and yet imitating their methods, now an old story to those who have read *Frenzied Finance, Lawless Wealth,* and other such exposures of the methods which produced our enormous American fortunes, were such younger men as Charles W. Morse (the victim of the 1907 panic), F. Augustus Heinze (another if less conspicuous victim of the same "panic"), E. R. Thomas, an ambitious young millionaire, himself born to money, David A. Sullivan, and Joseph G. Robin.

The person who made Robin essentially interesting to me long before I met him was one Lucien de Shay, a ne'er-do-well pianist and voice culturist, who was also a connoisseur in the matters of rugs, hangings, paintings and furniture, things in which Robin was just then most intensely interested, erecting as he was, a great house on Long Island and but newly blossoming into the world of art or fashion or culture or show—those various things which the American multi-millionaire always wants to blossom or bloom into and which he does not always succeed in doing. De Shay was one of those odd natures so common to the metropolis—half artist and half man of fashion who attach themselves so readily to men of strength and wealth, often as advisors and counselors in all matters of taste, social form and social progress.

127

How this particular person was rewarded I never quite knew, whether in cash or something else. He was also a semi-confidant of mine, furnishing me "tips" and material of one sort and another in connection with the various publications I was then managing. As it turned out later, Robin was not exactly a multi-millionaire as yet, merely a fledgling, although the possibilities were there and his aims and ambitions were fast nearing a practical triumph the end of which of course was to be, as in the case of nearly all American multi-millionaires of the newer and quicker order, bohemian or exotic and fleshly rather than cultural or esthetic pleasure, although the latter were never really exactly ignored.

But even so. He was a typical multi-millionaire in the showy and even gaudy sense of the time. For if the staid and conservative and socially well-placed rich have the great houses and the ease and the luxury of paraphernalia, the bohemian rich of the Robin type have the flair, recklessness and imagination which lend to their spendings and flutterings a sparkle and a shine which the others can never hope to match.

Said this friend of mine to me one day: "Listen, I want you to meet this man Robin. You will like him. He is fine. You haven't any idea what a fascinating person he really is. He looks like a Russian Grand Duke. He has the manners and the tastes of a Medici or a Borgia. He is building a great house down on Long Island that once it is done will have cost him five or six hundred thousand. It's worth seeing already. His studio here in the C——— studio building is a dream. It's thick with the loveliest things. I've helped buy them myself. And he isn't dull. He wrote a book at twenty, 'Icarus,' which is not bad either and which he says is something like himself. He has read your book (*Sister Carrie*) and he sympathizes with that man Hurstwood. Says parts of it remind him of his own struggles. That's why he wants to meet you. He once worked on the newspapers too. God knows how he is making his money, but I know how he is spending it. He's decided to live, and he's doing it splendidly. It's wonderful."

I took notice, although I had never even heard of the man. There were so very, very many rich men in America. Later I heard much more concerning him from this same De Shay. Once he had been so far down in the scale that he had to shine shoes for a living. Once he had walked the streets of New York in the snow, his shoes cracked and broken, no overcoat, not even a warm suit. He had come here a penniless emigrant from Russia. Now he controlled four banks, one trust company, an insurance company, a fire insurance company, a great real estate venture somewhere, and what not. Naturally all of this interested me greatly. When are we indifferent to a rise from nothing to something?

At De Shay's invitation I journeyed up to Robin's studio one Wednesday afternoon at four, my friend having telephoned me that if I could I must come at once, that there was an especially interesting crowd already assembled in the rooms, that I would meet a long list of celebrities. Two or three opera singers of repute were already there, among them an Italian singer and sorceress of great beauty, a veritable queen of the genus adventuress, who was setting the town by the ears not only by her loveliness but her voice. Her beauty was so remarkable that the Sunday papers were giving full pages to her face and torso alone. There were to be several light opera and stage beauties there also, a basso profundo to sing, writers, artists, poets.

I went. The place and the crowd literally enthralled me. It was so gay, colorful, thrillful. The host and the guests were really interesting—to me. Not that it was so marvelous as a studio or that it was so gorgeously decorated and furnished—it was impressive enough in that way—but that it was so gracefully and interestingly representative of a kind of comfort disguised as elegance. The man had everything, or nearly so—friends, advisors, servants, followers. A somewhat savage and sybaritic nature, as I saw at once, was here disporting itself in velvets and silks. The iron hand of power, if it was power, was being most gracefully and agreeably disguised as the more or less flaccid one of pleasure and friendship.

My host was not visible at first, but I met a score of people whom I knew by reputation, and listened to clatter and chatter of the most approved metropolitan bohemian character. The Italian sorceress was there, her gorgeous chain earrings tinkling mellifluously as she nodded and gesticulated. De Shay at once whispered in my ear that she was Robin's very latest flame and an expensive one too. "You should see what he buys her!" he exclaimed in a whisper. "God!" Actresses and society women floated here and there in dreams of afternoon dresses. The automobiles outside were making a perfect uproar. The poets and writers fascinated me with their praises of the host's munificence and taste. At a glance it was plain to me that he had managed to gather about him the very element it would be most interesting to gather, supposing one desired to be idle, carefree and socially and intellectually gay. If America ever presented a smarter drawing room I never saw it.

My friend De Shay, being the fidus Achates of the host, had the power to reveal the inner mysteries of this place to me, and on one or two occasions when there were not so many present and while the others were chattering in the various rooms—music, dining, ball, library and so forth—I was being shown the kitchen, pantry, wine cellar, and also various secret doors and passages whereby mine host by pressing a flower on a wall or a spring behind a picture could cause a door to fly open or close which gave entrance to or from a room or passage in no way connected with the others save by another secret door and leading always to a private exit. I wondered at once at the character of the person who could need, desire or value this. A secret bedroom, for instance; a lounging room! In one of these was a rather severe if handsome desk and a steel safe and two chairs—no more; a very bare room. I wondered at this silent and rather commercial sanctum in the center of this frou frou of gayety, no trace of sound of which seemed to penetrate here. What I also gained was a sense of an exotic, sybaritic and purely pagan mind, one which knew little of the conventions of the world and cared less.

On my first visit, as I was leaving, I was introduced to the host just within his picture gallery, hung with many fine examples of the Dutch and Spanish schools. I found him to be as described: picturesque and handsome, even though somewhat plump, phlegmatic and lethargic—yet active enough. He was above the average in height, well built, florid, with a huge, round handsome head, curly black hair, keen black eyes, heavy overhanging eyebrows, full red lips, a marked chin ornamented by a goatee. In any costume ball he would have made an excellent Bacchus or Pan. He appeared to have the free, easy and gracious manner of those who have known much of life and have achieved, in part at least, their desires. He smiled, wished to know if I had met all the guests, hoped that the sideboard had not escaped me, that I had enjoyed the singing. Would I come some evening when there was no crowd—or, better yet, dine with him and my friend De Shay, whose personality appeared to be about as agreeable to him as his own. He was sorry he could not give me more attention now.

Interestingly enough, and from the first, I was impressed with this man; not because of his wealth (I knew richer men) but because of a something about him which suggested dreams, romance, a kind of sense or love of splendor and grandeur which one does not often encounter among the really wealthy. Those cracked shoes were in my mind, I suppose. He seemed to live among great things, but in no niggardly, parsimonious or care-taking way. Here was ease, largess, a kind of lavishness which was not ostentation but which seemed rather to say, "What are the minute expenses of living and pleasuring as contrasted with the profits of skill in the world outside?" He suggested the huge and Aladdin-like adventures with which so many of the great financiers of the day, the true tigers of Wall Street, were connected.

It was not long thereafter that I was once more invited, this time to a much more lavish affair and something much more sybaritic in its tone, although I was really not conscious of what it was to be like when I went there. It began at twelve midnight, and to this day it glitters in my mind as among the few really barbaric and exotic things that I have ever witnessed. Not that the trappings or hangings or setting were so outré or amazing as that the atmosphere of the thing itself was relaxed, bubbling, pagan. There were so many daring and seeking people there. The thing sang and was talked of for months after—in whispers! The gayety! The abandon! The sheer intoxication, mental and physical! I never saw more daring costumes, so many really beautiful women (glitteringly so) in one place at one time, wonderful specimens of exotic and in the main fleshy or sensuous feminin-ity. There was, among other things, as I recall, a large nickeled ice-tray on wheels packed with unopened bottles of champagne, and you had but to lift a hand or wink an eye to have another opened for you alone, ever over and over. And the tray was always full. One wall of the dining room farther on was laden with delicate novelties in the way of food. A string quartet played for the dancers in the music room. There were a dozen corners in different rooms screened with banks of flowers and concealing divans. The dancing and singing were superb, individual, often abandoned in character, as was the conversation. As the morning wore on (for it did not begin until after midnight) the moods of all were either so mellowed or inflamed as to make intentions, hopes, dreams, the most secret and sybaritic, the order of expression. One was permitted to see human nature stripped of much of its repression and daylight reserve or cant. At about four in the morning came the engaged dancers, quite the pièce de résistance—with wreaths about heads, waists and arms for clothing and, well, really nothing more beyond their beautiful figures—scattering rose leaves or favors. These dancers the company itself finally joined, single file at first, pellmell afterwards—artists, writers, poets—dancing from room to room in crude Bacchic imitation of their leaders—the women too—until all were singing, parading, swaying and dancing in and out of the dozen rooms. And finally, liquor and food affecting them, I suppose, many fell flat, unable to do anything thereafter but lie upon divans or in corners until friends assisted them elsewhere—to taxis finally. But mine host, as I recall him, was always present, serene, sober, smiling, unaffected, bland and gracious and untiring in his attention. He was there to keep order where otherwise there would have been none.

I mention this merely to indicate the character of a long series of such events which covered the years 1907 to 1910. During that time, for the reason that I have first given (his curious pleasure in my company), I was part and parcel of a dozen such more or less vivid affairs and pleasurings, which stamped on my mind not only Robin but life itself, the possibilities and resources of luxury where taste and appetite are involved, the dreams of grandeur and happiness which float in some men's minds and which work out to a wild fruition—dreams so outré and so splendid that only the tyrant of an obedient empire, with all the resources of an enslaved and obedient people, could indulge with safety. Thus once, I remember, that a dozen of us—writers and artists—being assembled in his studio in New York one Friday afternoon for the mere purpose of idling and drinking, he, seeming to have nothing better to do for the time being, suddenly suggested, and as though it had but now occurred to him, that we all adjourn to his country house on Long Island, which was not yet quite finished (or, rather, furnished), but which was in a sufficient state of completion to permit of appropriate entertainment providing the necessaries were carried out there with us.

As I came to think of this afterward, I decided that after all it was not perhaps so unpremeditated as it seemed and that unconsciously we served a very useful purpose. There was work to do, suggestions to be obtained, an overseer, decorator and landscape gardener with whom consultations were absolutely necessary; and nothing that Robin ever did was without its element of calculation. Why not make a gala affair of a rather dreary November task—

Hence—

At any rate the majority of us forthwith agreed, since plainly it meant an outing of the most lavish and pleasing nature. At once four automobiles were pressed into service, three from his own garage and one specially engaged elsewhere. There was some telephoning *in re* culinary supplies to a chef in charge of the famous restaurant below who was *en rapport* with our host, and soon some baskets of food were produced and subsequently the four cars made their appearance at the entryway below. At dusk of a gray, cold, smoky day we were all bundled into these— poets, playwrights, novelists, editors (he professed a great contempt for actors), and forthwith we were off, to do forty-five miles between five-thirty and seven p.m.

I often think of that ride, the atmosphere of it, and what it told of our host's point of view. He was always so grave, serene, watchful yet pleasant and decidedly agreeable, gay even, without seeming so to be. There was something so amazingly warm and exotic about him and his, and yet at the same time something so cold and calculated, as if after all he were saying to himself, "I am the master of all this, am stage-managing it for my own pleasure." I felt that he looked upon us all not so much as intimates or friends as rather fine birds or specimens of one kind and another, well qualified to help him with art and social ideas if nothing more—hence his interest in us. Also, in his estimation no doubt, we reflected some slight color or light into his life, which he craved. We had done things too. Nevertheless, in his own estimation, he was the master, the Can Grande. He could at will "take us up or leave us out," or so he thought. We were mere toys, fine feathers, cap-and-bell artists. It was nice to "take us around," have us with him. Smothered in a great richly braided fur coat and fur cap, he looked as much the Grand Duke as one might wish.

But I liked him, truly. And what a delicious evening and holiday all told he made of it for us. By leaving a trail of frightened horses, men and women, and tearing through the gloom as though streets were his private racetrack—I myself as much frightened as any at the roaring speed of the cars and the possibilities of the road—we arrived at seven, and by eight were seated to a course dinner of the most gratifying character. There was no heat in the house as yet, but from somewhere great logs had been obtained and now blazed in the large fireplaces. There was no electricity as yet—a private plant was being installed—but candles and lamps blazed in lovely groups, casting a soft glow over the great rooms. One room lacked a door, but an immense rug took its place. There were rugs, hangings and paintings in profusion, many of them as yet unhung. Some of the most interesting importations of furniture and statuary were still in the cases in which they had arrived, with marks of ships and the names of foreign cities upon the cases. Scattered about the great living room, dining room, music room and library were enough rugs, divans and chairs as well as musical instruments—a piano among others— to give the place an air of completeness and luxury. The walls and ceilings had already been decorated—in a most florid manner, I must say. Outside were great balconies and verandahs commanding, as the following morning proved, a very splendid view of a very bleak sea. The sand dunes! The distant floor of the sea! The ships! Upstairs were nine suites of one and two rooms and bath. The basement was an intricate world of kitchen, pantry, engine room, furnace, wine cellars and what not. Outside was a tawny waste of sand held together in places by hummocks and of hills concealed by sand-binding grasses.

That night, because it was windy and dull and bleak, we stayed inside, I for one going outside only long enough to discover

134

that there were great wide verandahs of concrete about the house, fit for great entertainments in themselves, and near at hand hummocks of sand. Inside all was warm and flaring enough. The wine cellar seemed to contain all that one might reasonably desire. Our host once out here was most gay in his mood. He was most pleasantly interested in the progress of his new home, although not intensely so. He seemed to have lived a great deal and to be making the best of everything as though it were something to go through with. With much talking on the part of us all, the evening passed swiftly enough. Some of the men could play and sing. One poet recited enchanting bits of verse. For our inspection certain pieces of furniture and statuary were unpacked and displayed—a bronze faun some three feet in height, for one thing. All the time I was sensible of being in contact with someone who was really in touch with life in a very large way, financially and otherwise. His mind seemed to be busy with all sorts of things. There were two Syrians in Paris, he said, who owned a large collection of rugs suitable for an exhibition. He had an agent who was trying to secure the best of them for his new home. De Shay had recently introduced him to a certain Italian count who had a great house in Italy but could not afford its upkeep. He was going to take over a portion of its furnishings, after due verification, of course. Did I know the paintings of Monticelli and Mancini? He had just secured excellent examples of both. Some time when his new home was further along I must come out. Then the pictures would be hung, the statuary and furniture in place. He would get up a weekend party for a select group.

The talk drifted to music and the stage. At once I saw that because of his taste, wealth and skill, women formed a large and yet rather toy-like portion of his life, holding about as much relation to his inner life as do the concubines of an Asiatic sultan. Madame of the earrings, as I learned from de Shay, was a source of great expense to him, but at that she was elusive, not easily to be come at. The stage and Broadway were full of many beauties in various walks of life, many of whom he knew or to whom he could obtain access. Did I know thus and so—such-and-such an one?

"I'll tell you," he said after a time and when the wine glasses had been refilled a number of times, "we must give a party out

135

here some time, something extraordinary, a real one. De Shay and Bielow" (naming another artist) "and myself must think it out. I know three different dancers"—and he began to enumerate their qualities. I saw plainly that even though women played a minor part in his life, they were the fringe and embroidery to his success and power. At one a.m. we went to our rooms, having touched upon most of the themes dear to metropolitan lovers of life and art.

The next morning was wonderful—glittering, if windy. The sea sparkled beyond the waste of sand. I noted anew the richness of the furnishings, the greatness of the house. Set down in so much sand and facing the great sea, it was wonderful. There was no order for breakfast; we came down as we chose. A samovar and a coffee urn were alight on the table. Rolls, chops, anything, were brought on order. Possibly because I was one of the first about, my host singled me out—he was up and dressed when I came down—and we strolled over the estate to see what we should see.

Curiously, although I had seen many country homes of pretension and even luxury, I never saw one that appealed to me more on the ground of promise and, after a fashion, of partial fulfillment. It was so unpretentiously pretentious, so really grand in a limited and yet poetic way. Exteriorly its placement, on a rise of ground commanding that vast sweep of sea and sand, its verandahs, so very wide—great smooth floors of red concrete—bordered with stone boxes for flowers and handsomely designed stone benches, its long walks and drives but newly begun, its stretch of beach, say half a mile away and possibly a mile and a half long, to be left, as he remarked, "au naturel," driftwood, stones and all, struck me most favorably. Only one long pier for visiting yachts was to be built, and a certain stretch of beach, not over three hundred feet, cleared for bath houses and a smooth beach. On one spot of land, a high hummock reaching out into the sea, had already been erected a small vantage tower, open at the bottom for shade and rest, benches turning in a circle upon a concrete floor, above it a top looking more like a small bleak lighthouse than anything else. In this upper portion was a room reached by small spiral concrete stairs.

I could not help noting the reserve and *savoir faire* with which my host took all this. He was so healthy, assured, interested and,

136

I am glad to say, not exactly self-satisfied; at least he did not impress me in that way—a most irritating condition. Plainly he was building a very splendid thing. His life was nearing its apex. He must not only have had millions but great taste to have undertaken, let alone accomplished, as much as was already visible here. Pointing to a bleak waste of sand between the house and the sea—and it looked like a huge red and yellow bird perched upon a waste of sand—he observed, "When you come again in the spring that will contain a garden of 40,000 roses. The wind is nearly always off the sea here. I want the perfume to blow over the verandahs. I can rotate the roses so that a big percentage of them will always be in bloom."

We visited the stables, the garage, an artesian well newly driven, a drive that was to skirt the sea, a sunken garden some distance from the house and away from the sea.

Next spring I came once more—several times, in fact. The rose garden was then in bloom, the drives finished, the pictures hung. Although this was not a world in which society as yet deigned to move it was entirely conceivable that at a later period it might, and betimes it was crowded with people smart enough and more agreeable in the main than the hardy, strident members of the so-called really inner circles. There were artists, writers, playwrights, singers, actresses, and some nondescript figures of the ultra-social world—young men principally who seemed to come here in connection with beautiful young women, models and other girls whose beauty was their only recommendation to consideration.

The scene was not without brilliance. A butler and numerous flunkeys fluttered to and fro. Guests were received at the door by a footman. A housekeeper and various severe-looking maids governed in the matter of cleaning. One could play golf, tennis, bridge, motor, fish, swim, drink in a free and even disconcerting manner or read quietly in one angle or another of the grounds. There were affairs, much flirting and giggling, suspicious wanderings to and fro at night—no questions asked as to who came or whether one was married, so long as a reasonable amount of decorum was maintained. It was the same on other occasions, only the house and grounds were full to overflowing with guests and passing friends, whose machines parked in the drives. I saw

137

as many gay and fascinating costumes and heard as much clever and at times informative talk here as anywhere I have been.

During this fall and winter I was engaged to work which kept me very much to myself. During the period I read much of Robin, banks he was combining, new ventures he was undertaking. Yet all at once one winter's day, and out of a clear sky, the papers were full of an enormous financial crash of which he was the center. According to the newspapers, the first and foremost of a chain of banks of which he was the head, to say nothing of a bonding and realty company and some street railway project on Long Island, were all involved in the crash. Curiously, although no derogatory mention had previously been made of him, the articles and editorials were now most vituperative. Their venom was especially noticeable. He was a get-rich-quick villain of the vilest stripe; he had been juggling a bank, a trust company, an insurance company and a land and street railway speculative scheme as one would glass balls. The money wherewith he gambled was not his. He had robbed the poor, deceived them. Yet among all this and in the huge articles which appeared the very first day, I noted one paragraph which stuck in my mind, for I was naturally interested in all this and in him. It read:

Wall Street heard yesterday that Superintendent Hotchkiss got his first information concerning the state in which Robin's affairs were from quarters where resentment may have been cherished because of his activity in the Long Island Traction field. This is one of the Street's "clover patches" and the success which the newcomer seemed to be meeting did not provoke great pleasure.

Another item read:

A hitch in a deal that was to have transferred the South Shore to the New York and Queens County System, owned by the Long Island Railroad, at a profit of almost $2,000,000 to Robin, was the cause of all the trouble. Very active displeasure on the part of certain powers in Wall Street blocked, it is said, the closing of the deal for the railroad. They did not want him in this field, and were powerful enough to prevent it. At the same time pressure from other directions was brought to bear on him. The clearing-house refused

138

to clear for his banks. Robin was in need of cash, but still insisting on a high rate of remuneration for the road which he had developed to an important point. Their sinister influences entered and blocked the transfer until it was no longer possible for him to hold out.

Along with these two items was a vast mass of data, really pages, showing how, when, where he had done thus and so, "juggled accounts" between one bank and another, all of which he controlled however and most of which he owned, drew out large sums and put in their place mortgages on or securities in, new companies which he was organizing—tricks which were the ordinary routine of Wall Street and hence rather ridiculous as the sub-stone of so vast a hue and cry.

I was puzzled and, more than that, moved by the drama of the man's sudden end, for I understood a little of finance and its ways, also of what place and power had plainly come to mean to him. It must be dreadful. Yet how could it be, I asked myself, if he really owned fifty-one percent or more in so many companies that he could be such a dark villain? After all, ownership is ownership, and control, control. On the face of the reports themselves his schemes did not look so black. I read everything in connection with him with care.

As the days passed various other things happened. For one thing, he tried to commit suicide by jumping out of a window of his studio in New York; for another, he tried to take poison. Now of a sudden a bachelor sister, of whom I had never heard in all the time I had known him, put in an appearance as his nearest of kin—a woman whose name was not his own but a variation of it, an "-ovitch" having suddenly been tacked onto it. She took him to a sanitarium, from which he was eventually turned out as a criminal, then to a hospital, until finally he surrendered himself to the police. The names of great lawyers and other bankers began to enter the case. Alienists of repute, those fine chameleons of the legal world, were employed who swore first that he was insane, then that he was not. His sister, who was a physician and scientist of repute, asked the transfer of all his property to her on the ground that he was incompetent and that she was his next of kin. To this she swore, giving as her reasons for believing him insane that he had "illusions of grandeur" and that he believed himself "persecuted by eminent financiers," things which smacked more of sanity than anything else to me. At the same time he and she, as time rather indicated, had arranged this in part in the hope of saving something out of the great wreck. There were other curious features: Certain eminent men in politics and finance who from revelations made by the books of the various banks were in close financial if not personal relations with Robin denied this completely. Curiously, the great cry on the part of these was that he was insane, must be, and that he was all alone in his schemes. His life on Broadway, on Long Island, in his studio in New York, was ransacked for details. Enough could not be made of his gay, shameful, spendthrift life. No one else, of course, had ever been either gay or shameful before—especially not the eminent and hounding financiers.

Then from somewhere appeared a new element. In a staggeringly low tenement region in Brooklyn was discovered somehow or other a very old man and woman, most unsatisfactory as relatives of such imposing people, who insisted that they were his parents, that years before because he and his sister were exceedingly restless and ambitious, they had left them and had only returned occasionally to borrow money, finally ceasing to come at all. In proof of this, letters, witnesses, old photos, were produced. It really did appear as if he and his sister, although they had long vigorously denied it, really were the son and daughter of the two who had been petty bakers in Brooklyn, laying up a little competence of their own. I never knew who "dug" them up, but the reason why was plain enough. The sister was laying claim to the property as the next of kin. If this could be offset, even though Robin were insane, the property would at once be thrown into the hands of the various creditors and sold under a forced sale, of course—in other words, for a song—for their benefit. Naturally it was of interest to those who wished to have his affairs wound up to have the old people produced. But the great financier had been spreading the report all along that he was from Russia, that his parents, or pseudo-parents, were still there, but that really he was the illegitimate son of the Czar of Russia, boarded out originally with a poor family. Now, however, the old people were brought from Brooklyn and

140

compelled to confront him. It was never really proved that he and his sister had neglected them utterly or had done anything to seriously injure them, but rather that as they had grown in place and station they had become more or less estranged and so ignored them, having changed their names and soared in a world little dreamed of by their parents. Also a perjury charge was made against the sister which effectually prevented her from controlling his estate, a lease long enough to give the financiers time for their work. Naturally there was a great hue and cry over her, the scandal, the shame, that they should thus publicly refuse to recognize their parents as they did or had when confronted by them. Horrible! There were most heavily illustrated and tearful Sunday articles, all blazoned forth with pictures of his house and studio, his banks, cars, yacht, groups of guests, while the motives of those who produced the parents were overlooked. The pictures of the parents confronting Robin and his sister portrayed very old and feeble people, and were rather moving. They insisted that they were his parents and wept brokenly in their hands. But why? And he denying it! His sister, who resented all this bitterly and who stood by him valiantly, repudiated, for his sake of course, his and her so-called parents and friends.

I never saw such a running to cover of "friends" in all my life. Of all those I had seen about his place and in his company, scores on scores of people reasonably well known in the arts, the stage, the worlds of finance and music, all eating his dinners, riding in his cars, drinking his wines, there was scarcely anyone now who knew him anything more than "casually" or "slightly"—oh, so slightly! When rumors as to the midnight suppers, the Bacchic dancing, the automobile parties to his great country place and the spirited frolics which occurred there began to get abroad, there was no one whom I knew who had ever been there or knew anything about him or them. For instance, of all the people who had been close or closest and might therefore have been expected to be friendly and deeply concerned was de Shay, his fidus Achates and literally his pensioner—yet de Shay was almost the loudest in his denunciation or at least deprecation of Robin, his habits and methods! Although it was he who had told me of Mme. ——— and her relation to Robin, who urged me to come here, there and the other place, especially where Robin was the host, always assuring me that it would be so wonderful and that Robin was really such a great man, so generous, so worthwhile, he was now really the loudest or at least the most standoffish in his comments, pretending never to have been very close to Robin, and lifting his eyebrows in astonishment as though he had not even guessed what he had actually engineered. His "Did-you-hears," "Did-you-knows" and "Wouldn't-have-dreameds" would have done credit to a tea-party. He was so shocked, especially at Robin's robbing poor children and orphans, although in so far as my reading of the papers went I could find nothing that went to prove that he had any intention of robbing anybody—that is, directly. In the usual Wall Street high finance style he was robbing Peter to pay Paul, that is, he was using the monies of one corporation which he controlled to bolster up any of the others which he controlled, and was "washing one hand with the other," a proceeding so common in finance that to really radically and truly oppose it, or do away with it, would mean to bring down the whole fabric of finance in one grand crash.

Be that as it may. In swift succession there now followed the so-called "legal" seizure and confiscation of all his properties. In the first place, by alienists representing the District Attorney and the State banking department, he was declared sane and placed on trial for embezzlement. Secondly, his sister's plea that his property be put into her hands as trustee or administrator was thrown out of court and she herself arrested and confined for perjury on the ground that she had perjured herself in swearing that she was his next of kin when in reality his real parents, or so they swore, were alive and in America. Next, his banks, trust companies and various concerns, including his great country estate, were swiftly thrown into the hands of receivers (what an appropriate name!) and wound up "for the benefit of creditors." All the while Robin was in prison, protesting that he was really not guilty, that he was solvent, or had been until he was attacked by the State bank examiner or the department back of him, and that he was the victim of a cold-blooded conspiracy which was using the State banking department and other means to drive him out of financial life, and that solely because of his desire to grow and because by chance he had been impinging upon one of the choicest and most closely guarded fields of the ultra-rich of Wall Street—the street railway area in New York and Brooklyn.

One day, so he publicly swore to the grand jury by which he was being examined, as he was sitting in his great offices, in one of the great skyscrapers of New York, which occupied an entire floor and commanded vast panoramas in every direction (another evidence of the man's insane "delusion of grandeur," I presume), he was called to answer the telephone. One Mr. August Belmont, so his assistant said, one of the eminent financiers of Wall Street and America, was on the wire. Without any preliminary and merely asking was this Mr. Robin on the wire, the latter proceeded, "This is Mr. Belmont. Listen closely to what I am going to say. I want you to get out of the street railway business in New York or something is going to happen to you. I am giving you a reasonable warning. Take it." Then the phone clicked most savagely and ominously and superiorly at the other end.

"I knew at the time," went on Robin, addressing the grand jury, "that I was really listening to the man who was most powerful in such affairs in New York and elsewhere and that he meant what he said. At the same time I was in no position to get out without closing up the one deal which stood to net me two million dollars clear if I closed it. At the same time I wanted to enter this field and didn't see why I shouldn't. If I didn't it spelled not ruin by any means but a considerable loss, a very great loss, to me, in more ways than one. Oddly enough, just at this time I was being pressed by those with whom I was associated to wind up this particular venture and turn my attention to other things. I have often wondered, in the light of their subsequent actions, why they should have become so pressing just at this time. At the same time, perhaps I was a little vain and self-sufficient. I had once got the better of some agents of another great financier in a Western power deal, and I felt that I could put this thing through too. Hence I refused to heed the warning. However, I found that all those who were previously interested to buy or at least develop the property were now suddenly grown cold, and a little later when, having entered on several other matters, I needed considerable cash, the State banking department descended on me and, crying fraud and insolvency, closed all my banks.

"You know how it is when they do this to you. Cry 'Fire!' and you can nearly wreck a perfectly good theater building. Depositors withdraw, securities tumble, investigation and legal expenses begin, your financial associates get frightened or ashamed and desert you. Nothing is so squeamish or so retiring and nervous as money. Time will show that I was not insolvent at the time. The books will show a few technically illegal things, but so would the books or the affairs of any great bank, especially at this time, if quickly examined. I was doing no more than all were doing, but they wanted to get me out—and they did."

Regardless of proceedings of various kinds—legal, technical and the like—Robin was finally sent to the penitentiary, and spent some time there. At the same time his confession finally wrecked about nine other eminent men, financiers all. A dispassionate examination of all the evidence eight years later caused me to conclude without hesitation that the man had been the victim of a cold-blooded conspiracy, the object of which was to oust him from opportunities and to forestall him in methods which would certainly have led to enormous wealth. He was apparently in a position and with the brains to do many of the things which the ablest and coldest financiers of his day had been and were doing, and they did not want to be bothered with, would not brook, in short, his approaching rivalry. Like the various usurpers of regal powers in ancient days, they thought it best to kill a possible claimant to the throne in his infancy.

But that youth of his! The long and devious path by which he had come! Among the papers relating to the case and to a time when he could not have been more than eighteen, and when he was beginning his career as a book agent, was a letter written to his mother (August, 1892), which read:

My dear Parents:

Please answer me at once if I can have anything of you, or something of you or nothing. Remember this is the first and the last time in my life that I beg of you anything. You have given to the other child not $15 but hundreds, and now when I, the very youngest, ask of you, my parents, $15, are you going to be so hardhearted as to refuse me? Without these $15 it is left to me to be without income for two or three weeks.

For God's sake, remember what I ask of you, and send me at once so that I should cease thinking of it. Leon, as I have told you, will give me $10, $15 he has already paid for the contract, and your $15 will make $25. Out of this I need $10 for a ticket and $15 for two or three weeks' board and lodging.

Please answer at once. Don't wait for a minute, and send me the money or write me one word "not." Remember this only that if you refuse me I will have nothing in common with you.

Your son,
Joseph

There was another bit of testimony on the part of one Max Donath, a baker, who for some strange reason came forward to identify him as someone he had known years before in Williamsburgh, which read:

I easily recognize them [Robin and his sister] from their pictures in the newspapers. I worked for Robin's father, who was a baker in Williamsburgh, and frequently addressed letters that were written by Robin Senior and his wife to Dr. Louise Robinovitch who was then studying medicine in Philadelphia. Robin was then a boy going to school, but working in his father's bakery mornings and evenings. He did not want to do that, moaned a great deal, and his parents humored him in his attitude. He was very vain, liked to appear intellectual. They kept saying to their friends that he should have a fine future. Five years later, after I had left them once, I met the mother and she told me that Robin was studying banking and getting along fine.

Some seven years after the failure and trial by which he had so summarily been disposed of and after he had been released from prison, I was standing at a certain unimportant street corner in New York waiting for a car when I saw him. He was passing in the opposite direction, not very briskly, and, as I saw, plainly meditatively. He was not so well dressed. The clothes he wore while good were somehow different, lacking in that exquisite something which had characterized him years before. His hat— well, it was a hat, not a Romanoff shako nor a handsome panama such as he had affected in the old days. He looked tired, a little worn and dusty, I thought.

My first impulse was of course to hail him, my second not, since he had not seen me. It might have been embarrassing, and at any rate he might not have even remembered me. But as he walked I thought of the great house by the sea, the studio, the cars, the 40,000 roses, the crowds at his summer place, the receptions in town and out, Madame of the earrings (afterward married to a French nobleman), and then of the letter to his mother as a boy, the broken shoes in the winter time, his denial of his parents, the telephone message from the financial tiger. "Vanity, vanity," saith the preacher. The shores of our social seas are strewn with pathetic wrecks, the whitening bones of half-sand-buried ships.

At the next corner he paused, a little uncertain apparently as to which way to go, then turned to the left and was lost. I have never seen nor heard of him since.

Fulfilment

*H*EARING THE MAID TAP lightly on her door for the third
or fourth time, Ulrica uttered a semiconscious "Come." It
was her usual rising hour but today she was more depressed than
usual, although the condition was common enough at all times.
The heavy drag of a troubled mental state was upon her. Was
it never to end? Was she never to be happy again? After several
weeks of a decidedly acceptable loneliness, during which Harry
had been in the West looking after his interminable interests, he
was about to return. The weariness of that, to begin with! And
while she could not say that she really hated or even disliked him
deeply (he was too kind and considerate for that), still his existence, his able and different personality, constantly forced upon
or persuading her, had come to be a bore. The trouble was that
she did not truly love him and never could. He might be, as he
was, rich, resourceful and generous to a fault in her case, a man
whom the world of commerce respected, but how did that avail
her? He was not her kind of man. Vivian before him had proved
that. And other men had been and would be as glad to do as
much if not more.

Vivian had given all of himself in a different way. Only
Harry's seeking, begging eyes pleading with her (after Vivian's
death and when she was so depressed) had preyed upon and finally
moved her to sympathy. Life had not mattered then (only her
mother and sister), and she had become too weary to pursue any
career, even for them. So Harry with his wealth and anxiety to
do for her—

(*The maid entered softly, drew back the curtains and raised the
blinds, letting in a flood of sunshine, then proceeded to arrange the
bath.*)

It had been, of course, because of the magic of her beauty—how well she knew the magic of that!—plus an understanding and sympathy she had for the miseries Harry had endured in his youth, that had caused him to pursue her with all the pathetic vehemence of a man of fifty. He was not at all like Vivian, who had been shy and retiring. Life had seemed to frighten poor Vivian and drive him in upon himself, uncomplaining and dignified. In Harry's case it had acted contrariwise. Some men were so, especially the old and rich, those from whom life was slipping away and for whom youth, their lost youth, seemed to remain a colored and enthralling spectacle however wholly gone. The gifts he had lavished upon her, the cars, the jewels, this apartment, stocks and bonds, even that house in Seadale for her sister and mother! And all because of a beauty that meant so little to her now that Vivian was gone, and in the face of an indifference so marked that it might well have wearied any man.

How could she go on? (She paused in her thoughts to survey and follow her maid, who was calling for the second time.) Though he hung upon her least word or wish and was content to see her at her pleasure, to run her errands and be ever deferential and worshipful, still she could not like him, could barely tolerate him. Before her always now was Vivian with his brooding eyes and elusive, sensitive smile; Vivian, who had never a penny to bless himself with. She could see him now striding to and fro in his bare studio, a brush in one hand, or sitting in his crippled chair meditating before a picture or talking to her of ways and means which might be employed to better their state. The pathos!

"I cannot endure that perfume, Olga!"

In part she could understand her acceptance of Harry after Vivian (only it did not seem understandable always, even to her), for in her extreme youth her parents had been so very poor. Perhaps because of her longings and childish fears in those days she had been marked in some strange way that had eventually led her to the conviction that wealth was so essential. For her parents were certainly harassed from her sixth to her thirteenth years, when they recovered themselves in part. Some bank or concern had failed and they had been thrown on inadequate resources

148

and made to shift along in strange ways. She could remember an old brick house with a funereal air and a weedy garden into which they had moved and where for a long time they were almost without food. Her mother had cried more than once as she sat by the open window looking desolately out, while Ulrica, not quite comprehending what it was all about, had stared at her from an adjacent corner.

"Will Madame have the iris or the Japanese lilac in the water?"

She recalled going downtown once on an errand and slipping along shyly because her clothes were not good. And when she saw some schoolgirls approaching, hid behind a tree so they should not see her. Another time, passing the Pilkington at dinnertime, the windows being open and the diners visible, she had wondered what great persons they must be to be able to bask in so great a world. It was then perhaps that she had developed the obsession for wealth which had led to this. If only she could have seen herself as she now was she would not have longed so. (She paused, looking gloomily back into the past.) And then had come the recovery of her father in some way or other. He had managed to get an interest in a small stove factory and they were no longer so poor—but that was after her youth had been spoiled, her mind marked in this way.

And to crown it all, at seventeen had come Byram the inefficient. And because he was "cute" and had a suggestion of a lisp; was of good family and really insane over her, as nearly every youth was once she had turned fourteen, she had married him, against her parents' wishes, running away with him and lying about her age, as did he about his. And then had come trying times. Byram was no money-maker, as she might have known. He was inexperienced, and being in disfavor with his parents for ignoring them in his hasty choice of a wife, he was left to his own devices. For two whole years what had she not endured— petty wants which she had concealed from her mother, furniture bought on time and dunned for, collectors with whom she had to plead not to take the stove or the lamp or the parlor table, and grocery stores and laundries and meat markets which had to be avoided because of unpaid bills. There had even been an

149

ejectment for non-payment of rent, and job after job lost for one reason and another, until the whole experience had been discolored and made impossible even after comfort had been restored.

"I cannot endure the cries of the children, Olga. You will have to close that window."

No; Byram was no money-maker, not even after his parents in far-distant St. Paul had begun to help him to do better. And anyhow by then, because she had had time to sense how weak he was, what a child, she was weary of him, although he was not entirely to blame. It was life. And besides, during all that time there had been the most urgent pursuit of her by other men, men of the world and of means, who had tried to influence her with the thought of how easily her life could be made more agreeable. Why remain faithful to so young and poor a man when so much could be done for her. But she had refused. Despite Byram's lacks she had small interest in them, although their money and skill had succeeded in debasing Byram in her young and untrained imagination, making him seem even weaker and more ridiculous than he was. But that was all so long ago now and Vivian had proved so much more important in her life. While even now she was sorry for Harry and for Byram she could only think of Vivian, who was irretrievably gone. Byram was successful now and out of her life, but maybe if life had not been so unkind and they so foolish—

"You may have Henry serve breakfast and call the car!"

And then after Byram had come Newton, big, successful, important, a quondam employer of Byram, who had met her on the street one day when she was looking for work, just when she had begun to sense how inefficient Byram really was, and he had proved kind without becoming obnoxious or demanding. While declaring, and actually proving, that he wished nothing more of her than her goodwill, he had aided her with work, an opportunity to make her own way. All men were not selfish. He had been the vice-president of the Dickerson Company and had

150

made a place for her in his office, saying that what she did not know he would teach her since he needed a little sunshine there. And all the while her interest in Byram was waning, so much so that she had persuaded him to seek work elsewhere so that she might be rid of him, and then she had gone home to live with her mother. And Newton would have married her if she had cared, but so grieved was she by the outcome of her first love and marriage that she would not.

"The sedan, yes. And I will take my furs."

And then, living with her mother and making her own way, she had been sought by others. But there had been taking root and growing in her an ideal which somehow in the course of time had completely mastered her and would not even let her think of anything else, save in moments of loneliness and the natural human yearning for life. This somehow concerned some one man, not anyone she knew, not anyone she was sure she would ever meet, but one so wonderful and ideal that for her there could be no other like him. He was not to be as young or unsophisticated as Byram, nor as old and practical as Newton, though possibly as able (though somehow this did not matter), but wise and delicate, a spirit-mate, some such wondrous thing as a great musician or artist might be, yet to whom in spite of his greatness she was to be all in all. She could not have told herself then how she was to have appealed to him, unless somehow surely, because of her great desire for him, her beauty and his understanding of her need. He was to have a fineness of mind and body, a breadth, a grasp, a tenderness of soul such as she had not seen except in pictures and dreams. And such as would need her.

"To Thorne and Company's first, Fred."

Somewhere she had seen pictures of Lord Byron, of Shelley, Liszt and Keats, and her soul yearned over each, the beauty of their faces, the record of their dreams and seekings, their something above the common seeking and clayiness (she understood that now). They were of a world so far above hers. But before Vivian appeared, how long a journey! Life had never been

151

in any hurry for her. She had gone on working and seeking and dreaming, the while other men had come and gone. There had been, for instance, Joyce with whom, had she been able to tolerate him, she might have found a life of comfort in so far as material things went. He was, however, too thin or limited spiritually to interest a stirring mind such as hers, a material man, and yet he had along with his financial capacity more humanity than most, a kind of spiritual tenderness and generosity at times towards some temperaments. But no art, no true romance. He was a plunger in real estate, a developer of tracts. And he lacked that stability and worth of temperament which even then she was beginning to sense as needful to her, whether art was present or not. He was handsomer than Byram, a gallant of sorts, active and ebullient, and always he seemed to sense, as might a homing pigeon, the direction in which lay his own best financial opportunities and to be able to wing in that direction. But beyond that, what? He was not brilliant mentally, merely a clever "mixer" and maker of money, and she was a little weary of men who could think only in terms of money. How thin some clever men really were!

"I rather like that. I'll try it on."

And so it had been with him as it had been with Byram and Newton, although he sought her eagerly enough! and so it was afterward with Edward and Young. They were all worthy men in their way. No doubt some women would be or already had been drawn to them and now thought them wonderful. Even if she could have married any one of them it would only have been to have endured a variation of what she had endured with Byram; with them it would have been of the mind instead of the purse, which would have been worse. For poor Byram, inefficient and inexperienced as he was, had had some little imagination and longings above the commonplace. But these, as contrasted with her new ideal—

"Yes, the lines of this side are not bad."

152

Yes, in those days there had come to her this nameless unrest, this seeking for something better than anything she had yet known and which later, without rhyme or reason, had caused her to be so violently drawn to Vivian. Why had Vivian always grieved so over her earlier affairs? They were nothing, and she regretted them once she knew him.

"Yes, you may send me this one, and the little one with the jade pins."

And then after Young had come Karel, the son of rich parents and well-placed socially in Braleigh. He was young, well-informed, a snob of sorts, although a gentle one. The only world he knew was that in which his parents had been reared. Their ways had been and always would be his, conservatism run mad. At thirty the only place to be was in Braleigh. There he could meet his equals twenty times a day. They went to the same homes, the same hotels, the same parties the year round. It was all the life he wanted, and it was all the life she would have been expected to want. But by then she was being hopelessly held by this greater vision and something within had said: "No, no, no!"

"You were making over my ermine cape. Is it finished?"

And Loring! He, for a change, was a physician there in Braleigh and lived with his sister in Lankester Way, near her home, only hers was in a cheaper street. He was young and good-looking but seemed to think only of his practice, how it was to make him and achieve her perhaps, although it had all seemed so commonplace and practical to her. He was so keen as to his standing with the best people, always so careful of his ways and appearance, as though his life depended upon it. He might have married more to his social and financial advantage but he had wanted her. And she had never been able to endure him—never seriously tolerate his pursuit.

"Yes, if you would alter these sleeves I might like it."

Whenever he saw her he would come hustling up. "My, but it's nice to see you again, Ulrica. You are always the same, always charming, always beautiful—now don't frown. Have you changed your mind yet, Ulrica? You don't want to forget that I'm going to be one of the successful men here some day. Please do smile a little for me. I'll be just as successful as Joyce or any of them."

"And is it just success you think I want?" she had asked.

"Oh, I know it isn't just that, but I've had a hard time and so have you. I know it wouldn't do any good to offer you only success, but what I mean is that it makes everything so much easier. With you I could do anything—" and so he would ramble on.

"To McCafferey's, the Post Street entrance."

But the shrewd hard eyes and dapper figure and unvaried attention to *his interests* had all bored and after a time alienated her, since her ideal seemed to dwarf and discolor everyone and everything. Was there not something somewhere much bigger than all this, these various and unending men, she had asked herself, some man not necessarily so successful financially but different? She had felt that she would find him somewhere, must indeed if her life was to mean anything to her. Always her great asset, her beauty, had been looked upon as the one thing she must keep for this other. And so it had gone, man after man and flirtation after flirtation. It had seemed as though it would never end. Even after she had transferred her life to the great city, to work, to go upon the stage if need be, there were more of these endless approaches and recessions; but, like the others, they had come and gone, leaving only a faint impression. Not until that day at Althea's party in the rooming house in which they both lived had she found the one who touched her.

And then—

"And now to the Willoughby."

It was late afternoon and just as she was returning from her task of seeking work in connection with the stage that they met. There he was in Althea's room, tall, spare, angular, slightly sallow

154

and cloisterish, his heavy eyebrows low above his sunken eyes as though he sought to shut himself in to himself, and with those large dark eyes fixed ruminatively and yet somewhat uncertainly upon all, even her when she came. And from Althea she gathered that he was a painter of strange dark landscapes and decorations which many of those who knew seemed to think were wonderful but which as yet had achieved no recognition at all. Worse, he was from the Rockies, a sheep-rancher's son, but had not been able to endure ranching. His future was still very far before him, and, as one could sense, he was so innocent of any desire to be put forward; he seemed half the time to be adream. By some strange freak of luck he was still there when she entered, sitting in a corner not entirely at ease, because, as he told her later, he was strange to such affairs and did not know when to go.

The brightness of the buildings in the spring sun!

And she had looked at his hands, at his commonplace clothes, and then, a little troubled by his gaze, had withdrawn hers. Again and again her eyes sought his or his hers, as though they were furtively surveying each other; as though each was unable to keep his eyes off the other. And by degrees there was set up in her a tremendous something that was like music and fear combined, as though all at once she had awakened and comprehended. She was no longer the complete master of herself, as she had always imagined, but was now seized upon and possessed by this stranger! In brief, here he was, her dream, and now she could do nothing save gaze nervously and appealingly— for what? Those dark, somber eyes, the coarse black hair and sallow skin! Yes, it was he indeed, her love, her star, the one by whose mystic light she had been steering her course these many years. She sensed it. Knew it. He was here before her now as though saying: "Come." And she could only smile foolishly without speaking. Her hands trembled and her throat tightened until she almost choked. "I never saw anyone more beautiful than you," he had said afterwards when they talked, and she had thrilled so that it was an effort not to cry out. And then he had sighed like a child and said: "Talk to me, about anything—but don't go, will you?"

155

The air—the air—this day!

And so, realizing that he valued her for this one gift at least, her beauty, she had sought now to make him understand that she was his without, however, throwing herself beggingly before him. With her eyes, her smile, her every gesture, she had said: "I am yours! I am yours! Can't you see?" At last, in his shy way, he had seemed to comprehend, but even then, as he afterwards confessed, he could not believe that anything so wonderful could follow so speedily upon contact, that one could love, adore, at sight. She had asked where he lived and if she might come and see his work, and with repressed intensity he had said: "I wish you would! I wish you could come today!" It had made her sad and yet laugh, too, for joy.

That single tree blooming in this long, hard block!

There and then, with only the necessary little interludes which propriety seemed to demand, and with longing and seeking on the part of each, had begun that wondrous thing, their love. Only it seemed to have had no fixed beginning—to have been always—just been. For the day she had called him up his voice had so thrilled her that she could scarcely speak. She had still felt she had known him for so long. How could that have been?

"I was afraid you might not call," he had said tremulously, and she had replied: "And I was wondering if you really wanted me to."

And when she sought him out in his studio she had found it to be such a poor mean room over a stable, in a mean street among a maze of mean streets, and yet had thought it heaven. It was so like him, so bare and yet wonderful—a lovely spiritual mood set over against tawdry materials and surroundings.

"Drive me through the East Side, Fred."

Better, she had found him painting or perhaps merely pretending to. He had on that old long gray linen duster which later became so familiar a thing to her. And to one side of him and

156

his easel on a table were some of the colors of his palette, greens and purples and browns and blues. He had said so softly as he opened the door to her: "My painting is all bluffing today. I haven't been able to think of anything but you, how you might not come, how you would look—" And then, without further introduction or explanation, under the north light of his roof window filtering down dustily upon them, he had put his arms about her and she her lips to his, and they had clung together, thinking only of each other, their joy and their love. And he had sighed, a tired sigh, or one of great relief after a strain, such a strain as she herself had been under.

That one little cloud in the sky!

And then after a time, he had shown her the picture he was painting, a green lush sea-marsh with a ribbon of dark enamel-like water laving the mucky strand, and overhead heavy, somber, smoky clouds, those of a sultry summer day over a marsh. And in the distance, along the horizon, a fringe of trees showing as a filigree. But what a mood! Now it hung in the Wakefield Gallery—and— (Harry had helped to place it there for her!) But then he had said, putting his brushes aside: "But what is the use of trying to paint now that you are here?" And she had sighed for joy, so wonderful was it all.

The crowds in these East Side streets!

Yet what had impressed her most was that he made no apology for the bareness and cheapness of his surroundings. Outside were swarming push carts and crowds, the babble of the great foreign section, but it was all as though he did not hear. Over a rack at the back of the large bare room he had hung a strip of faded burnt orange silk and another of clear light green, which vivified what otherwise would have been dusty and gray. Behind this, as she later discovered, were his culinary and sleeping worlds.

And then, of course, had come other days.

But how like that first day was this one, so fresh and bright!

There was no question here of what was right or wrong, conventional or otherwise. This was love, and this her beloved. Had she not sought him in the highways and the byways? At the close of one afternoon, as she was insisting that she must continue her search for work, now more than ever since neither he nor she had anything, he had said sadly: "Don't go. We need so little, Ulrica. Don't. I can't stand it now." And she had come back. "No," she had replied, "I won't—I can't—not any more, if you want me."

And she had stayed.

And that wondrous, beautiful love-life! The only love-life she had ever known.

But just the same she had seen that she must redouble her efforts to make her way, and had. Six hundred dollars she had brought to the city was nearly all gone, and as for Vivian, his allotment was what he could earn, a beggar's dole. During the days that followed, each bringing them closer, he had confessed more and more of the difficulties that confronted him, how hard it was to sell his wares. And she—it was needful for her to reopen the pages of her past. She had not been happy or prosperous, she told him; fortune might have been hers for the taking but she could not endure those who came with it. Now that she had the misery of her soul's ache removed she must find something to do. The stage was her great opportunity. And plainly his life was one which had always been and must be based on the grudged dole that life offers to those who love its beauty and lift their eyes. So few, as yet, knew of his work or had been arrested by it. Yet if he persisted, as she felt—if that wondrous something in his work which had attracted the sensitive and selective did not fail—

The hot, bare redness of the walls of these streets, so flowerless, so bleak, and yet so alive and human!

But all too well she understood that his life, unless changed by her, would ever be the meager thing it had been. Beauty was his, but no more—a beauty of mind and of dreams and of the streets and the night and the sea and the movements of life itself, but of that which was material he had nothing. That was for

158

those whom she had been unable to endure. Only by a deft synthesis of those wondrous faculties which concern beauty was he able to perceive, respond to, translate the things which he saw and felt, and these were not of matter. Rather, they were epitomes, his pictures, of lands and skies and seas and strange valleys of dreams, worlds in miniature. But what transmutations and transferences! She was never weary of the pictures he made. Nor was she ever weary of the picture he made before his easel, tenuous and pale and concerned, his graceful hands at work with the colors he synthesized. The patience, the stability, the indifference to all but that which was his to do!

"Into Bartow Street, Fred."

And in him, too, was no impatience with life for anything it might have failed to provide. Instead, he seemed ever to be thinking of its beauties and harmonies, the wonder of its dawns and sunsets, the colors and harmonies of its streets, buildings, crowds, silences. Often of a morning when it was yet dark he would arise and open a door that gave out onto a balcony and from there gaze upon the sky and city. And at any time it was always an instinct with him to pause before anything that appealed to either of them as beautiful or interesting. And in his eye was never the estimating glint of one who seeks to capture for profit that which is elemental and hence evanescent, but only the gaze of the lover of beauty, the worshiper of that which is profitable to the soul only.

The very street! The very studio!

Although she was ignorant of the spirit or the technique of art she had been able to comprehend it and him, all that he represented as a portion of beauty itself, the vast and supernal beauty toward which the creative forces of life in their harsh and yet tender ways seem impelled at times.

Had she not understood very well that it was as beauty that she appealed to him, at first anyhow, an artistry of face and form plus a certain mood of appreciation or adoration or understanding which was of value to him? How often had he spoken of her

159

lavender-lidded eyes, the whiteness and roundness of her arms, the dark gold of her hair, the somber unrevealing blue of the iris of her eyes! How strange it was that these seemed to enthrall and hold him at times, leaving him, if not weak, at least childlike in her hands. He had never seemed to weary of her and during all their days together she could feel his unreasoning joy in her.

His one-time yellow curtains exchanged for green ones!

That she had proved and remained irresistible to him was evidenced by his welcoming and gratified eyes, the manner in which he paused to survey her whenever she came near, seeming to re-estimate her every least attribute with loving interest. Indeed, he seemed to need her as much as she needed him, to yearn with an intense hunger over her as a thing of beauty—he who to her was strength, beauty, ideals, power, all the substance of beauty and delight that she could crave.

Yes, here was where they had come to gaze at the towers of the bridge beyond.

And so for over a year it was that they clung together, seeking to make of their lives an ideal thing. Only it was after she came into his life that he had begun to worry—and because of what? It was no hardship for him to live upon what he could make, but now that she had come, with her beauty and her beauty's needs, it was no longer the same. As soon as she appeared he had seemed to sense his inefficiency as a creator of means. Bowdler, the wealthy dealer, had once told him that if he pleased him with something it might be worth five hundred dollars. Five hundred dollars! But when he took a painting to Bowdler he said he was overstocked, had too many of his things on hand—the very things that today—(now that Vivian was gone)—were selling for as much as ten and twelve thousand! And a single one of all those now being sold would have made them both happy for a whole year or more!

He had called this tree her parasol!

160

And she had been able to do so little for him! Realizing how little life had done for him she had decided then and there that all her efforts must be bent toward correcting this injustice. Life owed him more. And so it was that at last she had turned to the stage and sought earnestly, day after day and week after week, only to obtain very little of all she needed to make them happy, a small part in one of Wexford's many productions, he of the comedies and farces and beauty shows. Yet after some effort she had made him admit that she was distinctive and that he could use her. But then had come that long wait of nearly three months before the work began! And in the meantime what labor, the night and day work of rehearsals and appearances, the trying to get back to him each afternoon or night. And he had been so patient and hopeful and helpful, waiting for her after late hours of rehearsal to walk home with her and encouraging her in every way. And yet always there was a tang of something unreal about it all, hopes, as she so truly feared, that were never to be realized, dreams too good to come true. The hours had flown. The very pressure of his hand had suggested paradise, present and yet not to be.

She must be returning now. It was not wise for her to sit here alone.

And while those three months were dragging their slow days she had borrowed what money she could to keep them going. She had even borrowed from her mother! Yet they had been happy, wandering here and there, he always rejoicing in the success which her work promised to bring her. The studios facing the great park where she now lived at which they had looked, he seeming to think they were not for such as he. (The creatures who really dwelt there!)

Yes, she must be going. His train was due at four.

And then, at last, her trial period was over, Wexford had complimented her and her salary had been increased. She had begun to buy things for Vivian and his studio, much as he protested. But best of all for her the hope of better days still to come, greater fame for herself and so better days for Vivian, a real future in which he was to share—money—comfort for them both.

"To the apartment, Fred."

And then— In spite of all her wishes and fears, had come the necessity for her to go on the road with the show. And owing to their limited means he was compelled to remain behind. Worse, despite the fact that each knew that every thought was for the other, the thought of separation tortured them both. Wherever she was there was the thought of him, alone, at his easel and brooding. And herself alone. It had seemed at times as though she must die unless this separation could be ended.

If only Harry were not coming into her life again!

But it was not ended—for weeks. And then one day, after a brief silence had come the word that he had been ill. A wave of influenza was sweeping the city and had seized him. She was not to worry. But she did worry—and returned immediately, only to find him far along the path which he was never to retrace. He was so ill. And worse, a strange despondency based on the thought that he was never to get well, had seized him. He had felt when she left, or so he said, that something were sure to happen. They might not ever, really, be together again. It had been so hard for him to do without her.

He had added that he was sorry to be so poor a fighter, to bring her back from her work. Her work! And he ill!

The immense wall these hotels made along the park!

And then against the utmost protest of her soul had come the end, a conclusion so sudden and unexpected that it had driven despair like metal into her very soul. Hour after hour and under her very eyes, her protesting if not restraining hands and thoughts, he had grown weaker. Though he knew, he seemed to wish to deny it, until at last his big dear eyes fixed upon her, he had gone, looking as though he wished to say something.

This wretchedly wealthy West Side!

162

It was that look, the seeking in it, that wishing to remain with her that was written there, that had haunted her and did still. It was as though he had wished to say: "I do not want to go! I do not want to go!"

And then, half-dead, she had flung herself upon him. With her hands she had tried to draw him back, until she was led away. For days she was too ill to know, and only his grave—chosen by strangers!—had brought it all back. And then the long days! Never again would life be the same. For the first time in her life she had been happy. A bowl of joy had been placed in her eager fingers, only to be dashed from them. Yes, once more now she was alone and would remain so, thrust back upon herself. And worse, with the agonizing knowledge of what beauty might be. Life had lost its luster. What matter if others told of her beauty, if one or many sought to make her life less bare?

This stodgy porter always at the door in his showy braid! Why might not such as he die instead?

But then her mother and sister, learning of her despair, had come to her. Only since there was nothing that any pleasure, or aspect of life could offer her, the days rolled drearily—meaninglessly. And only because of what was still missing in her mother's life, material comfort, had she changed. It had been with the thought of helping her mother that after a year she had returned to the city and the stage, but exhausted, moping, a dreary wanderer amid old and broken dreams.

By degrees of course she had managed to pick up the threads of her life again. Who did not? And now nature, cynical, contemptuous of the dreams and longings which possess men, now lavished upon her that which she and Vivian had longed for in vain. Fame? It was hers. Money? A score of fortunes had sought her in vain. Friendship? She could scarcely drive it from the door. She was successful.

But what mattered it now? Was it not a part of the routine, shabby method of life to first disappoint one—sweat and agonize one—and then lavish luxury upon one—afterwards?

"I want nothing. And if anyone calls, I am not in."

And so it was that after a time Harry descending upon her with his millions, and seeking solace for himself through her sympathy, she had succumbed to that—or him—as a kindly thing to do. He too had confessed to a wretched dole of difficulties that had dogged his early years. He too had been disappointed in love, comfort—almost everything until too late. In his earliest years he had risen at four in a milltown to milk cows and deliver milk, only later to betake himself, barefooted and in the snow, to a mill to work. Later still he had worked in a jewelry factory, until his lungs had failed. And had then taken to the open road as a peripatetic photographer of street children in order to recover his health. But because of this work—the chemistry and physics of photography—he had interested himself in chemistry and physics, later taking a "regular job," as he phrased it, in a photographic supply house and later still opening a store of his own. It was here that he had met Kesselbloom, who had solved the mystery of the revolving shutter and the selenium bath. Financing him and his patents, Harry had been able to rise still more, to fly really, as though others were standing still. The vast Dagmar Optical and Photographic Company. It was now his, with all its patents. And the Baker-Wile Chemical Company. Yes, now he was a multimillionaire, and lonely—as lonely as she was. Strange that he and she should have met.

"No, I will not see anyone."

So now, through her, he was seeking the youth which could be his no more. Because of some strange sense of comradeship in misery, perhaps, they had agreed to share each other's unhappiness!

"You say Mr. Harris telephoned from the station?"

Yes, as he had told her in his brooding hours, at fifty it had suddenly struck him that his plethora of wealth was pointless. As a boy he had not learned to play, and now it was too late. Already he was old and lonely. Where lay his youth or any happiness?

And so now—nearly icy-cold the two of them, and contemning life dreams—they were still facing life together. And here

164

he was this day, at her door or soon would be, fresh from financial labors in one city and another. And returning to what? With a kind of slavish and yet royal persistence he still pursued her—to comfort—as well as to be comforted, and out of sheer weariness she endured him. Perhaps because he was willing to await her mood, to accept the least crumb of her favor as priceless. The only kinship that existed between them was this unhappy youth of his and her sympathy for it, and his seeming understanding and sympathy for the ills that had beset her. Supposing (so his argument had run) that the burden of this proposed friendship with him were to be made very light, the lightest of all burdens, that upon closer contact he proved not so hopeless or dull as he appeared, could she not—would she not—endure him? (The amazing contrarieties and strangenesses of things!) And so friendship, and later marriage under these strange conditions. Yet she could not love him, never had and never would. However it might have seemed at first—and she did sympathize with and appreciate him—still only the needs of her mother and sister and the fact that she herself needed someone to fall back upon, a support in this dull round of living, had caused her to go on as long as she had.

How deserted that wading-pool looked at evening, with all the children gone!

And now at this very moment he was below stairs waiting for her, waiting to learn whether she had smiled or her mood had relaxed so that he might come up to plead afresh for so little as she could give—her worthless disinterested company somewhere!

Well, perhaps it was unfair to serve one so who wished nothing more than to be kind and who had striven in every way for several years now to make himself useful if not agreeable to her, and yet— True, she had accepted of his largess, not only for herself but for her mother; but had she not had things of her own before that? And had she not been content? Was it charity from her or from him?

And still—

165

Those darkening shadows in the sky in the east!

And yet it was always "Ulrica" here and "Ulrica" there. Did she so much as refer to an old-time longing was it not he who attempted to make amends in some way or to bring about an belated fulfilment? Vivian's painting now in the museum, the talk as to his worth, his monument but now being erected—to whom, to whom were those things due—this belated honoring of her darling—?

"Oh, well, tell him to come up. And you may lay out my green evening dress, Olga."

Mathewson

*A*S AGAINST THE VITAL, the successful, the avaricious, the brutal—those who see life as something to take by storm or to win against by subtlety, or, what is worse, inequitable chance, I offer Mathewson.

I first saw him in the editorial offices of the *Globe-Democrat* in St. Louis, seated at the one and only copy reader's desk in the city news room, a long-visored green shade over his eyes. It was a late, airless summer afternoon and he was in his shirt sleeves. A slim and somewhat small, perhaps clerkly, figure. Dark, mellow and entirely unacquisitive eyes. Fine, long and somewhat pointed oval head, with a seemingly loose growth of limp black hair. Unobtrusive nose, sensitive mouth; pale, rather bloodless hands, and small, almost womanish, feet.

Interestingly enough, on that day the regular city editor was on vacation. A card over his desk stated: "All assignments given and copy received by Mr. Mathewson." When I approached him he was bent over a bit of copy. He looked up, neither genially nor the reverse, a note of inquiry in his eye. I stated who I was and he immediately replied: "Yes, Mr. Mitchell said you were to do the St. Louis terminal accident." At the same time he was writing, in a small, clear, almost printed hand, a street number in Carondelet, a then southern French suburb of the city. Also: "Residence of dead engineer. See Yardmaster (33-hundred something) South Broadway for details."

He handed me the memorandum and turned away. But from that single glance, as well as from the softness of his voice, the whiteness of his face and hands, his reticence, I sensed so much—gentility, apprehension, sensitivity, speculation and, more, brooding and very likely poetic thought. How different from the broad, solid, sullen, conventional, contentious Mitchell! And

167

Hartung, his assistant, young, nervous, frightened, a mouse-like soul! He also was out at the time.

I went, of course, and did the work. From the yardmaster, whatever his name was, I learned of a loosened rail which had plunged a switching engine pulling ten freight cars into five others standing on a siding. The engine was overturned. In some manner the engineer was pinioned and burned to death. It being a matter of night switching, he had been freed by dawn—freed to lie in a quickly provided coffin—the gift of the company—and taken to his home, where at two in the afternoon I was permitted to see him.

I tell all this because of a single incident which I wrote into my brief story and which elicited a comment from Wilson Mathewson. The incident followed my entry into the engineer's small brick house in Carondelet, for the purpose of viewing the body and questioning Mrs. Engineer.

In the front room, or parlor, in his wooden overcoat, was solemnly centered the dead man. At the back, as I could glimpse through a crack of light from a door not tightly closed, was a living room. There was a sewing machine and some nondescript furniture. Assuming that the dead man's wife was upstairs and would presently come down, I decided—reportorial custom and duty—that I should look into that room, and accordingly widened the crack. To my embarrassment, I saw in one corner, before what proved to be a clothes press, the doors of which were open, a short, stocky and decidedly worn and weary-looking woman, who was holding in her arms, pressed close to her body, a man's coat and trousers, plainly the large coat and trousers of the man in the coffin. She was sobbing, her head bent low over the clothes.

Instantly my mood changed. It seemed no longer important or meaningful that I question her. I felt that I had seen all, heard all, knew all that was significant in this case. In short, I desired to escape unseen—the only human apology I could make for my intrusion—and so did.

Once outside, however, and on my way to the office, I decided to capitalize this incident, as what incipient writer would not? For there was really nothing new in this type of story. News being plentiful, as news it would get but a minor paragraph. But if I could inject this wife clasping her husband's old working clothes and crying, at least it would make an impressive paragraph. Back in the office I wrote it, and Mathewson being out laid it on his desk. Having been interested by him and ambitious for myself as a reporter, I was eager to note what he would do with it. Perhaps it was too melodramatic and he would have preferred that I ask questions.

I went out for a bite to eat and later when I returned went over to him to see what else there was for me to do. The item I had written was in his fingers. He looked up oddly and with what seemed to me a mellow, appreciative light in his eyes. "I'm glad you did not question her. I was afraid you might." He turned and then added, from the depths of his work: "The evening assignments are not ready. Come back at six-thirty."

I sauntered out thinking what a mellow and arresting person this was, so different from Mitchell and quite all of the other city editors I had encountered in St. Louis or elsewhere. Then somewhere around the Laclede Hotel, I believe—I ran into Rodenberger, a fellow spirit of one of the other papers and much more worldly-wise than myself. He had been in St. Louis for years and had worked upon all of the papers. He would know about this Mathewson person. And in due course I asked him, the absence of my city editor and the substitution of this stranger being an item of no little interest in my beginner's world.

"Oh, Wilson Mathewson! Is he working over there? He must be behaving himself again. Queer bird, that! You might not think it, but he is one of the best newspapermen in the city. Maybe the best. Writes a beautiful story when he wants to. Only he don't often want to. He's been around here now for four or five years. But he doesn't work often." He symbolized the difficulty involved by curling his fingers into a cup and lifting the same to his lips.

Loquacious always, a man who drank and loafed not a little himself, Rodenberger launched upon a perhaps hearsay and possibly wholly untrue story of Mathewson's past. He had come from St. Joseph, Missouri, where his father, a wealthy printer, still dominated a large business. But Mattie (as Rodenberger called him) did not like St. Joseph nor the printing business, nor even newspaper work, for that matter. Too temperamental, too artistic. Yet here he was in St. Louis, and thought well of by local editors and publishers. For Mathewson could write better than any of them. And edit, too, providing he could stay sober.

The account fascinated me. An interesting personality, a fine writer, and yet a drunkard! No doubt he could write learnedly and tastefully of books, plays and personalities other than those involved in baseball and politics, the great American stimuli of the time. For Rodenberger had added that he did all this and more. But that he was highly unsocial and, worse, unconventional. That he lived in one of the most forlorn and decayed districts of the city, known as the "Black and Tan," and (whisper!) it was rumored that he had lived or did then live with a girl of color. More, it was believed by some that, on occasions at least, he took some drug or other. Morphine, maybe. A picture which instead of reducing him in my ever-erratic imagination only served to heighten him not a little. Ha! De Quincey! Poe! Defoe! In odd crannies of my mind, and for what reasons I could not have set forth at the time, were enshrined such erratic and perhaps depleted and defeated types. I have since learned why.

One of the things impressed upon me by additional contacts with Mathewson, as well as by reporters who either knew him slightly or knew of him, was that because of his frail body, his dark, liquid and inscrutable eyes, and his obviously total mental indifference to all the current commonplace activities of St. Louis of that day, to say nothing of his esthetic approach to the higher-mind matters of the time, he was a figure of real import as well as mystery to them. Wilson Mathewson! Wilson Mathewson! Wilson Mathewson!

His actual abode was a dark room over a harness-maker's shop in Second Street, north of Olive—a region adjoining the "Black and Tan"—a deserted neighborhood except for distant sounds emanating from the Black and Tan or the more distant business heart. A reporter who once carried a message to him from the city editor of the *Post-Dispatch* told me so. Nearly always he was sick, or doped, or drunk, but whether sick or not, usually mentally indisposed toward anything connected with the newspaper life of the city, since neither letters, telegrams nor personal calls when sent or made by editors or friends elicited any response. He had no known intimates, although plainly there were many who would have liked to be intimate with him, myself among them.

My interest in this man was so great that finding him, but a few days later, gone from the *Globe,* I went to look at the district and the house in which he was said to live, without, however, venturing to intrude myself upon him. And later, hearing from someone that on occasion he visited an out-of-the-way French wine restaurant in that same region, I went there, but did not see him. I should say, though, that it had been reported to me that he maintained some sort of contact with the old French host and his wife, that sometimes he wrote at a table there. Fascinating! I followed on his trail, but to no purpose. The best I could do was to establish the fact that at the house previously mentioned, the woman who rented a room to him was a certain Mrs. Schwarzkopf, a German widow about thirty-eight years old. She, with her two small girl children, maintained the flat or apartment on the second floor, one room of which was occupied by Mathewson. As he himself later deigned to comment to me she supported herself by renting this room to him and by doing night cleaning in a downtown office building, where she worked from six to eleven at night, the children being put to bed by a neighbor or by Mathewson himself if he was there at the time. I indulge in these preliminaries solely to show how truly magnetized I was by the man. He was, to me, so different. And St. Louis at that time, and to me at least, was so infernally dull.

The drowsy, muddy, sleepy Mississippi River. The dry and often intense and unbroken summer heat. The dull and commonplace business activities—shoes, dry goods, hardware, beer. And the inane and meaningless social groups: French, German, Irish, Old-South American, with their ridiculous money, family or religious standards, their large houses, brainless teas, dances, receptions or "at homes"; their marriages, deaths, births, anniversaries, as opposed to the dreadful slums, veritably sties and warrens along the waterfront and elsewhere and in which dwelt thousands upon thousands as socially forgotten as though they were dead! And then the holy churches! So blindly reverenced, their very bricks and stones along with their sleek and shrewd priests, ministers, rabbis, and what not, all bleeding the poor of their nickels and dimes. The city's rotten politics and politicians! And the immense and commonplace labor and whore districts! And the sacrosanct banks and trust companies! And whited sepulchres of newspapers! And the colleges, schools, universities!

Do I seem to rave? Life, in the main, is a cause for raving.

An article by Mathewson in one of the Sunday issues of the *Globe* or *Republic* (I forget which) not so long after that brought him violently to mind. It concerned Émile Zola, quite the dominant literary phenomenon of Europe and America of that day, although in America, of course, a phenomenon of decidedly disgraceful and even shameful imputation. For did he not deal with those painfully progressive human realities, the climaxes of which—here in America, at least—appeared to center, or should, in the police court, the jail, the bawdy district and the morgue? And of course, and for that very reason, of the utmost interest to a large number of the suppressed and restrained of our mawkishly conventional and for the most part pseudo-moral and religious land. Indeed, in sleek, almost wholly inesthetic and material-minded St. Louis, there was life quite as efflorescent with lechery and gluttony as ever in Paris, only here glazed over with an outward and better-than-thou pretence which compelled thousands to denounce this man Zola with a moral fervor only equaled by their secret vices. Unclean! Unclean! Unclean! He and all his works!

Yet this article by Mathewson, praise God, was entirely indifferent to that. It dealt with him wisely and impartially, and I, for my part, quite innocent of any responses other than those of wonder and a desire to increase my store of knowledge of life, now read of this man Zola with intense interest. His Paris, his people—the kind of people who appeared to be not so much different from what was all about me here in St. Louis! Indeed, in what respects, if any, I asked myself in following Mathewson's artfully etched thoughts and phrases, did Zola's French characters and scenes differ from those of America and St. Louis? French though he and his books were, he was writing of the same greeds, emotions, lusts, ambitions, successes and failures as characterized and directed the people of America. The only difference, as Mathewson pointed out in his article, was that by Zola's deliberate art as well as his insight, they were stripped bare of the pretence that "like a fog" (I particularly noted that phrase) enveloped Anglo-Saxon life and caused its citizens to see themselves as in a glass darkly.

172

Arrestingly enough, this résumé strengthened my impression of Mathewson as an individual of singular force and insight. For not only did he suggest clearly and startlingly the iron courage of Zola in presenting life as he saw it, but he made me aware of the tremendous stir that, for good or ill, Zola had made with his Rougon-Maquart family series, his *Thérèse Raquin, L'Assommoir,* and, of course, his *Nana.* Actually, as I read I gasped in wonder. For in the office as I recalled him he had seemed so frail, so pale and retiring, whereas in this article, smooth and stylized to no small degree, he conveyed a genuinely stirring mental force and acumen. Why had I not heard of Zola before? Why with such thoughts and understanding as this Mathewson had, should he seem so soft and delicate? And he probably wrote this on a small table in that dark, dingy, down-at-heels French restaurant. I was at once more puzzled and fascinated than before.

Just the same, during the months—six or seven all told— which followed the publication of the article, I saw Mathewson but twice, once in January coming out of the editorial office of the *Republic* (to which paper I had by then transferred my services), when he merely bowed to me courteously, and the second time perhaps three or four months later, very likely in the hottest part of May, one of those dry, lethargic St. Louis afternoons. I was making my reportorial rounds of the police stations at the time (few telephones in those days), and happened to be in the ribald, shiftless, drunken, levee district north of Olive and east of Third Street where he dwelt, when I encountered him shambling out of one of the cheaper and meaner of the really evil saloons or dives of that area. And looking—oh so different from the clean and even tidy individual I had seen in the *Republic* office! His hat and clothing soiled and limp, his face white, or bluewhite, and his dark eyes vacant. Also his kindly mouth was a little the worse for a relaxed lower jaw, and there were liquor stains on his clothes. How can this be, I thought? And why? Surely not the same man who so quietly and tactfully applauded my handling of the engineer's wife, not the one who had written so wisely and effectively of Zola!

I stopped and stared, for I could not be mistaken. And he, noting me, since I was directly before him, blocking his progress,

173

stared also. Then plainly, by his expression, remembering me, beginning, in answer to my inquiry, with: "Yes, Mathewson! Mathewson! What of it? Another young newspaperman staring at me and wondering. Well, what of it? I'm drunk. And what's more, I'm very drunk. But I remember you, young fellow. You used to be on the *Globe-Democrat.* And you had sense enough not to ask fool questions of an unhappy woman. I remember that. A whole lot more than most newspapermen remember even when they're not drunk. And what's more" . . . and here he hiccoughed and staggered and almost fell against me, "I've sense enough to get drunk like this once in a while and so escape the real damned drunkenness which is—well—which is . . ."

But here he paused, and with one hand lifted indicated a material and social circle which seemed to include the entire block, very likely the entire region, or St. Louis, or the world. And then finally, after hiccoughing and meditating and seeming to be trying to serialize his thoughts, he added: "Everything that you see around here. Me, you, these people, St. Louis . . . (hic) . . ."

"I see," I commented, but he paid no attention to me, rather staggering and nearly falling and then being helped by me to a nearby light post. "Look at 'em!" he went on. "Look at 'em!" (And once more waving a feeble hand.) "Ignorant! Dirty! Useless! Eating and drinking and loafing, and, and, reproducing themselves. For what? For what? So's there'll be more of 'em to eat and drink an' loaf an' reproduce. An' they're supposed to be sober. An' I'm drunk. An' everybody else that wants to eat and drink and . . . reproduce themselves in St. Louis an' everywhere. You're sober. An' I'm drunk. An' you want to reproduce. An' I don't. An' I want to think. An' they don't—or can't. An' they're sober. An' you're sober. An' I'm drunk. Ha! Ha!"

He attempted to lean forward and nearly fell. To emphasize his remarks he now lifted one arm semaphorewise and brought it down rather dramatically, but not heavily, upon me. Meanwhile I stared about me at the wretched cobbled street, with its low, old buildings, its nondescript population of negroes and whites, its degraded and if not evil merely dull and humdrum men and women, their stores, rooms, brothels, saloons, and their hot, smelly bodies, all sweating together in the heat. And although he once more staggered and fell against me, and I braced him

174

up and stood him against the post, the while a small crowd began to gather. I felt myself newly and differently affected, emotionally as well as mentally exalted. For the thought to which he had just given expression was to me, at that time in my life, so new and strange and, after a fashion, refreshing. For how true it was, or seemed, that we, or these people at least, were dreaming—a wild, bitter, troublesome and yet colorful and exciting dream! And perhaps the dream covered everything semi-miserable, semi-contented, semi-brutal, semi-decent everywhere, not only in St. Louis but in the world, of which by this time I had had some twenty-two years of experience.

Here in this drab, decayed, out-at-seat, down-at-heel, poverty-limited street, with its dirty children, black and white, and its stray cats and dogs, I was swelling with an excess of sympathy, wonder, respect, even awe. Drunkenness? Drunkenness? Who was really drunk? This small, limp, Chaplinesque figure, with his reflector-like temperament and laboratory-like mind and its scalpel-like thoughts, or myself, or these people of this street, or of St. Louis, or of the world?

"Better let me take you home," I pleaded. "I don't think you'd better try to go by yourself. I know where you live." "Do you?" he questioned. "Yes, I do." "All right then."

And, in due course, to the accompaniment of more talk of much the same nature, and some children and dogs, we were off—this very superior character whom, as I knew, I could so easily manage physically, and myself. And he consented—oh, blessed privilege—to let me lock my arm in his and lead him south on Second, where at last I found his door and got him up the staircase to the room on the second floor front which was his. On the ground floor, as I now recall, was the harness and saddle shop, with a huge wooden horse's head for a sign. And above, the room he occupied.

An old-time wire bell-pull and knob at the street door, below, which I jangled before entering, soon brought to a rear door, one flight up, a broad and decidedly commonplace if not unfriendly face. Also the shoulders of a typically German peasant woman whose soap-shined skin and sleeked yellow hair suggested your industrious, as well as cleanly char- or washwoman. I was about to speak, or await some comment from her, when a disturbed

"Ach, Himmel" sounded, and the head was gone. In a trice, though, came a clattering of heavy shoes inside her room, and after that his hall door opened. And then, "Pleece—in here he goess." Then she herself, with a number of "Ach, Himmels" now guided him deftly and quite gently to his bed, which occupied a corner of the room. The room, though very poorly lighted, was very clean. "He iss so—" she continued, almost pleadingly, "so goot a man, too. Ach, ach!" I felt a little sorry for her, since I gathered that he was a real support as well as care to her. She respected him and stood in awe of him, and, at the same time, cared for him—while he, drunk or sober, plainly dominated this menage entirely.

Although he was most quickly disposed of on this occasion —laid on the cheap, heavy wooden, but clean bed, with the black shades and curtains of the two front windows drawn —she was not yet through, but hurried for a bowl of water, a towel, some soap and a pair of pajamas, which I saw her extract from a closet in one corner. Then she proceeded to undress him—shoes, coat, trousers, all being carried into a rear room for future cleansing. In the meantime, seeing him so well looked after and, also, that by now he was making neither sound nor move, I decided I might as well go. I had my reportorial duties. But, oh, the thrill of being a part of all this, the pleasure of contacting so intimately a temperament I so much admired! Mrs. Schwarzkopf had said, "Now he iss all right. Now, already, you see he sleeps." But as I went, I was already thinking of returning the next morning to inquire. And so did —only not of him, since I feared to intrude so soon, but of her. And hearing that he was better but still resting, I departed satisfied. For now soon, as I argued, I might be permitted to tap on his door and, if admitted, struggle toward a friendship that I so much craved. I was not sure of the outcome, but I was eager to try.

And accordingly, after a lapse of nearly a week, I did, only to find him out—no sound from either his or Mrs. Schwarzkopf's door. Another visit, some five days later, was much more successful. It was in the afternoon between duties, and, to my surprise, I found him in bed. The downstairs door, to my satisfaction, stood open. And to my greater satisfaction, Mrs. Schwarzkopf was out. This was my chance, permitting a direct and uninter-rupted tapping at his own door.

At first, there was no response. Later, having coughed once or twice, I knocked again and was rewarded by a faint rustling within. Nervously, I waited, wondering how I was to begin, when a key in the door was suddenly turned, and I saw a room in semi-darkness, blinds drawn against the sun-bright afternoon outside. Mathewson, in a thin, gray dressing gown and a pair of heelless slippers, or "mules," admitted me—hesitatingly, and yet with an air of cordiality. He at once apologized for his bed as well as his room, both not a little disheveled. He had not been himself, he said, and had been resting. On the floor, as I noted, as well as on a chair near his bed were some of his clothes. On a flat-topped desk between the two front windows on which previously (my first visit) had been neatly arranged some papers and books, were now what looked to be medicine and whiskey bottles. Ex-cept for the pair of mules, his feet were bare, and they looked to me, as my eyes became accustomed to the light, to be drawn and bloodless, as did his face. His ordinarily smooth black hair was now tousled and askew. Altogether he looked not only dissipated, but sick, and for that reason, I felt more encouraged and hopeful of his consideration than otherwise. Being sick, he might find me useful, whereas sober and restrained, as I noted him to be in the offices of the *Globe-Democrat* and the *Republic,* he might find little enough time for me.

True to this thought on my part, he unceremoniously retreated to his bed and, flinging himself down, observed: "You'll have to excuse the appearance of this room. I could have it straightened, of course, if I could endure being in it when Mrs. Schwarzkopf does the straightening." He drew a sheet over him, and then wanted to know if I would be so good as to hand him a cigarette—a request which settled the problem as to whether I was to be endured, and on what terms.

Just the same, I was delighted. For by reason of the easy virtue of usefulness, I was being admitted to an intimacy which I had scarcely hoped for, with a man who not only held the respect of the really thinking newspapermen of the city, but had written so illuminatingly of Zola, and had made those precious remarks in regard to drunkenness and sobriety—. For want of something

177

better to say, I asked if there was anything else I could do, to which he replied that it depended on how much time I had. "You are still working for the *Republic,* aren't you?" "Yes, I am." "Well, then, I know you haven't any too much time, and you mustn't be wasting it on me. Suppose you sit down for a few moments, perhaps we can think of something to talk about."

The ease and kindly tolerance with which he sensed and accepted my neophytic mood quite startled me, and at the same time relieved me in regard to my relationship to him. Provided I proved myself sufficiently interesting, we were to pass into a not so much master-and-man as priest-and-neophyte—or teacher-and-student—relationship. And in substantiation of this, there followed some inquiries on his part. From whence was I come? What, if any, experience had I had previously to St. Louis? My origin? Views? Arrestingly enough, he troubled not at all to refer to his drunken appearance in the Black and Tan—or to be sensitive about it. On the contrary, he referred to some work he had been doing, but which had been interfered with by a sick headache. Another time, if I came, I would find him feeling better, and he would be glad to see me—a cool hint that all the time he could afford to give me was already exhausted. This left me with no alternative other than to rise and take my leave, feeling that he was by no means uninterested in or intolerant of me, but really sick, and might be pleased if I should come again. And so I determined to try him again—and soon.

One thing that blocked my adventurings in connection with him was the fact that he was not always to be found. My next sight of him was frustrated for at least three weeks. His stout German housekeeper, who hearing me tap—the first time after a calculated delay of ten days and the second after an additional week—assured me that he was not in. "He has not been here now for three weeks. I doaned know ven he will pe pack." "Has he moved?" I questioned. "No, no. He comes and goase ven he pleases."

I was disappointed but interested—slightly troubled by the thought of giving him up as one who was too difficult. Perhaps he was with his black girl. Perhaps in some wretched saloon or dope parlor, or maybe with his family in St. Joseph, or in some other city. Who could say? All the more interested, I waited another ten days, giving him ample time to purge his mind of me entirely if he was so inclined, or to receive me as genially as before. Then I again knocked at his door.

And now behold, on a late Saturday afternoon in mid-September, Mathewson, looking as though he had freed himself of all harm, and, incidentally, as though he rather more than less expected me. He mentioned that his housekeeper had informed him that I had called several times, a consideration which, as he chose to say, was very kind of me; something he did not deserve from anyone. "For you see," he said genially, and in higher spirits than ever I had seen him, "I am not a person who has ever done enough for anyone to deserve friendship. Besides, I am not sure that I know how to use it. I am either too limited or too extensive; I haven't decided which. At any rate, I don't fit into life as I find it here or anywhere. Do you use cigarettes?" I declined. "Cigars, maybe?" "No, thanks." "I never offer a young man a drink unless I am certain someone has corrupted him before. In my case, it's escape. It can't hurt me as much as the things I have to contemplate when I don't drink."

I took him to be jesting and asked, cheerfully, "Do you really think life is as bad as that?"

"It depends on how much you think about it. I am one of those unfortunates who cannot avoid thinking of it. If you don't, it's easy."

He had, after admitting me, returned to his bed. On this occasion, he was clothed in shirt and trousers—the shirt a clean silk one, open at the neck—and his heelless mules, of course, which he kicked off as he threw himself down. At the same time, his face seemed not as bloodless as it did before, and now the room as well as his table, the floor beside his bed and under it, was strewn with books and papers. He seemed to have been writing something, for on his writing desk were many scribbled sheets of something. I wished so much that I might read them. One thing I hastened to comment on this time, before I was dismissed, was his article on Zola. I calculated that it might gain for me an additional period of time. And at once he responded interestingly.

"Oh, yes, Zola. A real man. So far as I know the only writer who really sees and dares to present the real brutality of life. All the others are fooled by it. Or where they are not, they have no stomach for it. I believe he said so. In so far as literature is concerned, he is like a bull in an art-shop, knocking down a lot of fine fancies and lovely illusions. But it is because he sees what is and, in a way, is hurt or disgusted by it. But he will never be accepted here, or in England. I doubt if he will ever be translated in our time. Possibly. If you want to read him, you will have to study French unless you know it." And here he courteously paused as though he expected me to say that I did, a consideration, viewing my general lack of technical information or training, which caused me to smile. "I do not," I said.

"So much the better. Very likely you will move about this country, which certainly requires studying. At that, a foreign language offers you no better door to life than your native one. Life is life, much the same everywhere. I fancy Homer knew only Greek. Jesus, Hebrew—or a dialect of it. Shakespeare, English."

I felt very much encouraged, even to the point of ignoring all languages except English. Why not? "But returning to Zola," he continued, "here, of course, it's really useless to write about him. It merely starts some people looking for smut and others to saying unkind things, or having his books burned, or some old book dealer arrested." He smiled wanly, and then added, "But I'm afraid I'm making a very bad impression on you— drunkenness, Zola, no belief in life. You're very young and much less experienced than I am, possibly. Anyhow, I'm much older than I look, or the years I have lived." Having finished a drink of whiskey which he had taken from a small stand beside him, he now lit a cigarette, the while I thrilled to my very toes. For whether he sensed it or not, here was the very world and the very type of man I was most longing to know, and most calculated to adore at the time. His voice was so soft and agreeably modulated. And within his delicate but iron reserve appeared to snuggle a kindly resignation. It underlay all he said. He moved me far more than any rugged or vivid personality or experience of that day could have. In my mind, always, was his comment on the Black and Tan: *Not I, but they are drunk.* And now this latest: "A foreign language offers you no better door to life than your native one." I was determined to write that down once I was outside. My response to what he said about me was that he need not fear harming me. "Like yourself, I am after life," I remember boasting, "as much as life is after me"—at which he smiled.

"Well, you have an adversary worthy of your steel." To which he added, after a moment, "And one with more cruelty and subtlety than you or any of us." And I decided to write that down.

Much as I regretted it, my time was up. He was no man to mince words, at least with me, and so now said: "But you mustn't forget your job. Besides, I have something that I am trying to think out just now." Accordingly, I arose, excusing myself for my intrusion.

"Oh, no. Oh, no. You mustn't feel that you are intruding on me. I like you very much, and I like you to come. I really do. If I were a little stronger, I would invite you for walks. But as it is at present, I cannot. I am a man of many limitations, and I know them all. None better. But that mustn't keep you from coming—and soon." And by then he was on his feet, showing me graciously to the door. Strangely for all this seemingly timed and almost cavalier dismissal, I felt underlying it a friendly glow which manifested itself for one thing in his taking my arm and pressing it—a pressure which really assured me that he liked me.

After that, there were a number of visits, interstitial usually between assignments, afternoon and evening, because to call on him in the morning was to obtain no response whatsoever. Between four and six, if he were in, I was most likely to find him in a more receptive and even cordial mood, whereas at other times it was usually not so. Hence, as much as possible I calculated to reach there between those hours.

But the varying nature of these visits and my receptions! Once I called and found him working at his desk. This time the usually lowered curtains were up, and he himself was dressed and shaved and quite his public and journalistic self, even though I still sensed that same meditative and even somber strain, which marked if not marred the major part of his hours. This time he informed me that he was working on a paper for one of the Eastern magazines which he hoped might find favor in the editorial eye. After the Zola article some Eastern magazine had written him.

"The subject, of course, isn't new—Poe and Baudelaire (I had never heard of Baudelaire)—but it might interest a few people. Audiences for things," he continued dryly, "are very different. Consider a circus and then such a book as this," and he reached to his desk and picked up *Les Fleurs du Mal.* "It is quite a wonderful book, but the sideshow tent of any circus would hold all who have ever heard of it, I am sure." His lips made a thin, dry line.

I was so impressed as well as mentally uplifted by all of his thinking that he took on much the significance of a sacred image. I studied all the books about him—on the floor, desk, table by his bed—Baudelaire, Anatole France, Pierre Loti, de Maupassant—all in French—and then Shelley, Keats, Poe. Seeing me contemplating them, he added:

"The trouble is I don't work at it as continuously as I should." He touched his head and his stomach. "You see, I am not strong, and I do everything to make myself less so. It is a choice of evils—being well and strong and taking part in what I see, or making myself weak by trying to escape it. I find escape the lesser of the two." Once more the thin line of the lips.

"But when you can do the things you can do . . ." I began.

"For a few people in a side tent," he interrupted, and then walked over to the bed, threw himself down, and lighted a cigarette. "You are still young and too much in the net to see through it, although at some time or other you may . . . I wonder . . ."

I certainly was not seeing through it by any means, but even so I seemed to catch something of his meaning. "You mean you don't care for life at all?" I asked, startled by his indifference to so much that seemed to me altogether marvelous and fascinating.

"I might if I had been made differently. To enjoy it or thirst after it you need a good physical or mental capacity or both that are in tune with it. Physically, as I know, I am a very limited person, and possibly because of that and some other reasons, I am not in tune with it. Mostly what I see disgusts me. But, you see, you are young and strong and hungry and it looks different to you than it does to most people."

I tried to follow him in his mood, feeling a rebuke of sorts in what he said, but could not. The web was too thick to see through.

182

"But both Poe and Baudelaire seem to have sensed much of what I mean," he added.

I determined, in due time, to read both Poe and Baudelaire. Yet outside were the trucks and trolley cars and the circumambient noises of the city and when I went out into those again, the glare and flare of life recaptured me. He seemed marvelous, but so did life—even more so than he—at the time.

Another time—the next, for all I can remember—I called and tapped without getting an answer. Yet of a sudden as I was about to go, the door opened and there he was. Not drunk or unfriendly, but rather, as I sensed, in a moody, foggy, intermediate state which was decidedly not of liquor and could only mean one thing, a drug. The pupils of his elongated and inclusive brown eyes were widely, almost irritatingly, distended. And the kind if at times somewhat ironic mouth now seemed wholly ironic. His sensitive, white hands (I will never forget them) weaved about his mouth and eyes as he looked at me out of what dreams, what distant lotus land of reverie and forgetfulness—forgetfulness of the frightfulness of a raucous, clanking world that he could so little endure. With one thin and clean and bloodless hand he motioned me to go away. But what he said was even more arresting, "Never knock! Never knock! Never knock! It is this knocking! This infernal knocking! Never knock!" And then the door was closed. And he was gone. And truly awed, I descended the stairs.

But there came another day. A smoky, grey, November St. Louis morning—lowering, stifling, even acid with the fumes of the chemisms of the illusion of industry. And I was about to go to work at noon as usual—one more assignment—murder, rape, theft, trickery, fire, explosion, death, all mingled with churches and preachers and pillars of society and captains of industry and lust or love or marriage or hospitals or morgues. But first Mathewson. As usual he was on my mind, particularly since I had not seen him for a time. Besides, I was lonely—not girl lonely but mind lonely, really almost starved for the wonder of thought and sensory response that he represented. Was it not Sir William Hamilton who wrote: "On earth there is nothing great but man and in man there is nothing great but mind"? Or let me add, esthetic sensory response.

Hence an irresistible impulse to approach his door. And after knocking ("Never knock! Never knock!" How well I recalled that!), curious as well as happy because of his footstep and the realization that at least, and if no more, I was to see him. And, true enough, there he stood, not drunk, not doped, not even writing, but frail and pale and small in his almost beggarly grey dressing gown, a thin green cotton shirt underneath, and looking as frowsy and drawn as one who dissipated and afterwards seeks, in sleep or rest, to recuperate. And at once, after greeting me and retreating to his bed, reaching for a cigarette and then reclining, but only to get up again and without further comment going to a bookrack which stood to the right of his bed and opening up a small brown package, taking out a triangle of yellow American cheese. And after breaking off a small square of it, going to a far and somewhat more shadowy corner of the room and reaching down and placing it in the extreme corner. But with no comment of any kind until after returning to his bed and resuming his cigarette, he began with: "The trouble with both myself and Mrs. Schwarzkopf is that we forget. There is a little mouse that comes here quite regularly. He's a little thin. And Mrs. Schwarzkopf is very saving. I try to think to put cheese out for him or to have her do it, but I'm afraid she doesn't always do it." He puffed and gazed across the coverlet, quite as though he were ruminating to himself. Well, then, I thought, out of this rowdy world at least there is a mouse to come and keep him company, and he cares for that. Somehow it all fitted into the grey if not dreary world of his mind.

On another day a conversation of equal interest to me. That day was bright and cold. And I recall that because of a football game which I had been ordered to report and a new girl who was to accompany me to witness it, I had indulged myself in a new grey woolen suit, plus—for counterpoint—a dark brown coat and hat. Also a grey blue tie, a new pair of shoes, a new shirt, and I believe gloves and, so help me Heaven, spats! Anyhow, all told, a very material response to a very material zest in me for this very material world, as Mathewson instantly sensed when he saw me.

But Mathewson. There was the rub. My one esthetic jewel in this raucous material scene. And yet I secretly wished him to see me as I now was, reproof or no reproof. Only nearing his door, and sensing the contrast I presented to his esthetic asceticism, hesitating. What would he think? What say? Nonetheless, I knocked, and presently within the pallid step, and my name called in inquiry, which I took as a great compliment. Had he been expecting me then? Did so few others come? I never learned the answer to that. What I did learn was not a little more of his personal philosophy, so important to me then and since. And coming at just the right moment for me, as I see it now.

He was sufficiently arrested by my material equipment as well as by my still very youthful and illusioned vitality to comment at this time: "The sun in splendor!" As usual, he was in his leaden-colored dressing gown and heelless slippers, but plainly had been up and at work, since by his bedside was a small wooden kitchen table, probably borrowed from Mrs. Schwarzkopf, on which were various scraps of paper. And on the floor his usual collection of what to me were rare volumes: Loti, France, Baudelaire, de Maupassant, Poe, Keats, John Addington Symonds. I recall also a "Venus de Milo" by one Victor Rydberg. I have never read it. And also—new—Voltaire's *Candide*. And Blake's poems. While it could never have been said that there was any morning freshness about Mathewson, most assuredly he could and did, on occasion, achieve a greater or less alertness, which was as good as freshness. And on this occasion it certainly appeared greater. At least, as he retired to the edge of the bed to sit and light a fresh cigarette, he surveyed me quizzically. "The land of coffee, potatoes, and beefsteak," he commented dryly as he studied my clothing—a comment that for me at the moment was slightly enigmatic. (Later it classified itself, almost painfully.)

"I've been assigned to do a football game," I ventured, almost apologetically.

"Of course you have," he said. "Spring: swimming, racing, bicycling. Summer: baseball, racing, bicycling, rowing. Fall: football. Winter: dancing, skating, theater. The idea of life is contest in order to produce more contest." The thought arrested me, and I was about to say something when I noted, on his table, a scrap of paper on which was written: "Green slime on heaven's deserted walls." I was so struck by it that I could not think clearly of anything else. It countered so startlingly against all I had ever read or thought of heaven. Besides, written in his clear careful hand, it suggested itself as part of a poem he might be writing, at least an imposing quotation from some source. Fresh from the hard, noisy, dusty, homely streets of St. Louis, it resounded in my consciousness like a gloomy and yet entrancing bell. I was suddenly roused by his going on with: "But one must have the temperament and the strength to cope with it. I haven't. I never have had. It might have interested me if I had been differently made—like you, for instance. But I was not." He puffed languidly at his cigarette, then laid it aside. "But you have your football game, and I have my meditations and some of the thoughts I like to put down."

I ventured to protest that I was not wholly material, to which he replied: "I know that, or you would not be here."

Heartened by this comment, I ventured upon some thoughts in connection with himself—really a plea for recognition and a better mental understanding between the two of us. Among other things I recall saying that I thought his thoughts and all connected with him were of more importance to me than anything else I did in St. Louis—more important than anything mental I had encountered so far, and finally ventured to point to the poetic line on the scrap of paper and say that that was wonderful to me.

"Oh, that! Yes, I can understand that. You were probably brought up in some church." (I interpolated that I had been Catholic trained.) "So was I," he went on, "but apart from that, it isn't so important. Its wonder rests on your illusion about heaven—a place of gold and light and harps. The more important thing is that we're all shadows, ghosts, and the things that we do are not real or important. That's why this world outside is not important to me." With a movement of his hand he dismissed it. "But what I have the strength and taste, if not exactly need, for is thought. And thinking means so much to me, I can only hold to such ideas of reality as are agreeable to me. Most of the things about me are unreal—have no significance of any kind. Buddha saw it; so did Shakespeare. 'Sound and fury, signifying nothing.' But you're probably too young yet, too much a part of all this—" (once more a movement of the including hand) "—to sense it." He ceased and began looking for a cigarette.

186

There was something more of this, and finally I recall leaving with a feeling of strangeness about him and about life, since it was beginning to dawn upon me that what he was actually seeking was to escape life entirely—its noise, its notions, its people, ambitions, love even, and all because of the conviction that it all meant nothing, was nothing—a thing that was sensorially incomprehensible to me. What? Food nothing? Clothing nothing? Love nothing? Property nothing? Fame nothing? Impossible! And yet, in the face of all these—the clanging November streets of the city, my new clothes, the noisy factories, my girl, the football game, my work which seemed highly esteemed by those who employed me—in the face of all these came back like whispers these thoughts of his—that it was all nothing, nothing, as he said, a contest to produce more contest. Actually, for one moment at the football game that afternoon—my newest girl hanging on my arm, the two elevens bouncing against each other in an effort to break their respective lines—I had my first clear thought of unreality. Of what real significance was all this? To what end, except perhaps to build up more football players to play more games? In other words, to perpetuate a pleasure idea. But no more. And if that was of great importance, well then that was of great importance. But no more than that. Sound and fury signifying pleasure. But at least there was pleasure in this unreality for those able to share it. Mathewson had said he was not. That he was a man who knew his limitations. I was beginning to realize his point of view. He felt physically and mentally unfit or, perhaps better, out of key with life.

After that there were yet a number of other visits and conversations—I forget how many, perhaps as many as ten. They covered that winter, spring and the following summer. And during that time I grew in my understanding of him, and achieved enthusiasm and devotion for him. The interesting thing about him, though, was that he was rarely to be found, or at least I was but infrequently admitted, the landlady, Mrs. Schwarzkopf, sometimes waving to me with her fat German hand and implying—and that quite clearly—that he was out or "sick" or sleeping or perhaps drunk or doped. I assumed any or all, although I always wondered which. And when I was admitted, it was as regularly to find him in either a morbid or philosophically resigned state, his body so frail as to make his vigorous and flashing mind an anomaly—a lighthouse flare at the top of a wax candle. Somewhere in this period I recall asking him did he dismiss love as nothing, women as nothing, since I was so astonished by his monk-like solitude and his perpetual lone, if by no means lorn, thinking. On this occasion he used his right hand, a cigarette between his fore and middle finger, to indicate . . . what? I do not know. But his words were: "The perfume of women! A drug! The flesh of women! The same. The face of a woman is a formula, repeated endlessly throughout the ages. Her body another. Both calculated to excite desire, if you do not see it as a very commonplace pattern. I do. The flesh is a compound devised to satisfy the emotions or desire that the form and face automatically awake, but in what manner? Only consider! And worse, to be a part of all this, you must be fit for it—equipped with all the automatic responses. I am not. Besides, there is nothing individual about it, nothing personal. It is a fate. Really a disease. If you escape it, you are better off."

"Then were you ever in love?"

"Oh, yes. But, as I have said, I know my limitations. I am not particularly material. And, in this part of the world, love is likely to prove very material or insensitive."

He lay back and considered. I sensed something—the lack of a suitable temperament to love, or if not that, then some past defeat at the hands of an unattainable one. Could that be *the* explanation? My romantic temperament instantly assumed so. But today I am not so sure. More likely a lonely and sensitive esthete resignedly rejecting a world of mostly extreme and stupid insensitivity and lack of understanding.

Another thing gained by my visits was the knowledge that he was declining in health, slowly but surely. Now a week, now ten days, now two or even three weeks went by without a glimpse, and at the end of each lapse of time he seemed more lethargic, and if anything, more turned in on his own moods. During this time I saw parts of a paper or book that he was working on, but it never seemed to get on very far. His table, sacred as it was to Mrs. Schwarzkopf (all but untouchable to her, I think) appeared to retain for weeks at a stretch these dusty scraps as well as whole pages of paper, and nearly always in precisely the same

188

position. Because of this and them, and things he said to me, I am able to quote:

"Color and music are perhaps the two most valuable phases of life. But of these, color is the indispensable one."

"A heavy heart and an empty stomach. Take away the heavy heart and the empty stomach is endurable. But with it, what is food?"

"The struggle to live without violence is a dream; to live by violence is esthetic death."

"Religion is merely a dream of a life without brutality or torture."

"I watch them, wondering what lucky or unlucky number they have drawn."

"That snowy ghost of life—memory."

"When desire is strong enough to become a prayer, it is likely to become a reality."

•   •   •

The fall following this series of visits I was urged and for various reasons concluded to leave St. Louis. Up to the moment of decision I was fairly satisfied that I was not leaving, and on my last seeing Mathewson had said nothing. Subsequent to my final decision, which involved quick action, he was not to be found. The day I was leaving I wrote him a note full of regret and gratitude. I have often wondered not whether he received it, but what, if anything, he thought about it. I had no comment from him, but on the other hand I was moving eastward most of the time and little mail overtook me. In Pittsburgh a few months later I received a letter—not from Mathewson but from one who knew of him and had given me the most early information about him. This was Rodenberger. He asked if I had heard concerning Mathewson. He had been found dead in his Black and Tan room. It was said at first that he had committed suicide, since he had taken too much dope. A medical examination, or perhaps an autopsy, had revealed morphine. The body had been taken over by relatives in St. Joseph and St. Louis. Rodenberger included a clipping that revealed the story of his father's wealth and the commercial and social ideals of all those about him. He was by

189

no means poor and had he wished to use his wealth could have done so. As a matter of fact, at eighteen he had rejected all further contact with his father's business, preferring to travel and work as a newspaperman, later as a journalist and editor. There was no mention of any early or later romance. A solitary and eccentric by nature, he had chosen to live as he did, bringing drugs and drink to the aid of a philosophy or reaction which could not endure the reality it encountered. I think always of his line: "I know my limitations," and that about the heavy heart.

But one line in the Rodenberger letter interested me not a little. It read:

"I hear he was found lying on his right side, his arm curled up under his head, and the covers tucked under his chin, just as though he had fallen asleep and never waked."

Perfect, I thought!

But if I could have written his epitaph, it would have been: "The struggle to live without violence is a dream; to live by violence is esthetic death."

The "Mercy" of God

"Once, one of his disciples, walking with him in the garden, said:
'Master, how may I know the Infinite, the Good, and attain to
union with it, as thou hast?' And he replied: 'By desiring it utterly,
with all thy heart and with all thy mind.' And the disciple replied:
'But that I do.' 'Nay, not utterly,' replied the Master, 'or thou wouldst
not now ask how thou mayst attain to union with it. But come with
me,' he added, 'and I will show thee.' And he led the way to a stream,
and into the water, and there, by reason of his greater strength, he
seized upon his disciple and immersed him completely, so that present-
ly he could not breathe but must have suffocated and drowned had
it not been his plan to bring him forth whole. Only when, by reason
of this, the strength of the disciple began to wane and he would have
drowned, the Master drew him forth and stretched him upon the bank
and restored him. And when he was sufficiently restored and seeing
that he was not dead but whole, he exclaimed: 'But, Master, why
didst thou submerge me in the stream and hold me there until I was
like to die?' And the Master replied: 'Didst thou not say that above
all things thou desirest union with the Infinite?' 'Yea, true; but in
life, not death.' 'That I know,' answered the Master. 'But now tell
me: When thou wast thus held in the water what was it that thou didst
most desire?' 'To be restored to breath, to life.' 'And how much didst
thou desire it?' 'As thou sawest—with all my strength and with all
my mind.' 'Verily. Then when in life thou desirest union with the
All-Good, the Infinite, as passionately as thou didst life in the water,
it will come. Thou wilt know it then, and not before.' "

Keshub Chunder Sen

191

A FRIEND OF MINE, A QUITE celebrated neurologist, psychiatrist, and interpreter of Freud, and myself were met one night to discuss a very much talked-of book of his, a book of clinical studies relative to various obsessions, perversions and inhibitions which had afflicted various people in their day and which he, as a specialist in these matters, had investigated and attempted to alleviate. To begin with, I should say that he had filled many difficult and responsible positions in hospitals, asylums, and later, as a professor of these matters, occupied a chair in one of our principal universities. He was kindly, thoughtful, and intensely curious as to the workings of this formula we call life, but without lending himself to any—at least to very few—hard and fast dogmas. More interesting still, life appeared to interest but never to discourage him. He really liked it. Pain, he said, he accepted as an incentive, an urge to life. Strife he liked because it hardened all to strength. And he believed in action as the antidote to too much thought, the way out of brooding and sorrow. Youth passes, strength passes, life forms pass; but action makes all bearable and even enjoyable. Also he wanted more labor, not less, more toil, more exertion, for humanity. And he insisted that through, not round or outside, life lay the way to happiness, if there was a way. But with action all the while. So much for his personal point of view.

On the other hand he was always saying of me that I had a touch of the Hindu in me, the Far East, the Brahmin. I emphasized too much indifference to life—or, if not that, I quarreled too much with pain, unhappiness, and did not impress strongly enough the need of action. I was forever saying that the strain was too great, that there had best be less of action, less of pain. . . . As to the need of less pain, I agreed, but never to the need of less action; in verification of which I pointed to my own life, the changes I had deliberately courted, the various activities I had entered upon, the results I had sought for. He was not to be routed from his contention, nor I from mine.

Following this personal analysis we fell to discussing a third man, whom we both admired, an eminent physiologist, then connected with one of the great experimental laboratories of the world, who had made many deductions and discoveries in connection with the associative faculty of the brain and the mechanics of associative memory. This man was a mechanist, not an evolutionist, and of the most convinced type. To him nowhere in nature was there any serene and directive and thoughtful conception which brought about, and was still bringing about continually, all the marvels of structure and form and movement that so arrest and startle our intelligence at every turn. Nowhere any constructive or commanding force which had thought out, for instance, and brought to pass flowers, trees, animals, men— associative order and community life. On the contrary, the beauty of nature as well as the order of all living, such as it is, was an accident, and not even a necessary one, yet unescapable, a condition or link in an accidental chain. If you would believe him and his experiments, the greatest human beings that ever lived and the most perfect states of society that ever were have no more significance in nature than the most minute ephemera. The Macedonian Alexander is as much at the mercy of fate as the lowest infusoria. For every germ that shoots up into a tree thousands are either killed or stunted by unfavorable conditions; and although, beyond question, many of them—the most—bear within themselves the same power as the successful ones to be and to do, had they the opportunity, still they fail—a belief of my own in part, albeit a hard doctrine.

One would have thought, as I said to Professor Z—— at this meeting, that such a mental conviction would be dulling and destructive to initiative and force, and I asked him why he thought it had not operated to blunt and destroy this very great man. "For the very reasons I am always emphasizing," he replied. "Pain, necessity, life stung him into action and profound thought, hence success. He is the person he is by reason of enforced mental and physical action."

"But," I argued, "his philosophy makes him account it all as worthless, or, if not that, so fleeting and unstable as to make it scarcely worth the doing, even though he does it. As he sees it, happiness and tribulation, glory and obscurity, are all an accident. Science, industry, politics, like races and planets, are accidents. Trivial conditions cause great characters and geniuses

193

like himself to rest or to remain inactive, and mediocre ones are occasionally permitted to execute great deeds or frustrate them in the absence of the chance that might have produced a master. Circumstances are stronger than personalities, and the impotence of individuals is the tragedy of everyday life."

"Quite so," agreed my friend, "and there are times when I am inclined to agree with him, but at most times not. I used to keep hanging in one of my offices, printed and framed, that famous quotation from Ecclesiastes: 'I returned, and saw under the sun that the race is not to the swift, nor the battle to the strong, neither yet bread to the wise, nor yet favor to men of skill; but time and chance happeneth to them all.' But I took it down because it was too discouraging. And yet," he added after a time, because we both fell silent at this point, "although I still think it is true, as time has gone on and I have experimented with life and with people I have come to believe that there is something else in nature, some not as yet understood impulse, which seeks to arrange and right and balance things at times. I know that this sounds unduly optimistic and vainly cheerful, especially from me, and many—you, for one—will disagree, but I have sometimes encountered things in my work which have caused me to feel that nature isn't altogether hard or cruel or careless, even though accidents appear to happen."

"Accidents?" I said; "holocausts, you mean." But he continued:

"Of course, I do not believe in absolute good or absolute evil, although I do believe in relative good and relative evil. Take tenderness and pity, in some of their results at least. Our friend, on the contrary, sees all as accident, or blind chance and without much if any real or effective pity or amelioration, a state that I cannot reason myself into. Quite adversely, I think there is something that helps life along or out of its difficulties. I know that you will not agree with me; still, I believe it, and while I do not think there is any direct and immediate response, such as the Christian Scientists and the New Thought devotees would have us believe, I know there is a response at times, or at least I think there is, and I think I can prove it. Take dreams, for instance, which, as Freud has demonstrated, are nature's way of permitting a man to sleep in the presence of some mental worry

194

that would tend to keep him awake, or if he had fallen asleep, and stood in danger to wake him."

I waived that as a point, but then he referred to medicine and surgery and all the mechanical developments as well as the ameliorative efforts of life, such as laws relating to child labor, workingmen's compensation and hours, compulsory safety devices and the like, as specific proofs of a desire on the part of nature, working through man, to make life easier for man, a wish on her part to provide him, slowly and stumblingly, mayhap, with things helpful to him in his condition here. Without interrupting him, I allowed him to call to mind the Protestant Reformation, how it had ended once and for all the iniquities of the Inquisition; the rise of Christianity, and how, temporarily at least, it had modified if not entirely ended the brutalities of Paganism. Anesthetics, and how they had served to ameliorate pain. I could have pointed out that life itself was living on life and always had been, and that as yet no substitute for the flesh of helpless animals had been furnished man as food. (He could not hear my thoughts.) The automobile, he went on, had already practically eliminated the long sufferings of the horse; our anti-slavery rebellion and humane opposition in other countries had once and for all put an end to human slavery; also he called to mind the growth of humane societies of one kind and another, that ministered to many tortured animals. And humane laws were being constantly passed and enforced to better if not entirely cure inhuman conditions.

I confess I was interested, if not convinced. In spite of life itself existing on life, there was too much in what he said to permit anyone to pass over it indifferently. But there came to my mind just the same all the many instances of crass accident and brutish mischance which are neither prevented nor cured by anything—the thousands who are annually killed in railroad accidents and industrial plants, despite protective mechanisms and fortifying laws compelling their use; the thousands who die yearly from epidemics of influenza, smallpox, yellow fever, cholera and widespread dissemination of cancer, consumption and related ills. These I mentioned. He admitted the force of the point but insisted that man, impelled by nature, not only for his own immediate protection but by reason of a sympathy aroused through

195

pain endured by him, was moved to kindly action. Besides if nature loved brutality and inhumanity and suffering why in those atoms should it generate sympathy and tears and rejoicing at escape from suffering by man, why sorrow and horror at the accidental or intentional infliction of disaster on man by nature or man?

After a time he volunteered: "Let me give you a concrete instance. It has always interested me and it seems to prove that there is something to what I say. It concerns a girl I know, a very homely one, who lost her mind. At the beginning of her mental trouble her father called me in to see what, if anything, could be done. The parents of this girl were Catholics. He was a successful contractor and politician, the father of three children; he provided very well for them materially but could do little for them mentally. He was not the intellectual but the religious type. The mother was a cheerful, good-natured and conventional woman, and had only the welfare of her children and her husband at heart. When I first came to know this family—I was a young medical man then—this girl was thirteen or fourteen, the youngest of the three children. Of these three children, and for that matter of the entire family, I saw that this girl was decidedly the most interesting psychically and emotionally. She was intense and receptive, but inclined to be morbid; and for a very good reason. She was not good-looking, not in any way attractive physically. Worse, she had too good a mind, too keen a perception, not to know how severe a deprivation that was likely to prove and to resent it. As I came to know through later investigations—all the little neglects and petty deprivations which, owing to her lack of looks and the exceeding and of course superior charms of her sister and brother, were throughout her infancy and youth thrust upon her. Her mouth was not sweet—too large; her eyes unsatisfactory as to setting, not as to wistfulness; her nose and chin were unfortunately large, and above her left eye was a birthmark, a livid scar as large as a penny. In addition her complexion was sallow and muddy, and she was not possessed of a truly graceful figure; far from it. After she had reached fifteen or sixteen, she walked, entirely by reason of mental depression, I am sure, with a slow and sagging and moody gait; something within, I suppose, always whispering to her that hope was useless, that there

196

was no good in trying, that she had been mercilessly and irretrievably handicapped to begin with.

"On the other hand, as chance would have it, her sister and brother had been almost especially favored by nature. Celeste Ryan was bright, vivacious, colorful. She was possessed of a graceful body, a beautiful face, clear, large and blue eyes, light glossy hair, and a love for life. She could sing and dance. She was sought after and courted by all sorts of men and boys. I myself, as a young man, used to wish that I could interest her in myself, and often went to the house on her account. Her brother also was smart, well-favored, careful as to his clothes, vain, and interested in and fascinating to girls of a certain degree of mind. He and his sister liked to dance, to attend parties, to play and disport themselves wherever young people were gathered.

"And for the greater part of Marguerite's youth, or until her sister and brother were married, this house was a center for all the casual and playful goings-on of youth. Girls and boys, all interested in Celeste and her brother, came and went—girls to see the good-looking brother, boys to flirt with and dance attendance upon the really charming Celeste. In winter there was skating; in summer automobiling, trips to the beach, camping even. In most of these affairs, so long as it was humanly possible, the favorless sister was included; but, as we all know, especially where thoughtless and aggressive youth is concerned, such little courtesies are not always humanly possible. Youth will be served. In the main it is too intent upon the sorting and mating process, each for himself, to give the slightest heed or care for another. Vae Victis.

"To make matters worse, and possibly because her several deficiencies early acquainted her with the fact that all boys and girls found her sister and brother so much more attractive, Marguerite grew reticent and recessive—so much so that when I first saw her she was already slipping about with the air of one who appeared to feel that she was not as ingratiating and acceptable as she might be, even though, as I saw, her mother and father sought to make her feel that she was. Her father, a stodgy and silent man, too involved in the absurdities of politics and religion and the difficulties of his position to give very much attention to the intricacies and subtleties of his children's personalities, never did guess the real pain that was Marguerite's. He was a narrow and determined religionist, one who saw in religious abstention, a guarded and reserved life, the only keys to peace and salvation. In fact before he died an altar was built in his house and mass was read there for his especial spiritual benefit every morning. What he thought of the gayeties of his two eldest children at this time I do not know, but since these were harmless and in both cases led to happy and enduring marriages, he had nothing to quarrel with. As for his youngest child, I doubt if he ever sensed in any way the moods and torturous broodings that were hers, the horrors that attend the disappointed love life. He had not been disappointed in his love life, and was therefore not able to understand. He was not sensitive enough to have suffered greatly if he had been, I am sure. But his wife, a soft, pliable, affectionate, gracious woman, early sensed that her daughter must pay heavily for her looks, and in consequence sought in every way to woo her into an unruffled complacence with life and herself.

"But how little the arts of man can do toward making up for the niggardliness of nature! I am certain that always, from her earliest years, this ugly girl loved her considerate mother and was grateful to her; but she was a girl of insight, if not hard practical sense or fortitude, and loved life too much to be content with the love of her mother only. She realized all too keenly the crass, if accidental, injustice which had been done her by nature and was unhappy, terribly so. To be sure, she tried to interest herself in books, the theater, going about with a homely girl or two like herself. But before her ever must have been the spectacle of the happiness of others, their dreams and their fulfilments. Indeed, for the greater part of these years, and for several years after, until both her sister and brother had married and gone away, she was very much alone, and, as I reasoned it out afterwards, imagining and dreaming about all the things she would like to be and do. But without any power to compel them. Finally she took to reading persistently, to attending theaters, lectures and what not—to establish some contact, I presume, with the gay life scenes she saw about her. But I fancy that these were not of much help, for life may not be lived by proxy. And besides, her father, if not her mother, resented a too liberal thought-life. He believed that his faith and its teachings were the only proper solution to life.

"One of the things that interested me in connection with this case—and this I gathered as chief medical counsel of the family between Marguerite's fifteenth and twenty-fifth year—was that because of the lack of beauty that so tortured her in her youth she had come to take refuge in books, and then, because of these, the facts which they revealed in regard to a more worthwhile life than she could have, to draw away from all religion as worthless, or at least not very important as a relief from pain. And yet there must have been many things in these books which tortured her quite as much as reality, for she selected, as her father once told me afterward—not her mother, who read little or nothing—only such books as she should not read; books, I presume, that painted life as she wished it to be for herself. They were by Anatole France, George Moore, de Maupassant and Dostoyevsky. Also she went to plays her father disapproved of and brooded in libraries. And she followed, as she herself explained to me, one lecturer and another, one personality and another, more, I am sure, because by this method she hoped to contact, although she never seemed to, men who were interesting to her, than because she was interested in the things they themselves set forth.

"In connection with all this I can tell you of only one love incident which befell her. Somewhere around the time when she was twenty-one or -two she came in contact with a young teacher, himself not very attractive or promising and whose prospects, as her father saw them, were not very much. But since she was not pretty and rather lonely and he seemed to find companionship, and mayhap solace in her, no great objection was made to him. In fact as time went on, and she and the teacher became more and more intimate, both she and her parents assumed that in the course of time they would most certainly marry. For instance, at the end of his school-teaching year here in New York, and although he left the city, he kept up a long correspondence with her. In addition, he spent at least some of his vacation near New York, at times returning and going about with her and seeming to feel that she was of some value to him in some way.

"How much of this was due to the fact that she was provided

with spending money of her own and could take him here and there, to places to which he could not possibly have afforded to go alone I cannot say. None the less, it was assumed, because of their companionship and the fact that she would have some money of her own after marriage, that he would propose. But he did not. Instead, he came year after year, visited about with her, took up her time, as the family saw it (her worthless time!), and then departed for his duties elsewhere as free as when he had come. Finally this having irritated if not infuriated the several members of her family, they took her to task about it, saying that she was a fool for trifling with him. But she, although perhaps depressed by all this, was still not willing to give him up; he was her one hope. Her explanation to the family was that because he was poor he was too proud to marry until he had established himself. Thus several more years came and went, and he returned or wrote, but still he did not propose. And then of a sudden he stopped writing entirely for a time, and still later on wrote that he had fallen in love and was about to be married.

"This blow appeared to be the crowning one in her life. For in the face of the opposition, and to a certain degree contempt, of her father, who was a practical and fairly successful man, she had devoted herself to this man who was neither successful nor very attractive for almost seven years. And then after so long a period, in which apparently he had used her to make life a little easier for himself, even he had walked away and left her for another. She fell to brooding more and more to herself, reading not so much now, as I personally know, as just thinking. She walked a great deal, as her father told me, and then later began to interest herself, or so she pretended, in a course of history and philosophy at one of the great universities of the city. But as suddenly, thereafter, she appeared to swing between exaggerated periods of study or play or lecture-listening and a form of recessive despair, under the influence of which she retired to her room and stayed there for days, wishing neither to see nor hear from anyone—not even to eat. On the other hand again, she turned abruptly to shopping, dressmaking and the niceties which concerned her personal appearance; although even in this latter phase there were times when she did nothing at all, seemed to relax toward her old listlessness and sense of inconsequence and remained in her room to brood.

"About this time, as I was told afterwards, her mother died and, her sister and brother having married, she was left in charge of the house and of her father. It was soon evident that she had no particular qualifications for or interest in housekeeping, and a maiden sister of her father came to look after things. This did not necessarily darken the scene, but it did not seem to lighten it any. She liked this aunt well enough, although they had very little in common mentally. Marguerite went on as before. Parallel with all this, however, had run certain things which I have forgotten to mention. Her father had been growing more and more narrowly religious. As a matter of fact he had never had any sympathy for the shrewd mental development toward which her lack of beauty had driven her. Before she was twenty-three as I have already explained, her father had noted that she was indifferent to her church duties. She had to be urged to go to mass on Sunday, to confession and communion once a month. Also as he told me afterward, as something to be deplored, her reading had caused her to believe that her faith was by no means infallible or its ritual important; there were bigger and more interesting things in life. This had caused her father not only to mistrust but to detest the character of her reading, as well as her tendencies in general. From having some sympathy with her at first, as did her mother always, as the ugly duckling of the family, he had come to have a cold and stand-offish feeling. She was, as he saw it, an unnatural child. She did not obey him in respect to religion. He began, as I have hinted, to look into her books, those in the English tongue at least, and from a casual inspection came to feel that they were not fit books for anyone to read. They were irreligious, immoral. They pictured life as it actually was, scenes and needs and gayeties and conflicts, which, whether they existed or not, were not supposed to exist; and most certainly they were not to be introduced into his home, her own starved disposition to the contrary notwithstanding. They conflicted with the natural chill and peace of his religion and temperament. He forbade her to read such stuff, to bring such books into his home. When he found some of them later he burned them. He also began to urge the claims of his religion more and more upon her.

"Reduced by this calamity and her financial dependence, which had always remained complete, she hid her books away and read them only outside or in the privacy of her locked room—but she read them. The subsequent discovery by him that she was still doing this, and his rage, caused her to think of leaving home. But she was without training, without any place to go, really. If she should go she would have to prepare herself for it by teaching, perhaps, and this she now decided to take up.

"About this time she began to develop those characteristics or aberrations which brought me into the case. As I have said, she began to manifest a most exaggerated and extraordinary interest in her facial appearance and physical well-being, an interest not at all borne out rationally by her looks. Much to her father's and his sister's astonishment, she began to paint and primp in front of her mirror nearly all day long. Lipsticks, rouge, eyebrow pencils, perfumes, rings, pins, combs, and what not else, were suddenly introduced—very expensive and disconcerting lingerie, for one thing.

"The family had always maintained a charge account at at least two of the larger stores of the city, and to these she had recently repaired, as it was discovered afterwards, and indulged herself, without a by-your-leave, in all these things. High-heeled slippers, bright-colored silk stockings, hats, blouses, gloves, furs, to say nothing of accentuated and even shocking street costumes, began to arrive in bundles. Since the father was out most of the day and the elderly aunt busy with household affairs, nothing much of all this was noted, until later she began to adorn herself in this finery and to walk the streets in it. And then the due bills, sixty days late; most disturbing but not to be avoided. And so came the storm.

"The father and aunt, who had been wondering where these things were coming from, became very active and opposed. For previous to this, especially in the period of her greatest depression, Marguerite had apparently dressed with no thought of anything, save a kind of resigned willingness to remain inconspicuous, as much as to say: 'What difference does it make. No one is interested in me.' Now, however, all this had gone—quite. She had supplied herself with hats so wide and 'fancy' or 'fixy,' as her father said, that they were a disgrace. And clothing so noticeable or 'loud'—I forget his exact word—that anyone anywhere would be ashamed of her. There were, as I myself saw when I was eventually called in as specialist in this case, too many flowers, too much lace, too many rings, pins and belts and gewgaws connected with all this, which neither he nor his sister was ever quite able to persuade her to lay aside. And the colors! Unless she were almost forcibly restrained, these were likely to be terrifying, even laughter-provoking, especially to those accustomed to think of unobtrusiveness as the first criterion of taste—a green or red or light blue broad-trimmed hat, for instance, with no such color of costume to harmonize with it. And, whether it became her or not, a white or tan or green dress in summertime, or one with too much red or too many bright colors in winter. And very tight, worn with a dashing manner, mayhap. Even high-heeled slippers and thin lacy dresses in bitter windy weather. And the perfumes with which she saturated herself were, as her father said, impossible—of a high rate of velocity, I presume.

"So arrayed, then, she would go forth, whenever she could contrive it, to attend a theater, a lecture, a moving picture, or to walk the streets. And yet, strangely enough, and this was as curious a phase of the case as any, she never appeared to wish to thrust her personal charms, such as they were, on anyone. On the contrary, as it developed, there had generated in her the sudden hallucination that she possessed so powerful and self-troubling a fascination for men that she was in danger of bewildering them, enticing them against themselves to their moral destruction, as well as bringing untold annoyance upon herself. A single glance, one look at her lovely face, and presto! they were enslaved. She needed but to walk, and lo! beauty—her beauty, dazzling, searing, destroying—was implied by every motion, gesture. No man, be he what he might, could withstand it. He turned, he stared, he dreamed, he followed her and sought to force his attention on her. Her father explained to me that when he met her on the street one day he was shocked to the point of collapse. A daughter of his so dressed, and on the street! With the assistance of the maiden sister a number of modifications was at once brought about. All charge accounts were cancelled. Dealers were informed that no purchases of hers would be honored unless with the previous consent of her father. The worst of her sartorial offenses were unobtrusively removed from her room and burnt or given away, and plainer and more becoming things substituted.

"But now, suddenly, there developed a new and equally interesting stage of the case. Debarred from dressing as she would, she began to imagine, as these two discovered, that she was being followed and admired and addressed and annoyed by men, and that at her very door. Eager and dangerous admirers lurked about the place. As the maiden aunt once informed me, having wormed her way into Marguerite's confidence, she had been told that men 'were wild' about her and that go where she would, and conduct herself however modestly and inconspicuously, still they were inflamed.

"A little later both father and sister began to notice that on leaving the house or returning to it she would invariably pause, if going out, to look about first; if returning, to look back as though she were expecting to see someone outside whom she either did or did not wish to see. Not infrequently her comings-in were accompanied by something like flight, so great a need to escape some presumably dangerous or at least impetuous pursuer as to cause astonishment and even fear for her. There would be a feverish, fumbled insertion of the key from without, after which she would fairly jump in, at the same time looking back with a nervous, perturbed glance. Once in she would almost invariably pause and look back as though, having succeeded in eluding her pursuer, she was still interested to see what he was like or what he was doing, often going to the curtained windows of the front room to peer out. And to her then confidante, this same aunt, she explained on several occasions that she had 'just been followed again' all the way from Broadway or Central Park West or somewhere, sometimes by a most wonderful-looking gentleman, sometimes by a most loathsome brute. He had seen her somewhere and had pursued her to her very room. Yet, brute or gentleman, she was always interested to look back.

"When her father and aunt first noted this manifestation they had troubled to inquire into it, looking into the street or even going so far as to go to the door and look for the man, but there was no one, or perchance some passing pedestrian or neighbor who most certainly did not answer to the description of either

204

handsome gentleman or brute. Then sensibly they began to gather that this was an illusion. But by now the thing had reached a stage where they began to feel genuine alarm. Guests of the family were accused by her of attempting to flirt with her, of making appealing remarks to her as they entered, and neighbors of known probity and conventional rigidity of presuming to waylay her and forcing her to listen to their pleas. Thus her father and aunt became convinced that it was no longer safe for her to be at large. The family's reputation was at stake; its record for freedom from insanity about to be questioned.

"In due time, therefore, I was sent for, and regardless of how much they dreaded a confession of hallucination here, the confession was made to me. I was asked to say what if anything could be done for her, and if nothing, what was to be done with her. After that I was permitted to talk to Marguerite whom of course I had long known, but not as a specialist or as one called in for advice. Rather, I was presented to her as visiting again as of yore, having dropped in after a considerable absence. She seemed pleased to see me, only as I noticed on this, as on all subsequent occasions, she seemed to wish, first, not to stay long in my presence and more interesting still, as I soon noted, to wish to keep her face, and even her profile, averted from me, most especially her eyes and her glances. Anywhere, everywhere, save at me she looked, and always with the purpose, as I could see, of averting her glances.

"After she had left the room I found that this development was new to the family. They had not noticed it before, and then it struck me as odd. I suspected at once that there was some connection between this and her disappointed love life. The devastating effect of lack of success in love in youth had been too much for her. So this averted glance appeared to me to have something to do with that. Fearing to disturb or frighten her, and so alienate her, I chose to say nothing but instead came again and again in order to familiarize her with my presence, to cause her once more to take it as a matter of course. And to enlist her interest and sympathy, I pretended that there was a matter of taxes and some involved property that her father was helping me to solve.

"And in order to insure her presence I came as a rule just

before dinner, staying some little time and talking with her. To guarantee being alone with her I had her father and his sister remain out for a few minutes after I arrived, so as to permit me to seem to wait. And on these occasions I invented all sorts of excuses for coming into conversation with her. On all of these visits I noticed that she still kept her face from me. Having discussed various things with her, I finally observed: 'I notice, Marguerite, that whenever I come here now you never look at me. Don't you like me? You used to look at me, and now you keep your face turned away. Why is that?'

" 'Oh, of course I like you, doctor, of course,' she replied, 'only,' she paused, 'well, I'll tell you how it is: I don't want to have the same effect on you as I do on other men.'

"She paused and I stared, much interested. 'I'm afraid I don't quite understand, Marguerite,' I said.

" 'Well, you see, it's this way,' she went on, 'it's my beauty. All you men are alike you see: you can't stand it. You would be just the same as the rest. You would be wanting to flirt with me, too, and it wouldn't be your fault, but mine. You can't help it. I know that now. But I don't want you to be following me like the rest of them, and you would be if I looked at you as I do at the others.' She had on at the time a large hat, which evidently she had been trying on before I came, and now she pulled it most coquettishly low over her face and then sidled, laughingly, out of the room.

"When I saw and heard this," he went on, "I was deeply moved instead of being amused as some might imagine, for I recognized that this was an instance of one of those kindly compensations in nature about which I have been talking, some deep inherent wish on the part of some overruling Providence perhaps to make life more reasonably endurable for all of us. Here was this girl, sensitive and seeking, who had been denied everything—or, rather, the one thing she most craved in life: love. For years she had been compelled to sit by and see others have all the attention and pleasures, while she had nothing—no pleasures, no lovers. And because she had been denied them their import had been exaggerated by her; their color and splendor intensified. She had been crucified, after a fashion, until beauty and attention were all that her mind cried for. And then, behold the mercy of

206

the forces about which we are talking! They diverted her mind in order to save her from herself. They appeared at last to preserve her from complete immolation, or so I see it. Life does not wish to crucify people, of that I am sure. It lives on itself—as we see—is 'red of beak and claw' as the phrase has it—and yet, in the deep, who knows, there may be some satisfactory explanation for that too—who can tell? At any rate, as I see it basically, fundamentally, it is well-intentioned. Useless, pointless torture has no real place in it; or at least so I think." He paused and stared, as though he had clinched his argument.

"Just the same, as you say," I insisted, "it does live on itself, the slaughter houses, the stockyards, the butcher shops, the germs that live and fatten as people die. If you can get much comfort out of these you are welcome."

He paid no attention to me. Instead, he went on: "This is only a theory of mine, but we know, for instance, that there is no such thing as absolute evil, any more than there is absolute good. There is only relative evil and relative good. What is good for or to me may be evil to you, and vice versa, like a man who may be evil to you and good to me.

"In the case of this girl I cannot believe that so vast a thing as life, involving as it does, all the enormous forces and complexities, would single out one little mite such as she deliberately and specially for torture. On the contrary, I have faith to believe that the thing is too wise and grand for that. But, according to my theory, the machinery for creating things may not always run true. A spinner of plans or fabrics wishes them to come forth perfect of course, arranges a design and gathers all the colors and threads for a flawless result. The machine may be well oiled. The engine perfectly geared. Every precaution taken, and yet in the spinning here and there a thread will snap, the strands become entangled, bits, sometimes whole segments spoiled by one accident and another, but not intentionally. On the other hand, there are these flaws, which come from where I know not, of course, but are accidental, I am sure, not intended by the spinner. At least I think so. They cause great pain. They cause the worst disasters. Yet our great mother, Nature, the greatest spinner of all, does what she can to right things—or so I wish to believe. Like the spinner himself, she stops the machine, unites the broken

207

strands, uses all her ability to make things run smoothly once more. It is my wish to believe that in this case, where a homely girl could not be made into a beautiful one and youth could not be substituted for maturity, still nature brought about what I look upon as a beneficent illusion, a providential hallucination. Via insanity, Marguerite attained to all the lovely things she had ever longed for. In her unreason she had her beautiful face, her adoring cavaliers—they turned and followed her in the streets. She was beautiful to all, to herself, and must hide her loveliness in order to avert pain and disaster to others. How would you explain that? As reasoned and malicious cruelty on the part of nature? Or as a kindly intervention, a change of heart, a wish on the part of nature or something to make amends to her for all that she suffered, not to treat her or any of us too brutally or too unfairly? Or just accident? How?"

He paused once more and gazed at me, as much as to say: "Explain that, if you can." I, in turn, stared, lost for the time being in thoughts of this girl, for I was greatly impressed. This picture of her, trying, in her deranged imaginings as to her beauty, to protect others from herself, turning her face away from those who might suffer because of her indifference, because she in her day had suffered from the indifference of others, finding in hallucination, in her jumbled fancies, the fulfilment of all her hopes, her dreams, was too sad. I was too sad. I could not judge, and did not. Truly, truly, I thought, I wish I might believe.

• • •

"Master, how may I know the Infinite, the Good, and attain to union with it, as thou hast?" And the Master replied: "By desiring it utterly."

Ida Hauchawout

SHE IS IDENTIFIED IN MY MIND, and always will be somehow, with the rural setting in which I first saw her, a land, as it were, of milk and honey. When I think of her and the dreary, commonplace, brown farmhouse, in a doorway of which I first saw her framed, and later of the wee but cleanly cabin in which at last I saw her lying at rest, I think of smooth green hills that rise in noble billows, of valleys so wide and deep that they could hold a thousand cottage farms, of trees globe-like from being left unharried by the winds, of cattle red and black and white, great herds dotting the hills, and of barns so huge that they looked more like great hangars for flying machines than storehouses for hay and grain. Yes, everywhere was plenty, rich fields of wheat and corn and rye and oats, with here and there specializing farmers who grew only tomatoes or corn or peas or ran dairies, men who somehow seemed to grow richer than the others.

And then I think of "Fred" Hauchawout, her father, a man who evidently so styled himself, for the name was painted in big black letters over the huge door of his great red barn. This Hauchawout was a rude, crude, bear-like soul, stocky, high-booted, sandy-haired, gray-eyed and red-skinned, with as inhospitable a look as one might well conjure. Worse, he was clad always, on Sundays and every other day, so I heard, in brown overalls and jumper. In short, he was one of those dreadful tramping, laboring grubs who gather and gather and gather, sparing no least grain for pleasure by the way, and having so done, die and leave it all to children who have been alienated in youth and care no least whit whether their forebear is alive or dead, nor for anything save the goods which he has been able to amass. But in this latter sense Hauchawout was no huge success either. He was too limited in his ideas to do more than hide or reinvest in land or cattle or bank his moderate earnings at a low rate of interest. He was quoted locally as living up to his assertion that "no enimel gets fet py me," and he was known far and wide for having the thinnest and boniest and hardest-worked horses and cows in the neighborhood, from which he extracted the last ounce of labor and the last gill of milk.

He was the father of three sons and two daughters, so I was told, all of whom must have hated him; those I knew did, anyhow. One of the sons, when I first wandered into the region, had already gone to the far West, after pausing to throw a pitchfork at his father and telling him to go to hell, or so the story went. Another, whom I knew quite well, being a neighbor of a relative of mine, had married after being "turned out," as he said, by "the old man" because he wouldn't work hard enough. And yet he was a good enough worker to take over and pay for, in seven years, a farm of forty acres of fertile land, also eventually to acquire an automobile, a contraption which his father denounced as a "loafer's buggy."

The third son, Samuel, had also left his father because of a quarrel over his very human desire to marry and make his own way. Latterly, because he was greedy like his father and hoped to obtain an undue share of the estate at his death, or so his relatives said, he had made friends with his father and thereafter exchanged such greetings and visits as two such peculiar souls might enjoy. They were always fighting, the second son told me, being friendly one month and not the next, moods and different interests dictating their volatile and varying approaches and recessions.

In addition, though, there were two daughters: Effie, a woman of twenty-nine or thirty, who at the age of twenty-one had run away to a nearby large city and found work in a laundry and had never returned, since her father would not let her have a beau; and finally Ida, the subject of this sketch, whom I first saw when she was twenty-eight and who already showed the care and disappointment with which apparently her life had been freighted. For, besides being hard on "enimels," Hauchawout was hard on human beings and seemed to look upon them as mere machines like himself. It was said that he was up at dawn or earlier, with the first crow of the roosters, and the last to go

210

to bed at night. Henry Hauchawout, the son I knew best, once confessed to me that his father would "swear like hell" if all his children were not up within five minutes after he was. His wife, a worn and abused woman, had died at forty-three, and he had never married again, but not from loyalty. Did he not have Ida? He had no religion, of course, none other than the need of minding your own business and getting as much money as possible to bury away somewhere. And yet his children seemed not so hard; rather sentimental and human—reactions, no doubt, from the grinding atmosphere from which they had managed finally to extricate themselves.

But it is of Ida that I wish to speak—Ida, whom I first saw when my previously mentioned relative suggested that I go with him to find out if Hauchawout had any hay to sell. "You'll meet a character well worth the skill of any portrayer of fact," he added. It was Ida, however, who came to the door in answer to a loud "Hallo!" and I saw a woman prematurely old or overworked, drab and yet robust, a huge creature with small and rather nervous eyes, red sunburned face and hands, a small nose, and faded red hair done into a careless knot at the back of her head. At the request of my "in-law" to know where her father was, she pointed to the barn. "He just went out to feed the pigs," she added. We swung through a narrow gate and followed a well-fenced road to the barn, where just outside a great pen containing perhaps thirty pigs stood Hauchawout, a pail in each hand, his brown overalls stuck in his boots, gazing reflectively at his grunting property.

"Nice pigs, eh, Mr. Hauchawout!" commented my relative.

"Yes," he answered, with a marked accent, at the same time turning a quizzical and none too kindly eye upon me. "It's about time they go now. What they eat from now on makes me no money."

I glanced amusedly at my relative, but he was gazing politely at his host. "Any hay for sale, Mr. Hauchawout?"

"How much you t'ink you pay?" he asked, cannily.

"Oh, whatever the market price is. Seventeen dollars, I hear."

"Not py me. What I got I keep at dat price. Hay vill be vorth yust five tollars more if dis vedder keeps up." He surveyed the dry green-blue landscape, untouched by rains for these several weeks past.

My relative smiled. "Very well. You're quite right, if you think it's going to stay dry. You wouldn't take eighteen a ton, I suppose?"

"No, nor twenty. I t'ink hay goes to twenty-two before October. Anyhow, vot I got I can use next vinter if I can't sell him."

I stared at this crude, vigorous, self-protective soul. His house and barn seemed to confirm all I had heard. The house was small, yellow, porchless, inhospitable, and the walks at the front and side worn and flowerless. A thin dog and some chickens were in the shade of one fair-sized tree that graced a corner. Several horses were browsing in the barn lot, for it was Sunday and the sectarian atmosphere of this region rather enforced a strict observance of the day. They were as thin as even moderate health would permit. But Hauchawout, standing vigorous and ruddy before his large, newly painted barn, showed where his heart was. There was no flaw in that structure. It was a fine big barn and held all the other things he so much treasured.

But it was about his daughter that my relative chose to speak as we drove away.

"There's a woman whose life has been ruined by that old razorback," he reflected after volunteering various other details. "She's no beauty, and her chances were never very good, but he would never let anyone come near her, and now it's too late, I suppose. I often wonder why she hasn't run away, like her sister, also how she passes her time there with him. Just working all the time, I suppose. I doubt if he ever buys a newspaper. There was a story going the rounds here a few years ago about her and a farmhand who worked for Hauchawout. Hauchawout caught him tapping at her shutter at two in the morning and beat him up with a hoe-handle. Whether there was anything between them or not no one knows. Anyway, she's been here ever since, and I doubt if anybody courts her now."

•   •   •

I neither saw nor heard of this family for a period of five years, during which time I worked in other places. Then one summer, returning for a vacation, I learned that "the old man" had died and the property had been divided by law, no will having

212

been left by him. The lorn Ida, after a service of thirty-two or -three years in her father's behalf, cooking, sweeping, washing, ironing, feeding the animals, and helping her father to reap and pitch hay, had secured an equal fifth with the others, no more, a total of fifteen acres of land and two thousand dollars in cash. The land had already been leased on shares to her prosperous brother, the one with the automobile, and the cash placed out at interest. To eke out an existence, which was still apparently not much improved, Ida had gone to work, first as a laundress in a South Bixley (the county seat) laundry, at a later date as a canner of tomatoes in the summer canning season, and then as housekeeper in a well-to-do canner's family. She was reported by my host's wife as still husbandless, even loverless, though there was a rumor to the effect that now that she had property and money in the bank, she was being "set up to" by one Arlo Wilkens, a garrulous ne'er-do-well barber of Shrivertown, a drunken roistering, but now rather exploded and *passé* person of fifty; also one Henry Widdle, another ne'er-do-well of a somewhat more savory character, since he was credited with having neither the strength nor courage to be drunken or roistering. He was the son of a local farmer who himself owned no land and worked that of others. With no education of any description, this son had wandered off some years before, trying here and there to sell trees for a nursery and failing utterly, as he himself told me, and then going to work in a furniture factory in Chicago, which was too hard for him; and later wandering as far west as Colorado, where necessity compelled him to become a railroad hand for a time. ("I served my time on the Denver & Rio Grande," he used to say.) But finding this too hard also, he had quit, and returned to the comparative ease of his former life here, which had no doubt brightened by contrast. Once here again, he found life none too easy, but at the time I knew him he was earning a living by driving for a local contractor, that being "the easiest thing he could find," as a son of the relative aforementioned most uncharitably remarked.

While working in this region again for a summer under some trees that crowned a hill and close by a highroad which crossed one slope of it, I was often made aware of this swain by the squeak of the wheels of his wagon as he hauled his loads of stone or sand or lumber in one direction or another. And later I came to know him, he being well known, as are most country people the one to the other in a region such as this. Occasionally as the two sons of my host worked in a field of potatoes alongside the hill on which I worked, I could see them hailing this man as he passed, he for some reason appealing to them as a source of idle amusement or entertainment. Hearing laughter once I ambled over and joined the group, the possibility of countryside news enticing me. He proved to be an aimless, unpivoted, chartless soul, drifting nowhere in particular and with no least conception of either the order or the thoroughgoing intellectual processes of life, and yet not wholly uninteresting to me. Why, I often wondered. In so far as I could see he picked only vaguely at or fumbled unintelligently with such phases and aspects of life as he encountered. He spoke persistently and yet indefinitely of the things he had seen in his travels—the mountains of the West, the plains of Texas, where he had tried to sell trees, the worth of this region in which he lived—and yet he could report only fragmentarily of anything he had ever seen. The mountains of Colorado were "purty high," the scenery "purty fine in some places." In Texas it had been hot and dry, "not so many trees in most places, but I couldn't sell any." The people he had met everywhere were little more than moving objects or figures in a dream. His mind seemed to blur almost everything he saw. If he registered any definite vital impression of any kind, in the past or the present, I could not come to know. And yet he was a suitor, as he once admitted to us via our jesting, for the hand of the much-buffeted Ida; and, as I learned later in the same year, he did finally succeed in marrying her, thus worsting the aged and no doubt much more skillful Wilkens.

Still later in the same year, it was reported to me that they were building a small house or shack on Ida's acres, and with her money, and would be in it before spring. They were working together, so the letter ran, with the carpenters, Widdle hauling lumber and sand and brick and Ida working with hammer and nails. Still later I learned that they were comfortably housed, had a cow, some pigs and chickens, a horse and various implements, all furnished by Ida's capital, and that they were both working in the fields.

214

The thing that interested me was the fact that at last, after so many years, having secured a man, even of so shambling a character as Widdle, the fair Ida was prone to make a god of him. And what a god.

"Gee!" one of the sons commented to me once during my stay of a few weeks the following summer. "Widdle certainly has a cinch now. He don't need to work hard any more. Ida gets up in the morning and feeds the chickens and pigs and milks the cow and gets his breakfast while he lies in bed. He works in the field plowing sometimes, but she plows, too."

"Yeah, I've seen her pitch hay into the barn from the wagon, just as she did for her father," added the second youth.

"Ah, but the difference, the difference!" mine host, the father of these same sons, was jocosely at pains to point out. "Then it was against her will and without the enabling power of love, while now—"

"Love's not gonna make hay any lighter," sagely observed one of his sons.

"No, nor plowin' any easier. Ah, haw!" This from a farmhand, a fixture about the place. "An' I've seen her doin' that, too."

"What treachery to romance!" I chided. And otherwise did my best to stand up for romance, come what might.

Be that as it may, Widdle was about these days in a cheerful and even facetious frame of mind. When first I knew him, as a teamster, he had seemed to wear a heavy and sad look, as though the mystery of life, or perhaps better, the struggle for existence, pressed on him as much as it does on any of us. But now that his fortune had improved, he was a trifle more spruce, not so much in clothes, which were the usual farmer wear, but in manner. On certain days, especially in the afternoon, when his home chores were not too onerous or his wife was taking care of them for him, he came visiting to my woodland table on its hill, where a great and beautiful panorama spread before us. And once he inquired, though rather nibblish in his manner, as to the matter and manner of writing. Could a man make a living at that now, say? Did you have to write much or little in order to get along? Did I write for these here now magazines?

Rather ruefully I admitted that when I could I did. The way

of ye humble scribe, as I tried to make plain, was at times thorny. Still, I had no great reason to complain.

We then drifted to the business of farming, and here, I confess, I felt myself to be on much firmer ground. How was he getting along? Had he made much out of his first season's crop? How was his second progressing? Did he find fifteen acres difficult to manage? Was his wife well?

To the last question he replied that she was, doing very well indeed, but as for the second from the last: "Not so very. 'Course now," he went on musingly, "we ain't got the best implements yet, an' my wife's health ain't as good this summer as 't was last, but we're gettin' along all right. I got mebbe as much as a hundred barrels o' potatas comin' along, an' mebbe three hundred bushels o' corn. For myself, I'm more interested in this here chicken business, if I could once git it agoin' right. 'Course we ain't got all the up-to-date things we need, but I'm calc'latin' that next year, if everything goes right, I'll add a new pen an' a coupla runways to the coop I got there, an' try my hand at more chickens."

Never his wife's, I noticed, when it came to this end of the farming institution. And as an aside I could not help thinking of those breakfasts in bed and of his wife pitching hay and plowing as well as milking the cow and feeding the chickens while he slept.

The lorn Ida and her great love!

And then one day, expressing curiosity as to this *ménage*, I was taken there to visit. The place looked comfortable enough—a small, unpainted, two-room affair, with a lean-to at the back for a kitchen, a porch added only the preceding spring, so that milord might have a view of the thymy valley below, with its green fields and distant hills, while he smoked and meditated. It was very clean, as I noticed even from a distance, the doorway and the paths and all. And all about it, at points equidistant from the kitchen, were built a barn, a corncrib, a smokehouse, and a chicken coop, to say nothing of a new well-top, all unpainted as yet but all framed by the delicious green of the lawn. And Widdle, once he came forward, commented rather shyly on his treasures, walking about with me the while and pointing them out.

"What with all the other things I gotta do, I ain't got 'round to paintin' yet; but I 'low as how this comin' fall or spring mebbe

216

I'll be able to do sumpin' on it, if my wife's health keeps up. These chickens are a sight o' bother at times, an' we're takin' on another cow next week an' some pigs."

I thought of those glum days when he was still hauling sand and stone in his squeaky wagon.

And then came Ida, big, bony, silent, diffident, red-tanned by sun and weather, to whom this narrow fifteen-acre world was no doubt a paradise. Love had at last come to her. Widdle, le grand, was its embodiment. I could not help gazing at him and then at her, for after a still, bovine fashion she seemed fond, and not only that, but respectful of him. He talked and talked, while she only spoke when addressed—never first or spontaneously. Her father's training, I thought.

It being a Sunday afternoon, the only appropriate time to make a call in the farming world, when presumably the chores of the week were out of the way, and Widdle having resumed his seat on his front porch, still she was astir among her pots and pans, though eventually she came forward and made us welcome in her shy way. Wouldn't we sit down? Wouldn't we have a glass of milk? The worthy Widdle, scarcely cognizant of her presence as it seemed to me, went on smoking and dreaming and surveying his possessions. If ever a man looked at ease, he did, and his wife seemed to take great satisfaction in his comfort. She smiled as we talked to him or answered in monosyllables when we addressed her, having been so long repressed by her father, as I assumed, that she could not talk.

But my relative had called my attention to one thing which I was to note, and that was despite the fact that she was within three months of an accouchement, I would find her working as usual, which was true. She was obviously as near her day as that, and yet during our visit she went to look after the pigs and chickens, the while milord smoked on and talked. His one theme was the farm, his proposed addition to his chicken coop, a proposed enlargement of his pig pen, the fact that his farm would be better if he could afford to take over some five acres to the east, which were to be had, and so on. Several times he referred to his tour of the West and the fact that he had "served his time on the Denver & Rio Grande."

After that I could not help thinking of him from time to time,

217

for he illustrated to me so clearly the casual and accidental character of so many things in nature—the fact that fortune, strength, ease, beauty, fame, any power of mind or body, come in the main to the individual as gifts and are so often not even added to or developed by any effort of his. For here was this vague, casual weakling drawn back to this region by a kind of sixth sense which regulated his well-being, mayhap, and that after he had failed in all other things, only to find this repressed and yet now free victim, his wife, seeking, by the aid of her small means, some satisfaction in the world of love through him. But did he really care for her? I sometimes asked myself that question. Could he? Had he the capacity, the power of appreciation and understanding which any worthwhile love requires? I wondered.

· · ·

The events of the following September seemed to answer the question in a rather definite way, and yet I am not so sure that they did, either. Life is so casual; love, or the matter of affinity, such an indefinite thing with so many! I was sleeping in a large room which faced the front of the house—a room which commanded the slope of a hill and a distant and splendid valley beyond. Outside were evergreens and horse-chestnuts that rustled and whispered in the slightest breeze. At two or three of the clock of one of these fine moonlit nights I heard a knocking below and a voice calling: "Oh, Mis' K———! Oh, Mis' K———!"

Fearing that my hostess might not hear, I went to one of the open windows, but as I did so the door below opened and I heard her voice and then Widdle's, though I could not make him out in the pale light. He seemed, for once, somewhat concerned, and asked if she would not come over and see his wife.

"She's been taken powerful bad all of a sudden, Mis' K———," I heard him say. "She ain't been feelin' well for the last few days; been complainin' sorta, an' she's very bad now, an' I don't know what to do. It'd be a big favor if you'd come, Mis' K———. Mis' Agnew phoned fer a doctor fer me, but she don't seem to be able to get none yet."

So Ida's time had now come! Another child—and of such

218

parents—was about to enter the world—to be what? Do what? I wondered how the spinsterish Ida would make out. She was rather old now for motherhood, and so large and ungainly. How would she fare? How serve a nursing child? Not many minutes after I heard Mrs. K———, accompanied by one of her sons, leaving in the motor car, the humanitarian and social aspects of the situation seeming to arouse in her the greatest solicitude. Then I heard nothing more until the following noon, when she returned. By that time Mrs. Widdle was very ill indeed. She had worked in the fields up to three days before, as it now appeared, and only the day before her illness had attempted to do a week's washing. No help of any kind had ever been called in, no doctor consulted. Widdle, conscious of himself only, as it appeared to me, had gone on dreaming, possibly doing his share of the work but no more, and no doubt accepting cheerfully the sacrifices and ministrations of his wife until this latest hour.

It was also evident to all that conditions underlying possible motherhood for Mrs. Widdle were most unsatisfactory. During all the nine months of gestation she had given herself no least attention. A doctor called in at this late hour by my relative wagged his head most dolefully. Perhaps she would come through all right, but there was undue pressure on the kidneys. He suggested a nurse, but this Mrs. Widdle, ill as she was, would not hear of. It would cost so much. The end came swiftly on the following night, and with great agony. She was in nowise fitted to endure the strain, and an attempt to remove the child, accompanied by uric poisoning, did for her completely. Ether was given, and she remained unconscious until she died. And the child with her.

•   •   •

I saw her once, and once only, afterward, when I joined the family of my host and hostess in "viewing the body." Widdle, as I had long since learned, was in no great standing with either his relatives or his neighbors, being of that poor, drifting, dreaming caliber which offers no least foundation for a friendship, let alone a community of interest with either. Usually he was silent or slow of speech, with but a few ideas—and those mostly relative to his present state—upon which to meditate or speak. Consequently, few neighbors and no relatives, barring Ida's two brothers, were interested to call, and the latter in only the most perfunctory way. Such as did come or had offered assistance had arranged that the parlor, a most sacred place, should be devoted to the last ceremonies and the reception of visitors; and here the body, in a coffin, the like of which for color and decoration I had never seen before, lay in state. It was of lavender plush on the outside and lined with pink silk within, and to be carried, as one was forced to note, by six expensive handles of gilt. More, this parlor was obviously an esthetic realm as these two had seen it, and hence arresting to anyone's attention. For it was furnished with a gaudy yellow oak center table, now pushed to one side, some stiff and homely chairs with red plush seats, and a parlor wood-stove decorated with nickel and with red isinglass windows in front. On the walls, which were papered a bright pink, were two yarn mottoes handsomely framed in walnut, a picture of Widdle and his wife boxed in walnut and glass and surrounded by a wax wreath, and, for sharp contrast, a brightly colored calendar exhibiting a blonde movie queen rampant. Gracing the center table was a Bible and a yellow plush album, in which was not a single picture, for I looked. It must have been the yellow plush that had fascinated them, that ancient and honorable symbol of luxury.

But that coffin! I have no desire to intrude levity in connection with death, and, anyhow, it is said to presage misfortune. Also, I recognize too well the formless and untutored impulses toward beauty which struggle all too feebly in the most of us, animals and men. Out of such undoubtedly have risen Karnak and the Acropolis and the "Ode on a Grecian Urn." But at that time (and for all I know, the custom may endure to this hour), there was being introduced to the poorest sections of our American big cities (and from this experience I judged to the backwoods also) this concluding gayety in the matter of coffins calculated to engage the attention of any lover of color—in short, astonishing confections in yellow, blue, green, silver, and lavender plush, usually lined with contrasting shades of silk and equipped with handles of equally arresting hues—silver, gilt, black, or gray. Trust our American profiteer Barnums of the undertaking world to prepare something that would interest the afflicted simple, if not the dead, in their hour of bereavement. Beauty, as each interprets it for himself, must certainly be the anodyne that resolves all our pains. At any rate, this coffin, as described, was piled high with garden flowers. (And as I learned afterwards an attempt at mortuary verse by Widdle, concerning which more anon, was placed in one of his dead wife's hands.) But considering the general solidity and angularity of the frame, it could not but seem incongruous. Astonishing, in fact. Yet the coffin obviously selected for its beauty and as a special comfort to the bereaved living, the Honorable Henry Widdle. Indeed, unless I am greatly mistaken, Widdle was for the first time in his life indulging in a long repressed impulse toward luxury, which in its turn was disguising itself to him as deep grief.

But that figure in the coffin, the lorn Ida, no less, only now embedded in such voluptuous materiality and at so late a date— she who had followed the plow and pitched hay, and then, as a reward, had enjoyed one toiling, closing year of love or peace, or what you will! That hair so thick and coarse, but now smoothly plaited and laid—red hair. The large, bony head, with wide mouth and small nose, looking so tired. But none the less one strong arm snugly holding the minute infant that had never known life, close to her breast and her big, yearning face—the hand of the other arm holding Widdle's poem.

I turned away, arrested, humiliated, even terrified by this fresh evidence of the blank and humorless clanking of the cosmic urge that had brought about not only this, but so much that is inane or miserable or horrifying on this planet. For Ida's face showed lines which stilled all humor. They were not comic and not even sad, just fatefully mechanistic and so unbelievably grim. Sleep, I thought, sleep! It is best.

But the little house she had left, that little shell in which she had thought to intrench herself against misery and loneliness. Not a corner or a window or a shelf or a pan but had been scrubbed and shined and dusted repeatedly. The kitchen revealed a collection of utensils almost irritatingly clean; the dining-living room the same. And outside were all the things as she had left them, all in clean and orderly array. And on the front porch, viewing the scenery and greeting the few straggling visitors, Widdle himself in almost smiling serenity. For was he not now master of all he surveyed, the fifteen acres, house, barn, sheds, cattle—a man of affairs no less? And now for this great occasion in his best clothes, and looking for all the world as though he were holding a reception or conducting a function of some kind, the importance of which had been solemnly impressed upon his mind.

What interested me most, though, after seeing this other, was his attitude, the way in which he now faced death and this material as well as spiritual loss, also his attitude toward the future, now that this brief solution of most of his material difficulties had been removed. Anyone who postulates the mechanical or chemical origin of life, and behaviorism as the path of its development, would have been interested in this case. As I viewed Widdle then, he was really nothing more than a weak reflection of all the customs or emotional or mental mechanics of his day and realm. It was customary on such occasions to wear black, and he wore black, as much as he could find. He had heard or seen that funerals were occasions of state, hence this coffin, with such other evidences of grandeur as he could contrive, introduced into this meager home. He had noted that people grieved, so now he drew a long face and wore as sad a mien as he could muster, but not, I am sorry to report, a successful one.

And when, after due comments on the pathos of his great loss, I asked about his future, he showed a strong, if repressed, interest in the fact that all this which had been his wife's was now his, assuming that no undue wind arose to disturb him. Not only that but for some reason, due to no conscious effort on my part, he assumed that I was friendly to him and wished him well, and in consequence, not five minutes after I had come out of the house, he wished to know if I had seen the barn. I replied that I had not and expressed interest, and he took me to see it, solemnly and slowly, cortège style. But once there, his spirit seemed to expand or "limber up," as he would have said, and he then and there talked of the future that was his. The one horse he had there was good enough, but now that he was alone and might need to hire occasional help, he was thinking of buying another. Besides, his wife had helped him a good bit, and so he wasn't sure but that he would require the aid of a "hand"—become an employer, no less. Next came the pigs, which we examined with care. His wife had thought that four were enough for this fall, but next year, if his crops turned out right, he might try six or eight. There was money in the dairy business, too, if only a man had three or four cows; but there was a lot of trouble connected with feeding, milking, calving, and the like, and he wasn't sure that he understood this as well as had his wife. Did I know anything about the law governing a wife's property or her husband's just claim to it? I confessed that I did not but would be glad to inquire, if he wished, which he did.

"You know," he said, leaning against one of the posts of the pig pen, "my wife's relations ain't any too friendly to me, for some reason. I never could make it out, an' I was thinkin' mebbe they'd feel they have a claim on this, though when we bought she wouldn't have it any other way but joint. 'Squire,' she says to Squire Driggs over to Shrivertown, when she was havin' the property transferred to the two of us when we got married, 'I want this property fixed so that in case anything happens to either of us the other one gets it, money an' all.' That's what she said, an' that's what both of us signed onto over there to Shrivertown. I got the papers in the house here now. That's clear enough, ain't it? I'd like to bring the papers in to you sometime an' let you look at 'em. There ain't no way they could interfere with that, is there, do you think?"

I thought not, and said so. More, that I would see what a lawyer friend of mine would have to say since he appeared much perturbed. Indeed he seemed slightly strained when he first spoke but now became more calm. Then he led me to the chicken coop and the milk house. We stood at a fence and looked over that five-acre field adjoining, which some day he hoped to own. After a few more comments as to the merits of the departed, I left, and saw him but once after, some two weeks later, when, the funeral being over and the first fresh misery of his grief having passed, he came up to my table on the hilltop one sunny afternoon to spend a social moment or two, as I thought, but really to discuss the latter phases of his position as master and widower.

●   ●   ●

The afternoon was so fine. A sea of crystal light bathed the hills and valleys, and where I worked the ground was mottled with light sifting through leaves. Birds sang, and two woodchucks, bitten by curiosity, reconnoitered my realm. Then the brush crackled, and forward came Widdle out of nowhere and sidling slightly as he came.

"Nice view you have up here."

"Yes, I enjoy it very much. Have that stump over there. How've you been?"

"Oh, pretty fair, thank you. I was thinkin' you might like to look over them papers I spoke about. I have 'em here now." And he fished in his coat pocket.

I turned over the one paper he extracted, which was a memorandum to the effect that Ida Widdle, née Hauchawout, sole owner of such-and-such property, desired and hereby agreed that in the event of her death and the absence of any children, her husband, Henry Widdle, was to succeed her as sole owner and administrator. And this was witnessed by Notary Driggs of Shrivertown.

"There's no question in my mind as to the validity of that," I solemnly assured him. "It seems to me that a lawyer could make it very difficult for anyone to disturb you in your place. I can make a copy of it and find out. But why not see a lawyer? Or ask Justice Driggs?"

"Well," he said, turning his head slowly and as slowly taking the paper. "I don't like to go to any lawyer around here unless I have to nor no judge, either. They charge a lot. Besides, I'm afraid of 'em. They could make a lot o' trouble for a feller like me, not knowin' anything about these here things. But I don't calc'late to do nothin' about this unless I have to, not stir anything up, that is, but I thought you might know."

I stopped my work and meditated on his fate and how well chance had dealt with him in one way and another. Also his native shrewdness in regard to how he was to do. Lawyers, as he plainly saw, were dangerous. Judges and relatives also. After a time, during which it seemed to me that he might be thinking of the misused Ida, he searched in his pockets and finally extracted another paper, which I thought might be another agreement of some kind. This he held in his hands for a minute or more, then unfolding it very

224

carefully said: "You bein' a writer, I thought I'd bring up a little thing I've fixed up here about my wife an' ask you what you thought of it. It's what I put into her hand in the coffin. Course I've worked over it some since then. It's some poetry I've been thinkin' I'd put in *The Banner* over here to Bixley."

"The poetry laid in his dead wife's hand," I thought. Both my host and hostess had stated that an effusion had been placed there by Widdle and that presently—in some due and respectable hour—they would obtain the loan of it for my inspection. But now here it was before ever they had thought to secure it and I could scarcely repress my curiosity, as to the nature of this composition which was to be published, at his request, presumably, by *The Banner*.

"How do you mean, publish?" I inquired respectfully, and yet holding out my hand. "Suppose you let me see it."

"If you don't mind, I'd rather read it to you. It's in my writin' an' kind o' mixed up, but I can read it to you."

"By all means. But tell me something about it first. You say it's a poem about your wife. Did you compose it yourself?"

"Oh, yes. Only yesterday an' last night. Well, mebbe three days, countin' the time I put on it just after my wife died. Only I put the beginnin's of it in her coffin the day she was buried."

"Oh, I see," I commented. "Very good and thoughtful. And now you say it's going to be published in *The Banner*?"

"Yes, sir. That's where it's a-goin' to be published."

"But just how is that? Do you submit it, or how?"

"Oh, they always print death-rhymes," he went on in his slow explanatory way. "They charge ten cents a line. Everybody does it when anybody they're fond of dies—husband or wife or the like o' that."

"Oh, I see," I hazarded, a great light dawning. "It's a custom, and you feel in a way that you ought to do this."

"Yes, sir, that's it. If it don't cost too much, I thought I'd just put this in."

I prepared to give the matter attentive ear.

"Read it," I said, and he smoothed out the paper, the slanting afternoon light falling over him and it, and began:

"Dearest wife who now are dead,
I miss you as in the days before we were wed,
Gone is your kind touch, your loving care.
I look around, but can't find you anywhere.

The kind deeds that you scattered far and wide
Tell me that you are no longer by my side.
I look around now and seek you in vain;
My tears they fall like rain.

The house is silent without your dear tread,
Everywhere that you were you are now missed instead.
I am lonely now, but our Father above
Now has you in His care and love.

If gone from me you are happy there at rest,
And death that tortures me for you is best.
Dear husband, weep not for your departed wife,
For from heaven, looking down, I see you as in Life.

I see your woe and grief and misery,
And would be there with you if I could in glee,
So kind you were, dear husband, and so good,
The Father of All above knows what you've withstood;
He knows how hard you've tried, what efforts you
      have made,
To help and serve in love. Don't be afraid.

Face the world with courage, husband dear,
And never have any fear.
For if in life you may now be misunderstood,
Our Father who is in heaven knows that you were kind
      and good.

Your efforts were very many, your rewards were few.
The world should know how kind you were and true.
The tongues of men may slander, husband dear,
But do not let that trouble your ear.

226

I, your wife in heaven, know how we
While we were together on earth did love and agree,
And in heaven too, when it pleases God to call us,
We will love and be happy together as we did on
    earth always."

He paused and looked up, and I confess that by now my mouth had opened a little. The simplicity! The naive unconsciousness of possible ridicule, of anachronism, of false interpretation on the part of those who could not know! Could a mind be so obtuse as to believe that this was not ridiculous? I stared while he gazed, waiting for some favorable comment.

"Tell me," I managed at last, "did you write all of that yourself?"

"Well, you know how 'tis," he proceeded to explain. "The papers round here publish these here things right along, every week, that is. I see 'em in *The Banner,* an' I just took some of the lines from them, but a good many of 'em—most really—is my own."

"Very good," I said encouragingly. "Excellent. But you know you have quite a few lines there. At ten cents a line you are going to have a big bill to pay."

"That's so," he agreed, dubiously and ruefully, at the same time scratching his head. "I hadn't thought o' that. Let's see," and he began to count. "Three dollars and forty cents," he finally announced and then fell silent.

Aha, I thought, the frailty of these earthly affections! For, looking at him as he counted up the cost of his poetic flight and thinking of his wife—the dreary round of her days, the heavy labor up to the very hour of her death, that carefully enacted agreement as to the ultimate disposition of her property in case of her death, I could not help thinking of the pathos and futility of her as well as his life—of so much that we call life and effort, the absolute nonsense that living becomes in so many instances. Above me as I speculated was that great blazing ball we call the sun, spinning about in space and with its attendant planets. And upon the surface of this thing, "the earth," we, with our millions of little things we call "homes" and "possessions." And about and above and beneath us, immensities as well as mysteries, mysteries,

227

mysteries. And nowhere on all the earth, not even so much as a sane guess as to what we are or what the sun is or the "reason" for our being here. And yet, passion and lust and beauty and greed and yearning, this endless pother and bitterness and delight in order to retain this elusive and inexplicable something, "life," "us," "ours," in space. Birds a-wing, trees blowing and whispering, fields teeming with mysterious and yet needed things, and then, on every hand this wealth of tragedy. Life living on life, men and animals plotting and scheming as though there were only so much to be had and all of that in the possession of others.

And yet, despite the mystery and the suffering and the bitterness, here was this golden day, an enormous treasure in itself, and these lovely trees, these mountains blue, this wondrous, soothing panorama. Beauty, beauty, beauty, appealing and consoling to the heart—life's anodyne. And here, in the very heart of it, Ida Hauchawout, and her father, with his "no enimel gets fet py me," and his son who threw a pitchfork at him, and this poor clown before me with his death-rhymes now apparently too expensive and his fear of losing the little that had been left to him. *His* love. *His* loss. *His* gain. *His* desire to place *him*self right before the "world." Ha, ha! Ho, ho! This was what he was rhyming about. This was what he was worrying about.

But was he guilty of any wrong before the world? Not a bit that I could see. Was he entitled to what he had come by? As much as any of us are entitled to anything. Yet here he was, worrying, worrying, worrying, and trying to decide in the face of his loss or gain whether his verse, this tribute or self-justification, was worth three dollars and forty cents to him as a display in a miserable, meagerly circulated and quickly forgotten country newspaper.

Mesdames and Messieurs, are we all mad? Or am I? Or is *Life*? Is the whole thing what it appears to be to so many—aimless, insane, accidental jumble and gibberish? We articulate or put together out of old mysteries new mysteries, machines, methods, theories. But to what end? What about all the Hauchawouts and Widdles, past, present, and to come, their sons, daughters, and relatives, and all the fighting and the cruelty and the parading and the nonsense?

228

The crude and defeated Ida. And this fumbling, seeking, and rather to be pitied dub with his rhymes. Myself, writing and wondering about it all.

•   •   •

A letter written several years later by my relative's wife added this for my enlightenment:

"I think you ought to know that Widdle has been taken with religion and now interprets the Bible in his own fumbling way, coming to me occasionally for help. He plows his fields and meditates, expecting God any minute to come in the form of a dragon or giant and finish him and all men. He has figured out that the world will come to an end in this wise: God will appear as a dragon or a gigantic man, and wherever he places his foot, there life will cease to exist. That will be the end of the world. Yet he has no notion that the world is any larger than the United States at most. I said to him once: 'But Widdle, it would take Him a long time to step over all the world and crush out all life, wouldn't it?' 'Yes, that's so,' he replied, 'but I guess His feet are bigger than ours—maybe as big as a barn, an mebbe He can walk faster than we can.' He has lost himself completely in the Bible now and reads and meditates all the time, applying everything he reads to his own few acres. He still lives alone and does his own cooking, fearing, I think, a second wife who might take his possessions from him. But no legal trouble has ever been made him. People are a little sorry for him, I think. His chief dish is cornmeal mush, which he boils and pours into saucers or flat plates to the thickness he wants, because he doesn't know how to pour it into a deep dish and slice it."

Chains

$\mathcal{A}$ S GARRISON LEFT HIS LAST business conference in
K——, where the tall buildings and the amazing crowds
always seemed such a commentary on the power and force and
wealth of America and the world, and was on his way to the
railway station to take a train for G——, his home city, his
thoughts turned with peculiar emphasis and hope, if not actual
pleasure—and yet it was a pleasure, of a sad, distressed kind—
to Idelle. Where was she now? What was she doing at this particular moment. It was after four of a gray November afternoon,
just the time, as he well knew, winter or summer, when she so
much preferred to be glowing at an afternoon reception, a "thé
dansant," or a hotel grill where there was dancing, and always,
as he well knew, in company with those vivid young "sports"
or pleasure lovers of the town who were always following her.
Idelle, to do her no injustice, had about her that something, even
after three years of marriage, that drew them, some of the worst
or best—mainly the worst, he thought at times—of those who
made his home city, the great far-flung G——, interesting and
in the forefront socially and in every other way.

What a girl! What a history! And how strange that he should
have been attracted to her at all, he with his forty-eight years,
his superior (oh, very much!) social position, his conservative
friends and equally conservative manners. Idelle was so different,
so hoyden, almost coarse, in her ways at times, actually gross
and vulgar (derived from her French tanner father, no doubt, not
her sweet, retiring Polish mother), and yet how attractive, too,
in so many ways, with that rich russet-brown-gold hair of hers,
her brown-black eyes, almost pupil-less, the iris and pupil being
of the same color, and that trig, vigorous figure, always tailored
in the smartest way! She was a paragon—to him at least—or had
been to begin with.

How tingling and dusty these streets of K—— were, so vital always! How sharply the taxis of this Midwestern city turned corners!

But what a period he had endured since he had married her, three years before! What tortures, what despairs! If only he could make over Idelle to suit him! But what a wonderful thing that destroying something called beauty was, especially to one, like himself, who found life tiresome in so many ways—something to possess, a showpiece against the certain inroads of time, something wherewith to arouse envy in other persons.

At last they were reaching the station!

She did not deserve that he should love her. It was the most unfortunate thing for him that he did, but how could he help it now? How overcome it? How punish her for her misdeeds to him without punishing himself more? Love was such an inscrutable thing; so often one lavished it where it was not even wanted. God, he could testify to that! He was a fine example, really. She cared about as much for him as she did for the lamp-post on the corner, or an old discarded pair of shoes. And yet— He was never tired of looking at her, for one thing, of thinking of her ways, her moods, her secrets. She had not done and was not doing as she should—it was impossible, he was beginning to suspect, for her so to do—and still—

He must stop and send her a telegram before the train left!

What a pleasure it was, indeed, anywhere and at all times, to have her hanging on his arm, to walk into a restaurant or drawing room and to know that of all those present none had a more attractive wife than he, not one. For all Idelle's commonplace birth and lack of position to begin with, she was the smartest, the best dressed, the most alluring, by far—at least, he thought so—of all the set in which he had placed her. Those eyes! That hair! That graceful figure, always so smartly arrayed! To be sure, she was a little young for him. Their figures side by side were somewhat incongruous—he with his dignity and years and almost military bearing, as so many told him, she with that air of

232

extreme youthfulness and lure which always brought so many of the younger set to her side wherever they happened to be. Only there was the other galling thought: That she did not wholly belong to him and never had. She was too interested in other men, and always had been. Her youth, that wretched past of hers, had been little more than a lurid streak of bad, even evil—yes, evil—conduct. She had, to tell the truth, been a vile girl, sensuous, selfish, inconsiderate, unrepentant, and was still, and yet he had married her in spite of all that, knowing it, really. Only at first he had not known quite all.

"Yes, all three of these! And wait till I get my sleeper ticket!"

No wonder people had talked, though. He had heard it—that she had married him for his money, position, that he was too old, that it was a scandal, etc. Well, maybe it was. But he had been fond of her—terribly so—and she of him, or seemingly, at first. Yes, she must have been—her manner, her enthusiasm, if temporary, for him! Those happy, happy first days they spent together! Her quiet assumption of the role of hostess in Sicard Avenue at first, her manner of receiving and living up to her duties! It was wonderful, so promising. Yes, there was no doubt of it; she must have cared for him a little at first. Her brain, too, required a man of his years to understand—some phases of her moods and ideas, and as for him—well, he was as crazy about her then as now—more so, if anything—or was he? Wasn't she just as wonderful to him now as she had been then? Truly. Yes, love or infatuation of this kind was a terrible thing, so impossible to overcome.

"Car three, section seven!"

Would he ever forget the night he had first seen her being carried into the Insull General on that canvas ambulance stretcher, her temple bruised, one arm broken and internal injuries for which she had to be operated on at once—a torn diaphragm, for one thing—and of how she had instantly fascinated him? Her hair was loose and had fallen over one shoulder, her hands were limp. Those hands! That picture! He had been visiting his old friend

233

Dr. Dorsey and had wondered who she was, how she came to be in such a dreadful accident and had thought her so beautiful. Think of how her beauty might have been marred, only it wasn't, thank goodness!

His telegram should be delivered in one hour, at most—that would reach her in time!

Then and there he had decided that he must know her if she did not die, that perhaps she might like him as he did her, on the instant; had actually suffered tortures for fear she would not! Think of that! Love at first sight for him—and for one who had since caused him so much suffering—and in her condition, torn and bruised and near to death! It was wonderful, wasn't it?

How stuffy these trains were when one first entered them—coal smoky!

And that operation! What a solemn thing it was, really, with only himself, the doctor and three nurses in the empty operating room that night. Dorsey was so tall, so solemn, but always so courageous. He had asked if he might not be present, although he did not know her, and because there were no relatives about to bar him from the room, no one to look after her or to tell who she was, the accident having occurred after midnight in the suburbs, he had been allowed by Dorsey to come in.

"Yes, put them down here!"

He had pulled on a white slip over his business suit, and clean white cotton gloves on his hands, and had then been allowed to come into the observation gallery while Dorsey, assisted by the hospital staff, had operated. He saw her cut open—the blood—heard her groan heavily under ether! And all the time wondering who she was. Her history. And pitying her, too! Fearing she might not come to! How the memory of her pretty, shrewd face, hidden under bandages and a gas cone, had haunted him!

234

The train on this other track, its windows all polished, its dining-car tables set and its lamps already glowing!

That was another of those fool dreams of his—of love and happiness, that had tortured him so of late. From the first, almost without quite knowing it, he had been bewitched, stricken with this fever, and could not possibly think of her dying. And afterward, with her broken arm set and her torn diaphragm mended, he had followed her into the private room which he had ordered and had charged to himself (Dorsey must have thought it queer!) and then had waited so restlessly at his club until the next morning, when, standing beside her bed, he had said: "You don't know me, but my name is Garrison—Upham Brainerd Garrison. Perhaps you know of our family here in G———, the Willard Garrisons. I saw you brought in last night. I want to be of service to you if I may, to notify your friends, and be of any other use that I can. May I?"

How well he remembered saying that, formulating it all beforehand, and then being so delighted when she accepted his services with a peculiar, quizzical smile—that odd, evasive glance of hers!

Men struck car wheels this way, no doubt, in order to see that they were not broken, liable to fly to pieces when the train was running fast and so destroy the lives of all!

And then she had given him her address—her mother's, rather, to whom he went at once, bringing her back with him. And so glad he was to know that there was only her mother, no husband or— And the flowers he had sent. And the fruit. And the gifts generally, everything he thought she might like! And then that queer friendship with Idelle afterwards, his quickly realized dream of bliss when she had let him call on her daily, not telling him anything of herself, of course, evading him rather, and letting him think what he would, but tolerating him! Yes, she had played her game fair enough, no doubt, only he was so eager to believe that everything was going to be perfect with them—smooth, easy, lasting, bliss always. What a fool of love he really was!

What a disgusting fat woman coming in with all her bags! Would this train never start?

At that time—how sharply it had all burned itself into his memory!—he had found her living as a young widow with her baby daughter at her mother's, only she wasn't a widow really. It was all make-believe. Already she had proved a riant scoffer at the conventions, a wastrel, only then he did not know that. Where he thought he was making an impression on a fairly unsophisticated girl, or at least one not roughly used by the world, in reality he was merely a new sensation to her, an incident, a convenience, something to lift her out of a mood or a dilemma in which she found herself. Although he did not know it then, one of two quarreling men had just attempted to kill her via that automobile accident and she had been wishing peace, escape from her own thoughts and the attentions of her two ardent wooers, for the time being, at the time he met her. But apart from these, even, there were others, or had been before them, a long line apparently of almost disgusting—but no, he could not say quite that—creatures with whom she had been—well, why say it? And he had fancied for the moment that he was the big event in her life—or might be! He!

But even so, what difference did all that make either, if only she would love him now? What would he care who or what she was, or what she had done before, if only she really cared for him as much as he cared for her—or half as much—or even a minute portion! But Idelle could never care for anyone really, or at least not for him, or him alone, anyway. She was too restless, too fond of variety in life. Had she not, since the first six or seven months in which she had known and married him, little more than tolerated him? She did not really need to care for anybody; they all cared for her, sought her.

At last they were going!

Too many men of station and means—younger than himself, as rich or richer, far more clever and fascinating in every way than he would ever be (or she would think so because she really liked a gayer, smarter type than he had ever been or ever could

236

be now)—vied with him for her interest, and had with each other before ever he came on the scene. She was, in her queer way, a child of fortune, a genius of passion and desire, really. Life would use her well for some time yet, whatever she did to him or any other person, or whatever he sought to do to her in revenge, if he ever did, because she was interesting and desirable. Why attempt to deny that? She was far too attractive yet, too clever, too errant, too indifferent, too spiritually free, to be neglected by anyone yet, let alone by such seeking, avid, pleasure lovers as always followed her. And because she wouldn't allow him to interfere (that was the basis on which she had agreed to marry him, her personal freedom) she had always been able to go and do and be what she chose, nearly, just as she was going and doing now.

These wide yards and that ruck of shabby yellow-and-black houses, begrimed and dirty externally, and internally no doubt, with souls in them nearly as drab, perhaps. How much better it was to be rich like himself and Idelle; only she valued her station so lightly!

Always, wherever he went these days, and his affairs prevented him from being with her very much, she was in his mind—what she was doing, where she was going, with whom she might be now—ah, the sickening thought, with whom she might be now, and where—with that young waster Keene, possibly, with his millions, his shooting preserve and his yacht; or Browne, equally young and still in evidence, though deserted by her to marry him, Garrison; or Coulstone, with whom Idelle had had that highly offensive affair in Pittsburgh five years before, when she was only eighteen. Eighteen! The wonder year! He, too, was here in G——— now after all these years, this same Coulstone, and after Idelle had left him once! Yes, he was hanging about her again, wanting her to come back and marry him, although each of them had remarried!

That flock of crows flying across that distant field!

Of course, Idelle laughed at it, or pretended to. She pretended to be faithful to him, to tell him all this was unavoidable gossip,

237

the aftermath of a disturbing past, before ever she saw him. But could he believe her? Was she not really planning so to do— leave him and return to Coulstone, this time legally? How could he tell? But think of the vagaries of human nature and character, the conniving and persuasive power of a man of wealth like Coulstone. He had left his great business in Pittsburgh to come here to G——— in order to be near her and annoy him (Garrison) really—not her, perhaps—with his pleas and crazy fascination and adoration when she was now safely and apparently happily married! Think of the strangeness, the shame, the peculiarity of Idelle's earlier life! And she still insisted that this sort of thing was worthwhile! All his own station and wealth and adoration were not enough—because he could not be eight or ten people at once, no doubt. But why should he worry? Why not let her go? To the devil with her, anyhow! She merely pretended to love him in her idle, wanton spirit, because she could—well, because she could play at youth and love!

Barkersburg—a place of 30,000, and the train not stopping! The sun, breaking through for just one peep at this gray day, under those trees!

The trouble with his life, as Garrison now saw it, was that throughout it for the last twenty years, and before that even, in spite of his youth and money, he had been craving the favor of just such a young, gay, vigorous, attractive creature as Idelle or Jessica—she of his earlier years—and not realizing it, until he met Idelle, his desire. And this craving, of course, had placed him at a disadvantage in dealing with women like them. Years before—all of fourteen now, think of it!—there had been that affair between himself and Jessica, daughter of the rich and fashionable Balloghs, of Lexington, which had ended so disastrously for him. He had been out there on Colonel Ledgebrook's estate attending to some property which belonged to his father when she had crossed his path at the Colonel's house, that great estate in Bourbon County. Then, for the first time really, he had realized the delight of having a truly beautiful girl interested in him, and him alone, of being really attracted to him— for a little while. It was wonderful.

238

The smothered clang of that crossing bell!

But also what a failure! How painful to hark back to that, and yet how could he avoid it? Although it had seemed to end so favorably—he having been able to win and marry her—still in reality it had ended most disastrously, she having eventually left him as she did. Jessica, too, was like Idelle in so many ways, as young, as gay, nearly as forceful, not as pretty, and not with Idelle's brains. You had to admit that in connection with Idelle. She had more brains, force, self-reliance, intuition, than most women he knew anything about, young or old.

But to return to Jessica. At first she seemed to think he was wonderful, a man of the world, clever, witty, a lover of light, frivolous, foolish things, such as dancing, drinking, talking idle nonsense, which he was not at all. Yes, that was where he had always failed, apparently, and always would. He had no flair, and clever women craved that.

That flock of pigeons on that barn roof!

At bottom really he had always been slow, romantic, philosophic, meditative, while trying in the main to appear something else, whereas these other men, those who were so successful with women at least, were hard and gay and quick and thoughtless, or so he thought. They said and did things more by instinct than he ever could, were successful—well, just because they were what they were. You couldn't do those things by just trying to. And gay, pretty, fascinating women, such as Idelle or Jessica, the really worthwhile ones, seemed to realize this instinctively and to like that kind and no other. When they found a sober and reflective man like himself, or one even inclined to be, they drew away from him. Yes, they did; not consciously always, but just instinctively. They wanted only men who tingled and sparkled and glittered like themselves. To think that love must always go by blind instinct instead of merit—genuine, adoring passion!

This must be Phillipsburg coming into view! He couldn't mistake that high, round water tower!

239

Ah, the tragedy of seeing and knowing this and not being able to remedy it, of not being able to make oneself over into something like that! Somehow, Jessica had been betrayed by his bog-fire resemblance to the thing which she took him to be. He was a bog fire and nothing more, in so far as she was concerned, all she thought he was. Yet because he was so hungry, no doubt, for a woman of her type he had pretended that he was "the real thing," as she so liked to describe a gay character, a man of habits, bad or good, as you choose; one who liked to gamble, shoot, race, and do a lot of things which he really did not care for at all, but which the crowd or group with which he was always finding himself, or with whom he hoped to appear as somebody, was always doing and liking.

These poor countrymen, always loitering about their village stations!

And the women they ran with were just like them, like Jessica, like Idelle—smart, showy and liked that sort of man—and so—

Well, he had pretended to be all that and more, when she (Jessica) had appeared out of that gay group, petite, blonde (Idelle was darker), vivacious, drawn to him by his seeming reality as a man of the world and a gay cavalier. She had actually fallen in love with him at sight, as it were, or seemed to be at the time—she!—and then, see what had happened! Those awful months in G——— after she had returned with him! The agonies of mind and body!

If only that stout traveling man in that gray suit would cease staring at him! It must be the horn-rimmed glasses he had on which interested him so! These Midwestern people!

Instantly almost, only a few weeks after they were married, she seemed to realize that she had made a mistake. It seemed not to make the slightest difference to her, after the first week or so, that they were married or that he was infatuated with her or that he was who he was or that her every move and thought were beautiful to him. On the contrary, it seemed only to irritate her

240

all the more. She seemed to sense then—not before—that he was really the one man not suited to her by temperament or taste or ideas, not the kind she imagined she was getting, and from then on there were the most terrible days, terrible—

That pretty girl turning in at that village gate!

Trying, depressing, degrading really. What dark frowns used to flash across her face like clouds at that time—she was nineteen to his thirty-four, and so pretty!—the realization, perhaps, that she had made a mistake. What she really wanted was the gay, anachronistic, unthinking, energetic person he had seemed to be under the stress of life at Ledgebrook's, not the quiet, reasoning, dreamy person he really was. It was terrible!

Tall trees made such shadowy aisles at evening!

Finally she had run away, disappearing completely one morning after telling him she was going shopping, and then never seeing him any more—ever—not even once! A telegram from Harrisburg had told him that she was going to her mother's and for him not to follow her, please; and then before he could make up his mind really what to do had come that old wolf Caldwell, the famous divorce lawyer of G———, representing her mother, no doubt, and in smooth, ingratiating, persuasive tones had talked about the immense folly of attempting to adjust natural human antipathies, the sadness of all human inharmonies, the value of quiet in all attempts at separation, the need he had to look after his own social prestige in G———, and the like, until finally Caldwell had persuaded him to accept a decree of desertion in some Western state in silence and let her go out of his life forever! Think of that!

The first call for dinner! Perhaps he had better go at once and have it over with! He wanted to retire early tonight!

But Jessica—how she had haunted him for years after that! The whole city seemed to suggest her at times, even after he heard that she was married again and the mother of two children, so strong was the feeling for anything one lost. Even to this day certain corners in G——, the Brandingham, where they had lived temporarily at first; Mme. Gateley's dressmaking establishment, where she had had her gowns made, and the Tussockville entrance to the park—always touched and hurt him like some old, dear, poignant melody.

How this train lurched as one walked! The crashing couplings between these cars!

And then, after all these busy, sobering years, in which he had found out that there were some things he was not and could not be—a gay, animal man of the town, for instance, a "blood," a waster; and some things that he was—a fairly capable financial and commercial man, a lover of literature of sorts, and of horses, a genial and acceptable person in many walks of society—had come Idelle.

Think of the dining car being crowded thus early! And such people!

He was just settling down to a semi-resigned acceptance of himself as an affectional, emotional failure in so far as women were concerned, when she had come—Idelle—this latest storm which had troubled him so much. Idelle had brains, beauty, force, insight—more than Jessica ever had had, or was he just older?— and that was what made her so attractive to men, so indifferent to women, so ready to leave him to do all the worshiping. She could understand him, apparently, at his time of life, with his sober and in some ways sad experiences, and sympathize with him most tenderly when she chose, and yet, strangely enough, she could ignore him also and be hard, cruel, indifferent. The way she could neglect him at times—go her own way! God!

Not a bad seat, only now it was too dark to see anything outside! These heavy forks!

But to return to that dreadful pagan youth of hers, almost half-savage: take that boy who shot himself at the age of sixteen

242

for love of her, and all because she would not run away with him, not caring for him at all, as she said, or she would have gone! What a sad case that was—as she had told it, at least. The boy's father had come and denounced her to her parents in her own home, according to her, and still she denied that it had been her fault. And those other two youths, one of whom had embezzled $10,000 and spent it on her and several other boys and girls! And that other one who had stolen five hundred in small sums from his father's till and safe and then wasted it on her and her companions at country inns until he was caught! Those country clubs! Those little rivers she described, with their canoes—the automobiles of these youths—the dancing, eating, drinking life under the moon in the warmth of spring and summer under the trees! And he had never had anything like that, never! When one of the boys, being caught, complained of her to his parents as the cause of his evil ways she had denied it, or so she said, and did still to this day, saying she really did not know he was stealing the money and calling him coward or crybaby. Idelle told him of this several years ago as though it had some humorous aspects, as possibly it had, to her—who knows? but with some remorse, too, for she was not wholly indifferent to the plight of these youths, although she contended that what she had given them of her time and youth and beauty was ample compensation. Yes, she was a bad woman, really, or had been—a bad girl, say what one would, a child of original evil impulse. One could not deny that really. But what fascination also, even yet, and then no doubt—terrible! He could understand the actions of those youths, their recklessness. There was something about sheer beauty, evil though it might be, which overcame moral prejudices or scruples. It had done so in his case, or why was he living with her? And so why not in theirs?

How annoying to have a train stop in a station while you were eating!

Beauty, beauty, beauty! How could one gainsay the charm or avoid the lure of it? Not he, for one. Trig, beautiful women, who carried themselves with an air and swing and suggested by their every movement passion, alertness, gayety of mind! The church bells might ring and millions of religionists preach of a life hereafter with a fixed table of rewards and punishments, but what did anyone know of the future, anyhow? Nothing! Exactly nothing, in spite of all the churches. Life appeared and disappeared again; a green door opened and out you went, via a train wreck, for instance, on a night like this. All these farmers here tilling their fields and making their little homes and towns—where would they be in forty or fifty years, with all their moralities? No, here and now was life, here and now beauty—here and now Idelle, or creatures like her and Jessica.

He would pay his bill and go into the smoker for a change. It would be pleasant to sit there until his berth was made up.

Then, take that affair of the banker's son, young Gratiot it was, whom he knew well even now here in G———, only Gratiot did not know that he knew—or did he? Perhaps he was still friendly with Idelle, although she denied it. You could never really believe her. He it was, according to her, who had captured her fancy with his fine airs and money and car when she was only seventeen, and then robbed her (or could you call it robbery in Idelle's case, seeking, restless creature that she was?) of her indifferent innocence. No robbery there, surely, whatever she might say. How wonderful she must have been then, though! How courageously—or at least according to her—she had gone through that whole experience, entering upon it in the first instance with bravado (his waiting car in those side streets near her home!), then evading observation and detection by her parents by going all alone across the river to Pittsburgh while pretending to visit a girl friend! That awful wooden house in a back street of Pittsburgh, with its broken wooden shutters! The hag who waited on her! The fears, doubts, determination not to flinch or tell, whatever happened!! Somebody ought to, or could, make a story out of that, only no one would ever read it—no decent person at least. It seemed at times as though she might almost have been the unconscious victim of her own disposition, a something working through her like a devil or demon, at other times as though she were incurably, hopelessly bad, as in the light, of her present drifting back into her old ways. And yet she had

244

her good qualities, too. Note her generosity to her mother, her persistent love and genuine understanding of and sympathy with her, and her generosity in all ways to so many others—waiters, chauffeurs, porters, clerks. She was never vicious, snappish, cynical, unfair to them—just pleasant, or at most unconscious of them.

Those fascinating coke ovens blazing in the dark beside the track, mile after mile!

Somehow her telling him these things at first, or rather shortly after they were married and when she was going to make a clean breast of everything and lead a better life, had thrown a wonderful glamour over her past.

"Gay Stories"! What a name for a magazine! And that stout old traveling man reading it!

What a strange thing it was to be a girl like that—with passions and illusions like that! perhaps, after all, life only came to those who sought it with great strength and natural gifts. But how hard it was on those who hadn't anything of that kind! Nevertheless, people should get over the follies of their youth—Idelle should, anyhow. She had had enough, goodness knows. She had been one of the worst—hectic, vastly excited about life, irresponsible—and she should have sobered by now. Why not? Look at all he had to offer her! Was that not enough to effect a change? While it made her interesting at times, this leftover enthusiasm, still it was so ridiculous, and made her non-desirable, too, either as wife or mother. Yet no doubt that was what had made her so fascinating to him, too, at this late day and to all those other men in Pittsburgh and elsewhere—that blazing youthfulness. Strange as it might seem, he could condone Idelle's dreadful deeds even now, just as her mother could, if she would only behave herself, if she would only love him and him alone—but would she? She seemed so determined to bend everything to her service, regardless—to yield nothing to him.

No use! He couldn't stand these traveling men in this smoking room! He must have the porter make up his berth!

And then had come Coulstone, the one who was still hanging about her now, the one with whom she had had that dreadful affair in Pittsburgh, the affair that always depressed him to think about even now. Of course, there was one thing to be said in extenuation of that, if you could say anything at all—which you couldn't really—and that was that Idelle was no longer a good girl then, but experienced and with all her blazing disposition aroused. She had captured the reins of her life then and was doing as she pleased—only why couldn't he have met her then instead of Coulstone? He was alive then. And his own life had always been so empty. When she had confessed so much of all this to him afterward—not this Coulstone affair exactly, but the other things—why hadn't he left her then? He might have and saved himself all this agony—or could he have then? He was twice her age when he married her and knew better, only he thought he could reform her—or did he? Was that the true reason? Could he admit the true reason to himself?

"Yes, make it up right away, if you will!" Now he would have to wait about and be bored!

But somehow, strange as it may seem, fairly worthy people like himself seemed to compound these horrible errors in youth— in women, anyhow, when they were attractive, and in later years also—by accepting the committers of them into love and marriage and respectable social situations, just as he had, and so legitimizing it all, when really one should not do it, of course. It wasn't right, fair to others, like himself—only he had, just the same. Some people wouldn't—his father, for instance, and men of his stamp, but still there were hundreds of others like himself, the younger generation, who would too, just the same. Times were different now to what they had been in his father's day. he had done so, no doubt, largely because this was the closest he could get to the scorching exuberance of youth and pleasure such as Idelle and her kind represented—and there must be others like him, lots of them.

246

That clanging crossing bell in the darkness!

But to come back to the story of Coulstone and all that hectic life in Pittsburgh. Coulstone, it seems, had been one of four or five very wealthy young managing vice-presidents of the Iverson-Centelever Frog and Switch Company, of Pittsburgh. And Idelle, because her father had suddenly died after her affair with young Gratiot, never knowing a thing about it, and her mother, not knowing quite what to do with her, had (because Idelle seemed to wish it) sent her to stay with an aunt in Pittsburgh. But the aunt having to leave for a time shortly after Idelle reached there, a girl friend had, at Idelle's instigation, apparently, suggested that she stay with her until the aunt's return, and Idelle had then persuaded her mother to agree to that.

That tall, lanky girl having to sleep in that upper berth opposite! European sleeping cars were so much better!

Her girl friend was evidently something like Idelle, or even worse. At any rate, Idelle appeared to have been able to wind her around her finger. For through her she had found some method of being introduced to a few of these smart new-rich men of the town (or letting them introduce themselves), among them two of these same vice-presidents, one of whom was Coulstone. According to Idelle, he was a lavish and even reckless spender, wanting it to appear generally that he could do anything and have anything that money could buy, and liking to be seen in as many as a dozen public places in one afternoon or evening, especially at weekends, only there weren't so many in Pittsburgh at the time.

This must be Centerfield, the state capital of E——, they were now passing without a pause! These expresses cut through so many large cities!

From the first, so Idelle said, he had made violent love to her, though he was already married (unhappily, of course), and she, caring nothing for the conventions and not being of the kind that obeys any laws (willful, passionate, reckless), had received him probably in exactly the spirit in which he approached her, if not more so. That was the worst of her, her constant, willful, pagan pursuit of pleasure, regardless of anybody or anything, and it still held her in spite of him. There was something revolting about the sheer animality of it, that rushing together of two people, regardless. Still, if it had been himself and Idelle now—

How fortunate that he had been able to obtain a section! At least he would have air!

There had been a wild season, according to her own admissions or boastings—he could never quite tell which—extending over six or seven months, during which time Idelle had pretended to her mother, so she said, to prefer to live with her girl friend rather than return home, when in reality she was living with this same Coulstone, or being maintained by him at least in one of the best apartment houses in Pittsburgh. She had had, according to her, her machine, her servants, clothes without end, and what not—a dreamworld of luxury and freedom which he had provided and from which she never expected to wake, and her mother totally ignorant of it all the while! There had been everything she wished at her finger tips—hectic afternoons, evenings and midnights; affairs at country clubs or hotel grills, where the young bloods of the city and their girls congregated; wild rides in automobiles; visits to the nearest smartest watering places, and the like. Or was she lying? He could scarcely think so, judging by her career with him and others since.

Ah, what a comfort to fix oneself this way and rest, looking at the shadowy moonlit landscape passing by!

Idelle had often admitted or boasted that she had been wildly happy—and that was the worst of it—that she had not quite realized what she was doing, but that she had no remorse either, even now—that she had lived! (And why should she have, perhaps? Weren't all people really selfish at bottom—or were they?) Only, owing to her almost insatiable pagan nature, there were other complications right then and there—think of that!—an older rival millionaire, if you please, richer by far than Coulstone, and more influential locally . . . and younger ones, too, who

248

sought her but really did not win her, she having no time or plan for them. As it happened, the older one, having been worsted in the contest but being partially tolerated by her, had become frantically jealous and envious, although "he had no right," as she said, and had finally set about making trouble for the real possessor, and succeeded to the extent of exposing him and eventually driving him out of the great concern with which he was connected and out of Pittsburgh, too, if you please, on moral grounds (!), although he himself was trying to follow in Coulstone's footsteps! And all for the love or possession of a nineteen-year-old girl, a petticoat, a female ne'er-do-well! How little the world in general knew of such things—and it was a blessed thing, too, by George! Where would things be if everybody went on like that?

The rhythmic clack of these wheels and trucks over these sleeper joints—a poetic beat, of sorts!

But Idelle was so naive about all this now, or pretended to be, so careless of what he or anyone else might think in case they ever found out. She did not seem to guess how much he might suffer by her telling him all this, or how much pain thinking about it afterward might cause him. She was too selfish intellectually. She didn't even guess, apparently, what his mood might be toward all this, loving her as he did. No—she really didn't care for him, or anyone else—couldn't, or she couldn't have done anything like that. She would have lied to him rather. She had been, and was—although now semi-reformed—a heartless, careless wastrel, thinking of no one but herself. She had not cared about the wives of either of those two men who were pursuing her in Pittsburgh, or what became of them, or what became of any of the others who had pursued her since. All she wanted was to be danced attendance on, to be happy, free, never bored. The other fellow never counted with Idelle much. In this case the wife of the younger lover, Coulstone, had been informed, the conservatives of the city appealed to, as it were. Coulstone, seeing the storm and being infatuated with his conquest, suggested Paris or a few years on the Riviera, but, strangely enough, Idelle would have none of it, or him, then. She wouldn't agree to be tied down for

249

so long! She had suffered a reversal of conscience or mood—even—or so she said—went to a priest, went into retirement here in G———, having fled her various evil pursuers, and all but betrayed the sad, lonely father who was seeking only to comfort her—only she had suffered a qualm and betrayed him too, at the last, fearing her own intentions in regard to him, the horror of offending against the religious mood which she had once held in regard to this great church, the vicars and representatives generally.

How impressive the outlying slopes of these mountains they were just entering!

And yet he could understand that, too, in some people, anyhow—the one decent thing in her life maybe, a timely revolt against a too great and unbroken excess. But, alas, it had been complicated by the fact that she wasn't ready to leave her mother or to do anything but stay in America. Besides things were becoming rather complicated. The war on Coulstone threatened to expose her. Worse yet—and so like her, life had won her back. Her beauty, her disposition, youth and age pursuing her—one slight concession to indulgence or pleasure after another and the new mood or bent toward religiosity was entirely done away with. Coulstone had hunted her up, found her again. He had renewed his attentions, his proffers of money, as his right—the child, you know, now on the scene. Her sensual sex nature had conquered, of course.

That little cabin on that slope, showing a lone lamp in the dark!

And then—then—

Morning, by George! Ten o'clock! He had been asleep all this time! He would have to hurry and dress now!

But where was he in regard to Idelle? Oh yes! . . . How she haunted him all the time these days! Coulstone, angered at her refusal to come with him again (she could not bring herself to do that, for all her religiosity, she said, not caring for him so

250

much any more), but frightened by the presence of others, had eventually transferred all his interests from Pittsburgh to G——, and at this very time, on the ground of some form of virtue or duty—God only knows what!—five years later, indeed—was here in G—— with his wife and attempting to persuade her that she ought to give him a divorce in order to permit him to marry Idelle and so legitimize her child! And he, Garrison, already married to her! The insanity of mankind!

He must be hurrying through his breakfast; they would soon be nearing G—— now . . . and he must not forget to stop in at Kiralfy's when he reached G—— and buy some flowers for her!

But Idelle was not to be taken that way. She did not care for Coulstone any more, or so she said. Besides nothing would cure her varietism then or now but age, apparently. And who was going to wait for age to overtake her? Not he, anyhow. Why, the very event that threw her into his arms—couldn't he have judged by that if he had had any sense? Wasn't that just such another affair as that of Coulstone and old Candia, only in this case it concerned much younger men—wasters in their way, too—one of whom, at least, was plainly madly in love with her, while the other was just intensely interested. Why was it that Idelle's affairs always had to be a complex of two or more contending parties?

The condition of these washrooms in the morning!

According to her own story, she had first fallen in love, or thought she had, with the younger of the two, Gaither Browne, of the Harwood Brownes here in G—— and then while he was still dancing attendance on her (and all the while Coulstone was in the background, not entirely pushed out of her life) young Gatchard Keene had come along with his motor cars, his yacht, his stable of horses, and she had begun to flirt with him also. Only, by then—and she didn't care particularly for him, either—

What a crowded breakfast car—all the people of last night, and more from other cars attached since, probably!

251

—she had half promised young Browne that she would marry him, or let him think she might; had even confessed a part of her past to him (or so she said) and he had forgiven her, or said it didn't matter. But when Keene came along and she began to be interested in him Browne did not like this new interest in the least, became furiously jealous indeed. So great was his passion for her that he had threatened to kill her and himself if she did not give up Keene, which, according to her, made her care all the more for Keene. When Browne could stand it no longer and was fearful lest Keene was to capture the prize—which he was not, of course, Idelle being a mere trifler at all stages—he had invited her out on that disastrous automobile ride—

A mere form, eating, this morning! No appetite—due to his troubled thoughts, of course, these days!

—which had ended in her being carried into his presence at the Insull General. Browne must have been vividly in love with her to prefer to kill himself and her in that fashion rather than lose her, for, according to her, he had swung the car squarely into the rocks at Saltair Brook, only it never came out in the papers, and neither Idelle nor Browne would tell.

All railway cars seemed so soiled toward the end of a ride like this!

She professed afterwards to be sorry for Browne and inquired after him every day, although, of course, she had no sympathy for him or Keene either—for no man whom she could engage in any such contest. She was too wholly interested in following her own selfish bent. Afterward, when Keene was calling daily and trying to find out how it really did happen, and Coulstone was still in evidence and worrying over her condition (and old Candia also, he presumed—how could he tell whom all she had in tow at that time?), she refused to tell them, or any of a half dozen others who came to inquire. Yet right on top of all that she had encouraged him, Garrison, to fall in love with her, and had even imagined herself, or so she sneeringly charged, whenever they quarreled, in love with him, ready to reform and lead a better

252

life, and had finally allowed him to carry her off and marry her in the face of them all! What were you to make of a creature like that? Insanity, on his or her part? Or both? Both, of course.

Kenelm! They were certainly speeding on! Those four wooden cows in that field, advertising a brand of butter!

But she could be so agreeable when she chose to be, and was so fascinatingly, if irritatingly, beautiful all the time!

There was no doubt, though, that things were now reaching such a state that there would have to be a change. He couldn't stand this any longer. Women like Idelle were menaces, really, and shouldn't be tolerated. Most men wouldn't stand for her, although he had. But why? Why? Well, because he loved her, that was why, and you couldn't explain love. And the other reason—the worst of all—was the dread he had been suffering of late years of being left alone again if she left him. Alone! It was a terrible feeling, this fear of being left alone in the future, and especially when you were so drawn to someone who, whatever her faults, could make you idyllically happy if she only would. Lord, how peculiar these love passions of people were, anyhow! How they swayed one! Tortured one! Here he was haunted all the time now by the knowledge that he would be miserable if she left him, and that he needed someone like her to make him happy, a cheerful and agreeable beauty when she chose to be, fascinating even when she was not, and yet knowing that he would have to learn to endure to be alone if ever he was to get the strength to force her to better ways. Why couldn't he? Or why couldn't she settle down and be decent once? Well, he would have to face this out with her, once and for all now. He wasn't going to stand for her carrying on in this fashion. She must sober down. She had had her way long enough now, by God! He just wasn't going to pose as her husband and be a shield for her any longer! No sir, by George!

Only thirty-eight miles more! If she were not there now, as she promised!

Beginning today she would have to give him a decent deal or he would leave her. He wouldn't—he couldn't—stand for it any longer. Think of that last time he had come on from K———, just as he was coming today, and she had agreed to be at home— because he had made her promise before going that she would— and then, by George, when he got off the train and walked into the Brandingham with Arbuthnot to telephone, having just told Arbuthnot that he expected to find her out at the house, wasn't she there with young Keene and four or five others, drinking and dancing?

"Why, there's your wife now, Garrison," Arbuthnot had laughingly jested, and he had had to turn it all off with that "Oh, yes, that's right! I forgot! She was to meet me here. How stupid of me!"

Why hadn't he made a scene then? Why hadn't he broken things up then? Because he was a blank-blanked fool, that's why, allowing her to pull him around by the nose and do as she pleased! Love, that's why! He was a damned fool for loving her as much as he did, and in the face of all he knew!

Nearing Shively! Colonel Brandt's stock-farm! Home soon now! That little town in the distance, no connection with the railroad at all!

On that particular occasion, when at last they were in a taxi, she had begun one of her usual lies about having come downtown for something—a romper for Tatty—only when he ventured to show her what she was doing to herself and him socially, that he was being made a fool of, and that he really couldn't stand it, hadn't she flown into the usual rage and exclaimed: "Oh, all right! Why don't you leave me then? I don't care! I don't care! I'm bored! I can't help it! I can't always sit out in Sicard Avenue waiting for you!"

In Sicard Avenue. And that on top of always refusing to stay out there or to travel with him anywhere or to meet him and go places! Think of that for a happy married life, will you? Love! Love! Yes, love! Hell!

Well, here was Lawndale now, only eighteen miles—that meant about eighteen minutes from here, the way they were running now—and he would soon see her now if she was at home.

254

If she only were, just this one time, to kiss him and laugh and ask about the trip and how he had made out, and let him propose some quiet dinner somewhere for just the two of them, a quiet dinner all to themselves, and then home again! How delightful that would be! Only— No doubt Charles would be at the station with the jitney, as he always called the yellow racer. He would have to summon all his ease to make his inquiry, for one had to keep one's face before the servants, you know—but then it was entirely possible that Charles wouldn't know whether she was home or not. She didn't always tell the servants. If she wasn't there, though—and after that letter and telegram— Well—now—this time!—by God!—

Wheelwright! They were running a little later, perhaps, but they would enter the station nearly on time!

But take, again, that last affair, that awful scene in the Shackamaxon at C———, when without his knowing it she had gone down there with Bodine and Arbuthnot and that wretched Aikenhead. Think of being seen in a public place like the Shackamaxon with Aikenhead and two such other wasters (even if Mrs. Bodine were along—she was no better than the others!), when she was already married and under so much suspicion as it was. If it weren't for him she would have been driven out of society long ago! Of course she would have! Hadn't General and Mrs. de Pasy cut her dead on that occasion?—only when they saw that he had joined her they altered their expressions and were polite enough, showing what they *would* do if they had to deal with her alone.

That brown automobile racing this train! How foolish some automobilists were!

Well, that time, coming home and finding her away, he had run down to C——— on the chance of finding her there—and sure enough there she was dancing with Aikenhead and Bodine by turns, and Mrs. Bodine and that free Mrs. Gildas and Belle Geary joining them later. And when he had sought her out to let her know he was back quite safe and anxious to see her, hadn't

she turned on him with all the fury of a wildcat—"Always following me up and snooping around after me to catch me in
something!" and that almost loud enough for all the others to
hear! It was terrible! How could anybody stand for such a thing!
He couldn't, and retain his self-respect. And yet he had—yes, he
had, more shame to him! But if it hadn't been that he had been
so lonely just beforehand and so eager to see her, and hadn't had
those earrings for her in his pocket—thinking they would please
her—perhaps he wouldn't have done as he did, backed down so.
As it was—well, all he could think of at the moment was to
apologize—to his own wife!—and plead that he hadn't meant
to seem to follow her up and "snoop around." Think of that!
Hang it all, why hadn't he left her then and there? Supposing
she didn't come back? Supposing she didn't? What of it? What
of it? Only—

"This way out, please."

Well, here was G——— at last, and there was Charles, well
enough, waiting as usual. Would she be home now? Would she?
Perhaps, after all, he had better not say anything yet, just go
around to Kiralfy's and get the flowers. But to what end, really,
if she weren't there again? What would he do this time? Surely
this must be the end if she weren't there, if he had any strength
at all. He wouldn't be put upon in this way again, would he?—
after all he had told himself he would do the last time if ever it
happened again! His own reputation was at stake now, really.
It depended on what he did now. What must the servants think—
his always following her up and she never being there or trou-
bling about him in the least?

"Ah, Charles, there you are! To Kiralfy's first, then home!"

She was making him a laughingstock, or would if he didn't
take things in hand pretty soon today, really—a man who hung
onto a woman because she was young and pretty, who tolerated
a wife who did not care for him and who ran with other men—a
sickening, heartless social pack—in his absence. She was pulling
him down to her level, that's what she was doing, a level he had

256

never deemed possible in the old days. It was almost unbelievable—and yet— But he would go in and get the flowers, anyway!

"Back in a minute, Charles!"

And now here was Sicard Avenue, again, dear old Sicard, with its fine line of trees on either side of its broad roadway, and their own big house set among elms and with that French garden in front—so quiet and aristocratic! Why couldn't she be content with a place like this, with her present place in society? Why not? Why not be happy in it? She could be such an interesting social figure if she chose, if she would only try. But no, no—she wouldn't. It would always be the same until—until—

The gardener had trimmed the grass again, and nicely!

"No, suh, Mr. Garrison," George was already saying in that sing-song darky way of his as he walked up the steps ahead of him, and just as he expected or feared he would. It was always the way, and always would be until he had courage enough to leave once and for all—as he would today, by George! He wouldn't stand for this one moment longer—not one. "Mrs. Garrison she say she done gone to Mrs. Gildas' " (it might just as well have been the Bodines, the Del Guardias or the Cranes—they were all alike), "an' dat yo' was to call her up dere when yo' come in or come out. She say to say she lef' a note fo' yo' on yo' dresser."

Curse her! Curse her! Curse her! To be treated like this all the time! He would fix her now, though, this time! Yes, he would. This time he wouldn't change his mind.

And the brass on the front door not properly cleaned either!

"George," this to his servant as the latter preceded him into his room—their room—where he always so loved to be when things were well between them, "never mind the bags now. I'll call you later when I want you," and then, as the door closed, almost glaring at everything about him. There in the mirror, just

257

above his military brushes, was stuck a note—the usual wheedling, chaffering rot she was inclined to write him when she wanted to be very nice on such occasions as this. Now he would see what new lying, fool communication she had left for him, where he would be asked to come now, what do, instead of her being here to receive him as she had promised, as was her duty really, as any decent married woman would—as any decent married man would expect her to be. Oh, the devil!

That fly buzzing in the window there, trying to get out!

What was the use of being alive, anyway? What the good of anything—money or anything else? He wouldn't stand for this any longer, he couldn't—no, he couldn't, that was all there was to it! She could go to the devil now; he wouldn't follow her any more—never, never, never—the blank-blank-blank-blank—! This was the end! This was the way she was always doing! But never again now, not once more! He'd get a divorce now! Now, by George, for once he would stand his ground and be a man, not a social door mat, a humble beggar of love, hanging around hat in hand waiting for her favors! Never again, by God! Never!! Never!!! Only—

That letter of hers on the dresser there waiting for him, as usual!

"Dearest Old Judge: This isn't the real one. This is just a hundred-kiss one, this. The real one is pinned to your pillow over there—our pillow—where it ought to be, don't you think? I don't want you to be unhappy at not finding me home, Judgie, see? And I don't want you to get mad and quarrel. And I do want you to be sure to find the other letter. So don't be angry, see? But call me up at the Gildas'. I'm dying to see you, dearie, really and truly I am! I've been so lonesome without you! (Yes!) You're sure to find me out there. And you're not to be angry—not one little frown, do you hear? I just couldn't help it, dearest! So read the other letter now!

"Idelle"

258

If only his hands wouldn't tremble so! Damn her! Damn her!
Damn her! To think she would always treat him like this! To think
he was never to have one decent hour of her time to himself, not one!
Always this running here, there and everywhere away from him, as
it were!

He crumpled up the note and threw it on the floor, then went
to the window and looked out. There over the way at her own
spacious door was young Mrs. Justus just entering her car—a
simple, home-loving little woman, who would never dream of
the treacheries and eccentricities of Idelle; who, if she even guessed
what manner of woman she was, would never have anything more
to do with her. Why couldn't he have loved a girl like her—why
not? And just beyond, the large quiet house of the Walterses,
those profoundly sober people of the very best ways and means,
always so kind and helpful, anxious to be sociable, of whom Idelle
could think of nothing better to say than "stuffy." Anything kind
and gentle and orderly was just stuffy to her, or dull. That was
what she considered him, no doubt. That's because she was what
she was, curses on her! She couldn't stand, or even understand,
profoundly worthy people like the Justuses or the Walterses.
(There was May Walters now at her dining-room window.) And
then there were the Hartleys. . . . But that other note of hers—
what did it say? He ought to read that now, whether he left or
no; but he would leave this time, well enough!

He turned to the twin bed and from the fretted counterpane
unpinned the second lavender-colored and scented note—the kind
Idelle was always scribbling when she was doing things she
shouldn't. It didn't make one hanged bit of difference now what
she wrote, of course—only— He wouldn't follow her this time;
no, he wouldn't! He wouldn't have anything more to do with
her ever! He would quit now, lock the doors in a few minutes,
discharge the servants, cut off her allowance, tell her to go to
blazes. He would go and live at a club, as he had so often threatened before to himself—or get out of G———, as he had also
threatened. He couldn't stand the comment that would follow,
anyhow. He had had enough of it. He hated the damned city!
He had never had any luck in it. Never had he been happy here,
in spite of the fact that he had been born and brought up here,

259

and twice married here—never! Twice now he had been treated like this by women right here in this city, his home town, where everybody knew! Twice he had been made a fool of, but this time—

The letter, though!

"Dearest and best of hubbies," he read in spite of himself, setting his firm, even jaws as he did so. He looked older, grayer, sadder by years. "I know you're going to be disappointed at not finding me here, and in spite of anything I can say, probably terribly angry, too. (I wish you wouldn't be, darling!) But, sweetheart, if you'll only believe me this time (I've said that before when you wouldn't, I know, and it wasn't my fault, either), it wasn't premeditated, really, it wasn't! Honest, cross my heart, dear, twenty ways, and hope to die!"

(What did she really care for his disappointment or what he suffered, curse her!)

"Only yesterday at four Betty called up and insisted that I should come. There's a big house party on, and you're invited, of course, when you get back. Her cousin Frank is coming and some friends of his,"

(Yes, he knew what friends!)

"and four of my old girl chums, so I just couldn't get out of it, nor would I, particularly since she wanted me to help her, and I've asked her so many times to help us—now, could I?"

Idelle's way in letters, as in person, was always bantering. To the grave with Betty Gildas and all her house parties, in so far as he was concerned, the fast, restless, heartless thing! Why couldn't she have been here just this once, when he wanted her so much and had wired and written in plenty of time for her to be!

But no, she didn't care for him. She never had. She merely wanted to fool him along like this, to keep his name, his position, the social atmosphere he could give her. This whole thing was a joke to her—this house, his friends, himself, all—just nothing! Her idea was to fool him along in this way while she continued to run with these other shabby, swift, restless, insatiable creatures like herself, who liked cabarets, thés dansants, automobile runs to this, that and the other wretched place, country-house parties, country clubs, country this, country that, or New York and all its shallow and heartless mockery of simplicity and peace. Well, he was through. She was always weary of him, never anxious to be with him for one moment even, but never weary of any of them, you bet—of seeking the wildest forms of pleasure! Well, this was the end now. He had had enough. She could go her own way from now on. Let the beastly flowers lie there—what did he care? He wouldn't carry them to her. He was through now. He was going to do what he said—leave. Only—

He began putting some things in another bag, in addition to the ones he had—his silk shirts, extra underwear, all his collars. Once and for all now he wouldn't stand this—never! Never!

Only—

As he fumed and glared, his eye fell on his favorite photo of Idelle—young, rounded, sensuous, only twenty-four to his forty-eight, an air and a manner flattering to any man's sense of vanity and possession—and then, as a contrast, he thought of the hard, smiling, self-efficiency of so many of her friends—Coulstone, for one, still dogging her heels in spite of him, and Keene, young and wealthy, and Arbuthnot—and who not else?—anyone and all of whom would be glad to take her if he left her. And she knew this. It was a part of her strength, even her charm—curse her! Curse her! Curse her!

But more than that, youth, youth, the eternal lure of beauty and vitality, her smiling softness at times, her geniality, her tolerance, their long talks and pleasant evenings and afternoons. And all of these calling, calling now. And yet they were all at the vanishing point, perhaps never to come again, if he left her! She had warned him of that. "If I go," she had once said—more than once, indeed—"it's for good. Don't think I'll ever come back, for I won't." And he understood well enough that she would not. She didn't care for him enough to come back. She never would, if she really went.

He paused, meditating, biting his lips as usual, flushing,

frowning, darkening—a changeable sky his face—and then—

"George," he said after the servant had appeared in answer to his ring, "tell Charles to bring the jitney around again, and you pack me the little brown kit bag out of these others. I'm going away for a day or two, anyhow."

"Yes, suh!"

Then down the stairs, saying that Idelle was a liar, a wastrel, a heartless butterfly, worthy to be left as he proposed to leave her now. Only, once outside in his car with Charles at the wheel, and ready to take him wherever he said, he paused again, and then—sadly— "To the Gildases, and better go by the Skillytown road. It's the shortest!"

Then he fell to thinking again.

The Second Choice

SHIRLEY DEAR:

You don't want the letters. There are only six of them, anyhow, and think, they're all I have of you to cheer me on my travels. What good would they be to you—little bits of notes telling me you're sure to meet me—but me—think of me! If I send them to you, you'll tear them up, whereas if you leave them with me I can dab them with musk and ambergris and keep them in a little silver box, always beside me.

Ah, Shirley dear, you really don't know how sweet I think you are, how dear! There isn't a thing we have ever done together that isn't as clear in my mind as this great big skyscraper over the way here in Pittsburgh, and far more pleasing. In fact, my thoughts of you are the most precious and delicious things I have, Shirley.

But I'm too young to marry now. You know that, Shirley, don't you? I haven't placed myself in any way yet, and I'm so restless that I don't know whether I ever will, really. Only yesterday, old Roxbaum—that's my new employer here—came to me and wanted to know if I would like an assistant overseership on one of his coffee plantations in Java, said there would not be much money in it for a year or two, a bare living, but later there would be more—and I jumped at it. Just the thought of Java and going there did that, although I knew I could make more staying right here. Can't you see how it is with me, Shirl? I'm too restless and too young. I couldn't take care of you right, and you wouldn't like me after a while if I didn't.

But ah, Shirley sweet, I think the dearest things of you! There isn't an hour, it seems, but some little bit of you comes back—a dear, sweet bit—the night we sat on the grass in Tregore Park and counted the stars through the trees; that first evening at Sparrows Point when we missed the last train and had to walk to Langley. Remember the tree-toads, Shirl? And then that warm April Sunday

263

in Atholby woods! Ah, Shirl, you don't want the six notes! Let me keep them. But think of me, will you, sweet, wherever you go and whatever you do? I'll always think of you, and wish that you had met a better, saner man than me, and that I really could have married you and been all you wanted me to be. By-by, sweet. I may start for Java within the month. If so, and you would want them, I'll send you some cards from there—if they have any.

Your worthless,
Arthur.

She sat and turned the letter in her hand, dumb with despair. It was the very last letter she would ever get from him. Of that she was certain. He was gone now, once and for all. She had written him only once, not making an open plea but asking him to return her letters, and then there had come this tender but evasive reply, saying nothing of a possible return but desiring to keep her letters for old times' sake—the happy hours they had spent together.

The happy hours! Oh, yes, yes, yes—the happy hours!

In her memory now, as she sat here in her home after the day's work, meditating on all that had been in the few short months since he had come and gone, was a world of color and light—a color and a light so transfiguring as to seem celestial, but now, alas, wholly dissipated. It had contained so much of all she had desired—love, romance, amusement, laughter. He had been so gay and thoughtless, or headstrong, so youthfully romantic, and with such a love of play and change and to be saying and doing anything and everything. Arthur could dance in a gay way, whistle, sing after a fashion, play. He could play cards and do tricks, and he had such a superior air, so genial and brisk, with a kind of innate courtesy in it and yet an intolerance for slowness and stodginess or anything dull or dingy, such as characterized— But here her thoughts fled from him. She refused to think of anyone but Arthur.

Sitting in her little bedroom now, off the parlor on the ground floor in her home in Bethune Street, and looking out over the Kessels' yard, and beyond that—there being no fences in Bethune Street—over the "yards" or lawns of the Pollards, Bakers, Cryders, and others, she thought of how dull it must all have seemed to him, with his fine imaginative mind and experiences, his love of change and gayety, his atmosphere of something better than she had ever known. How little she had been fitted, perhaps, by beauty or temperament to overcome this—the something—dullness in her work or her home, which possibly had driven him away. For, although many had admired her to date, and she was young and pretty in her simple way and constantly receiving suggestions that her beauty was disturbing to some, still, he had not cared for her—he had gone.

And now, as she meditated, it seemed that this scene, and all that it stood for—her parents, her work, her daily shuttling to and fro between the drug company for which she worked and this street and house—were typical of her life and what she was destined to endure always. Some girls were so much more fortunate. They had fine clothes, fine homes, a world of pleasure and opportunity in which to move. They did not have to scrimp and save and work to pay their own way. And yet she had always been compelled to do it, but had never complained until now—or until he came, and after. Bethune Street, with its commonplace front yards and houses nearly all alike, and this house, so like the others, room for room and porch for porch, and her parents, too, really like all the others, had seemed good enough, quite satisfactory indeed, until then. But now, now!

Here, in their kitchen, was her mother, a thin, pale but kindly woman, peeling potatoes and washing lettuce, and putting a bit of steak or a chop or a piece of liver in a frying pan day after day, morning and evening, month after month, year after year. And next door was Mrs. Kessel doing the same thing. And next door Mrs. Cryder. And next door Mrs. Pollard. But, until now, she had not thought it so bad. But now—now—oh! And on all the porches or lawns all along this street were the husbands and fathers, mostly middle-aged or old men like her father, reading their papers or cutting the grass before dinner, or smoking and meditating afterward. Her father was out in front now, a stooped, forbearing, meditative soul, who rarely had anything to say—leaving it all to his wife, her mother, but who was fond of her in his dull, quiet way. He was a pattern-maker by trade, and had come into possession of this small, ordinary home via years of toil and saving, her mother helping him. They had no particular religion, as he often said, thinking reasonable human conduct a sufficient passport to heaven, but they had gone occasionally to the Methodist Church over in Nicholas Street, and she had once joined it. But of late she had not gone, weaned away by the other commonplace pleasures of her world.

And then in the midst of it, the dull drift of things, as she now saw them to be, he had come—Arthur Bristow—young, energetic, good-looking, ambitious, dreamful, and instanter, and with her never knowing quite how, the whole thing had been changed. He had appeared so swiftly—out of nothing, as it were.

Previous to him had been Barton Williams, stout, phlegmatic, good-natured, well-meaning, who was, or had been before Arthur came, asking her to marry him, and whom she allowed to half assume that she would. She had liked him in a feeble, albeit, as she thought, tender way, thinking him the kind, according to the logic of her neighborhood, who would make her a good husband, and, until Arthur appeared on the scene, had really intended to marry him. It was not really a love match, as she saw now, but she thought it was, which was much the same thing, perhaps. But, as she now recalled, when Arthur came, how the scales fell from her eyes! In a trice, as it were, nearly, there was a new heaven and a new earth. Arthur had arrived, and with him a sense of something different.

Mabel Gove had asked her to come over to her house in Westleigh, the adjoining suburb, for Thanksgiving eve and day, and without a thought of anything, and because Barton was busy handling a part of the work in the dispatcher's office of the Great Eastern and could not see her, she had gone. And then, to her surprise and strange, almost ineffable delight, the moment she had seen him, he was there—Arthur, with his slim, straight figure and dark hair and eyes and clean-cut features, as clean and attractive as those of a coin. And as he had looked at her and smiled and narrated humorous bits of things that had happened to him, something had come over her—a spell—and after dinner, they had all gone round to Edith Barringer's to dance, and there as she had danced with him, somehow, without any seeming boldness on his part, he had taken possession of her, as it were, drawn her close, and told her she had beautiful eyes and hair and such a delicately rounded chin, and that he thought she danced gracefully and was sweet. She had nearly fainted with delight.

"Do you like me?" he had asked in one place in the dance, and, in spite of herself, she had looked up into his eyes, and from that moment she was almost mad over him, could think of nothing else but his hair and eyes and his smile and his graceful figure.

Mabel Gove had seen it all, in spite of her determination that no one should, and on their going to bed later, back at Mabel's home, she had whispered:

"Ah, Shirley, I saw. You like Arthur, don't you?"

"I think he's very nice," Shirley recalled replying, for Mabel knew of her affair with Barton and liked him, "but I'm not crazy over him." And for this bit of treason she had sighed in her dreams nearly all night.

And the next day, true to a request and a promise made by him, Arthur had called again at Mabel's to take her and Mabel to a "movie" which was not so far away, and from there they had gone to an ice-cream parlor, and during it all, when Mabel was not looking, he had squeezed her arm and hand and kissed her neck, and she had held her breath, and her heart had seemed to stop.

"And now you're going to let me come out to your place to see you, aren't you?" he had whispered.

And she had replied, "Wednesday evening," and then written the address on a little piece of paper and given it to him.

But now it was gone, gone!

This house, which now looked so dreary—how romantic it had seemed that first night *he* called—the front room with its commonplace furniture, and later in the spring, the veranda, with its vines just sprouting, and the moon in May. Oh, the moon in May, and June and July, when he was here! How she had lied to Barton to make evenings for Arthur, and occasionally to Arthur to keep him from contact with Barton. She had not even mentioned Barton to Arthur because—because—well, because Arthur was so much better, and somehow (she admitted it to herself now) she had not been sure that Arthur would care for her long, if at all, and then—well, and then, to be quite frank, Barton might be good enough. She did not exactly hate him because she had found Arthur—not at all. She still liked him in a way—he was so kind and faithful, so very dull and straightforward and thoughtful of her, which Arthur was certainly not. Before Arthur had appeared, as she well remembered, Barton had seemed to be plenty good enough—in fact, all that she desired in a pleasant, companionable way, calling for her, taking her places, bringing her flowers and candy, which Arthur rarely did, and for that, if nothing more, she could not help continuing to like him and to feel sorry for him, and, besides, as he had admitted to herself before, if Arthur left her— Weren't his parents better off than hers—and hadn't he a good position for such a man as he—one hundred and fifty dollars a month and the certainty of more later on? A little while before meeting Arthur, she had thought this very good, enough for two to live on at least, and she had thought some of trying it at some time or other—but now—now—

And that first night he had called—how well she remembered it—how it had transfigured the parlor next this in which she was now, filling it with something it had never had before, and the porch outside, too, for that matter, with its gaunt, leafless vine, and this street, too, even—dull, commonplace Bethune Street. There had been a flurry of snow during the afternoon while she was working at the store, and the ground was white with it. All the neighboring homes seemed to look sweeter and happier and more inviting than ever they had as she came past them, with their lights peeping from under curtains and drawn shades. She had hurried into hers and lighted the big red-shaded parlor lamp, her one artistic treasure, as she thought, and put it near the piano, between it and the window, and arranged the chairs, and then bustled to the task of making herself as pleasing as she might. For him she had gotten out her one best filmy house dress and done up her hair in the fashion she thought most becoming— and that he had not seen before—and powdered her cheeks and nose and darkened her eyelashes, as some of the girls at the store did, and put on her new satin slippers, and then, being so arrayed, waited nervously, unable to eat anything or to think of anything but him.

And at last, just when she had begun to think he might not be coming, he had appeared with that arch smile and a "Hello! It's here you live, is it? I was wondering. George, but you're twice as sweet as I thought you were, aren't you?" And then, in the little entryway, behind the closed door, he had held her and kissed her on the mouth a dozen times while she pretended to push against his coat and struggle and say that her parents might hear.

And, oh, the room afterward, with him in it in the red glow of the lamp, and with his pale handsome face made handsomer thereby, as she thought! He had made her sit near him and had held her hands and told her about his work and his dreams—all that he expected to do in the future—and then she had found herself wishing intensely to share just such a life—his life— anything that he might wish to do; only, she kept wondering, with a slight pain, whether he would want her to—he was so young, dreamful, ambitious, much younger and more dreamful than herself, although, in reality, he was several years older.

And then followed that glorious period from December to this late September, in which everything which was worth happening in love had happened. Oh, those wondrous days the following spring, when, with the first burst of buds and leaves, he had taken her one Sunday to Atholby, where all the great woods were, and they had hunted spring beauties in the grass, and sat on a slope and looked at the river below and watched some boys fixing up a sailboat and setting forth in it quite as she wished she and Arthur might be doing—going somewhere together—far, far away from all commonplace things and life! And then he had slipped his arm about her and kissed her cheek and neck, and tweaked her ear and smoothed her hair—and oh, there on the grass, with the spring flowers about her and a canopy of small green leaves above, the perfection of love had come— love so wonderful that the mere thought of it made her eyes brim now! And then there had been days, Saturday afternoons and Sundays, at Atholby and Sparrows Point, where the great beach was, and in lovely Tregore Park, a mile or two from her home, where they could go of an evening and sit in or near the pavilion and have ice cream and dance or watch the dancers. Oh, the stars, the winds, the summer breath of those days! Ah, me! Ah, me!

Naturally, her parents had wondered from the first about

her and Arthur, and her and Barton, since Barton had already assumed a proprietary interest in her and she had seemed to like him. But then she was an only child and a pet, and used to presuming on that, and they could not think of saying anything to her. After all, she was young and pretty and was entitled to change her mind; only, only—she had had to indulge in a career of lying and subterfuge in connection with Barton, since Arthur was headstrong and wanted every evening that he chose—to call for her at the store and keep her downtown to dinner and a show.

Arthur had never been like Barton, shy, phlegmatic, obedient, waiting long and patiently for each little favor, but, instead, masterful and eager, rifling her of kisses and caresses and every delight of love, and teasing and playing with her as a cat would a mouse. She could never resist him. He demanded of her her time and her affection without let or hindrance. He was not exactly selfish or cruel, as some might have been, but gay and unthinking at times, unconsciously so, and yet loving and tender at others—nearly always so. But always he would talk of things in the future as if they really did not include her—and this troubled her greatly—of places he might go, things he might do, which, somehow, he seemed to think or assume that she could not or would not do with him. He was always going to Australia sometime, he thought, in a business way, or to South Africa, or possibly to India. He never seemed to have any fixed clear future for himself in mind.

A dreadful sense of helplessness and of impending disaster came over her at these times, of being involved in some predicament over which she had no control, and which would lead her on to some sad end. Arthur, although plainly in love, as she thought, and apparently delighted with her, might not always love her. She began, timidly at first (and always, for that matter), to ask him pretty, seeking questions about himself and her, whether their future was certain to be together, whether he really wanted her—loved her—whether he might not want to marry someone else or just her, and whether she wouldn't look nice in a pearl satin wedding dress with a long creamy veil and satin slippers and a bouquet of bridal wreath. She had been so slowly but surely saving to that end, even before he came, in connection with Barton; only, after *he* came, all thought of the import of it had

270

been transferred to him. But now, also, she was beginning to ask herself sadly, "Would it ever be?" He was so airy, so inconsequential, so ready to say: "Yes, yes," and "Sure, sure! That's right! Yes, indeedy; you bet! Say, kiddie, but you'll look sweet!" But, somehow, it had always seemed as if this whole thing were a glorious interlude and that it could not last. Arthur was too gay and ethereal and too little settled in his own mind. His idea of travel and living in different cities, finally winding up in New York or San Francisco, but never with her exactly until she asked him, was too ominous, although he always reassured her gaily: "Of course! Of course!" But somehow she could never believe it really, and it made her intensely sad at times, horribly gloomy. So often she wanted to cry, and she could scarcely tell why.

And then, because of her intense affection for him, she had finally quarreled with Barton, or nearly that, if one could say that one ever really quarreled with him. It had been because of a certain Thursday evening a few weeks before about which she had disappointed him. In a fit of generosity, knowing that Arthur was coming Wednesday, and because Barton had stopped in at the store to see her, she had told him that he might come, having regretted it afterward, so enamored was she of Arthur. And then when Wednesday came, Arthur had changed his mind, telling her he would come Friday instead, but on Thursday evening he had stopped in at the store and asked her to go to Sparrows Point, with the result that she had no time to notify Barton. He had gone to the house and sat with her parents until ten-thirty, and then, a few days later, although she had written him offering an excuse, had called at the store to complain slightly.

"Do you think you did just right, Shirley? You might have sent word, mightn't you? Who was it—the new fellow you won't tell me about?"

Shirley flared on the instant.

"Supposing it was? What's it to you? I don't belong to you yet, do I? I told you there wasn't anyone, and I wish you'd let me alone about that. I couldn't help it last Thursday—that's all— and I don't want you to be fussing with me—that's all. If you don't want to, you needn't come any more, anyhow."

"Don't say that, Shirley," pleaded Barton. "You don't mean that. I won't bother you, though, if you don't want me any more."

And because Shirley sulked, not knowing what else to do, he had gone and she had not seen him since.

And then sometime later when she had thus broken with Barton, avoiding the railway station where he worked, Arthur had failed to come at his appointed time, sending no word until the next day, when a note came to the store saying that he had been out of town for his firm over Sunday and had not been able to notify her, but that he would call Tuesday. It was an awful blow. At the time, Shirley had a vision of what was to follow. It seemed for the moment as if the whole world had suddenly been reduced to ashes, that there was nothing but black charred cinders anywhere—she felt that about all life. Yet it all came to her clearly then that this was but the beginning of just such days and just such excuses, and that soon, soon he would come no more. He was beginning to be tired of her and soon he would not even make excuses. She felt it, and it froze and terrified her.

And then, soon after, the indifference which she feared did follow—almost created by her own thoughts, as it were. First, it was a meeting he had to attend somewhere one Wednesday night when he was to have come for her. Then he was going out of town again, over Sunday. Then he was going away for a whole week—it was absolutely unavoidable, he said, his commercial duties were increasing—and once he had casually remarked that nothing could stand in the way where she was concerned—never! She did not think of reproaching him with this; she was too proud. If he was going, he must go. She would not be willing to say to herself that she had ever attempted to hold any man. But, just the same, she was agonized by the thought. When he was with her, he seemed tender enough; only, at times, his eyes wandered and he seemed slightly bored. Other girls, particularly pretty ones, seemed to interest him as much as she did.

And the agony of the long days when he did not come any more for a week or two at a time! The waiting, the brooding, the wondering, at the store and here in her home—in the former place making mistakes at times because she could not get her mind off him and being so reminded of them, and here at her own home at nights, being so absent-minded that her parents remarked on it. She felt sure that her parents must be noticing that Arthur was not coming any more, or as much as he had—for she pretended

272

to be going out with him, going to Mabel Gove's instead—and that Barton had deserted her too, he having been driven off by her indifference, never to come any more, perhaps, unless she sought him out.

And then it was that the thought of saving her own face by taking up with Barton once more occurred to her, of using him and his affections and faithfulness and dullness, if you will, to cover up her own dilemma. Only, this ruse was not to be tried until she had written Arthur this one letter—a pretext merely to see if there was a single ray of hope, a letter to be written in a gentle enough way and asking for the return of the few notes she had written him. She had not seen him now in nearly a month, and the last time she had, he had said he might soon be compelled to leave her awhile—to go to Pittsburgh to work. And it was his reply to this that she now held in her hand—from Pittsburgh! It was frightful! The future without him!

But Barton would never know really what had transpired, if she went back to him. In spite of all her delicious hours with Arthur, she could call him back, she felt sure. She had never really entirely dropped him, and he knew it. He had bored her dreadfully on occasion, arriving on off days when Arthur was not about, with flowers or candy, or both, and sitting on the porch steps and talking of the railroad business and of the whereabouts and doings of some of their old friends. It was shameful, she had thought at times, to see a man so patient, so hopeful, so good-natured as Barton, deceived in this way, and by her, who was so miserable over another. Her parents must see and know, she had thought at these times, but still, what else was she to do?

"I'm a bad girl," she kept telling herself. "I'm all wrong. What right have I to offer Barton what is left?" But still, somehow she realized that Barton, if she chose to favor him, would only be too grateful for even the leavings of others where she was concerned, and that even yet, if she but deigned to crook a finger, she could have him. He was so simple, so good-natured, so stolid and matter of fact, so different to Arthur whom (she could not help smiling at the thought of it) she was loving now about as Barton loved her—slavishly, hopelessly.

And then, as the days passed and Arthur did not write any more—just this one brief note—she at first grieved horribly, and then in a fit of numb despair attempted, bravely enough from one point of view, to adjust herself to the new situation. Why should she despair? Why die of agony where there were plenty who would still sigh for her—Barton among others? She was young, pretty, very—many told her so. She could, if she chose, achieve a vivacity which she did not feel. Why should she brook this unkindness without a thought of retaliation? Why shouldn't she enter upon a gay and heartless career, indulging in a dozen flirtations at once—dancing and killing all thought of Arthur in a round of frivolities? There were many who beckoned to her. She stood at her counter in the drug store on many a day and brooded over this, but at the thought of which one to begin with, she faltered. After her late love, all were so tame, for the present anyhow.

And then—and then—always there was Barton, the humble or faithful, to whom she had been so unkind and whom she had used and whom she still really liked. So often self-reproaching thoughts in connection with him crept over her. He must have known, must have seen how badly she was using him all this while, and yet he had not failed to come and come, until she had actually quarreled with him, and any one would have seen that it was literally hopeless. She could not help remembering, especially now in her pain, that he adored her. He was not calling on her now at all—by her indifference she had finally driven him away—but a word, a word— She waited for days, weeks, hoping against hope, and then—

•　　　•　　　•

The office of Barton's superior in the Great Eastern terminal had always made him an easy object for her blandishments, coming and going, as she frequently did, via this very station. He was in the office of the assistant train dispatcher on the ground floor, where passing to and from the local, which, at times, was quicker than a street car, she could easily see him by peering in; only, she had carefully avoided him for nearly a year. If she chose now, and would call for a message-blank at the adjacent telegraph window which was a part of his room, and raised her voice as she often had in the past, he could scarcely fail to hear, if he did not see her. And if he did, he would rise and come over—of that she was sure, for he never could resist her. It had been a wile of hers in the old days to do this or to make her presence felt by idling outside. After a month of brooding, she felt that she must act—her position as a deserted girl was too much. She could not stand it any longer really—the eyes of her mother, for one.

It was six-fifteen one evening when, coming out of the store in which she worked, she turned her step disconsolately homeward. Her heart was heavy, her face rather pale and drawn. She had stopped in the store's retiring room before coming out to add to her charms as much as possible by a little powder and rouge and to smooth her hair. It would not take much to reallure her former sweetheart, she felt sure—and yet it might not be so easy after all. Suppose he had found another? But she could not believe that. It had scarcely been long enough since he had last attempted to see her, and he was really so very, very fond of her and so faithful. He was too slow and certain in his choosing— he had been so with her. Still, who knows? With this thought, she went forward in the evening, feeling for the first time the shame and pain that comes of deception, the agony of having to relinquish an ideal and the feeling of despair that comes to those who find themselves in the position of suppliants, stooping to something which in better days and better fortune they would not know. Arthur was the cause of this.

When she reached the station, the crowd that usually filled it at this hour was swarming. There were so many pairs like Arthur and herself laughing and hurrying away or so she felt. First glancing in the small mirror of a weighing scale to see if she were still of her former charm, she stopped thoughtfully at a little flower stand which stood outside, and for a few pennies purchased a tiny bunch of violets. She then went inside and stood near a window, peering first furtively to see if he were present. He was. She could see his stolid, genial figure at a table, bent over his work, a green shade over his eyes. Stepping back a moment to ponder, she finally went forward and, in a clear voice, asked,

"May I have a blank, please?"

The infatuation of the discarded Barton was such that it brought him instantly to his feet. In his stodgy, stocky way he rose, his eyes glowing with a friendly hope, his mouth wreathed in smiles, and came over. At the sight of her, pale, but pretty—

paler and prettier, really, than he had ever seen her—he thrilled dumbly.

"How are you, Shirley?" he asked sweetly, as he drew near, his eyes searching her face hopefully. He had not seen her for so long that he was intensely hungry, and her paler beauty appealed to him more than ever. Why wouldn't she have him? he was asking himself. Why wouldn't his persistent love yet win her? Perhaps it might. "I haven't seen you in a month of Sundays, it seems. How are the folks?"

"They're all right, Bart," she smiled archly, "and so am I. How have you been? It has been a long time since I've seen you. I've been wondering how you were. Have you been all right? I was just going to send a message."

As he had approached, Shirley had pretended at first not to see him, a moment later to affect surprise, although she was really suppressing a heavy sigh. The sight of him, after Arthur, was not reassuring. Could she really interest herself in him any more? Could she?

"Sure, sure," he replied genially; "I'm always all right. You couldn't kill me, you know. Not going away, are you, Shirl?" he queried interestedly.

"No; I'm just telegraphing to Mabel. She promised to meet me tomorrow, and I want to be sure she will."

"You don't come past here as often as you did, Shirley," he complained tenderly. "At least, I don't seem to see you so often," he added with a smile. "It isn't anything I have done, is it?" he queried, and then, when she protested quickly, added: "What's the trouble, Shirl? Haven't been sick, have you?"

She affected all her old gaiety and ease, feeling as though she would like to cry.

"Oh, no," she returned; "I've been all right. I've been going through the other door, I suppose, or coming in and going out on the Langdon Avenue car." (This was true, because she had been wanting to avoid him.) "I've been in such a hurry, most nights, that I haven't had time to stop, Bart. You know how late the store keeps us at times."

He remembered, too, that in the old days she had made time to stop or meet him occasionally.

"Yes, I know," he said tactfully. "But you haven't been to

276

any of our old card-parties either of late, have you? At least, I haven't seen you. I've gone to two or three, thinking you might be there."

That was another thing Arthur had done—broken up her interest in these old store and neighborhood parties and a banjo-and-mandolin club to which she had once belonged. They had all seemed so pleasing and amusing in the old days—but now— In those days Bart had been her usual companion when his work permitted.

"No," she replied evasively, but with a forced air of pleasant remembrance; "I have often thought of how much fun we had at those, though. It was a shame to drop them. You haven't seen Harry Stull or Trina Task recently, have you?" she inquired, more to be saying something than for any interest she felt.

He shook his head negatively, then added:

"Yes, I did, too; here in the waiting room a few nights ago. They were coming downtown to a theater, I suppose."

His face fell slightly as he recalled how it had been their custom to do this, and what their one quarrel had been about. Shirley noticed it. She felt the least bit sorry for him, but much more for herself, coming back so disconsolately to all this.

"Well, you're looking as pretty as ever, Shirley," he continued, noting that she had not written the telegram and that there was something wistful in her glance. "Prettier, I think," and she smiled sadly. Every word that she tolerated from him was as so much gold to him, so much of dead ashes to her. "You wouldn't like to come down some evening this week and see *The Mouse-Trap*, would you? We haven't been to a theater together in I don't know when." His eyes sought hers in a hopeful, doglike way.

So—she could have him again—that was the pity of it! To have what she really did not want, did not care for! At the least nod now he would come, and this very devotion made it all but worthless, and so sad. She ought to marry him now for certain, if she began in this way, and could in a month's time if she chose, but oh, oh—could she? For the moment she decided that she could not, would not. If he had only repulsed her—told her to go— ignored her—but no; it was her fate to be loved by him in this moving, pleading way, and hers not to love him as she wished to love—to be loved. Plainly, he needed someone like her, whereas she, she— She turned a little sick, a sense of the sacrilege of gaiety at this time creeping into her voice, and exclaimed:

"No, no!" Then seeing his face change, a heavy sadness come over it, "Not this week, anyhow, I mean" ("Not so soon," she had almost said). "I have several engagements this week and I'm not feeling well. But"—seeing his face change, and the thought of her own state returning—"you might come out to the house some evening instead, and then we can go some other time."

His face brightened intensely. It was wonderful how he longed to be with her, how the least favor from her comforted and lifted him up. She could see also now, however, how little it meant to her, how little it could ever mean, even if to him it was heaven. The old relationship would have to be resumed in toto, once and for all, but did she want it that way now that she was feeling so miserable about this other affair? As she meditated, these various moods racing to and fro in her mind, Barton seemed to notice, and now it occurred to him that perhaps he had not pursued her enough—was too easily put off. She probably did like him yet. This evening, her present visit, seemed to prove it.

"Sure, sure!" he agreed. "I'd like that. I'll come out Sunday, if you say. We can go any time to the play. I'm sorry, Shirley, if you're not feeling well. I've thought of you a lot these days. I'll come out Wednesday, if you don't mind."

She smiled a wan smile. It was all so much easier than she had expected—her triumph—and so ashenlike in consequence, a flavor of Dead Sea fruit and defeat about it all, that it was pathetic. How could she, after Arthur? How could he, really?

"Make it Sunday," she pleaded, naming the farthest day off, and then hurried out.

Her faithful lover gazed after her, while she suffered an intense nausea. To think—to think—it should all be coming to this! She had not used her telegraph-blank, and now had forgotten all about it. It was not the simple trickery that discouraged her, but her own future which could find no better outlet than this, could not rise above it apparently, or that she had no heart to make it rise above it. Why couldn't she interest herself in someone different to Barton? Why did she have to return to him? Why not wait and meet some other—ignore him as before? But no, no; nothing mattered now—no one—it might as well be Barton really as anyone, and she would at least make him happy and at the same time solve her own problem. She went out into the train shed and climbed into her train. Slowly, after the usual pushing and jostling of a crowd, it drew out toward Latonia, that suburban region in which her home lay. As she rode, she thought.

"What have I just done? What am I doing?" she kept asking herself as the clacking wheels on the rails fell into a rhythmic dance and the houses of the brown, dry, endless city fled past in a maze. "Severing myself decisively from the past—the happy past—for supposing, once I am married, Arthur should return and want me again—suppose! Suppose!"

Below at one place, under a shed, were some market-gardeners disposing of the last remnants of their day's wares—a sickly, dull life, she thought. Here was Rutgers Avenue, with its line of red streetcars, many wagons and tracks and counter-streams of automobiles—how often had she passed it morning and evening in a shuttle-like way, and how often would, unless she got married! And here, now, was the river flowing smoothly between its banks lined with coal pockets and wharves—away, away to the huge deep sea which she and Arthur had enjoyed so much. Oh, to be in a small boat and drift out, out into the endless, restless, pathless deep! Somehow the sight of this water, tonight and every night, brought back those evenings in the open with Arthur at Sparrows Point, the long line of dancers in Eckert's Pavilion, the woods at Atholby, the park, with the dancers in the pavilion—she choked back a sob. Once Arthur had come this way with her on just such an evening as this, pressing her hand and saying how wonderful she was. Oh, Arthur! Arthur! And now Barton was to take his old place again—forever, no doubt. She could not trifle with her life longer in this foolish way, or his. What was the use? But think of it!

Yes, it must be—forever now, she told herself. She must marry. Time would be slipping by and she would become too old. It was her only future—marriage. It was the only future she had ever contemplated really, a home, children, the love of some man whom she could love as she loved Arthur. Ah, what a happy home that would have been for her! But now, now—

But there must be no turning back now, either. There was no other way. If Arthur ever came back—but fear not, he wouldn't! She had risked so much and lost—lost him. Her little venture into true love had been such a failure. Before Arthur had come all had been well enough. Barton, stout and simple and frank and direct, had in some way—how, she could scarcely realize now—offered sufficient of a future. But now, now! He had enough money, she knew, to build a cottage for the two of them. He had told her so. He would do his best always to make her happy, she was sure of that. They could live in about the state her parents were living in—or a little better, not much—and would never want. No doubt there would be children, because he craved them—several of them—and that would take up her time, long years of it—the sad, gray years! But then Arthur, whose children she would have thrilled to bear, would be no more, a mere memory—think of that!—and Barton, the dull, the commonplace, would have achieved his finest dream—and why?

Because love was a failure for her—that was why—and in her life there could be no more true love. She would never love anyone again as she had Arthur. It could not be, she was sure of it. He was too fascinating, too wonderful. Always, always, wherever she might be, whoever she might marry, he would be coming back, intruding between her and any possible love, receiving any possible kiss. It would be Arthur she would be loving or kissing. She dabbed at her eyes with a tiny handkerchief, turned her face close to the window and stared out, and then as the environs of Latonia came into view, wondered (so deep is romance): What if Arthur should come back at some time—or now! Supposing he should be here at the station now, accidentally or on purpose, to welcome her, to soothe her weary heart. He had met her here before. How she would fly to him, lay her head on his shoulder, forget forever that Barton ever was, that they had ever separated for an hour. Oh, Arthur! Arthur!

But no, no; here was Latonia—here the viaduct over her train, the long business street and the cars marked "Center" and "Langdon Avenue" running back into the great city. A few blocks away in tree-shaded Bethune Street, duller and plainer than ever, were her parents' cottage and the routine of that old life which was now, she felt, more fully fastened upon her than ever before—the lawnmowers, the lawns, the front porches all alike. Now would come the going to and fro of Barton to business as her father and she now went to business, her keeping house, cooking, washing, ironing, sewing for Barton as her mother now did these things for her father and herself. And she would not be in love really, as she wanted to be. Oh. Dreadful! She could never escape it really, now that she could endure it less, scarcely for another hour. And yet she must, must, for the sake of—for the sake of—she closed her eyes and dreamed.

She walked up the street under the trees, past the houses and lawns all alike to her own, and found her father on their veranda reading the evening paper. She sighed at the sight.

"Back, daughter?" he called pleasantly.

"Yes."

"Your mother is wondering if you would like steak or liver for dinner. Better tell her."

"Oh, it doesn't matter."

She hurried into her bedroom, threw down her hat and gloves, and herself on the bed to rest silently, and groaned in her soul. To think that it had all come to this!—Never to see him any more!—To see only Barton, and marry him and live in such a street, have four or five children, forget all her youthful companionships—and all to save her face before her parents, and her future. Why must it be? Should it be, really? She choked and stifled. After a little time her mother, hearing her come in, came to the door—thin, practical, affectionate, conventional.

"What's wrong, honey? Aren't you feeling well tonight? Have you a headache? Let me feel."

Her thin cool fingers crept over her temples and hair. She suggested something to eat or a headache powder right away.

"I'm all right, mother. I'm just not feeling well now. Don't bother. I'll get up soon. Please don't."

"Would you rather have liver to steak tonight, dear?"

"Oh, anything—nothing—please don't bother—steak will do—anything"—if only she could get rid of her and be at rest!

Her mother looked at her and shook her head sympathetically, then retreated quietly, saying no more. Lying so, she thought and thought—grinding, destroying thoughts about the beauty of the past, the darkness of the future—until able to endure them no longer she got up and, looking distractedly out of the window into the yard and the house next door, stared at her future fixedly. What should she do? What should she really do? There was Mrs. Kessel in her kitchen getting her dinner as usual, just as her own mother was now, and Mr. Kessel out on the front porch in his shirt sleeves reading the evening paper. Beyond was Mr. Pollard in his yard, cutting the grass. All along Bethune Street were such houses and such people—simple, commonplace souls all—clerks, managers, fairly successful craftsmen, like her father and Barton, excellent in their way but not like Arthur the beloved, the lost—and here was she, perforce, or by decision of necessity, soon to be one of them, in some such street as this no doubt, forever and— For the moment it choked and stifled her.

She decided that she would not. No, no no! There must be some other way—many ways. She did not have to do this unless she really wished to—would not—only— Then going to the mirror she looked at her face and smoothed her hair.

"But what's the use?" she asked of herself wearily and resignedly after a time. "Why should I cry? Why shouldn't I marry Barton? I don't amount to anything, anyhow. Arthur wouldn't have me. I wanted him, and I am compelled to take someone else—or no one—what difference does it really make who? My dreams are too high, that's all. I wanted Arthur, and he wouldn't have me. I don't want Barton and he crawls at my feet. I'm a failure, that's what's the matter with me."

And then, turning up her sleeves and removing a fichu which stood out too prominently from her breast, she went into the kitchen and, looking about for an apron, observed:

"Can't I help? Where's the tablecloth?" and finding it among napkins and silverware in a drawer in the adjoining room, proceeded to set the table.

282

Sanctuary

I

PRIMARILY, THERE WERE THE conditions under which she was brought to fifteen years of age: the crowded, scummy tenements; the narrow green-painted halls with their dim gas jets, making the entrance look more like that of a morgue than a dwelling place; the dirty halls and rooms with their green or blue or brown walls painted to save the cost of paper; the bare wooden floors, long since saturated with every type of grease and filth from oleomargarine and suet leaked from cheap fats or meats, to beer and whiskey and tobacco juice. A little occasional scrubbing by some would-be hygienic tenant was presumed to keep or make clean some of the chambers and halls.

And then the streets outside—any of the streets by which she had ever been surrounded—block upon block of other red, bare, commonplace tenements crowded to the doors with human life, the space before them sped over by noisy, gassy trucks and vehicles of all kinds. And stifling in summer, dusty and icy in winter; decorated on occasion by stray cats and dogs, pawing in ashcans, watched over by lordly policemen, and always running with people, people, people—who made their living heaven knows how, existing in such a manner as their surroundings suggested.

In this atmosphere were always longshoremen, wagon drivers, sweepers of floors, washers of dishes, waiters, janitors, workers in laundries, factories—mostly in indifferent or decadent or despairing conditions. And all of these people existed, in so far as she ever knew, upon that mysterious, evanescent and fluctuating something known as the weekly wage.

Always about her there had been drunkenness, fighting, complaining, sickness or death; the police coming in, and arresting one and another; the gas man, the rent man, the furniture man, hammering at doors for their due—and not getting it—in due

283

time the undertaker also arriving amid a great clamor, as though lives were the most precious things imaginable.

It is entirely conceivable that in viewing or in meditating upon an atmosphere such as this, one might conclude that no good could come out of it. What! a dungheap grow a flower? Exactly, and often, a flower—but not to grow to any glorious maturity probably. Nevertheless a flower of the spirit at least might have its beginnings there. And if it shrank or withered in the miasmatic atmosphere—well, conceivably, that might be normal, although in reality all flowers thus embedded in infancy do not so wither. There are flowers and flowers.

Viewing Madeleine Kinsella at the ages of five, seven, eleven and thirteen even, it might have been concluded that she was a flower of sorts—admittedly not a brave, lustrous one of the orchid or gardenia persuasion, but a flower nevertheless. Her charm was simpler, more retiring, less vivid than is usually accorded the compliment of beauty. She was never rosy, never colorful in the high sense, never daring or aggressive. Always, from her infancy on, she seemed to herself and others to be slipping about the corners and out-of-the-way places of life, avoiding it, staring at it with wide, lamblike eyes, wondering at things, often fearfully.

Her face, always delicately oval and pale, was not of the force which attracted. Her eyes, a milkish blue-gray with a suggestion of black in the iris, her hair black, her hands long-fingered and slim, were not of a type which would appeal to the raw youth of her world. Unconsciously, and ever, her slender, longish body sank into graceful poses. Beside the hard, garish, colorful, strident types of her neighborhoods—the girls whom the boys liked—she was not fascinating, and yet, contemplated at odd moments as she grew, she was appealing enough—at times beautiful.

What most affected her youth and her life was the internal condition of her family, the poverty and general worthlessness of her parents. They were as poor as their poorest neighbors, and quarrelsome, unhappy and mean-spirited into the bargain. Her father came dimly into her understanding at somewhere near her seventh or eighth year as an undersized, contentious and drunken and wordy man, always more or less out of a job,

284

irritated with her mother and her sister and brother, and always, as her mother seemed to think, a little the worse for drink.

"You're a liar! You're a liar! You're a liar! You're a liar!"— how well she remembered this sing-song echoing reiteration of his, in whatever basement or hole they were living in at the time! "You're a liar! I never did it! You're a liar! I wasn't there!"

Her mother, often partially intoxicated or morose because of her own ills, was only too willing to rejoin in kind. Her elder sister and brother, much more agreeable in their way and as much put upon as herself, were always coming in or running out somewhere and staying while the storm lasted; while she, shy and always a little frightened, seemed to look upon it all as unavoidable, possibly even essential. The world was always so stern, so mysterious, so nonunderstandable to Madeleine.

Again it might be, and often was, "Here, you, you brat, go an' get me a can o' beer! Gwan, now!" which she did quickly and fearfully enough, running to the nearest wretched corner saloon with the "can" or "growler," her slim little fingers closed tightly over the five-cent piece or dime entrusted to her, her eyes taking in the wonders and joys of the street even as she ran. She was so small at the time that her little arms were unable to reach quite the level of the bar, and she had to accept the aid of the bartender or some drinker. Then she would patiently wait while one of them teased her as to her size or until the beer was handed. down.

Once, and once only, three "bad boys," knowing what she was going for and how wretched and shabby was her father, not able to revenge himself on anyone outside his family, had seized her en route, forced open her hand and run away with the dime, leaving her to return fearsomely to her father, rubbing her eyes, and to be struck and abused soundly and told to fight—"Blank-blank you, what the hell are you good for it you can't do that?"

Only the vile language and the defensive soberness of her mother at the time saved her from a worse fate. As for the boys who had stolen the money, they only received curses and awful imprecations, which harmed no one.

Wretched variations of this same existence were endured by the other two members of the family, her brother Frank and her sister Tina.

The former was a slim and nervous youth, given to fits of

savage temper like his father and not to be ordered and controlled exactly as his father would have him. At times, as Madeleine recalled, he appeared terribly resentful of the conditions that surrounded him and cursed and swore and even threatened to leave; at other times he was placid enough, at least not inclined to share the dreadful scenes which no one could avoid where her father was.

At the age of twelve or thirteen he secured work in a box factory somewhere and for a while brought his wages home. But often there was no breakfast or dinner for him, and when his father and mother were deep in their cups or quarreling things were so generally neglected that even where home ties were strong no one of any worldly experience could have endured them, and he ran away.

His mother was always complaining of "the lumbago" and of not being able to get up, even when he and Tina were working and bringing home a portion of their weekly wage or all of it. If she did, it was only to hover over the wretched cookstove and brew herself a little tea and complain as before.

Madeleine had early, in her ignorant and fearsome way, tried to help, but she did not always know how and her mother was either too ill or too disgruntled with life to permit her to assist, had she been able.

As it had been with Frank so it as with Tina, only it came sooner.

When Madeleine was only five Tina was a grown girl of ten, with yellow hair and a pretty, often smiling face, and was already working somewhere—in a candy store—for a dollar and a half a week. Later, when Madeleine was eight and Tina thirteen, the latter had graduated to a button-works and was earning three.

There was something rather admirable and yet disturbing connected dimly with Tina in Madeleine's mind, an atmosphere of rebelliousness and courage which she had never possessed and which she could not have described, lacking as she did a mind that registered the facts of life clearly. She only saw Tina, pretty and strong, coming and going from her ninth to her thirteenth year, refusing to go for beer at her father's order and being cursed for it, even struck at or thrown at by him, sometimes by her mother, and often standing at the foot of the stairs after work hours or on a Sunday afternoon or evening, looking at the crowded street or walking up and down with other girls and boys, when her mother wanted her to be doing things in the house—sweeping, washing dishes, making beds—dreary, gray tasks all.

"Fixin' your hair again! Fixin' your hair again! Fixin' your hair again!" she could hear her father screaming whenever she paused before the one cracked mirror to arrange her hair. "Always in front of that blank-blank mirror fixin' her hair! If you don't get away from in front of it I'll throw you an' the mirror in the street! What the hell are you always fixin' your hair for? Say? What're you always fixin' your hair for? Say! What? What're you always fixin' your hair for?"

But Tina was never cast down apparently, only silent. At times she sang and walked with an air. She dressed herself as attractively as possible, as if with the few things she had she was attempting to cast off the burden of the life by which she was surrounded. Always she was hiding things away from the others, never wanting them to touch anything of hers. And how she had hated her father as she grew, in bitter moments calling him a "sot" and a "fool."

Tina had never been very obedient, refusing to go to church or to do much of anything about the house. Whenever her father and mother were drinking or fighting she would slip away and stay with some girl in the neighborhood that she knew. And in spite of all this squalor and misery and the fact that they moved often and the food was bad, Tina, once she was twelve or thirteen, always seemed able to achieve an agreeable appearance.

Madeleine often remembered her in a plaid skirt she had got somewhere, which looked beautiful on her, and a little gilt pin which she wore at her neck. And she had a way of doing her yellow hair high on her forehead, which had stuck in Madeleine's mind perhaps because of her father's rude comments on it.

II

It is not surprising that Madeleine came to her twelfth and thirteenth years without any real understanding of the great world about her and without any definite knowledge or skill. Her drunken mother was now more or less dependent upon her,

her father having died of pneumonia and her brother and sister having disappeared to do for themselves.

Aside from petty beginners' tasks in shops or stores, or assisting her mother at washing or cleaning, there was little that she could do at first. Mrs. Kinsella, actually compelled by the need for rent or food or fuel after a time, would get occasional work in a laundry or kitchen or at scrubbing or window-cleaning, but not for long. The pleasure of drink would soon rob her of that.

At these tasks Madeleine helped until she secured work in a candy factory in her thirteenth year at the wage of three-thirty a week. But even with this little money paid in regularly there was no assurance that her mother would add sufficient to it to provide either food or warmth. Betimes, and when Madeleine was working, her mother cheered her all too obvious sorrows with the bottle, and at nights or weekends rewarded Madeleine with a gabble which was all the more painful because no material comfort came with it.

The child actually went hungry at times. Usually, after a few drinks, her mother would begin to weep and recite her past ills: a process which reduced her timorous and very sympathetic daughter to complete misery. In sheer desperation the child sought for some new way in her own mind. A reduction in the working-force of the candy factory, putting her back in the ranks of the work-seekers once more, and a neighbor perceiving her wretched state and suggesting that some extra helpers were wanted in a department store at Christmastime, she applied there, but so wretched were her clothes by now that she was not even considered.

Then a man who had a restaurant in a nearby street gave her mother and Madeleine positions as dishwashers, but he was compelled to discharge her mother, although he wished to retain Madeleine. From this last, however, because of the frightening attentions of the cook, she had to flee, and without obtaining a part of the small pittance which was due her. Again, and because in times past she had aided her mother to clean in one place and another, she was able to get a place as a servant in a family.

Those who know anything of the life of a domestic know

how thoroughly unsatisfactory it is—the leanness, the lack of hope. As a domestic, wherever she was—and she obtained no superior places for the time being—she had only the kitchen for her chief chamber or a cubby-hole under the roof. Here, unless she was working elsewhere in the house or chose to visit her mother occasionally, she was expected to remain. Pots and pans and scrubbing and cleaning and bed-making were her world. If anyone aside from her mother ever wanted to see her (which was rare) he or she could only come into the kitchen, an ugly and by day inconvenient realm.

She had, as she soon came to see, no privileges whatsoever. In the morning she was expected to be up before anyone else, possibly after working late the night before. Breakfast had to be served for others before she herself could eat—what was left. Then came the sweeping and cleaning. In one place which she obtained in her fifteenth year the husband annoyed her so, when his wife was not looking, that she had to leave; in another it was the son. By now she was becoming more attractive, although by no means beautiful or daring.

But wherever she was and whatever she was doing, she could not help thinking of her mother and Tina and Frank and her father, and of the grim necessities and errors and vices which had seemed to dominate them. Neither her brother nor her sister did she ever see again. Her mother, she felt (and this was due to a sensitiveness and a sympathy which she could not possibly overcome), she would have with her for the rest of her days unless, like the others, she chose to run away.

Daily her mother was growing more inadequate and less given to restraint or consideration. As "bad" as she was, Madeleine could not help thinking what a "hard" time she had had. From whatever places she obtained work in these days (and it was not often any more) she was soon discharged, and then she would come inquiring after Madeleine, asking to be permitted to see her. Naturally, her shabby dress and shawl and rag of a hat, as well as her wastrel appearance, were an affront to any well-ordered household. Once in her presence, whenever Madeleine was permitted to see her, she would begin either a cozening or a lachrymose account of her great needs.

"It's out o' oil I am, me dear," or "Wurra, I have no wood"

or "bread" or "meat"—never drink. "Ye won't let yer pore old mother go cold or hungry, now, will ye? That's the good girl now. Fifty cents now, if ye have it, me darlin', or a quarter, an' I'll not be troublin' ye soon again. Even a dime, if ye can spare me no more. God'll reward ye. I'll have work o' me own to-morra. That's the good girl now—ye won't let me go away without anything."

Oscillating between shame and sympathy, her daughter would take from the little she had and give it to her, tremulous for fear the disturbing figure would prove her undoing. Then the old woman would go out, lurching sometimes in her cups, and disappear, while an observant fellow servant was probably seeing and reporting to the mistress, who, of course, did not want her to come there and so told the girl, or, more practical still, discharged her.

Thus from her fourteenth to her sixteenth year she was shunted from house to house and from shop to shop, always in the vain hope that this time her mother might let her alone.

And at the very same time, life, sweetened by the harmonies of youth in the blood, was calling—that exterior life which promised everything because so far it had given nothing. The little simple things of existence, the very ordinary necessities of clothing and ornament, with which the heart of youth and the inherent pride of appearance are gratified, had a value entirely disproportionate to their worth. Yes, already she had turned the age wherein the chemic harmonies in youth begin to sing, thought to thought, color to color, dream to dream. She was being touched by the promise of life itself.

And then, as was natural, love in the guise of youth, a rather sophisticated gallant somewhat above the world in which she was moving, appeared and paid his all but worthless court to her. He was physically charming, the son of a grocer of some means in the vicinity in which she was working, a handsome youth with pink cheeks and light hair and blue eyes, and vanity enough for ten. Because she was shy and pretty he became passingly interested in her.

"Oh, I saw you cleaning the windows yesteday," this with a radiant, winning smile; or "You must live down toward Blake Street. I see you doing down that way once in a while."

Madeleine acknowledged rather shamefacedly that it was true. That so dashing a boy should be interested in her was too marvelous.

In the evenings, or at any time, it was easy for a youth of his skill and *savoir-faire* to pick her out of the bobbing stream of humanity in which she occasionally did errands or visited her mother in her shabby room, and to suggest that he be permitted to call upon her. Or, failing that, because of her mother's shabby quarters and her mother herself, that the following Sunday would be ideal for an outing to one of those tawdry, noisy beaches to which he liked to go with other boys and girls in a car.

A single trip to Wonderland, a single visit to one of its halls where music sounded to the splash of the waves and where he did his best to teach her to dance, a single meal in one of its gaudy, noisy restaurants, a taste of its whirly pleasures, and a new color and fillip were given to hope, a new and seemingly realizable dream of happiness implanted in her young mind. The world was happier than she had thought, or could be made so; not all people fought and screamed at each other. There were such things as tenderness, soft words, sweet words.

But the way of so sophisticated a youth with a maid was brief and direct. His mind was of that order which finds in the freshness of womankind a mere passing delight, something to be deflowered and then put aside. He was a part of a group that secured happiness in rifling youth, the youth of those whose lives were so dull and bleak that a few words of kindness, a little change of scene, the mere proximity of experience and force such as they had never known, were pay ample for anything which they might give or do.

And of these Madeleine was one.

Never having had anything in her own life, the mere thought of a man so vigorous and handsome, one with knowledge enough to show her more of life than she had ever dreamed of, to take her to places of color and light, to assure her that she was fitted for better things even though they were not immediately forthcoming, was sufficient to cause her to place faith where it was least worthy of being placed. To win his way there was even talk of marriage later on, that love should be generous and have faith—and then—

III

Plainclothesman Amundsen, patrolling hawk-like the region of Fourteenth and K streets, not so far from Blake, where Madeleine had lived for a time, was becoming interested in and slightly suspicious of a new face.

For several days at odd hours, he had seen a girl half-slinking, half-brazening her way through a region the very atmosphere of which was blemishing to virtue. To be sure, he had not yet seen her speak to anyone; nor was there that in her glance or manner which caused him to feel that she might.

Still—with the assurance of his authority and his past skill in trapping many he followed discreetly, seeing where she went, how she lingered for awhile nervously, then returned as she had come. She was very young, not more than seventeen.

He adjusted his tie and collar and decided to attempt his skill.

"Excuse me, Miss. Out for a little stroll? So am I. Mind my walking along with you a little way? Wouldn't like to come and have a drink, would you? I work in an automobile place over here in Grey Street, and I'm just off for the afternoon. Live here in the neighborhood?"

Madeleine surveyed this stranger with troubled eyes. Since the day her youthful lover had deserted her, and after facing every conceivable type of ill, but never being willing to confess or fall back upon her drunken, dreaming mother for aid, she had tested every device. The necessities and expenses incident to a prospective, and to her degrading state, as well as the continued care of her mother, had compelled her, as she had finally seen it, to come to this—for a time anyhow. A street girl, finding her wandering and crying, had taken her in hand and shown her, after aiding her for weeks, how to make her way.

Her burden that she feared so much was artificially if ruthlessly and criminally disposed of. Then she was shown the way of the streets until she could gain a new foothold in life; only, as she had since learned, it was difficult for her to accommodate herself to this fell traffic. She was not of it spiritually. She really did not intend to continue in it; it was just a temporary makeshift, born of fear and a dumb despair.

But neither Detective Amundsen nor the law was ready to believe that. To the former she seemed as worthless as any— one of those curious, uncared-for flowers never understood by the dull.

In a nearby café she had listened to his inquiries, the fact that he had a room in a nearby hotel, or could secure one. Contemning a fate which drove her to such favors, and fully resolved to leave it soon, to make something better of her life in the future, she went with him..

Then came the scarring realization that he was an officer of the law, a cynical, contemptuous hawk smirking over her tears and her explanations. It was absolutely nothing to him that she was so young and could scarcely have been as hardened as he pretended. She was compelled to walk through the streets with him to the nearest police station, while he nodded to or stopped to explain to his brothers of the cloth the nature of his latest conquest.

There was the registering of her under the false name that she chose, rather than be exposed under her true one, before a brusque and staring sergeant in shirtsleeves; a cell with a wooden bench, the first she had ever known; a matron who searched her; then a swift and confusing arraignment before a judge whose glance was seemingly so cold that it was frightening.

"Nellie Fitzpatrick; Officer Amundsen, Eighth Precinct."

The friend who had taught her the ways of the streets had warned her that if caught and arrested it might mean months of incarceration in some institution, the processes or corrective meaning of which she did not quite comprehend. All that she had grasped fully was that it meant a severance from her freedom, the few little things, pitiful as they were, that she could call her own. And now here she was, in the clutches of the law, and with no one to defend her.

The testimony of the officer was as it had been in hundreds of cases before this; he had been walking his beat and she had accosted him, as usual.

There being no legal alternative, the magistrate had held her for sentence, pending investigation, and the investigation proving, as it only could, that her life would be better were some corrective measures applied to it, she was sent away. She had never had any training worthy the name. Her mother was an irresponsible inebriate. A few months in some institution where she could be taught some trade or craft would be best.

And so it was that for a period of a year she was turned over to the care of the Sisterhood of the Good Shepherd.

IV

The gray and bony walls of that institution starkly dominated one of the barest and most unprepossessing regions of the city. Its northern facade fronted a stone yard, beyond which were the rocks of the racing Sound and a lighthouse. To the east, rocks and the river, a gray expanse in winter picked over by gulls, mourned over by the horns of endless craft. To the south, bare coal yards, wagon yards, tenements.

Twice weekly, sentenced delinquents of various ages—the "children," of whom Madeleine was one; the "girls" ranged from eighteen to thirty; the "women," ranging from thirty to fifty; and the old people, ranging from fifty until the last years of life— were brought here in an all but air-tight cage, boxed like a great circus van, and with only small barred air holes at the top. Inside the van were bare, hard benches, one against either wall. A representative of the probation and control system of the city, a gaunt female of many years, sat within; also an officer of such prodigious proportions that the mere sight of him might well raise the inquiry of why so much unnecessary luggage. For amusement in dull hours he smoothed his broad mouth with the back of his red, hairy hand, and dreamed of bygone days.

The institution itself was operated by a Mother Superior and thirty nuns, all of the order mentioned, all expert in their separate ways in cooking, housekeeping, laundering, buying, lace-making, teaching, and a half dozen other practical or applied arts.

Within the institution were separate wings or sections for each of the four groups before mentioned, sections in which each had its separate working, eating, sleeping and playing rooms. Only one thing was shared in common: the daily, and often twice or thrice daily, religious ceremonies in the great chapel, a lofty, magi-decorated and be-altared and be-candled chamber, whose tall, thin spire surmounted with a cross might easily be seen from many of the chambers in which the different groups worked. There were masses in the mornings, vespers and late prayers in the afternoons, often late prayers at night or on holidays, when additional services of one kind or another were held. To the religious-minded these were of course consoling. To the contrary-minded they became at times a strain.

Always, and over all the work and all the routine relaxations or pleasures of the institution, there hung the grim insistence of the law, its executive arm, upon order, seemliness, and, if not penance, at least a servility of mind which was the equivalent thereof. Let the voices of the nuns be never so soft, their foot-falls light, their manners courteous, their ways gentle, persuasive, sympathetic, their mood tender; back of it all lay the shadow of the force which could forthwith return any or all to the rough hands of the police, the stern and not-to-be-evaded dictum of the courts.

This much more than any look of disappointment or displeasure, if such were ever necessary, spoke to these delinquents or victims, whatever their mood, and quieted them in their most rebellious hours. Try as they would, they could not but remember that it was the law that had placed them here and now detained them. That there reigned here peace, order, sweetness and harmony, was well enough, comforting in cases, yet and always the life here had obviously a two-fold base: one the power of the law itself, the other the gentle, appealing, beautiful suasion of the nuns.

But to so inexperienced and as yet unreasoning a child as Madeleine all of this savored at this time of but one thing: the sharp, crude, inconsiderate and uninquiring forces of law or life, which seemed never to stop and inquire how or why, but only to order how, and that without mercy. Like some frightened animal faced by a terrifying enemy, she had thus far been able to think only of some darksome corner into which she might slip and hide, a secret place so inconspicuous and minute that the great savage world without would not trouble to care or follow.

And well enough the majority of the Sisterhood, especially those in immediate authority over her, understood the probable direction and ramifications of her present thoughts.

They knew her mood, for had they not during the years past dealt with many such? And stern as was the law, they were not unmindful of her welfare. So long as she was willing and obedient there was but one thing more: that somehow her troubled or resentful or congealed and probably cruelly injured mind should be wooed from its blind belief in the essential injustice of life, to be made to feel, as they themselves were ready to believe, that all paths were not closed, all forces not essentially dark or evil.

For them there was hope of sorts for all, a way out, and many—even she—might find ways and means of facing life, better possibly than any she had ever known.

V

Sister St. Agnes, for instance, who controlled the spotlessly clean but barnlike and bleak room in which were a hundred machines for the sewing of shirtwaists, was a creature of none too fortunate a history herself.

Returning at the age of eighteen and at the death of her father from a convent in which she had been placed by him in order to escape the atmosphere of a home which he himself had found unsatisfactory, she had found a fashionable mother leading a life of which she could scarcely conceive, let alone accept. The taint, the subterfuge, the self-indulgent waste, had as soon sickened her as had the streets Madeleine.

Disappointed, she felt herself after a time incapable of enduring it and had fled, seeking first to make her way in a world which offered only meager wages and a barren life to those incapable of enduring its rugged and often shameless devices; later, again wearied of her own trials, she had returned to the convent in which she had been trained and asked to be schooled for service there. Finding the life too simple for a nature grown more rugged, she had asked to be, and had been, transferred to the House of the Good Shepherd, finding there for the first time, in this institution, duties and opportunities which somehow matched her ideals.

And by the same token the Mother Superior of this same

institution, Mother St. Bertha, who often came through and inquired into the story of each one, was of a history and of an order of mind which was not unlike that of Sister St. Agnes, only it had even more of genuine pathos and suffering in it. The daughter of a shoe manufacturer, she had seen her father fail, her mother die of consumption, a favorite brother drink and carouse until he finally fell under the blight of disease and died. Before this, one of his flames, a pathetic figure, having been neglected by him and her family, in fear of exposure had committed suicide. The subsequent death of her father, to whom she had devoted her years, and the failing of her own dreams of a personal love, had saddened her, and she sought out and was admitted to this order in the hope that she, too, might still make especial use of a life that promised all too little in the world outside.

Her great comfort was in having someone or something to love, the satisfaction of feeling that lives which otherwise might have come to nothing had by some service of hers been lifted to a better state. And in that thought she worked here daily, going about among those incarcerated in different quarters, seeing to it that their tasks were not too severe, their comforts and hopes, where hope still remained, in nowise betrayed.

But to Madeleine at first the solemn habits of the nuns, as well as the gray gingham apron she had to don, the grayer woolen dress, the severe manner in which she had to dress her hair, her very plain shoes, the fact that she had to rise at six-thirty, attend mass and then breakfast at eight, work from eight-thirty to twelve-thirty, and again from one-thirty to four; lunch regularly at twelve-thirty and sup at six, attend a form of prayer service at four-thirty, play at simple games with her new companions between five and six and again between seven and nine, and then promptly retire to a huge sleeping-ward set with small white iron beds in long rows, and lit, after the retiring bell had sounded, by small oil cups or candles burning faintly before various images, all smacked of penance, the more disturbing because it was strange, a form of personal control which she had not sought and could not at once accept.

Nor could she help thinking that some severer form of punishment was yet to be meted out to her, or might ensue by reason of one unavoidable error or another. Life had always been so with her. But, once here a time, things proved not so bad.

The large workroom with its hundred machines and its tall windows, which afforded a stark view of the coal pockets to the south, and the river with its boats and gulls, proved not unpleasing. The clean, bright windows, polished floors and walls—washed and cleaned by the inmates themselves, the nuns not disdaining to do their share—and the habits of the Sisters, their white-fringed hoods, black robes and clinking beads and their silent tread and low speech, impressed her greatly.

The fact that there was no severe reproof for any failure to comprehend at first, but only slow and patient explanations of simple things, not difficult in themselves to do; that aside from the routine duties, the marching in line with hands crossed over breast and head up, as well as genuflections at mass, prayers before and after meals, at rising and on retiring and at the peal of the Angelus, morning, noon and night, there was no real oppression, finally caused her to like it.

The girls who were here with her, shy or silent or cold or indifferent at first, and each with her world of past experiences, contacts and relationships locked in her heart, were still—placed as they were elbow to elbow at work, at meals, at prayer, at retiring—incapable of not achieving some kind of remote fellowship which eventually led to speech and confidences.

Thus the young girl who sat next at her right in the sewing-room—Viola Patters by name, a brave, blonde, cheerful little thing—although she had endured much that might be called ill-fortune, was still interested in life.

By degrees and as they worked the two reached an understanding. Viola confessed that her father, who was a non-union painter by trade, had always worked well enough when he could get work, but that he managed badly and could not always get it. Her mother was sickly and they were very poor and there were many children.

Viola had first worked in a box factory, where she had been able to earn only three dollars or less at piece work—"pasting corners," as she described it—and once she had been sworn at and even thrown away from a table at which she had been working because she didn't do it right, and then she quit. Then her father in turn swearing at her for her "uppishness," she had got

298

work in a five-and-ten-cent store, where she had received three dollars a week and a commission of one per cent on her sales, which were not sufficient to yield more than a dollar more. Then she had secured a better place in a department store at five dollars a week, and there it was that she had come by the handsome boy who had caused her so much trouble.

He was a taxi driver, who always had a car at his disposal when he worked, only it was very seldom that he cared to work. Although he married her swiftly enough and took her away from her family, still he had not supported her very well, and shortly after they were married he was arrested and accused with two others of stealing a machine and selling it, and after months and months of jail life he had been sentenced to three years in the penitentiary.

In the meantime he had called upon her to aid him, pressed her to raise sums of which she had never previously dreamed— and by ways of which she had never previously dreamed—was pleaded with, all but ordered—and still she loved him. And then in executing the "how" of it she had been picked up by the police and sent here, as had Madeleine, only she never told, not even to Madeleine, what the police had never discovered—that at the suggestion of her first love she had included robbery among her arts.

"But I don't care," she had whispered finally as they worked. "He was good to me, anyhow, when he had work. He was crazy about me, and he liked to go places and dance and eat and see shows when he had money, and he always took me. Gee, the times we had! And if he wants me to stick to him when he gets out, I will. He ain't half as bad as some. Gee, you oughta hear some of the girls talk!"

And so it was finally that Madeleine was induced to tell her story.

There were other girls here who, once this bond of sympathy was struck, were keen enough to tell their tales—sad, unfortunate, harried lives all—and somehow the mere telling of them restored to Madeleine some of her earlier faint confidence or interest in life. It was "bad," but it was vivid. For in spite of their unfortunate beginnings, the slime in which primarily and without any willing of their own they had been embedded and from which nearly all were seeking to crawl upwards, and bravely enough, they had heart for and faith in life.

In all cases, apparently, love was their star as well as their bane. They thought chiefly of the joy that might be had in joining their lives with some man or being out in the free world, working again possibly, at least in touch in some feeble way with the beauty and gayety of life, as beauty and gayety manifested themselves to them.

And so by degrees, the crash of her own original hopes echoing less and less loudly in the distance, the pain of her great shame and rude awakening passed farther and farther from her. The smoothness and regularity of this austere life, indifferent as it seemed at times, consoled her by its very security and remoteness from the world. It was lean and spare, to be sure, but it offered safety and rest to the mind and heart. Now, rising in her dim, silent ward of a morning, repeating her instructed prayers, marching in silence to chapel, to breakfast, to work, hearing only the soft hum of the machines, marching again to chapel, playing each day, but not too noisily, and finally retiring in the same ordered and silent way to her tiny bed, she was soothed and healed.

And yet, or perhaps because of this, she could not help thinking of the clangor and crash of the world without. It had been grim and painful to her, but in its rude, brutal way it had been alive. The lighted streets at night! The cars! That dancing pavilion in which once she had been taught to dance by the great blue sea! The vanished touches of her faithless lover's hands—his kisses—brief, so soon over! Where was he now in the great strange world outside? With whom? What was she like? And would he tire of her as quickly? Treat her as badly? Where was Tina? Frank? Her mother? What had happened to her mother? Not a word had she heard.

To Sister St. Agnes, after a time, sensing her to be generous, faithful, patient, she had confided all concerning herself and her mother, crying on her shoulder, and the Sister had promised to learn what she could. But the investigation proving that her mother had been sent to the workhouse, she deemed it best to say nothing for the present. Madeleine would find her quickly enough on returning to the world. Why cloud the new budding life with so shameful a memory?

300

VI

And then once more, in due time, and with the memory of these things clinging fast to her, she was sent forth into the world, not quite as poorly armed as before, perhaps, but still with the limited equipment which her own innate disposition and comprehension compelled.

After many serious and presumably wise injunctions as to the snares and pitfalls of this world, and accompanied by a black-habited nun, who took her direct to one of those moral and religious families whose strict adherence to the tenets of this particular faith was held to provide an ideal example, she was left to her own devices and the type of work she had previously followed, the nuns themselves being hard put to it to discover anything above the most menial forms of employment for their various charges. Theirs was a type of schooling and training which did not rise above a theory of morality requiring not so much skill as faith and blind obedience.

And again here, as in the institution itself, the idea of a faith, a religion, a benign power above that of man and seeking his welfare, surrounded her as the very air itself or as an aura, although she personally was by no means ready to accept it, never having given it serious thought.

Everywhere here, as in the institution itself, were little images or colored pictures of saints, their brows circled by stars or crowns, their hands holding sceptres or lilies, their bodies arrayed in graceful and soothing robes of white, blue, pink and gold. Their faces were serene, their eyes benignly contemplative, yet to Madeleine they were still images only, pretty and graceful, even comforting, but at so great variance to life as she knew it as to be little more than pretty pictures.

In the great church which they attended, and to which they persuaded her to accompany them, were more of these same candle-lit pictures of saints, images and altars starred with candles, many or few, at which she was wont to stare in wonder and awe. The vestments of the priest and the acolytes, the white-and-gold and red-and-gold of the chasuble and the stole and the cope, the

301

gold and silver crosses, chalices and winecups, overawed her in-experienced and somewhat impressionable mind without convincing it of the immanence of superior forces whose significance or import she could in nowise guess. God, God, God—she heard of Him and the passion and death of the self-sacrificing Lord Jesus.

And here, as there, the silence, the order, the cleanliness and regularity, as well as simplicity, were the things which most in-vested her reason and offered the greatest contrasts to her old life.

She had not known or sensed the significance of these things before. Now, day by day, like the dripping of water, the ticking of time, they made an impression, however slight. Routine, routine, routine, and the habit and order and color of a vast and autocratic religion, made their lasting impression upon her.

And yet, in spite of an occasional supervisory visit on the part of one or other of the nuns of the probation department, she was not only permitted but compelled to work out her life as best she might, and upon such wages as she could command or devise. For all the prayers and the good-will of the nuns, life was as insistent and driving as ever. It did not appear to be so involved with religion. In spite of the admonitions of the church, the family for whom she was working saw little more in its religious obligation than that she should be housed and fed ac-cording to her material merits. If she wished to better herself, as she soon very clearly saw she must, she would have to develop a skill which she did not now have and which, once developed, would make her of small use here. At the same time, if the months spent in the institution had conveyed to her the reasonableness of making something better of her life than hitherto she had been able to do, the world, pleasure, hope, clanged as insistently and as wooingly as ever before.

But how? How? was the great problem. Hers was no resourceful, valiant soul, capable of making its own interesting way alone. Think as she would, and try, love, and love only, the admiration and ministering care of some capable and affec-tionate man, was the only thing that seemed likely to solve for her the various earthly difficulties which beset her.

But even as to this, how, in what saving or perfect way, was love to come to her? She had made one mistake which in the development of any honest relationship with another would have to be confessed. And how would it be then? Would love, admiration, forgive? Love, love, love, and the peace and comfort of that happy routine home life which she imagined she saw operative in the lives of others—how it glimmered afar, like a star!

And again there was her mother.

It was not long after she had come from the institution that sheer loneliness, as well as a sense of daughterly responsibility and pity, had urged her to look up her mother, in order that she might restore to herself some little trace of a home, however wretched it might be. She had no one, as she proceeded to argue. At least in her own lonely life her mother provided, or would, an ear and a voice, sympathetic if begging, a place to go.

She had learned on returning to their last living-place on one of her afternoons off, that her mother had been sent away to the "Island," but had come back and since had been sent to the city poor-farm. This last inquiry led eventually to her mother's discovery of her and of her fixing herself upon her once more as a dependent, until her death somewhat over a year later.

But in the meantime, and after all, life continued to call and call and to drive her on, for she was still full of the hope and fever of youth.

Once, before leaving the institution in which they had worked together, Viola Patters had said to her in one of those bursts of confidence based on attraction:

"Once you're outta here an' I am, too, I'd like to see you again, only there ain't no use your writin' me here, for I don't believe they'd give it to me. I don't believe they'd want us to run together. I don't believe they like me as well as they do you. But you write me, wherever you are, care of—" and here she gave a definite address—"an' I'll get it when I get out."

She assured Madeleine that she would probably be able to get a good place, once she was free of the control of the Sisters, and then she might be able to do something for her.

Often during these dark new days she thought of this, and being hard-pressed for diverting interests in her life she finally wrote her, receiving in due time a request to come and see her.

But, as it proved, Viola was no avenue of improvement for her in her new mood. She was, as Madeleine soon discovered, part of a small group which was making its way along a path which she had promised herself henceforth to avoid. Viola was more comfortably placed in quarters of her own than Madeleine had ever been, but the method by which she was forwarding her life she could not as readily accept.

Yet her own life, move about as she might and did after a time from one small position to another, in store or factory, in the hope of bettering herself, held nothing either. Day by day as she worked she sensed all the more clearly that the meager tasks at which she toiled could bring her nothing of permanent value. Her mother was dead now, and she more alone than ever. During a period of several years, in which she worked and dreamed, leading a thin, underpaid life, her mind was ever on love and what it might do for her—the pressure of a seeking hand, the sanctuary of an enveloping heart.

And then, for the second time in her brief life, love came, or seemed to—at least in her own heart if nowhere else.

She had by now, and through her own efforts, attained to a clerkship in one of the great stores at the salary of seven dollars a week, on which she was trying to live. And then, behold, one day among her customers one of those suave and artful masters of the art of living by one's wits, with a fortune of looks, to whom womanhood is a thing to be taken by an upward curl of a pair of mustachios, the vain placement of ringed locks, spotless and conspicuous linen, and clothes and shoes of a newness and luster all but disturbing to a very work-a-day world. His manners and glances were of a winsomeness which only the feminine heart— and that unschooled in the valuelessness of veneer—fully appreciates.

Yes, the sheer grace of the seeking male, his shallow and heartless courtesy, the luster of his eye and skin, a certain something of shabby-grand manner, such as she had never known in the particularly narrow world in which she moved, was sufficient to arrest and fix her interest.

He leaned over and examined the stationery and pencils which she sold, commenting on prices, the routine of her work, smiled archly and suggested by his manner entire that she was one in whom he could be deeply interested. At the same time a certain animal magnetism, of the workings of which she was no more

304

conscious than might be any stick or stone, took her in its tow.

Here was one out of many, a handsome beau, who was interested in her and her little life. The oiled and curled hair became the crown of a god; the mustachios and the sharp, cruel nose harmonies of exquisite beauty. Even the muscular, prehensile hands were rhythmic, musical in their movements. She had time only to sense the wonder of his perfect self before he went away. But it was to return another day, with an even more familiar and insinuating grace.

He was interested in her, as he frankly said the next time, and she must be his friend. At lunch-time one day he was waiting to take her to a better restaurant than she would ever have dreamed of entering; on another day it was to dinner that she accompanied him.

According to him, she was beautiful, wonderful. Her flower-like life was being wasted on so rude a task. She should marry him, and then her difficulties would be solved. He was one who, when fortune was with him, so he said, made much, much money. He might even take her from the city at times to see strange places and interesting scenes.

As for her own stunted life, from most of the details of which she forebore, he seemed in nowise interested. It was not due to any lack on her part in the past that her life had been so ill. . . .

Love, love, love. . . . The old story. In a final burst of admiration and love for his generosity she told him of her one great error, which caused him a few moments of solemn cogitation and was then dismissed as nothing of importance, a pathetic, childish mistake. Then there followed one of those swift and seemingly unguarded unions, a commonplace of the tangled self-preserving underworld of poverty. A clergyman was found whose moral assurances seemed to make the union ideal. Then a room in a commonplace boarding house, and the newer and better life which eventually was to realize all was begun.

VII

To those familiar with the brazen and relentless methods of a certain type of hawk of the underworld, which picks

305

fledglings from the nest and springlings from the fields and finds life itself only a hunting ground in which those mentally or physically weaker than itself may be enslaved, this description will seem neither strained nor inadequate. Fagins of sex, creatures who change their women as they would their coats, they make an easy if reprehensible bed of their lives, and such of their victims as have known them well testify that for a while at least in their care or custody they were not unhappy.

So it was with Madeleine and her lover. With amused and laughing tolerance toward her natural if witless efforts to build up a home atmosphere about their presumably joint lives, to build for a future in which they should jointly share, he saw in them only something trivial or ridiculous, whereas to her it was as though the heavens had opened and she was surveying a new world. For in his love and care there was to be peace. Latterly, if not now—for already he complained of conditions which made it impossible for him to work—the results of their several labors were to be pooled in order to prepare for that something better which would soon be achieved—a home, an ideally happy state somewhere. Even children were in mind.

The mere fact that he shortly complained of other temporary reverses which made it necessary for him and her to keep close watch over their resources, and that for the time being, until he "could arrange his affairs," she must find some employment which would pay much better than her old one, gave her no shock.

Indeed, it was an indescribable joy for her to do for her love, for love had come, that great solvent of all other earthly difficulties, that leveler of all but insurmountable barriers. Even now love was to make her life flower at last. There was an end to loneliness and the oppressive indifference of the great sea of life.

But, as in the first instance, so now the awakening was swift and disconcerting. Realizing the abject adoration in which she held his surface charms and that his thin, tricky soul was the beginning and the end of things for her, it was all the easier to assure her, and soon insist, that the easiest and swiftest way of making money, of which she was unfortunately aware, must be resorted to, for a great necessity had come upon him. The usual tale of a threatening disaster, a sudden loss at cards which might

306

end in imprisonment for him and their enforced separation, was enough.

Swiftly he filled her ears with tales of rescues by women of many of his men friends similarly circumstanced, of the "fools" and "marks" that filled the thoroughfares to be captured and preyed upon by women. Why hesitate? Consider the meager, beggarly wages she had previously earned, the nothingness of her life before. Why jeopardize their future now? Why be foolish, dull? Plainly it was nothing to love, as he saw it. Should it be so much to her? In this wise she was persuaded.

But now it was not the shame and the fear of arrest that troubled her, but the injury which love had done and was doing to her, that cut and burned and seared and scarred.

Love, as she now began dimly to realize once more, should not be so. More than anything else, if love was what she had always dreamed, should it not protect and save and keep her for itself? And now see. Love was sending her out again to loiter in doorways and before windows and to "make eyes."

It was this that turned like a wheel in her brain and heart. For in spite of the roughness of her emotional experiences thus far, she had faith to believe that love should not be so, should not do so.

Those features which to this hour, and long after, like those features of her first love, seemed so worship-worth, those eyes that had seemed to beam on her with love, the lips that had smiled so graciously and kissed hers, the hands and arms that had petted and held her, should not be part of the compulsion that sent her here.

No, love should be better than that. He himself had told her so at first—that she was worth more than all else to him— and now see!

And then one night, fully a year and a half later, the climax. Being particularly irritated by some money losses and the need of enduring her at all, even though she might still prove of some value as a slave, he turned on her with a savage fury.

"What, only . . . ! Get to hell outa here! What do yuh think I am—a sucker? And let go my arm. Don't come that stuff on me. I'm sick of it. Don't hang on my arm, I tell yuh! I'm tired, damn tired! Get out! Go on—beat it, an' don't come back, see?

I'm through—through—yuh hear me? I mean what I say. I'm through, once an' fer all. Beat it, an' fer good. Don't come back. I've said that before, but this time it *goes*! Go on, now quick—Scat!—an' don't ever let me see yuh around here any more, yuh hear?—yuh damned piece o' mush, yuh!"

He pushed her away, throwing open the door as he did so, and, finding her still pleading and clinging, threw her out with such force that she cut her left eye and the back of her left hand against the jamb of the door.

There was a cry of "Fred! Fred! Please! Please!"—and then the door was slammed and she was left leaning disconsolately and brokenly against the stair rail outside.

And now, as before, the cruelty and inscrutability of life weighed on her, only now, less than before, had she hope wherewith to buoy herself. It was all so dark, so hopeless. Often in this hour she thought of the swift, icy waters of the river, glistening under a winter moon, and then again of the peace and quiet of the House of the Good Shepherd, its shielding remoteness from life, the only true home or sanctuary she had ever known. And so, brooding and repressing occasional sobs, she made her way toward it, down the long streets, thinking of the pathetically debasing love-life that was now over—the dream of love that never, never could be again, for her.

VIII

The stark red walls of the institution stood as before, only dim and gray and cold under a frosty winter moon. It was three of a chill, cold morning. She had come a long way, drooping, brooding, half-freezing and crying. More than once on the way the hopelessness of her life and her dreams had given her pause, causing her to turn again with renewed determination toward the river—only the vivid and reassuring picture she had retained of this same grim and homely place, its restricted peace and quiet, the sympathy of Sister St. Agnes and Mother St. Bertha, had carried her on.

En route she speculated as to whether they would receive her now, so objectionable and grim was her tale. And yet she

308

could not resist continuing toward it, so reassuring was its memory, only to find it silent, not a single light burning. But, after all, there was one, at a side door—not the great cold gate by which she had first been admitted but another to one side, to her an all but unknown entrance; and to it after some brooding hesitation she made her way, ringing a bell and being admitted by a drowsy nun, who ushered her into the warmth and quiet of the inner hallway. Once in she mechanically followed to the bronze grille which, as prison bars, obstructed the way, and here on one of the two plain chairs placed before a small aperture she now sank wearily and looked through.

Her cut eye was hurting her and her bruised hands. On the somewhat faded jacket and crumpled hat, pulled on indifferently because she was too hurt to think or care, there was some blown snow. And when the Sister Secretary in charge of the room after midnight, hearing footsteps, came to the grille, she looked up wanly, her little red, rough hands crossed on her lap.

"Mother," she said beseechingly, "may I come in?"

Then remembering that only Mother St. Bertha could admit her, added wearily:

"Is Mother St. Bertha here? I was here before. She will know me."

The Sister Secretary surveyed her curiously, sensing more of the endless misery that was ever here, but seeing that she was sick or in despair hastened to call her superior, whose rule it was that all such requests for admission should be referred to her. There was no stir in the room in her absence. Presently pattened feet were heard, and the face of Mother St. Bertha, wrinkled and aweary, appeared at the square opening.

"What is it, my child?" she asked curiously if softly, wondering at the crumpled presence at this hour.

"Mother," began Madeleine tremulously, looking up and recognizing her, "don't you remember me? It is Madeleine. I was here four years ago. I was in the girls' ward. I worked in the sewing room."

She was so beaten by life, the perpetual endings to her never more than tremulous hopes, that even now and here she expected little more than an indifference which would send her away again.

"Why, yes, of course I remember you, my child. But what

309

is it that brings you now, dear? Your eye is cut, and your hand."

"Yes, mother, but please don't ask—just now. Oh, please let me come in! I am so tired! I've had such a hard time!"

"Of course, my child," said the Mother, moving to the door and opening it. "You may come in. But what has happened, child? How is it that your cheek is cut, and your hands?"

"Mother," pleaded Madeleine wearily, "must I answer now? I am so unhappy! Can't I just have my old dress and my bed for tonight—that little bed under the lamp?"

"Why, yes, dear, you may have them, of course," said the nun tactfully, sensing a great relief. "And you need not talk now. I think I know how it is. Come with me."

She led the way along bare, dimly lit corridors and up cold solid iron stairs, echoing to the feet, until once more, as in the old days, was reached the severe but spotless room in which were the baths and the hampers for soiled clothes.

"Now, my child," she said, "you may undress and bathe. I will get something for your eye."

And so here at last, once more, Madeleine put aside the pathetic if showy finery that for a time had adorned and shamed her: a twilled skirt she had only recently bought in the pale hope of interesting *him,* the commonplace little hat for which she had paid ten dollars, the striped shirtwaist, once a pleasure to her in the hope that it would please *him.*

In a kind of dumbness of despair she took off her shoes and stockings and, as the Mother left, entered the warm, clean bath which had been provided. She stifled a sob as she did so, and others as she bathed. Then she stepped out and dried her body and covered it with the clean, simple slip of white which had been laid on a chair, brushing her hair and touching her eye, until the Mother Sister returned with an unguent wherewith to dress it.

Then she was led along other silent passages, once dreary enough but now healing in their sense of peace and rest, and so into the great room set with row upon row of simple white iron beds, covered with their snowy linen and illuminated only by the minute red lamps or the small candles burning before their idealistic images here and there, beneath which so many like herself were sleeping. Over the bed which she had once occupied, and which by chance was then vacant, burned the one little lamp which she recognized as of old—her lamp, as she had always thought of it—a thin and flickering flame, before an image of the Virgin. At sight of it, she repressed a sob.

"You see, my child," said the Mother Superior poetically, " it must have been waiting for you. Anyhow it is empty. Perhaps it may have known you were coming."

She spoke softly so that the long rows of sleepers might not be disturbed, then proceeded to turn down the coverlets.

"Oh, Mother," Madeleine suddenly whispered softly as she stood by the bed, "won't you let me stay always? I never want to go out any more. I have had such a hard time. I will work so hard for you if you will let me stay!"

The experienced Sister looked at her curiously. Never before had she heard such a plea.

"Why, yes, my child," she said. "If you wish to stay I'm sure it can be arranged. It is not as we usually do, but you are not the only one who has gone out in the past and come back to us. I am sure God and the Blessed Virgin will hear your prayer for whatever is right. But now go to bed and sleep. You need rest. I can see that. And tomorrow, or any time, or never, as you choose, you may tell me what has happened."

She urged her very gently to enter and then tucked the covers about her, laying finally a cool, wrinkled hand on her forehead. For answer Madeleine seized and put it to her lips, holding it so.

"Oh, Mother," she sobbed as the Sister bent over her, "don't ever make me go out in the world again, will you? You won't, will you? I'm so tired! I'm so tired!"

"No, dear, no," soothed the Sister, "not unless you wish it. And now rest. You need never go out in the world again unless you wish."

And withdrawing the hand from the kissing lips, she tiptoed silently from the room.

Bridget Mullanphy

*I*THINK OF HER ALWAYS as an integral part of one of those blowsy, ash-can-decorated thoroughfares of New York's lower West Side, gray granite blocks paving it, dirt and garbage lying disgustingly uncollected, a dead cat or dog, maybe; dirty children; dirty, dark hallways giving into the respective walls at regular intervals; a ruck of trucks and carts clattering to and fro; but at the end the bright North River, a metal stream, flowing at the base of the Palisades, which rise like a gray wall above it, and above that a gray or blue sky, ribbon-wide.

On the low step gracing the sidewalk entrance of one of these squalid tenements, Mrs. Mullanphy, gray-haired, burly, squarish rather than rotund, a slight indentation at the middle of her sleeveless "wrapper" indicating a former waistline, almost always tied around with a dirty, faded gingham apron. She has been sweeping and is now resting upon the handle of her broom. A slattern of a girl in a green blouse and brown skirt, holding a baby on one arm, is talking to her. I am about to address her, Jimmie, my man of all work, having deserted me these several weeks, when the following scene takes place:

MRS. MULLANPHY (*looking along the hall toward an invisible stair—invisible because of shadow—and then up at a second- or third-story window*): The likes of them! The likes of them! It's them that is the clean ones, is it, with a peck of dirt under the bed and the same blanket from one year's end to the other! 'Tis never they have a blanket on the line. (*A head appears at one of the upper windows, second story left. It is a big head, broad-faced between parted wings of dark red hair. Its owner wears a triangle of red-and-brown-squared shawl—a small shawl in no way protecting an immense bosom held in by a nightgown or "wrapper."*)

RED HEAD: And who is it that talks of dirt, with ashes

313

under the stove—pans of them—and fish heads on the floor! And the health department wonderin' at the sickness in the block! (*The head disappears.*)

MRS. MULLANPHY (*looking up defiantly and shouting*): The health department, is it? The health department? And with yer own child after dyin' from dirt and little else. And yer old man out of a job three months out of four. And yer son that drinks till 'tis himself that can't find his way through the hall and up the stairs at night but must be fallin' against the doors of other folks when they're tryin' to sleep. (*To the girl who is holding the baby*) 'Tis a bit warm, ain't it? (*Then giving a square rag of a carpet an extra flick with her broom.*)

THE GIRL WITH THE BABY: Yes, it is. Terry! Terry! Come away from that dead cat!

RED HEAD (*reappearing at the window above*): 'Tis me son, is it? And work, is it? And your old man out of work these three months now, and scabbin' in the place of better men when he does. And where is the cup of sugar borried of me these six months and not returned yet? And before that, me salt and me starch? (*The head disappears.*)

MRS. MULLANPHY: Out of work, is it? And you with yer darter on the streets of the city this day! And with men runnin' to where ye lived before till it was the vice society that was called in and yerselves put out by the police! And no rent, and yer furniture put out! Where is the can of coffee I loaned ye six weeks this Monday? Salt, is it? And yer darter out to get money from men and yer drunken son fallin' through the halls!

•   •   •

So there you are! I would not, I assure you, present this, nor much that is to follow, save for the strange irritability of it all; the vague, blundering, I might even say fantastic, and reasonless pother and ado that *is* life, here as well as elsewhere. And what the meaning or purpose of the creative force when it could descend to such folderol and nonsense as this, I used to ask myself on observing and listening to such a scene.

But let us return to the same doorstep a few months later. Now it is a cold, gray, almost dark November afternoon. I am

314

again on my way to engage Mrs. Mullanphy to do some cleaning for me. I encounter little Delia Mullanphy, aged four (although the eldest daughter of this household is in her thirties), playing house with a little boy in the dust and dirt of the sidewalk under an arc light blazing thus early on this dusky afternoon.

"And now ye're to come home at six, see?" the child is saying as she rises and pushes her little boy companion away to give him a good start on his homecoming. And he, once strategically placed as a homecomer, comes swaggering and staggering, but listen.

"Ain't dinner ready yet, hey? You—! It's six o'clock and there ain't nothin' on the table, eh! I'll give you a punch in the jaw, you!" And with this making a vigorous, if childish, lunge. But at this strenuous point in the game I choose to interrupt with an inquiry. It is all so realistic that I fear he will strike her, wondering at the same time how two such infants come by such knowledge as this.

The second floor front right as you go up is occupied by Mrs. Mullanphy, her husband, thirty-year-old daughter and four-year-old daughter. Mullanphy père, as I understand from Mrs. Mullanphy's irrepressible patter, works very occasionally as a teamster. He works, that is, when the spirit moves him. Cornelia, the elder daughter, as I also occasionally hear from my talkative cleaning woman, works out at times; at other times she sews at home. Mrs. Mullanphy herself scrubs, washes, anywhere and everywhere, as the spirit or necessity moves her. For Mullanphy, as I also well know by now, is exceedingly unreliable—a temperamental and in the main befogged Irishman who seems in part to be afraid of and in another part not to consider or be moved by his wife in any way. In truth, I cannot exactly explain how this is—a sort of marital enigma which I have never been able to solve for myself. As I ascend the stairs, however, I hear a voice, unmistakably that of my cleaning lady, and I stop to listen to the following:

"And who is it that talks of family? Is it the Finnertys? God knows what they sprang from! Family, is it? With a son in the protectory! 'Tis me fond boast that a Mullanphy is as good as anyone, and better. They can be looked up for what they are these hundreds of years back."

(Upon my word, I thought! Such noble lineage! This is a

cleaning woman worth having.) But then came the reply, hurled down from an upper window and treasured by me to this day:

"'Tis yer proud boast, is it? And your nieces carryin' things to ye that don't belong to them! 'Tis the police that should be told of it! And yerself pretendin' to be the mother of a child not yer own! Ye old harridan! And 'tis well we can guess whose it is! And who's the father of yer darter's child? And where is he? And why isn't she with him this day, and the child, too? A widow, is it? A foine widow! And her and yerself leavin' Barry Street and no father there! Widow! And she the young lady yet, still lookin' for a man! Foine family, is it? Heaven preserve the rest of us from such foineness!" The voice died heavily away.

But enough of the long rigmarole of charges and rejoinders that invariably flew about these tenement rooms and halls, principally, as I was always pained to note, between Mrs. Mullanphy and her neighbors whenever I was in that region. How flesh and blood could continuously endure them is beyond me. My own interest might honestly be said to have been literary. I was so thoroughly fascinated by this outspoken Irish realism which nowhere else apparently could I find in such undiluted and plentiful quantities that I liked to come here. Otherwise not. For as I had already observed of other nations and races, they were much more secretive. But the Irish never. On the contrary, in such a world as this, it did seem as though all of the customary reserves and punctilio of better neighborhoods or ordinary social life anywhere no longer held. Either they had never existed for those who dwelt in this environment or they had broken down. And in addition, whatever the reason—poverty and lack of training in the amenities being the principal ingredients, I am sure—a state of troublesome and devastating espionage and criticism held. No one could do anything that was not more or less the subject of observation and comment. At the slightest indication of exclusiveness, public opprobrium and denunciation seemed sure to follow. Such a thing as privacy could scarcely be said to exist. Having so few mental employments, those who dwelt in these gaunt sties and pits of the world had little beyond vagrom and errant notions in regard to life, and spied and quarreled from sheer ennui. They could not think sanely and consecutively. Their interests, vivid enough at the moment, were, after all, mere mental flutterings. They were concerned only with what was immediately before them, the things that at the moment they could see, hear, taste, smell, feel. A low order of animal life, most assuredly, and yet interesting as animal by reason of the sharp contrast afforded to the more ordered and constructive superimposed intellectual life of other regions.

But now as to Cornelia Mullanphy, the thin, amiable and yet eccentric, anemic and high-strung daughter who, if such taunts as Mrs. Finnerty's were to be believed, was the true mother of the little Delia Mullanphy whom Mrs. Mullanphy claimed to be her own. Because of fear of scandal in this region, no doubt, as well as, possibly, previous neighborhoods in which the family had lived, the parentage of Delia had to be concealed. I am not sure. At any rate Cornelia was perhaps thirty-three or -four, and not so ill-looking. Being neglected and lonely, she would occasionally, as I often had the chance to observe for myself, leave the corner ordinarily occupied by her and her sewing machine, to visit one of the neighbors. Then would her mother's wrath pour down on her on her return.

"Keep out of yer neighbors' rooms, you! Isn't it them that's laughin' and makin' fun of us the while? Indeed, it's Katie Tooney herself, her that ye think is yer friend, that only last week was callin' down fer all the neighbors to know that ye're not married but a man's plaything and Delia's not my child but yours!"

"It's a lie! It's a lie!" flared Cornelia, furiously. "She never said it, and you know she didn't. You make up lies—you with yer church! Have you no peace ever! Shut yer jaw!"

"Shut me jaw, is it? Yer own mother, and me that took ye back when ye had no one, when ye couldn't get a man to look at ye! It's me that's to shut me jaw, is it?"

But in spite of Mrs. Mullanphy's raucous family and neighborly controversies, she could be as careful and silent about my place and among my spare belongings as any one could wish. Indeed at times my humble effects seemed positively to overawe her, especially such things as paintings, candelabra, silverware. There was one painting in particular, a large and well-composed nude after the manner of the neo-impressionists of 1912, which seemed actually to terrify her. Curiously enough, in her world the nude, in the form of prints, illustrations and paintings was plainly taboo. Perhaps her church or priest condemned them. At any rate I cannot recall that ever I saw her give this particular picture one direct glance, unless it was the first one. Invariably she passed it, where it hung above a low shelf of books, with averted face and downcast eyes. The frame might need dusting, and the objects on the shelf below it, yet although everything else in the rooms was scrupulously cleaned and polished by her, these things were left untouched. She objected to the painting. It disagreed with her. Or if not that, as I have said, her church did not countenance such things.

Considering her amazing tempers and moods, however, her church, as it seemed to me, appeared to have an almost uncanny and even amazing hold on Bridget. She was a devout Catholic, blending, to my confusion always, a kind of blind animal faith in her religion with the temperamental, material, and as I often thought, pagan notions and actions that elsewhere governed others who were wholly pagan. In short, oil and water mixed.

And because of this I once ventured to interrogate her as follows:

"Mrs. Mullanphy," I said, "I notice that you go to church very regularly. You must be a good Christian."

"And why not?" she bristled. "'Tis from me church that I gets me stren'th. And if it wasn't for me faith, I couldn't go on at all, 'tis that hard on me life is."

"True enough," I agreed. "Life does press hard on most of us. But I notice that in spite of your religion you have a pretty rough time of it where you are. Are all your neighbors so bad?"

"And am I to hold my tongue and that bein' said about me that's not so?" she demanded, her choler rising. "'Tis not within morshall (*mortal* was what she meant) patience. 'Tis not human." And she brandished the handle of an oil mop then in her hand as one might a spear, at the same time crumpling a dusting cloth in the other hand as though it were something tangible with which to fight.

"I know, I know," I said placatingly. "No doubt they say a lot of things about you they shouldn't. Everybody has to endure that sort of thing. But how about what the Bible says about

318

loving your neighbor as yourself, and turning the left cheek if someone smites you on the right. Doesn't that command you to keep the peace?"

"The Bible! The Bible!" she blurted, defiantly. "Sure, and I know me Bible as well as anyone, and better." (I knew she could not read.) "And I know what me church says about it, too. I can get the straight of it from me priest any day. But what about me neighbors lovin' me and lettin' me alone when I'm not doin' anything to any of them, bad end to them! Will ye tell me that? 'Tis the Bible itself says an eye for an eye and a tooth for a tooth, and I'm not forgettin' that either. 'Tis in the same book."

"Very true," I agreed. "It does say that. But this other is what Jesus said. An eye for an eye and a tooth for a tooth is from the Old Testament. But Jesus said that he was giving a new law."

"And 'tis not anyone that need be tellin' me, fer 'tis well I know it," she replied, pugnaciously. "But who'll be sayin' that I'm not within me right in defendin' me own? Isn't it meself that is forever tryin' to keep the pace wherever I am, loanin' of me salt and me coffee and me butter and the suds of me wash or the boilin's of me meat? Sure, and there would be none better than meself as a neighbor did I have them about me that had the sense. 'Tis better than this I was used to before I come to where I am today—the roilin's and the scrapin's of New York."

"You were better born, you mean?"

"Indade and I was. The scrapin's that I have to live with this day."

"Quite so, quite so," I dishonestly soothed. "I can see that you are better than those about you, and that you do better too, really."

"Well, I'm not meanin' to say that I'm that much better than another. But sure, I 'm not called to do more than me best nor more than any other. And the Lard himself never intended that anyone should be more than human. He'd never have made a purgatory if he had."

"Grand," I thought. "The acme of logic. What more need I say now?" And so desisted. But hers, as you many see, was a typically confused, evasive and pagan mind coated over by a lot of religious dogma which she did not really comprehend but which she sought to blend in some confused way with the sordid routine of her daily life. Yet, as anyone could also see, the blending went hard. Still, Heaven, I am sure, was a real enough place to Mrs. Mullanphy—the heaven of a patriarchal whiskered God, the Father; of the Jesus of mediaeval pictures, and the kindly Virgin of the starry crown and lilies. If she has since died and not found them seated upon a throne and surrounded by clouds as she imagined them to be, then there is one very much troubled and puzzled Irish spirit roaming about somewhere in space.

But I speak of this religious tendency not irreverently or to poke fun, as some may think—I am too sorry for blind, stumbling, seeking humanity to do anything of that sort—but because this profound religiosity of hers contrasted so oddly with her general outlook and method of procedure; with the grand frays and ebullitions of temperament that were the order of each week, excluding Sundays, which as I know were more solemnly observed—Mrs. Mullanphy attending mass and observing her other church duties with a regularity which all Catholics would no doubt look upon as commendable.

Yet in order to round out this decidedly Hogarthian atmosphere, I am, perforce, and almost against my will, compelled to introduce two other persons connected with her, and when I would so much prefer to describe her only. Those same were apparently two grandnieces, bizarre and hoyden creatures both, who made their livings, in so far as I could gather, at housework here and there in the great city and who some time after I had known Bridget were either imported by or else had out of a clear sky descended on my heroine from Ireland. Only and except for a certain lightness or brightness which they contributed to the Mullanphy atmosphere from time to time, they really constituted a moral problem and one somewhat different, I must say, from that of Cornelia and the mysterious child. I do not mean to imply that they were not good girls in the sense that their limited intelligence could grasp good. But . . . well . . . in so far as I could gather from one and another person observing this somewhat complicated scene, they were not strictly honest. That is . . . but there, let me proceed to the painting of them and let the peculiar data take care of itself.

Molly McGragh, for instance, was tall and pale, with a round face, gray eyes and lightish brown hair, not very attractive, but with a fairly genial manner and temperament and rather addicted to gossip. By way of contrast, her sister Katie, younger by at least two years, was cheerful, good-natured, amusing, flamboyant. Where Molly was usually sober and plain in gray or white, Katie was arresting always in a suit of terra cotta or strawberry, with a red or green hat adorned with white feathers, a boa, a parasol, and I know not what else. Whenever she came, which was often, she came quite noisily. Indeed, the first day I saw her it was her voice that startled the air and myself. "Ha, he! 'Tis yerself!" (To Cornelia) "Where's the Mullanphys? Where's the grafters? Out airin' thimselves? 'Tis as well. They should get the air once in a while." Then going to the rear air shaft and waving to a tenant occupying rooms to the rear: "Ho, ho, is it yerself, Mrs. Hanfy? And how the divil are ye?"

And then Molly: "The grafters is out, is they? The two of us swears we'll never come here again. But 'tis the nature of us brings us, I do suppose, Cornelia. We're that soft-hearted. But 'tis unnecessary to ask ye how ye are. Ye're lookin' good."

To which Cornelia, from her dusty corner and sewing machine, replied: "Sure, I'm all right. Sit down, will ye? The old man ain't workin' again. I suppose he'll be findin' somethin' pretty soon though or we won't be here long, any of us."

"Not workin', ye say?" This from Molly. "He's been idle long enough now, I'm thinkin'. And always watchin' everybody else to see whether they're workin' or not. 'Tis strange how 'tis with some folks. 'Tis a mystery to me how it is that without work he gets the drink."

But if you were to assume from this that Bridget and her husband and the McGraghs were very much at outs, you are very much mistaken. You could not judge by what you heard any more than you could believe your own eyes. The approach of one to another in this peculiar world, to say nothing of their attitude toward life, toward friendship, and what not else, was literally topsy-turvy. Thus, should the Mullanphys père and mère happen to appear in the midst of such a condemnation as I have described, you would hear "me darlin's" and "How are ye, auntie dear? Sure, 'tis weeks since we've been over, but 'tis not fer not wantin' to come. Only Chuesday of last week 'twas me that was sayin' to Katie that we must be goin' to see our Aunt Bridget and be takin' her a little somethin' to let her know we're not ungrateful fer all she did fer us. But last week 'twas Mrs. Whitebait herself was sick on our day off. But today the two of us was sayin', sick or not sick we would come this day, and here we be."

"And sure, me darlin's," Mrs. Mullanphy would rejoice. "'Tis welcome ye are, too, as the flowers in May. And to dinner it is that ye'll be stayin', the two of ye. Whist, now, 'tis not much that will be in the house, I'm fearin', with Mullanphy out of work this long while, but 'twill be somethin'. The store is but a step and I can run over this minute, or Cornelia can, and will be bringin' all we need before ye can say six or ten!"

And forthwith Cornelia, who had just been declaring that her parents were slave drivers, that they "borried" from her, and that they never gave her anything for the work she did, would begin suggesting appetizing dishes that she could prepare. And the McGraghs themselves would insist on paying for what was needed, since that was obviously what Mrs. Mullanphy intended, at the same time giving each other a sly look which seemed to suggest "grafter."

But the amazing turns these same feasts and presumably gay conversations would take, and almost entirely due to the temperament of Mrs. Mullanphy, as I used to think. For first, and now that a good dinner loomed ahead of her (the McGraghs or Cornelia having gone to the store), she would proceed to indulge in a bit of cheering banter either from the front or rear window or across the open air shaft. Ah, how often have I listened. "And is the old man's corns better, Mrs. Hanfy? Ah, 'tis the sad infliction!" Then pausing to sniff, "And what is it ye may be cookin'? Yes, I see the smoke of it. Lamb? Eggplant, ye say? Oh, steak." Then leaning still farther out of the window and talking louder: "'Tis not a lover of steak I am meself. What? Corned-beef hash?" Turning and facing whoever might chance to be inside, she might add, somewhat censoriously and yet not entirely so: "She don't like the smoke seen comin' from out of her room. She's closed the window on me."

But we will assume that the arrangements for dining are progressing satisfactorily enough. The young nieces have bought and paid for the proposed feast. Cornelia, given the cash, has brought it. Mullanphy, a sleepily intoxicated person and usually somewhat dour, life seeming not too much or too important to him at any time, may be stalking about in an odd, silent way, his hat on the back of his head—never off—and his coat, winter or summer, slipped back off his shoulder and hanging rather limply and crumpled between the arms. Sober and working or drunk and idle, he was, as I had observed in the course of time, never quite able to face his wife bravely and roughly and yet never wholly afraid of her—a cross between a man who has never been wholly subdued and one who is still afraid to say too much.

Suddenly, in the midst of this, and after setting out to do all the cooking, and apparently not wishing to be interfered with in that quarter, Mrs. Mullanphy would bethink herself of the fact that whosoever might have paid for the dinner, it was she and none other who was cooking it, the McGraghs and others lolling about. Presto! "Mullanphy! Mullanphy! Will ye be standin' there and lettin' the steak burn up on me? And me with a dozen other things on me hands at once, and the coffee not boiled yet!"

Yet despite this and for all his awe of and therefore respect for his somewhat difficult and threatening wife, Mullanphy would know well enough that this shot was not for him. Rather, and as seemingly direct as it was, he would look blankly back from one of the front windows where he was standing, but without a word. On the other hand, Katie and Molly, and even Cornelia, for whom the remark was really intended, would run from whatever they were doing and come to the rescue, only decidedly resentful and ready to fight.

"Sure, Aunt Bridget," Katie might exclaim in an injured tone, "if ye want us to help you in the first place, why didn't ye say so? Certainly ye needn't make it look as though we didn't want to help." Then Mrs. Mullanphy, throwing up both hands and shaking her head, would wail: "If I'm not the unfortunate woman! If I'm not the persecuted one with ye, Katie McGragh! To think and I cannot talk but ye must be mistakin' the meaning of me. 'Tis Mullanphy himself who well knows 'tis his place to give me help, and dinner for six on the fire. If I do lose me temper, 'tis not with ye, or Cornelia either, but with him that should be helpin' me and never does."

And yet Mullanphy would stand there without a word. And Katie and Molly and Cornelia merely exchanging looks. And then presently, of course, there would be peace for the time being and more gassing about the neighbors until, and possibly because of, the loud talk and the air carrying the sounds across the halls and through the windows, there would be renewed argument between one neighbor and another and Mrs. Mullanphy and the nieces and Mullanphy or all, separately or collectively by turns. The "roilin's and scrapin's" as it were.

But to return to these nieces. One of the phases of Mrs. Mullanphy's dealings with them which puzzled me not a little, and concerning which as yet I have said nothing, was her somewhat lax and certainly far from religious or even moral attitude toward their rather moral-less point of view in regard to what can only be described as the property of others. And that in the face of her continued religious and conventional criticism of others. For her nieces, as well as her daughter, as I gradually came to know, were inclined to purloin things from their various employers (quite numerous during the course of several years)—food, clothing etcetera—and presently bring the same to Mrs. Mullanphy, who, as she was wont to declare, got her "stren'th" from her church. Only she took these same spoils, as I am very truly able to state, with some weak, if moral, reflection to the effect that extreme necessity tends to excuse deeds of this kind, however little it may repeal moral law. But how do I know all this? Well, for one thing, at one time there was one who lived on the floor above the Mullanphys and with whom they as well as myself were friendly, and who told me many amusing tales of strange goings-on in this respect. On the other hand, there were my own personal observations, based on a desire to know, as well as overheard scraps and long conversations with one or another of these same characters in these same halls or rooms.

But regardless of this, some of the facts in regard to these dishonestly-come-by gains relate to a certain afternoon in October, at which time the two nieces arrived from where they had been working—deserted because of unsatisfactory conditions—bearing between them half of a ham, a quarter of a side of bacon, two dozen eggs, a can of coffee, a package of tea, a tablecloth, and a few more such items, all of which and themselves included were received with open arms by Mrs. Mullanphy—who subsequently fell out with them because they stayed too long with her before getting another place. And yet the friendship and perhaps the generous purloining continued unbroken. Again there was Cornelia, who, I was once told, returned fairly laden with spoils from her place of employment one afternoon when Mr. and Mrs. Mullanphy and one of the nieces were present. One of her trophies—which she brought forth from under the voluminous cape she wore—was a yellow plush album containing portraits of people in no way related to her.

"'Tis the color of it that I like most," was her reported comment.

"And ye divil!" her mother's only reply, the while she admired the binding.

"When I only get a dollar and me meals for seven or eight hours' slavin', 'tis small blame to me to help meself," the intrepid robber is alleged to have announced.

On the other hand, Mrs. Mullanphy was not without a form of charity for others, as the following incident will show.

On the ground floor of her place lived the Kiltys—husband, wife, and fragile daughter of eleven or twelve. A grown-up son had disappeared. At one time, not so long after the above, they were about to be dispossessed for non-payment of rent. Michael Kilty, the father, was in many respects even worse than Mullanphy. He was no good at all. A bricklayer by trade, for one reason or another—drink, indifference, laziness—he had degenerated to the point where he was almost always out of work, and out of the masons' union also, an organization which had apparently dismissed him for his various sins. In the face of this he did not hesitate to "scab," a thing which infuriated the union men. Even when he did work, though, he would often disappear and leave his wife for six or eight weeks at a time. At other times, having loafed a long time and not having a cent on him, he would come home in rags, or sick, or at least pretending to be, and would hang around promising to do better when he got well and would then send his wife out to do washing until she too would fall ill. Yet for some reason she would endure all this, and more—ill treatment of a physical nature, even so much as a beating from time to time.

On one occasion this model father, having been away for a long time and his wife in his absence having fallen ill and because of this having been unable to work, the Kilty furniture was about to be set out on the streets. But Mrs. Mullanphy, having had few, if any, fights with Mrs. Kilty, whom she considered a deserving and much put-upon woman, was, at the last moment, moved to sympathy. What, the poor sick things to be set out on the sidewalk? Sure, all the landlords were bloodsuckers and divils! Was not hers a true Irish heart, and would a true Irish heart go back on any other true Irish heart in its hour of distress? Scarcely. So, in the afternoon of the day the notice had been served on the Kiltys, and after the news had been spread and discussed throughout the building and no one had come to the rescue, she made her way down to their floor.

"Sure," she announced on her arrival, and referring to landlords and real estate dealers in general, "'tis the divil's own brood they are, fattenin' on the bodies of the pore! 'Tis none of them that has the heart of a snake, or the dacency either, to see how it is with the pore. But what is it the paper says, anyhow—the notice? One of ye read it to me, 'tis me eyes that are bad." (As I said before, she could not read.)

"'Pay tomorrow at noon or be required to vacate said premises,'" read Norah Kilty. "'This letter is in legal form and no other notice will be necessary.'"

"'Tis not worth the paper 'tis written on," exclaimed Mrs. Mullanphy, who because of many previous instances in which she herself, you may be sure, had been the subject of such a notice, had acquired at least the rudiments of proper legal procedure in all such cases. "Sure, the old divil's written ye this to save expenses. It costs from two-fifty to eight dollars for the regular notice, accordin' to the fees of the marshal and the marshal's men. And the landlord has to put everything out on the street in perfect order or ye can collect on him. Yes, indeed so 'tis. And what's more, Mrs. Kilty, 'tis often a good plan in these cases to loosen up the back of a mirror or some such thing so 'twill fall out and break, fer nothin' is supposed to be broke. Nothin'! And 'tis such things as might be helpin' ye to get a start, ye understand? The court would be holdin', maybe, that what with damage and all that, a little somethin' might be due ye, ye see? 'Tis not that I speak of this by any experience of me own, y'understand, but 'tis not the first case of dispossess I see, either."

"Oh, wurra, wurra! Oh me, oh me!" wailed Mrs. Kilty. " 'Tis not the wit I have to do it. 'Tis not the wit nor the strenth either. And me old man out of work this three months now. And me son Tim away and down with pneumony in Philadelphy. And meself that upset with trouble and not knowin' how to do next. If only me husband was the sober man he might be, and with a better heart for the jobs he do get . . . !"

"But what becomes of the furniture once it do be set out, Mrs. Mullanphy, if ye know?" This from Mrs. Hanfy, another inquisitive and sympathetic neighbor who had edged in and was eager to know the ins and out of dispossess proceedings generally.

"Sure, and I know very little of these cases except as I have seen 'em here and there in me time," replied Mrs. Mullanphy, loftily and aloofly. "We was never dispossessed ourselves, but 'tis me recollection that unless the furniture be took away again be the tenant, the Bureau of Encumbrances moves it to the City Yard. 'Tis the laa, I believe. Only, be what I hear—'tis all hear-say, y'understand—ye must go down and see about it within twenty-four hours else the Bureau of Encumbrances can do whatever they please with it. But whisht ye!" she added, as Mrs. Kilty burst into a fresh fit of weeping. "'Tis the judge of the district that can do somethin' fer ye, too. 'Tis to him ye must go with the notice. This be the Eight District—Charlless Street—if I'm not mistaken, and 'tis to the judge of the court there ye must go. Me darter Cornelia will be goin' with ye if ye like. But, sure, any policeman can be tellin' ye where to go. Maybe ye can get a stay from the judge. Sometimes if ye be after tellin' him a sad story, 'tis easy to take a week's time at least. And between that and the work ye may get and the expenses to the landlord ye may bring on him by way of damage to yer furniture, ye can maybe make out. 'Tis me that has seen it done before." Yet in the face of this Mrs. Kilty continued to cry, whereupon Mrs. Mullanphy continued:"And sure, and ye're not the first whose furniture was set out on the street fer want of a bit of rent. In these days, and with the wolves that is ownin' property, 'tis small wonder."

" 'Tis hard, 'tis hard," interpolated Mrs. Hanfy at this point.

"Sure an' 'tis," continued Mrs. Mullanphy. "But listen, 'tis easy to tell a sad story. Sure, any one can do it. 'Twould be better, of course, if ye had a child or two—a baby in arms is the best—but since ye have a husband and son sick and out of work, 'tis as well. So don't be taken on so. Besides, there be lots of children in the house. Let ye but ask fer the loan of two. Ye pay yer rent to the agent, don't ye, the same as the rest of us? Well then, they'll not be after knowin' whether the children are yer own or not. Once ye're before the judge, ye can say ye have the little ones to look after and no place to go this night. 'Tis no judge in New York will turn ye out, and ye with children to look after. 'Tis meself would be lettin' ye have the rent an' I had it. But Delia ye may take fer one if ye will. For I'll not be seein' ye turned out on the streets at that. If the judge won't be givin' ye more time, ye can come with me for a day or two. Room fer yer things I have not, but as for you and Norah, yes. No doubt your husband will be lookin' fer another place the while, and yerself too, and findin' somethin'."

But as it turned out, Mrs. Kilty being sick and not having the courage to go before the judge with a borrowed child as her own, the furniture was set out on the sidewalk and removed by the Bureau of Encumbrances. And Mrs. Kilty and her daughter having been escorted to the Mullanphy apartment, it was not twenty-four hours before Kilty returned, and finding his wife thus comfortably housed and no rent to pay, fixed himself, by a process of blather and a hard luck story and promises, upon the Mullanphys also. But after three or four days of this, and no sign on the part of Kilty that he was developing any intention to work (although Mrs. Kilty was out seeking something to do), Mrs. Mullanphy's "true Irish" rose. Only, instead of taking the situation directly in hand and ordering them out, her curiously involute and roundabout nature dictated an entirely different course. Better to hint, and hint broadly, as in the case of her nieces, but more for the benefit of Kilty than for his wife and daughter. And with her husband, whether by prearrangement or not I could never guess, serving as a foil or false target. Thus all would be gathered in the combination dining room and kitchen. Kilty would be lounging near the mantel, behind the stove, where it was warmest. Mrs. Mullanphy, her aproned sides slanting wide, would be seated at the table. Mrs. Kilty and her daughter, mayhap, would be engaged in cleaning up after dinner, Mrs. Mullanphy having done the work of preparing it.

Sewing or mending, but contemplating with dissatisfied eyes the imperturbable Kilty, who would be calmly smoking a pipe and meditating, hands on stomach, she would finally reach the point where the sight of him would be too much for her, and would begin, presumably addressing her husband:

"Oh, but it's you that knows how to live without hurtin' yer health, it is. The idler that ye are, Mullanphy the loafer." Whereupon Mullanphy, knowing full well that this was not for him but Kilty, would shift perhaps a trifle uneasily and yet not wholly uncomfortably, and perhaps after a time, seeing his wife's eyes fixed steadily upon him, would turn to Kilty, who without a trace of embarrassment, might continue to rest as before, and inquire: "Ye've found nothin' in yer line today again, I suppose, Kilty?"

"Not today, no," would the imperturbable Kilty reply. "There's plenty of work for union men, of course, if only me card was good, but not for the likes of me in the shape I'm in now. I did go into four places, though. There's a job over at the car company, I hear. None but non-union men there. I'm goin' over there in the mornin'. If it's not more than four hundred brick a day, I can manage in me present state, I think."

And at this Mullanphy, his duty done, might resume his former contemplative position. But not so his wife, who was not to be put off so easily.

"Ah, four hundred brick; 'tis a lot for one man to lay, I suppose. But 'tis a gentleman's life *you* lead, Mullanphy, just the same, and without even that much work, makin' yerself comfortable where it's warm and no meals to pay for. 'Tis you I mean, Mullanphy; always idle, always 'tis somethin' that stops ye from findin' somethin'. Sure, and 'tis a wonder to me that any women find anythin' to do these days, 'tis so hard men be findin' it to get anything at all."

But the shrewd Kilty was by no means so easily to be routed. On the contrary, slyer and more dissolute than Mullanphy, and as cunning and much more callous than even Mrs. Mullanphy (who was cunning enough), and with the effrontery of the devil himself, he would "stick" or "sit tight," as we say, the while such broadsides as the above were leveled at him. But not so either his wife or daughter, who daily sought work. Yet in this instance the last straw was finally laid by himself when some three of four days later—and after this much sponging—he finally arrived on the scene one evening, drunk and with a drunken companion, cut and bleeding from having been thrown out of a saloon. It was Mrs. Mullanphy who, peeling potatoes at the time, saw him first; and then Mullanphy, breaking the slats of a greengrocer's box on the window sill with a flat iron. Mrs. Kilty and her daughter were sitting about rather helplessly. Cornelia was working out and had not returned as yet. Little Delia was playing in the street below.

Mrs. Mullanphy's first impulse as the door opened and the two bums stood revealed, one holding the other up, was to shout: "Mullanphy, by the Blessed Mother of God!" The stranger's cheek and forehead were badly cut and smeared with blood and Kilty was saying most helpfully: "Wait'll I tie a rag around yer head. That'll fix it. Wait'll ye wash the blood off, then ye'll be all right when yer head's tied up."

But Mrs. Mullanphy did not think so. "Jesus, Mary and all the Blessed Saints!" she exclaimed. "I could never stand the sight o' blood. I'm faint, Mullanphy. Will no one be puttin' the likes of that out o' here? Will ye be lettin' the likes o' that in here?"

Whereupon Mullanphy drew dubiously if by no means threateningly nearer.

But Kilty, drunk, was by no means to be dismayed at this reception. On the contrary, he was all cheer and hope. "Will ye let me explain, Mrs. Mullanphy?" he pleaded genially, the while he sustained his companion as best he might. "He's only been cut, see? Some bums up at the job where we was workin' jumped on him. We was workin' on a job, see, and some bums . . ."

"Yes, 'tis well I know who the bums was! And as for the job, I know that, too. Job, indeed! Mullanphy, will ye be after lettin' the two of them come in here? Ain't it enough that they be eatin' us out of house and home but must be searchin' the streets for bums, as if there wasn't a houseful here now? And me workin' and slavin', and yerself and Cornelia, too, fer the likes o' them. Have ye no spunk at all? Must I be slavin' here and not enough to eat in the house as 'tis?"

At this the shameless and undaunted Kilty had the drunken effrontery to come forward and exclaim: "'Tisn't dinner he's after,

330

Mrs. Mullanphy. 'Tisn't that. He's had his dinner, see? We both have. 'Tis his face; 'tis his face he wants to wash up. I'm only bringin' him in to wash his face, see?"

"And to stay the night, yes, like yerself. And to breakfast in the mornin'. And to supper the morrow night again. And after that for weeks and months like yerself and yer family that ye won't support. 'Tis more than morshall patience can bear. And scarce room to move and breathe as 'tis, Mullanphy."

And Mullanphy, now coming forward, added: "Say, now, this *is* too much, Kilty. Man, ye can't expect to bring yerself and him in the fix he's in here. 'Tis to the hospital he should go."

"Yes, after he's fixed his face. Yes, sure, after he's fixed his head."

"No, not after he fixes his head, but right now!" This from the now thoroughly aroused Mrs. Mullanphy. "And yerself and yer wife and yer darter. To be sure, I pities them more than I do you, but 'tis the lot of ye must go. Is Mullanphy and meself to be workin' to feed a regiment? Is there no end to the lot o' ye, and will ye be searchin' the streets fer more? Then out of me sight with the lot of ye! And go laughin' to yerself fer the fool you've made of Bridget Mullanphy!"

By this time Mrs. Kilty and Norah, seeing the trouble that had been brought upon them by this worthless head of their family, were meekly packing up their belongings, making bundles of little things and rolling them up. Incidentally putting on extra skirts, one above the other, and pointing out silently to each other the things they had forgotten.

"Be sure, Mrs. Mullanphy," coaxed the artful Kilty, "ye don't want to get so excited. You're takin' the wrong meanin' out o' this."

"Wrong meaning', is it? And me provisions laid away for the winter gone this long time, and no money to pay the rent that's due this Chuesday next? Daylight robbers! Midnight robbers! That's what ye are! Not yer wife, but you!"

"Ah, well," conceded Kilty, realizing at last the futility of coaxing, "if ye don't want us to stay here, that's all right. We can go someplace else. Sure, we can. Come on, Mike, I can take ye to a hospital." And down the steps they lurched.

"And 'tis good riddance to the both of ye!" shouted Mrs.

Mullanphy after them. "But who's to give me back me butter, of which ye ate five pounds, and me fish and me steak and me flour? Where's the bottle of relish that lasted but the one meal? That the divil might have choked ye with it! Robbers! Robbers!"

"We're very sorry, Mrs. Mullanphy," pleaded the humble Norah Kilty, frightened out of her wits at this storm. "We're goin' now. 'Tis that sorry we are to have been the cause of so much trouble." And Mrs. Kilty added: "Yes, we are that. We're goin' right now. 'Tis more than sorry I am fer all the trouble I've brought on ye, and 'twasn't fer him I wouldn't have stayed the time I did, but 'twas he that made me."

"And well I know it, the robber! But 'tis not fer yerself that I'm talkin', but fer him, the robber! 'Tis the likes of him and his bums that has brought ye where ye are this day, Mrs. Kilty. But the good Lord himself wouldn't be after feedin' him and his drunken friends and the lot of ye into the bargain. But 'tis tonight ye'll be stayin', or tomorrow maybe, the two of ye, now that he's gone." Her tone softened.

But no, the Kiltys would not, and sensibly enough under the circumstances. Instead they went crying down the stairs after Kilty had disappeared with his friend and were neither seen nor heard of more, in so far as I know.

About this time, the agent of the building in which I rented a floor chanced to ask me whether I knew anyone who would, for the gift of one or two rooms in the basement, rent free, perform the duties of a janitress. I immediately suggested Mrs. Mullanphy. For despite all of her rowing with her neighbors and their charges in regard to her cleanliness or lack of cleanliness, she was really comparatively clean. More, having heard her asseverate so often how much better she would do if surrounded by those who would let her alone, I suggested to this agent that if he would instruct her sharply as to possible visitors and the heinousness of loud talking, let alone shouting or quarreling— for which there was small opportunity in this very different vicinity—I thought all would be well. And should she fail to behave herself, of course she was to be compelled to vacate at once.

And following this advice of mine, and with a clear understanding of what was desired, as I assumed, came Mrs.

Mullanphy and Mullanphy also, his coat below his shoulders, as always, and Cornelia and little Delia, and in due time the two nieces, Molly and Katie McGragh—with such rags of furniture as I will not trouble to describe. Only finding me master of the parlor floor and others like myself living above, the entire family, for a short time at least, was very quiet, Mrs. Mullanphy, for one, devoting herself to washing and cleaning for all, the others working, and no quarrels that I could hear between them. Only— and just the same—and quarreling or no quarreling—tragedy, as I might have expected, since with or because of the combination of personal ties about them, neither Mrs. Mullanphy nor her daughter was suitable for the work in hand. Their social standards were a little too decayed. Also, and via this same tragedy, a clear white light on the mystery of Cornelia and little Delia.

For one hot summer afternoon, after all had been in this new place some four or five months, there arrived outside Mrs. Mullanphy's basement door a small, pinched, intense and decidedly distrait-looking Irish woman, who after knocking and ringing with great violence at the Mullanphy door and the two basement windows—which seemed for the occasion to have been closed and shuttered against her—took a position before one of them (and this same just below one of mine which was directly above) and began calling. But what? For a long time I did not know what this droning voice was, and only by opening one of my windows did I at last gather the import of it.

"Come out, now! Come out, ye ——! Come out, ye ——! Come out, and I'll teach ye to let me husband alone! Ye ——, you! Ye ——, you! Come on out now! Come on out!"

And so on and on and over and over, like a droning fly with the little woman rattling at the shutters or the iron basement gates, betimes, but no faintest noise or sign from within. Yet that some of the Mullanphy family were below I well knew, for only a little time before there had been voices which had been audible enough through a rear areaway. None the less, silence. And with the little woman trying, as I could see, to peer through the blinds.

After a considerable time, however, during which a street crowd began to gather—first a few small children, then men and women—and the noise of this same becoming loud with inquiry or wonder—that same basement hall door under the outside stoop

333

opened and Cornelia Mullanphy stepped forth. A strange girl, or woman, that Cornelia, grotesque and a little sad, as I always thought, with her thin, angular body, high cheek bones, red hair, and her of course confused and befuddled because inadequate mind. And always, as I had long noted, in staccato colors, a green or red or yellow shirtwaist, coupled with a brown or dark green skirt. And this very day the same—bizarre, flamboyant. Also her manner, as I had often noted, was a little flighty. And this day the same—a girl or woman who seemed weakly and so helplessly drawn to men, but one who had, none the less, never proved very attractive to any, or at least few, and, in consequence, I assume, spiritually distrait. And behind her on this occasion her mother, unusually nervous and pale, as I thought (the neighborhood overawing her somewhat, I presume), and saying as she came: "Have no words with her, I say! Have no words with her, fer the love o' God! 'Tis nonsense to have words with her, I say!"

But for all of that, the intense and dour Cornelia paying no attention, her face very white, her eyes narrowed. Instead exclaiming—and that most defiantly for her: "Who're ye callin' those names to, say? Who?" And glaring. As a matter of fact, she was quite dramatic, far more picturesque and intense than ever she had seemed before.

" 'Tis well ye know who I'm talkin' to, ye ——, you!" exclaimed the little woman from a higher level, to which at the sound of the basement door opening she had retreated. " 'Tis yerself that I'm callin', ye ——! 'Tis you that'll not be lettin' me man alone, but must be runnin' after him, and him the father of two children, and you not able to get a man of yer own! 'Tis well I know of ye from Barry Street, ye ——! And with a child of yer own that has no father but must be owned by her mother for ye!"

"Say that again and I'll slap yer face fer ye!" declared the infuriated Cornelia, stepping close.

" 'Tis me that says it, and 'tis you that knows it's true!" insisted the stranger. "'Tis Cornelia Dempsey ye are that lived in Barry Street, and not Mullanphy, and 'tis me man that ye're tryin' to take from me this day, since ye can't get one of yer own, ye —— you!"

334

At this, smack came the hand of the intense, white Cornelia square across the mouth and cheek of the older woman, and then smack again from the other side. "I'll show ye whether ye'll rattle me windows and say what ain't so!"

At first the intruder appeared to be completely stunned by this—beaten, no less, for she fell back, white and weak—the crowd, of course of whom I made one, gazing in amaze. Then: "Aha!" hissed the little woman, laying at the same time a thin, worn hand across her mouth and cheek. "Aha!" And then, "But wait! You'll strike me, will ye? And after tryin' to steal me husband from me! But wait! 'Tis not the last of me or you! I'll be back!" And off she started up the hot, sunlit street, at first walking very fast and then as her shame and rage grew, breaking into an odd, awkward lope until as she approached the nearest corner she turned, and disappeared. But not for long, as she said. She was soon back. Only in the meantime, the cautious Bridget, now very much excited, had seized her irate daughter by the shoulders and pulled her down into and through the basement door and closed it.

But as I say, in a few minutes (the doors and windows below stairs still tightly closed and the place silent) the little woman returned. But this time with nothing less than an ax in her hand—a large, hard, glistening ax. And behind her, trailing, two children, her own as I could tell, but following without her consent. For, as I pictured it all to myself, she must have rushed into her home and out again, her children amazedly seeing her seize the ax and then following after her. But as I could now see, her mood was really murderous—no thought of fear or compromise this time. And at once she began as before, only in much louder tone, the while she banged at the shutters with the ax. "Come out, now . . ." etc., etc.

Indeed so white was she and panting, that as she struck the first blow I seized my telephone and called for the police, explaining, as soon as I had the neighborhood station house, that the situation was desperate. Also that a large crowd was gathering. Whereupon an officer was promised at once. Then I returned to the window and listened to such an outburst as I had scarcely ever heard before—never in that neighborhood—the wronged Irish wife now shouting her ills at the top of her voice, and banging the shutters with such violence as finally to break one through. The scandal, the disgrace, I thought. And now, no doubt, murder into the bargain. And I had brought them here. Ye Gods—my own studio in danger of being forfeited. I was in real distress, as I can tell you.

By this time, however, the policeman for whom I had first called had arrived, also teamsters from a livery stable over the way, and storekeepers, saloonkeepers—the riffraff as well as the well-dressed pedestrians, and children from all the neighboring houses—a huge crowd which blocked traffic and stared in amazement at this odd figure with her ax and two children. Yet not a sound from the rooms below; not a whisper. And the police now demanding in sharp, aggressive tones: "And what's the trouble here now? Why will ye be here in broad daylight destroyin' property? Is it murder ye want to do? Let me have the ax now." And, much to my personal relief, seizing and securing the ax even as he spoke.

But the little woman still continuing to shout. And the two children crying. And the crowd now buzzing, murmuring, even laughing or catcalling—some yoo-hooing and even whistling—the result of a fiasco, I assume. None the less, as I saw it, a most scandalous scene, and one that I by my recommendation to my landlord had brought about. And what would he say now when he heard of this? What excuse could I offer? For he was a none too liberal, in fact highly conventional landlord, who seemed always to think that I too was conventional. Ah, my honorable life! My previous good name! I feared the worst for myself as well as the family below, but wondered still more about the attitude of Mrs. Mullanphy. Why the quiet? Why no defiance, no martial display of dustpan and broom, or mop and washrag? A most amazing stillness this—one such as I would not have deemed possible in her case, and especially under such circumstances. And yet so it was.

In due course, though, the police had succeeded not only in disarming and removing the violent visitor—taking her away and advising her, I suppose, to see a lawyer and file an action—but in dispersing the crowd also. None the less, and for hours after that, and even several days, not the lifting of a curtain or the opening of a door, nor even after evening fell. Yet up the rear areaway, between six and seven the next evening, the most subdued of voices—where I could scarcely detect—in whispered conversation. And sometime after midnight, more talk. And then Mullanphy and Mrs. Mullanphy and Cornelia going out. But where? And then two days after—and due, no doubt, to a suggestion on the part of the landlord—a small, dusty moving van, removing their few and humble belongings. And then silence. They were gone. Moved. But with no word to me or anyone. And after that I never saw either Cornelia or Delia or the two nieces again.

But a curious thing. Some three or four years later I began to use for cleaning purposes a sometimes drunken, and always impoverished and down-at-heels, yet rather intelligent and interesting Village character—Johnny Morton by name—who did odd jobs such as scrubbing, cleaning, washing windows, and the like for various Greenwich Villagers. Some seemed to find him amusing as well as useful and so were pleased to have him around, although quite frequently he was either too drunk or weak from dissipation to fulfill his stipulated agreements at fifty cents an hour and so earn his daily bread. Worse, he was, among other things, as I subsequently learned, an ex-convict and a dope addict, one who rather more than less bore the marks of both. His was a wasted and worthless look at times, so querulous, blue-nosed, nervous, and generally rickety as to be pitiable. But when sober he was genial and obliging, and useful enough, courteous as well as humorous. For a long time when he was about my place I paid not the least attention to him. He did my work and did it fairly well, and I paid him and let him go. But then one day, being in an unusually genial and communicative mood, he announced: "I used to live around here, you know." He was industriously polishing a brass coal box in the middle of my studio floor at the time.

"Yes?"

"Yep, sure. I was born over here on Barrow Street." A slight sniff. He was always sniffing as though afflicted with a perpetual cold, or scratching as though afflicted with fleas, or wiping his nose with his coat sleeve.

"Barrow Street can at least lay claim to something then," I commented.

337

"Yep, sure. My old man used to be head harness man in that old stable at Tenth and Waverly."

"Really? Well, just what do you mean—harness man?"

"He kept all the harness in order, you know, shined and oiled all the harnesses of the horses, forty–fifty sets a day. I used to help him when I was a kid. Many's the kick I'd get fer not keepin' 'em shined right."

"Indeed! Pleasant youthful memories," I commented.

"Yep, sure. That's right. (Sniff.) The old man was pretty quick that way. Bad tempered. He used to drink and he was all the worse when he was drunk. He's not so bad now, though, I hear. He's gettin' older."

"Natural enough," I commented. "Age will do that. You see him occasionally then, I take it."

"Yep."

"But you don't live at home?"

"Who, me? Oh, no!" This last with a swipe of coat sleeve across his nose. "They wouldn't have me. I ain't lived at home for years now, ever since I ran away. The old man wouldn't have me now, nor the old woman either, I guess. I wouldn't ask 'em to. But I see 'em around just the same. They got sore about something I did. But I could get along with my mother if it wasn't for the old man. She ain't so bad."

(Fairly complimentary to one's mother, I thought, all things considered.) "And what is your real name, Johnny?" I ventured. "I never did think to ask you before."

"Who, me? Oh, well, I go by the name of Morton now, since the family don't like to have me around any more, but my real name is Dempsey. My mother and father changed their name, too, to Mullanphy. But Dempsey is the real name. I got 'em into some trouble, see, and they changed the name."

Aha, I said to myself! Then a little after: "Jabez Mullanphy, by any chance? I used to know a man around here by that name."

"Why, sure, he's me father. Yuh know him? He used to be a teamster after he left the livery stable." He seemed to be a little startled himself.

"Yes, I think I know him, and your mother, too. They lived here in Bank Street once, didn't they, about five or six years ago?"

"Yep, sure. Did my mother ever do any work for you?"

"Well, not directly. I lived in a house where she did some work though."

"Well, I guess that's her. Big woman with gray hair?"

"Yes."

"My mother wouldn't be so bad," he volunteered, rather indifferently now that the interest of this discovery had paled, "if she didn't have such an awful temper. Gee, but she's got a rough temper! But the old man made her that way, I guess. He never would do what he ought to do, nor me, either—work or anything."

At this point, and without any particular emotion that I could see, he launched into a long dissertation on family ties, family duties, and the like. I gathered that, besides the daughter Cornelia, there was this same Johnny, but no other child. Hence little Delia must be Cornelia's, and so the mystery was at last solved. But no word from Johnny as to the child. He did not say and I would not ask him. After that he drifted out of my life and I never saw him again.

But about three years after this conversation I chanced to change cars one noon hour at Times Square. The crowds! The rush! You know. Nearing the stairs leading down to the Seventh Avenue platform I heard a voice, a familiar one, as it seemed to me, bewailing and anxious.

"Oh-h-h-h, where is he? Where's me man? Mullanphy, in God's name, where are ye? Where's he gone to? In God's name, Mullanphy! I've lost him! My God! Ow-w-w, what'll I do now? And not a nickel on me! Ow! And where's he gone? Me old man! I'm lost! Oh-h-h!"

And turning, sure enough, there stood Mrs. Mullanphy in the flesh. A little stouter, a little grayer even—not much— a little dustier, maybe, but lurching and pitching like a ship in a heavy sea, ascending the steps inside the subway while I was descending them. And behind her, at a distance but following because he heard her shrieks and wondered what it was all about, Mullanphy himself. The same blank and yet equivocal expression on his face, his hat for once not on the back of his head, a rag of a gray overcoat over his shoulders. And trying to catch up with his bulky wife, who was lurching directly away from him and who had evidently lost track of him in the crush. Finally, catching up with her, he yelled: "Where're ye goin', ye old fool? Can't ye see I'm right here? Didn't ye just folly me down these steps a minute ago?"

"And why the divil didn't ye stay near me?" came the old, quick, defiant and irritated reply. "And what'll ye be galootherin' here and there fer and me not able to keep up with ye? And without a cent in me pocket and me not knowin' where 'tis ye're goin' anyhow! Give me me fare! Give me me fare, and thin ye can go where ye like and I'll go where I like."

A large percentage of the crowd, hurrying as it was, paused to chortle and guffaw. Fine, I thought! The old Mullanphy spirit! Not dead yet. And despite so many ills. Hurrah! Her goodly soul has not been utterly crushed, thanks be! She does live. And she can fight, hale and forceful as ever.

Yet with the nervous fear of being recognized and seized upon as an old friend in the midst of this exciting confab, I dashed into an inrushing express which was just stopping, and which plainly they were not taking, and was whisked away. But not without a backward and even sentimental look. For had there not been Barrow Street? The sisters McGragh, the dour-minded Cornelia, that awful scene in Tenth Street? Great! Life vigorous and willful if degraded, pitiful and strange. Yet why, as I consoled myself, renew our old and always amicable relations? Was she not doing well enough, apparently? And I also. I thought so. Comparatively so, at any rate. But oh, that hearty, defiant Irishness, so to say. The upstanding vigor amidst all ills.

And because of these speculative musings in regard to this same Bridget Mullanphy, her troubles and her temper, I was carried two stations past my getting-off place. And proceeded to grumble at her for that.

Muldoon, the Solid Man

I MET HIM IN CONNECTION with a psychic depression which only partially reflected itself in my physical condition. I might almost say that I was sick spiritually. At the same time I was rather strongly imbued with a contempt for him and his cure. I had heard of him for years. To begin with, he was a wrestler of repute, or rather ex-wrestler, retired undefeated champion of the world. As a boy I had known that he had toured America with Modjeska as Charles, the wrestler, in *As You Like It.* Before or after that he had trained John L. Sullivan, the world's champion prize fighter of his day, for one of his most successful fights, and that at a time when Sullivan was unfitted to fight anyone. Before that, in succession, from youth up, he had been a peasant farmer's son in Ireland, a scullion in a ship's kitchen earning his way to America, a "beef slinger" for a packing company, a cooks' assistant and waiter in a Bowery restaurant, a bouncer in a saloon, a rubber-down at prize fights, a policeman, a private in the army during the Civil War, a ticket-taker, ex-hibition wrestler, "short-change man" with a minstrel company, later a circus, until having attained his greatest fame as champion wrestler of the world, and as trainer of John L. Sullivan, he finally opened a sporting sanitarium in some county in upper New York State which later evolved into the great and now decidedly fashionable institution in Westchester, near New York.

It has always been interesting to me to see in what awe men of this type or profession are held by many in the more intellectual walks of life as well as by those whose respectful worship is less surprising   those who revere strength, agility, physical courage, so-called brute or otherwise. There is a kind of retiring worshipfulness, especially in men and children of the lower walks, for this type, which must be flattering in the extreme.

However, in so far as Muldoon was concerned at this time,

the case was different. Whatever he had been in his youth he was not that now, or at least his earlier rawness had long since been glazed over by other experiences. Self-education, an acquired politeness among strangers and a knowledge of the manners and customs of the better-to-do, permitted him to associate with them and to accept if not copy their manners and to a certain extent their customs in his relations with them. Literally, he owned hundreds of the best acres of the land about him, in one of the most fashionable residence sections of the East. He had already given away to some Sisters of Mercy a great estate in northern New York. His stables contained every type of fashionable vehicle and stalled and fed sixty or seventy of the worst horses, purposely so chosen, for the use of his "guests." Men of all professions visited his place, paid him gladly the six hundred dollars in advance which he asked for the course of six weeks' training, and brought, or attempted to, their own cars and retinues, which they lodged in the vicinity but could not use. I myself was introduced or rather foisted upon him by my dear brother, whose friend if not crony— if such a thing could have been said to exist in his life—he was. I was taken to him in a very somber and depressed mood and left; he rarely if ever received guests in person or at once. On the way, and before I had been introduced, I was instructed by my good brother as to his moods, methods, airs and tricks, supposed or rumored to be so beneficial in so many cases. They were very rough—purposely so.

The day I arrived, and before I saw him, I was very much impressed with the simplicity yet distinction of the inn or sanitarium or "repair shop," as subsequently I learned he was accustomed to refer to it, perched upon a rise of ground and commanding a quite wonderful panorama. It was spring and quite warm and bright. The cropped enclosure which surrounded it, a great square of green fenced with high, well-trimmed privet, was good to look upon, level and smooth. The house, standing in the center of this, was large and oblong and gray, with very simple French windows reaching to the floor and great wide balustraded balconies reaching out from the second floor, shaded with awnings and set with rockers. The land on which this inn stood sloped very gradually to the Sound, miles away to the southeast, and the spires of churchs and the gables of villages rising in between, as well as various toy-like sails upon the water, were no small portion of its charm. To the west for a score of miles the green-covered earth rose and fell in undulating beauty, and here again the roofs and spires of nearby villages might in fair weather be seen nestling peacefully among the trees. Due south there was a suggestion of water and some peculiar configuration, which by day seemed to have no significance other than that which attached to the vague outlines of a distant landscape. By night, however, the soft glow emanating from myriads of lights identified it as the body and length of the merry, night-reveling New York. Northward the green waves repeated themselves unendingly until they passed into a dim green-blue haze.

Interiorly, as I learned later, this place was most cleverly and sensibly arranged for the purpose for which it was intended. It was airy and well-appointed, with, on the ground floor, a great gymnasium containing, outside of an alcove at one end where hung four or five punching bags, only medicine balls. At the other end was an office or receiving room, baggage or storeroom, and locker and dining room. To the east at the center extended a wing containing a number of showerbaths, a lounging room and sun parlor. On the second floor, on either side of a wide airy hall which ran from an immense library, billiard and smoking room at one end to Muldoon's private suite at the other, were two rows of bedrooms, perhaps a hundred all told, which gave in turn, each one, upon either side, on to the balconies previously mentioned. These rooms were arranged somewhat like the rooms of a passenger steamer, with its center aisle and its outer decks and doors opening upon it. In another wing on the ground floor were kitchens, servants' quarters, and what not else. Across the immense lawn or campus to the east, four-square to the sanitarium, stood a rather grandiose stable, almost as impressive as the main building. About the place, and always more or less in evidence, were servants, ostlers, waiting-maids and always a decidedly large company of men of practically all professions, ages, and one might say nationalities. That is as nationalities are represented in America, by first and second generations.

The day I arrived I did not see my prospective host or manager or trainer for an hour or two after I came, being allowed

343

to wait about until the very peculiar temperament which he possessed would permit him to come and see me. When he did show up, a more savage and yet gentlemanly-looking animal in clothes *de rigueur* I have never seen. He was really very princely in build and manner, shapely and grand, like those portraits that have come down to us of Richelieu and the Duc de Guise—fawn-colored riding trousers, bright red waistcoat, black-and-white check riding coat, brown leather riding boots and leggings with the essential spurs, and a riding quirt. And yet really, at that moment he reminded me not so much of a man, in his supremely well-tailored riding costume, as of a tiger or a very ferocious and yet at times purring cat, beautifully dressed, as in our children's storybooks, a kind of tiger in collar and boots. He was so lithe, silent, cat-like in his tread. In his hard, clear, gray animal eyes was that swift, incisive, restless, searching glance which sometimes troubles us in the presence of animals. It was hard to believe that he was all of sixty, as I had been told. He looked the very well-preserved man of fifty or less. The short trimmed mustache and goatee which he wore were gray and added to his grand air. His hair, cut a close pompadour, the ends of his heavy eyebrow hairs turned upward, gave him a still more distinguished air. He looked very virile, very intelligent, very indifferent, intolerant and even threatening.

"Well," he exclaimed on sight, "you wish to see me?"

I gave him my name.

"Yes, that's so. Your brother spoke to me about you. Well, take a seat. You will be looked after."

He walked off, and after an hour or so I was still waiting, for what I scarcely knew—a room, something to eat possibly, someone to speak a friendly word to me, but no one did.

While I was waiting in this rather nondescript antechamber, hung with hats, caps, riding whips and gauntlets, I had an opportunity to study some of the men with whom presumably I was to live for a number of weeks. It was between two and three in the afternoon, and many of them were idling about in pairs or threes, talking, reading, all in rather commonplace athletic costumes—soft woolen shirts, knee trousers, stockings and running or walking shoes. They were in the main evidently of the so-called learned professions or the arts—doctors, lawyers, preachers, actors, writers, with a goodly sprinkling of merchants, manufacturers and young and middle-aged society men, as well as politicians and monied idlers, generally a little the worse for their pleasures or weaknesses. A distinguished judge of one of the superior courts of New York and an actor known everywhere in the English-speaking world were instantly recognized by me. Others, as I was subsequently informed, were related by birth or achievement to some one fact or another of public significance. The reason for the presence of so many people rather above than under the average in intellect lay, as I came to believe later, in their ability or that of someone connected with them to sincerely appreciate or to at least be amused and benefited by the somewhat different theory of physical repair which the lord of the manor had invented, or for which at least he had become famous.

I have remarked that I was not inclined to be impressed. Sanitariums with their isms and theories did not appeal to me. However, as I was waiting here an incident occurred which stuck in my mind. A smart conveyance drove up, occupied by a singularly lean and haughty-looking individual, who, after looking about him, expecting someone to come out to him no doubt, clambered cautiously out, and after seeing that his various grips and one trunk were properly deposited on the gravel square outside, paid and feed his driver, then walked in and remarked:

"Ah—Where is Mr. Muldoon?"

"I don't know, sir," I replied, being the only one present. "He was here, but he's gone. I presume someone will show up presently."

He walked up and down a little while, and then added: "Um—rather peculiar method of receiving one, isn't it? I wired him I'd be here." He walked restlessly and almost waspishly to and fro, looking out of the window at times, at others commenting on the rather casual character of it all. I agreed.

Thus, some fifteen minutes having gone by without anyone approaching us, and occasional servants or "guests" passing through the room or being seen in the offing without even so much as a vouchsafing a word or appearing to be interested in us, the new arrival grew excited.

"This is very unusual," he fumed, walking up and down. "I wired him only three hours ago. I've been here now fully three-quarters of an hour! A most unheard-of method of doing business, I should say!"

Presently our stern, steely-eyed host returned. He seemed to be going somewhere, to be nowise interested in us. Yet into our presence, probably into the consciousness of this new "guest," he carried that air of savage strength and indifference, eyeing the stranger quite sharply and making no effort to apologize for our long wait.

"You wish to see me?" he inquired brusquely once more.

Like a wasp, the stranger was vibrant with rage. Plainly he felt himself insulted or terribly underrated.

"Are you Mr. Muldoon?" he asked crisply.

"Yes."

"I am Mr. Squiers," he exclaimed. "I wired you from Buffalo and ordered a room," this last with an irritated wave of the hand.

"Oh, no, you didn't order any room," replied the host sourly and with an obvious desire to show his indifference and contempt even. "You wired to know if you *could engage* a room."

He paused. The temperature seemed to drop perceptibly. The prospective guest seemed to realize that he had made a mistake somewhere, had been misinformed as to conditions here.

"Oh! Um—ah! Yes! Well, have you a room?"

"I don't know. I doubt it. We don't take everyone." His eyes seemed to bore into the interior of his would-be guest.

"Well, but I was told—my friend, Mr. X——," the stranger began a rapid, semi-irritated, semi-apologetic explanation of how he came to be here.

"I don't know anything about your friend or what he told you. If he told you you could order a room by telegraph, he's mistaken. Anyhow, you're not dealing with him, but with me. Now that you're here, though, if you want to sit down and rest yourself a little I'll see what I can do for you. I can't decide now whether I can let you stay. You'll have to wait a while." He turned and walked off.

The other stared. "Well," he commented to me after a time, walking and twisting, "if a man wants to come here I suppose he has to put up with such things, but it's certainly unusual, isn't it?" He sat down, wilted, and waited.

346

Later a clerk in charge of the registry book took us in hand, and then I heard him explaining that his lungs were not in good shape. He had come a long way—Denver, I believe. He had heard that all one needed to do was to wire, especially one in his circumstances.

"Some people think that way," solemnly commented the clerk, "but they don't know Mr. Muldoon. He does about as he pleases in these matters. He doesn't do this any more to make money but rather to amuse himself, I think. He always has more applicants than he accepts."

I began to see a light. Perhaps there was something to this place after all. I did not even partially sense the drift of the situation, though, until bedtime when, after having been served a very frugal meal and shown to my very simple room, a kind of cell, promptly at nine o'clock lights were turned off. I lit a small candle and was looking over some things which I had placed in a grip, when I heard a voice in the hall outside: "Candles out, please! Candles out! All guests in bed!" Then it came to me that a very rigorous régime was being enforced here.

The next morning as I was still soundly sleeping at five-thirty a loud rap sounded at my door. The night before I had noticed above my bed a framed sign which read: "Guests must be dressed in running trunks, shoes and sweater, and appear in the gymnasium by six sharp!" "Gymnasium at six! Gymnasium at six!" a voice echoed down the hall. I bounced out of bed. Something about the very air of the place made me feel that it was dangerous to attempt to trifle with the routine here. The tiger-like eyes of my host did not appeal to me as retaining any softer ray in them for me than for others. I had paid my six hundred . . . I had better earn it. I was down in the great room in my trunks, sweater, dressing gown, running shoes in less than five minutes.

And that room! By that time as odd a company of people as I have ever seen in a gymnasium had already begun to assemble. The leanness! the osseosity! the grandiloquent whiskers parted in the middle! the mustachios! the goatees! the fat, Hoti-like stomachs! the protuberant knees! the thin arms! the bald or semi-bald pates! the spectacles or horn glasses or pince-nezes!—laid aside a few moments later, as the exercises began. Youth and strength in the pink of condition, when clad only in trunks, a sweater and running shoes, are none too acceptable—but middle age! And out in the world, I reflected rather sadly, they all wore the best of clothes, had their cars, servants, city and country houses perhaps, their factories, employees, institutions. Ridiculous! Pitiful! As lymphatic and flabby as oysters without their shells, myself included. It was really painful.

Even as I meditated, however, I was advised, by many who saw that I was a stranger, to choose a partner, any partner, for medicine ball practice, for it might save me being taken or called by *him*. I hastened so to do. Even as we were assembling or beginning to practice, keeping two or three light medicine balls going between each pair, our host entered—that iron man, that mount of brawn. In his cowled dressing gown he looked more like some great monk or fighting abbot of the medieval years than a trainer. He walked to the center, hung up his cowl and revealed himself lithe and lion-like and costumed like ourselves. But how much more attractive as he strode about, his legs lean and sturdy, his chest full, his arms powerful and graceful! At once he seized a large leather-covered medicine ball, as had all the others, and calling a name to which responded a lean whiskerando with a semi-bald pate, thin legs and arms, and very much caricatured, I presume, by the wearing of trunks and sweater. Taking his place opposite the host, he was immediately made the recipient of a volley of balls and brow-beating epithets.

"Hurry up now! Faster! Ah, come on! Put the ball back to me! Put the ball back! Do you want to keep it all day? Great God! What are you standing there for? What are you standing there for! What do you think you're doing—drinking tea? Come on! I haven't all morning for you alone. Move! Move, you ham! You call yourself an editor! Why you couldn't edit a handbill! You can't even throw a ball straight! Throw it straight! Throw it straight! For Christ's sake where do you think I am—out in the office? Throw it straight! Hell!" and all the time one and another ball, grabbed from anywhere, for the floor was always littered with them, would be thrown in the victim's direction, and before he could well appreciate what was happening to him he was being struck, once in the neck and again on the chest by the rapidly delivered six-ounce air-filled balls, two of which at least he and the host were supposed to keep in constant motion between them. Later, a ball striking him in the stomach, he emitted a weak "ooph!" and laying his hands over the affected part ceased all effort. At this the master of the situation only smirked on him leoninely and holding up a ball as if to throw it continued, "What's the matter with you now? Come on! What do you want to stop for? What do you want to stand there for? You're not hurt. How do you expect to get anywhere if you can't keep two silly little balls like these going between us?" (There had probably been six or eight.) "Here I am sixty and you're forty, and you can't even keep up with me. And you pretend to give the general public advice on life! Well, go on; God pity the public, is all I say," and he dismissed him, calling out another name.

Now came a fat, bald soul, with dewlaps and a protruding stomach, who later I learned was a manufacturer of clothing—six hundred employees under him—down in health and nerves, really all "shot to pieces" physically. Plainly nervous at the sound of his name, he puffed quickly into position, grabbing wildly after the purposely eccentric throws which his host made and which kept him running to left and right in an all but panicky mood.

"Move! Move!" insisted our host as before, and, if anything, more irritably. "Say, you work like a crab! What a motion! If you had more head and less guts you could do this better. A fine specimen you are! This is what comes of riding about in taxis and eating midnight suppers instead of exercising. Wake up! Wake up! A belt would have kept your stomach in long ago. A little less food and less sleep, and you wouldn't have any fat cheeks. Even your hair might stay on! Wake up! Wake up! What do you want to do—die?" and as he talked he pitched the balls so quickly that his victim looked at times as though he were about to weep. His physical deficiencies were all too plain in every way. He was generally obese and looked as though he might drop, his face a flaming red, his hands trembling and missing, when a "Well, go on," sounded and a third victim was called. This time it was a well-known actor who responded, a star, rather spry and well set up, but still nervous, for he realized quite well what was before him. He had been here for weeks and was in pretty fair trim, but still he was plainly on edge. He ran and began receiving and tossing as swiftly as he could, but as with the others so it was his turn now to be given such a grilling and tongue-lashing as falls to few of us in this world, let alone among the successful in the realm of the footlights. "Say, you're not an actor—you're a woman! You're a stewed onion! Move! Move! Come on! Come on! Look at those motions now, will you? Look at that one arm up! Where do you suppose the ball is? On the ceiling? It's not a lamp! Come on! Come on! It's a wonder when you're killed as Hamlet that you don't stay dead. You are. You're really dead now, you know. Move! Move!" and so it would go until finally the poor thespian, no match for his master and beset by flying balls, landing upon his neck, ear, stomach, finally gave up and cried:

"Well, I can't go any faster than I can, can I? I can't do any more than I can!"

"Ah, go on! Go back into the chorus!" called his host, who now abandoned him. "Get somebody from the baby class to play marbles with you," and he called another.

By now, as may well be imagined, I was fairly stirred up as to the probabilities of the situation. He might call me! The man who was playing opposite me—a small, decayed person who chose me, I think, because he knew I was new, innocuous and probably awkward—seemed to realize my thoughts as well as his own. By lively exercise with me he was doing his utmost to create an impression of great and valuable effort here. "Come on, let's play fast so he won't notice us," he said most pathetically at one point. You would have thought I had known him all my life.

But he didn't call us—not this morning at any rate. Whether owing to our efforts or the fact that I at least was too insignificant, too obscure, we escaped. He did reach me, however, on the fourth or fifth day, and no spindling failure could have done worse. I was struck and tripped and pounded until I all but fell prone upon the floor, half convinced that I was being killed, but I was not. I was merely sent stumbling and drooping back to the sidelines to re-cover while he tortured someone else. But the names he called me! The comments on my none too smoothly articulated bones—and my alleged mind! As in my schooldays when, a laggard in the fierce and seemingly malevolent atmosphere in which I was taught my A B C's, I crept shamefacedly and beaten from the scene.

It was in the adjoining bathroom, where the host daily personally superintended the ablutions of his guests, that even more of his remarkable method was revealed. Here a goodly portion of the force of his method was his skill in removing any sense of ability, agility, authority or worth from those with whom he dealt. Apparently to him, in his strength and energy, they were all children, weaklings, failures, numbskulls, no matter what they might be in the world outside. They had no understanding of the most important of their possessions, their bodies. And here again, even more than in the gymnasium, they were at the disadvantage of feeling themselves spectacles, for here they were naked. However grand an osseous, leathery lawyer or judge or doctor or politician or society man may look out in the world addressing a jury or a crowd or walking in some favorite place, glistening in his raiment, here, whiskered, thin of legs, arms and neck, with bulging brow and stripped not only of his gown but everything else this side of his skin—well, draw your own conclusion. For after performing certain additional exercises—one hundred times up on your toes, one hundred times (if you could) squatting to your knees, one hundred times throwing your arms out straight before you from your chest or up from your shoulders or out at right angles, right and left from your body and back to your hips until your fingers touched and the sweat once more ran—you were then ready to be told (for once in your life) how to swiftly and agilely take a bath.

"Well, now, you're ready, are you?" this to a noble jurist who, like myself perhaps, had arrived only the day before. "Come on, now. Now you have just ten seconds in which to jump under the water and get yourself wet all over, twenty seconds in which to jump out and soap yourself thoroughly, ten seconds in which to get back in again and rinse off all the soap, and twenty seconds in which to rub and dry your skin thoroughly—now start!"

The distinguished jurist began, but instead of following the advice given him for rapid action huddled himself in a shivering position under the water and stood all but inert despite the previous explanation of the host that the sole method of escaping the weakening influence of cold water was by counteracting it with activity, when it would prove beneficial.

He was such a noble, stalky, bony affair, his gold eyeglasses laid aside for the time being, his tweeds and carefully laundered linen all dispensed with during his stay here. As he came, meticulously and gingerly and quite undone by his efforts, from under the water, where he had been most roughly urged by

351

Muldoon, I hoped that he and not I would continue to be seized upon by this savage who seemed to take infinite delight in disturbing the social and intellectual poise of us all.

"Soap yourself!" exclaimed the latter most harshly now that the bather was out in the room once more. "Soap your chest! Soap your stomach! Soap your arms, damn it! Soap your arms! And don't rub them all day either! Now soap your legs, damn it! Soap your legs! Don't you know how to soap your legs? Don't stand there all day! Soap your legs! Now turn around and soap your back—soap your back! For Christ's sake, soap your back! Do it quick—quick! Now come back under the water again and see if you can get it off. Don't act as though you were cold molasses! Move! Move! Lord, you act as though you had all day—as though you had never taken a bath in your life! I never saw such an old poke. You come up here and expect me to do some things for you, and then you stand around as though you were made of bone! Quick now, move!"

The noble jurist did as demanded—that is, as quickly as he could—only the mental inadequacy and feebleness which he displayed before all the others, of course, was the worst of his cruel treatment here, and in this as in many instances it cut deep. So often it was the shock to one's dignity more than anything else which hurt so, to be called an old poke when one was perhaps a grave and reverend senior, or to be told that one was made of bone when one was a famous doctor or merchant. Once under the water this particular specimen had begun by nervously rubbing his hands and face in order to get the soap off, and when shouted at and abused for that had then turned his attention to one other spot—the back of his left forearm.

Mine host seemed enraged. "Well, well!" he exclaimed irascibly, watching him as might a hawk. "Are you going to spend all day rubbing that one spot? For God's sake, don't you know enough to rub your whole body and get out from under the water? Move! Move! Rub your chest! Rub your belly! Hell, rub your back! Rub your toes and get out!"

When routed from the ludicrous effort of vigorously rubbing one spot he was continually being driven on to some other, as though his body were some vast complex machine which he had never rightly understood before. He was very much flustered

352

of course and seemed wholly unable to grasp how it was done, let alone please his exacting host.

"Come on!" insisted the latter finally and wearily. "Get out from under the water. A lot you know about washing yourself! For a man who has been on the bench for fifteen years you're the dullest person I ever met. If you bathe like that at home, how do you keep clean? Come on out and dry yourself!"

The distinguished victim, drying himself rather ruefully on an exceedingly rough towel, looked a little weary and disgusted. "Such language!" someone afterwards said he said to someone else. "He's not used to dealing with gentlemen, that's plain. The man talks like a blackguard. And to think we pay for such things! Well, well! I'll not stand it, I'm afraid. I've had about enough. It's positively revolting, positively revolting!" But he stayed on, just the same—second thoughts, a good breakfast, his own physical needs. At any rate weeks later he was still there and in much better shape physically if not mentally.

About the second or third day I witnessed another such spectacle, which made me laugh—only not in my host's presence—nay, verily! For into this same chamber had come another distinguished personage, a lawyer or society man, I couldn't tell which, who was washing himself rather leisurely, as was *not* the prescribed way, when suddenly he was spied by mine host, who was invariably instructing someone in this swift one-minute-or-less system. Now he eyed the operation narrowly for a few seconds, then came over and exclaimed:

"Wash your toes, can't you? Wash your toes! Can't you wash your toes?"

The skilled gentleman, realizing that he was now living under very different conditions from those to which presumably he was accustomed, reached down and began to rub the tops of his toes but without any desire apparently to widen the operation.

"Here!" called the host, this time much more sharply, "I said wash your toes, not the outside of them! Soap them! Don't you know how to wash your toes yet? You're old enough, God knows! Wash between 'em! Wash under 'em!"

"Certainly I know how to wash my toes," replied the other irritably and straightening up, "and what's more, I'd like you to know that I am a gentleman."

"Well, then, if you're a gentleman," retorted the other, "you ought to know how to wash your toes. Wash 'em—and don't talk back!"

"Pah!" exclaimed the bather now, looking twice as ridiculous as before. "I'm not used to having such language addressed to me."

"I can't help that," said Muldoon. "If you knew how to wash your toes perhaps you wouldn't have to have such language addressed to you."

"Oh, hell!" fumed the other. "This is positively outrageous! I'll leave the place, by George!"

"Very well," rejoined the other, "only before you go you'll have to wash your toes!"

And he did, the host standing by and calmly watching the performance until it was finally completed.

It was just this atmosphere which made the place the most astonishing in which I have ever been. It seemed to be drawing the celebrated and successful as a magnet might iron, and yet it offered conditions which one might presume they would be most opposed to. No one here was really anyone, however much he might be outside. Our host was all. He had a great blazing personality which dominated everybody, and he did not hesitate to show before one and all that he did so do.

Breakfast here consisted of a cereal, a chop and coffee—plentiful but very plain, I thought. After breakfast, between eight-thirty and eleven, we were free to do as we chose: write letters, pack our bags if we were leaving, do up our laundry to be sent out, read, or merely sit about. At eleven, or ten-thirty, according to the nature of the exercise, one had to join a group, either one that was to do the long or short block, as they were known here, or one that was to ride horseback, all exercises being so timed that by proper execution one would arrive at the bathroom door in time to bathe, dress and take ten minutes' rest before luncheon. These exercises were simple enough in themselves, consisting, as they did in the case of the long and the short blocks (the long block seven, the short four miles in length), of our walking, or walking and running betimes, about or over courses laid up hill and down dale, over or through unpaved mudroads in many instances, along dry or wet beds of brooks or streams, and across stony or weedy fields, often still damp with dew or the

354

spring rains. But in most cases, when people had not taken any regular exercise for a long time, this was by no means easy. The first day I thought I should never make it, and I was by no means a poor walker. Others, the new ones especially, often gave out and had to be sent for, or came in an hour later to be most severely and irritatingly ragged by the host. He seemed to all but despise weakness and had apparently a thousand disagreeble ways of showing it.

"If you want to see what poor bags of mush some people can become," he once said in regard to some poor specimen who had seemingly had great difficulty in doing the short block, "look at this. Here comes a man sent out to do four measly country miles in fifty minutes, and look at him. You'd think he was going to die. He probably thinks so himself. In New York he'd do seventeen miles in a night running from barroom to barroom or one lobster palace to another—that's a good name for them, by the way—and never say a word. But out here in the country, with plenty of fresh air and a night's rest and a good breakfast, he can't even do four miles in fifty minutes! Think of it! And he probably thinks of himself as a man—boasts before his friends, or his wife, anyhow. Lord!"

A day or two later there arrived here a certain major of the United States Army, a large, broad-chested, rather pompous person of about forty-eight or -nine, who from taking his ease in one sinecure and another had finally reached the place where he was unable to endure certain tests (or he thought so) which were about to be made with a view to retiring certain officers grown fat in the service. As he explained to Muldoon, and the latter was always open and ribald afterward in his comments on those who offered explanations of any kind, his plan was to take the course here in order to be able to make the difficult tests later.

Muldoon resented this, I think. He resented people using him or his methods to get anywhere, do anything more in life than he could do, and yet he received them. He felt, and I think in the main that he was right, that they looked down on him because of his lowly birth and purely material and mechanical career, and yet having attained some distinction by it he could not forego this work which raised him, in a way, to a position of dominance over these people. Now the sight of presumably so efficient a person in need of aid or exercise, to be built up, was all that was required to spur him on to the most waspish or wolfish attitude imaginable. In part at least he argued, I think (for in the last analysis he was really too wise and experienced to take any such petty view, although there is a subconscious "past-lack" motivating impulse in all our views), that here he was, an ex-policeman, ex-wrestler, ex-prize fighter, ex-private, ex-waiter, beef-carrier, bouncer, trainer; and here was this grand major, trained at West Point, who actually didn't know any more about life or how to take care of his body than to be compelled to come here, broken down at forty-eight, whereas he, because of his stamina and Spartan energy, had been able to survive in perfect condition until sixty and was now in a position to rebuild all these men and wastrels and to control this great institution. And to a certain extent he was right, although he seemed to forget or not to know that he was not the creator of his own great strength, by any means, impulses and tendencies over which he had no control having arranged for that.

However that may be, here was the major a suppliant for his services, and here was he, Muldoon, and although the major was paying well for his minute room and his probably greatly decreased diet, still Muldoon could not resist the temptation to make a show of him, to picture him as the more or less pathetic example that he was, in order perhaps that he, Muldoon, might shine by contrast. Thus on the first day, having sent him around the short block with the others, it was found at twelve, when the "joggers" were expected to return, and again at twelve-thirty when they were supposed to take their places at the luncheon table, that the heavy major had not arrived. He had been seen and passed by all, of course. After the first mile or two probably he had given out and was making his way as best he might up hill and down dale, or along some more direct road, to the "shop," or maybe he had dropped out entirely, as some did, via a kindly truck or farmer's wagon, and was on his way to the nearest railway station.

At any rate, as Muldoon sat down at his very small private table, which stood in the center of the dining room and far apart from the others (a vantage point, as it were), he looked about and, not seeing the new guest, inquired, "Has anyone seen that alleged army officer who arrived here this morning?"

No one could say anything more than that they had left him two or three miles back.

"I thought so," he said tersely. "There you have a fine example of the desk general and major—we had 'em in the army—men who sit in a swivel chair all day, wear a braided uniform and issue orders to other people. You'd think a man like that who had been trained at West Point and seen service in the Philippines would have sense enough to keep himself in condition. Not at all. As soon as they get a little way up in their profession they want to sit around hotel grills or society ballrooms and show off, tell how wonderful they are. Here's a man, an army officer, in such rotten shape that if I sent a good horse after him now it's ten to one he couldn't get on him. I'll have to send a truck or some such thing."

He subsided. About an hour later the major did appear, much the worse for wear. A groom with a horse had been sent out after him, and, as the latter confided to someone afterward, he "had to help the major on." From that time on, on the short block and the long, as well as on those horseback tours which every second or third morning we were supposed to take, the major was his especial target. He loved to pick on him, to tell him that he was "nearly all guts"—a phrase which literally sickened me at that time—to ask him how he expected to stay in the army if he couldn't do this or that, what good was he to the army, how could any soldier respect a thing like him, and so on *ad infinitum* until, while at first I pitied the major, later on I admired his pluck. Muldoon foisted upon him his sorriest and boniest nag, the meanest animal he could find, yet he never complained; and although he forced on him all the foods he knew the major could not like, still there was no complaint; he insisted that he should be out and around of an afternoon when most of us lay about, allowed him no drinks whatever, although he was accustomed to them. The major, as I learned afterwards, stayed not six but twelve weeks and passed the tests which permitted him to remain in the army.

But to return to Muldoon himself. The latter's method always contained this element of nag and pester which, along with his brazen reliance on and pride in his brute strength at sixty, made all these others look so puny and ineffectual. They might have brains and skill but here they were in his institution, more or less undone nervously and physically, and here he was, cold, contemptuous, not caring much whether they came, stayed or went, and laughing at them even as they raged. Now and then it was rumored that he found some single individual in whom he would take an interest, but not often. In the main I think he despised them one and all for the puny machines they were. He even despised the life and the pleasures and dissipations or swinish indolence which, in his judgment, characterized most men. I recall once, for instance, his telling us how as a private in the United States Army when the division of which he was a unit was shut up in winter quarters, huddled about stoves, smoking (as he characterized them) "filthy pipes" or chewing tobacco and spitting, actually lousy, and never changing their clothes for weeks on end—how he, revolting at all this and the disease and fevers ensuing, had kept out of doors as much as possible, even in the coldest weather, and finding no other way of keeping clean the single shift of underwear and the one uniform he possessed he had, every other day or so, washed all, uniform and underwear, with or without soap as conditions might compel, in a nearby stream, often breaking the ice to get to the water, and dancing about naked in the cold, running and jumping, while they dried on bushes or the branch of a tree.

"Those poor rats," he added most contemptuously, "used to sit inside and wonder at me or laugh and jeer, hovering over their stoves, but a lot of them died that very winter, and here I am today."

And well we knew it. I used to study the faces of many of the puffy, gelatinous souls, so long confined to their comfortable offices, restaurants and homes that two hours on horseback all but wore them out, and wonder how this appealed to them. I think that in the main they took it as an illustration of either one of two things: insanity, or giant and therefore not-to-be-imitated strength.

But in regard to them Muldoon was by no means so tolerant. One day, as I recall, there arrived at the sanitarium a stout and mushy-looking Hebrew, with a semi-bald pate, protruding paunch and fat arms and legs, who applied to Muldoon for

358

admission. And, as much to irritate his other guests, I think, as to torture this particular specimen into some semblance of vitality, he admitted him. And thereafter, from the hour he entered until he left about the time I did, Muldoon seemed to follow him with a wolfish and savage idea. He gave him a most damnable and savage horse, one that kicked and bit, and at mounting time would place Mr. Itzky (I think his name was) up near the front of the procession where he could watch him. Always at mount-time, when we were permitted to ride, there was inside the great stable a kind of preliminary military inspection of all our accouterments, seeing that we had to saddle and bridle and bring forth our own steeds. This particular person could not saddle a horse very well nor put on his bit and bridle. The animal was inclined to rear and plunge when he came near, to fix him with an evil eye and bite at him.

And above all things Muldoon seemed to value strain of this kind. If he could just make his guests feel the pressure of necessity in connection with their work he was happy. To this end he would employ the most contemptuous and grilling comment. Thus to Mr. Itzky he was most unkind. He would look over all most cynically, examining the saddles and bridles, and then say, "Oh, I see you haven't learned how to tighten a belly-band yet," or "I do believe you have your saddle hind-side to. You would if you could, that's one thing sure. How do you expect a horse to be sensible or quiet when he knows that he isn't saddled right? Any horse knows that much, and whether he has an ass for a rider. I'd kick and bite too if I were some of these horses, having a lot of damned fools and wasters to pack all over the country. Loosen that belt and fasten it right" (there might be nothing wrong with it) "and move your saddle up. Do you want to sit over the horse's rump?"

Then would come the fateful moment of mounting. There was of course the accepted and perfect way—his way: left foot in stirrup, an easy balanced spring and light descent into the seat. One should be able to slip the right foot into the right stirrup with the same motion of mounting. But imagine fifty, sixty, seventy men, all sizes, weights and differing conditions of health and mood. A number of these people had never ridden a horse before coming here and were as nervous and frightened as children. Such

359

mounts! Such fumbling around, once they were in their saddles, for the right stirrup! And all the while Muldoon would be sitting out front like an army captain on the only decent steed in the place, eyeing us with a look of infinite and weary contempt that served to increase our troubles a thousandfold.

"Well, you're all on, are you? You all do it so gracefully I like to sit here and admire you. Hulbert there throws his leg over his horse's back so artistically that he almost kicks his teeth out. And Effingham does his best to fall off on the other side. And where's Itzky? I don't even see him. Oh, yes, there he is. Well" (this to Itzky, frantically endeavoring to get one fat foot in a stirrup and pull himself up) "what about you? Can't you get your leg that high? Here's a man who for twenty-five years has been running a cloak-and-suit business and employing five hundred people, but he can't get on a horse! Imagine! Five hundred people dependent on that for their living!" (At this point, say, Itzky succeeds in mounting.) "Well, he's actually on! Now see if you can stick while we ride a block or two. You'll find the right stirrup, Itzky, just a little forward of your horse's belly on the right side—see? A fine bunch this is to lead out through a gentleman's country! Hell, no wonder I've got a bad reputation throughout this section! Well, forward, and see if you can keep from falling off."

Then we were out through the stable door and the privet gate at a smart trot, only to burst into a headlong gallop a little farther on down the road. To the seasoned riders it was all well enough, but to beginners, those nervous about horses, fearful about themselves! The first day, not having ridden in years and being uncertain as to my skill, I could scarcely stay on. Several days later, I by then having become a reasonably seasoned rider, it was Mr. Itzky who appeared on the scene, and after him various others. On this particular trip I am thinking of, Mr. Itzky fell or rolled off and could not again mount. He was miles from the repair shop and Muldoon, discovering his plight, was by no means sympathetic. We had a short ride back to where he sat lamely by the roadside viewing disconsolately the cavalcade and the country in general.

"Well, what's the matter with you now?" It was Muldoon, eyeing him most severely.

"I hef hurt my foot. I kent stay on."

"You mean you'd rather walk, do you, and lead your horse?"

"Vell, I kent ride."

"All right, then, you lead your horse back to the stable if you want any lunch, and hereafter you run with the baby-class on the short block until you think you can ride without falling off. What's the good of my keeping a stable of first-class horses at the service of a lot of mush-heads who don't even know how to use 'em? All they do is ruin 'em. In a week or two, after a good horse is put in the stable, he's not fit for a gentleman to ride. They pull and haul and kick and beat, when as a matter of fact the horse has a damned sight more sense than they have."

We rode off, leaving Itzy alone. The men on either side of me—we were riding three abreast—scoffed under their breath at the statement that we were furnished decent horses. "The nerve! This nag!" "This bag of bones!" "To think a thing like this should be called a horse!" But there were no outward murmurs and no particular sympathy for Mr. Itzky. He was a fat stuff, a sweat-shop manufacturer, they would bet; let him walk and sweat.

So much for sympathy in this gay realm where all were seeking to restore their own little bodies, whatever happened.

So many of these men varied so greatly in their looks, capacities and troubles that they were always amusing. Thus I recall one lean iron manufacturer, the millionaire president of a great "frog and switch" company, who had come on from Kansas City, troubled with anemia, neurasthenia, "nervous derangement of the heart" and various other things. He was over fifty, very much concerned about himself, his family, his business, his friends; anxious to obtain the benefits of this celebrated course of which he had heard so much. Walking or running near me on his first day, he took occasion to make inquiries in regard to Muldoon, the life here, and later on confidences as to his own condition. It appeared that his chief trouble was his heart, a kind of phantom disturbance which made him fear that he was about to drop dead and which came and went, leaving him uncertain as to whether he had it or not. On entering he had confided to Muldoon the mysteries of his case, and the latter had examined him, pronouncing him ("Rather roughly," as he explained to me), quite fit to do "all the silly work he would have to do here."

361

Nevertheless while we were out on the short block his heart was hurting him. At the same time it had been made rather clear to him that if he wished to stay here he would have to fulfill all the obligations imposed. After a mile or two or three of quick walking and jogging he was saying to me, "You know, I'm not really sure that I can do this. It's very severe, more so than I thought. My heart is not doing very well. It feels very fluttery."

"But," I said, "if he told you you could stand it, you can, I'm sure. It's not very likely he'd say you could if you couldn't. He examined you, didn't he? I don't believe he'd deliberately put a strain on anyone who couldn't stand it."

"Yes," he admitted doubtfully, "that's true perhaps."

Still he continued to complain and complain and to grow more and more worried, until finally he slowed up and was lost in the background.

Reaching the gymnasium at the proper time I bathed and dressed myself quickly and waited on the balcony over the bathroom to see what would happen in this case. As a rule Muldoon stood in or near the door at this time, having just returned from some route or "block" himself, to see how the others were faring. And he was there when the iron manufacturer came limping up, fifteen minutes late, one hand over his heart, the other to his mouth, and exclaiming as he drew near, "I do believe, Mr. Muldoon, that I can't stand this. I'm afraid there is something the matter with my heart. It's fluttering so."

"To hell with your heart! Didn't I tell you there was nothing the matter with it? Get into the bath!"

The troubled manufacturer, overawed or reassured as the case might be, entered the bath and ten minutes later might have been seen entering the dining room, as comfortable apparently as anyone. Afterwards he confessed to me on one of our jogs that there was something about Muldoon which *gave him confidence* and made him believe that there wasn't anything wrong with his heart—which there wasn't, I presume.

The intensely interesting thing about Muldoon was this different, very original and forthright if at times brutal point of view. It was a blazing material world of which he was the center, the sun, and yet always I had the sense of very great life. With no knowledge of or interest in the superior mental sciences or arts

362

or philosophies, still he seemed to suggest and even live them. He was in his way an exemplification of that ancient Greek regimen and stark thought which brought back the Ten Thousand from Cunaxa. He seemed even to suggest in his rough way historical perspective and balance. He knew men, and apparently he sensed how at best and at bottom life was to be lived, with not too much emotional or appetitive swaying in any one direction, and not too little either.

Yet in "trapseing" about this particular realm each day with ministers, lawyers, doctors, actors, manufacturers, papa's or mamma's young hopefuls and petted heirs, young scapegraces and so-called "society men" of the extreme "upper crust," stuffed and plethoric with money and as innocent of sound knowledge or necessary energy in some instances as anyone might well be, one could not help speculating as to how it was that such a man, as indifferent and all but discourteous as this one, could attract them (and so many) to him. They came from all parts of America—the Pacific, the Gulf, the Atlantic and Canada—and yet, although they did not relish him or his treatment of them, once here they stayed. Walking or running or idling about with them one could always hear from one or another that Muldoon was too harsh, a "bounder," an "upstart," a "cheap pugilist" or "wrestler" at best (I myself thought so at times when I was angry), yet here they were, and here I was, and staying. He was low, vulgar—yet here we were. And yet, meditating on him, I began to think that he was really one of the most remarkable men I had ever known, for these people he dealt with were of all the most difficult to deal with. In the main they were of that order or condition of mind which springs from (1), too much wealth too easily acquired or inherited; or (2), from a blazing material success, the cause of which was their own savage self-interested viewpoint. Hence a colder and in some respects a more critical group of men I have never known. Most of them had already seen so much of life in a libertine way that there was little left to enjoy. They sniffed at almost everything, Muldoon included, and yet they were obviously drawn to him. I tried to explain this to myself on the ground that there is some iron power in some people which literally compels this, whether one will or no; or that they were in the main so tired of life and so truly selfish and egotistic that it required some such different iron or caviar mood plus such a threatening regimen to make them really take an interest. Sick as they were, he was about the only thing left on which they could sharpen their teeth with any result.

As I have said, a part of Muldoon's general scheme was to arrange the starting time for the walks and jogs about the long and short blocks so that if one moved along briskly he reached the sanitarium at twelve-thirty and had a few minutes in which to bathe and cool off and change his clothes before entering the dining room, where, if not at the bathroom door beforehand, Muldoon would be waiting, seated at his little table, ready to keep watch on the time and condition of all those due. Thus one day, a group of us having done the long block in less time than we should have devoted to it, came in panting and rejoicing that we had cut the record by seven minutes. We did not know that he was around. But in the dining room as we entered he scoffed at our achievement.

"You think you're smart, don't you?" he said sourly and without any preliminary statement as to how he knew we had done it in less time. "You come out here and pay me one hundred a week and then you want to be cute and play tricks with your own money and health. I want you to remember just one thing: my reputation is just as much involved with the results here as your money. I don't need anybody's money, and I do need my orders obeyed. Now you all have watches. You just time yourselves and do that block in the time required. If you can't do it, that's one thing; I can forgive a man too weak or sick to do it. But I haven't any use for a mere smart aleck, and I don't want any more of it, see?"

That luncheon was very sad.

Another thing in connection with these luncheons and dinners, which were sharply timed to the minute, were these crisp table speeches, often made *in re* some particular offender or his offense, at other times mere sarcastic comments on life in general and the innate cussedness of human nature, which amused at the same time that they were certain to irritate some. For who is it that is not interested in hearing the peccadilloes of his neighbor aired?

Thus while I was there, there was a New York society man

364

by the name of Blake, who unfortunately was given to severe periods of alcoholism, the results of which were, after a time, nervous disorders which sent him here. In many ways he was as amiable and courteous and considerate a soul as one could meet anywhere. He had that smooth, gracious something about him—good nature, for one thing, a kind of understanding and sympathy for various forms of life—which left him highly noncensorious, if genially examining at times. But his love of drink, or rather his mild attempts here to arrange some method by which in this droughty world he could obtain a little, aroused in Muldoon not so much opposition as an amused contempt, for at bottom I think he really liked the man. Blake was so orderly, so sincere in his attempts to fulfill conditions, only about once every week or so he would suggest that he be allowed to go to White Plains or Rye, or even New York, on some errand or other—most of which requests were promptly and nearly always publicly refused. For although Muldoon had his private suite at one end of the great building, where one might suppose one might go to make a private plea, still one could never find him there. He refused to receive complaints or requests or visits of any kind there. If you wanted to speak to him you had to do it when he was with the group in its entirety—a commonsense enough policy. But just the same there were those who had reasonable requests or complaints, and these, by a fine intuition as to who was who in this institution and what might be expected of each one, he managed to hear very softly, withdrawing slowly as they talked or inviting them into the office. In the main however the requests were very much like those of Blake—men who wanted to get off somewhere for a day or two, feeling, as they did after a week or two or three, especially fit and beginning to think no doubt of the various comforts and pleasures which the city offered.

But to all these he was more or less adamant. By hook or by crook, by special arrangements with friends or agents in nearby towns and the principal showy resorts of New York, he managed to know, providing they did leave the grounds, either with or without his consent, about where they were and what they had done, and in case any of his rules or their agreements were broken their privileges were thereafter cut off or they were promptly ejected; their trunks being set out on the roadway in front of the estate and they being left to make their way to shelter elsewhere as best they might.

On one occasion, however, Blake had been allowed to go to New York over Saturday and Sunday to attend to some urgent business, as he said, he on his honor having promised to avoid the white lights. Nevertheless he did not manage so to do but instead, in some comfortable section of that region, was seen drinking enough to last him until perhaps he should have another opportunity to return to the city.

On his return to the "shop" on Monday morning or late Sunday night, Muldoon pretended not to see him until noonday lunch, when, his jog over the long block done with and his bath taken, he came dapperly into the dining room, wishing to look as innocent and fit as possible. But Muldoon was there before him at his little table in the center of the room, and patting the head of one of the two pure-blooded collies that always followed him about on the grounds or in the house, began as follows:

"A dog," he said very distinctly and in his most cynical tone and apparently apropos of nothing, which usually augured that the lightning of his criticism was about to strike somewhere, "is so much better than the average man that it's an insult to the dog to compare them. The dog's really decent. He has no sloppy vices. You set a plate of food before a regularly-fed, blooded dog, and he won't think of gorging himself sick or silly. He eats what he needs, and then stops. So does a cat" (which is of course by no means true, but still—). "A dog doesn't get a red nose from drinking too much." By now all eyes were turning in the direction of Blake, whose nose was faintly tinged. "He doesn't get gonorrhea or syphilis." The united glances veered in the direction of three or four young scapegraces of wealth, all of whom were suspected of these diseases. "He doesn't hang around hotel bars and swill and get his tongue thick and talk about how rich he is or how old his family is." (This augured that Blake did such things, which I doubt, but once more all eyes shifted to him.) "He doesn't break his word. Within the limits of his poor little brain he's faithful. He does what he thinks he's called upon to do.

"But you take a man—more especially a gentleman—one of these fellows who is always very pointed in emphasizing that he is a gentleman" (which Blake never did). "Let him inherit eight or ten millions, give him a college education, let him be socially well connected, and what does he do? Not a damned thing if he can help it except contract vices—run from one saloon to another, one gambling house to another, one girl to another, one meal to another. He doesn't need to know anything necessarily. He may be the lowest dog physically and in every other way, and still he's a gentleman—because he has money, wears spats and a high hat. Why, I've seen fifty poor boob prize fighters in my time who could put it all over most of the so-called gentlemen I have ever seen. They kept their word. They tried to be physically fit. They tried to stand up in the world and earn their own living and be somebody." (He was probably thinking of himself.) "But a gentleman wants to boast of his past and his family, to tell you that he must go to the city on business—his lawyers or some directors want to see him. Then he swills around at hotel bars, stays with some of his lady whores, and then comes back here and expects me to pull him into shape again, to make his nose a little less red. He thinks he can use my place to fall back on when he can't go any longer, to fix him up to do some more swilling later on.

"Well, I want to serve notice on all so-called gentlemen here, and *one gentleman* in particular" (and he heavily and sardonically emphasized the words), "that it won't do. This isn't a hospital attached to a whorehouse or a saloon. And as for the trashy little six hundred paid here, I don't need it. I've turned away more men who have been here once or twice and have shown me that they were just using this place and me as something to help them go on with their lousy drinking and carousing, than would fill this building. Sensible men know it. They don't try to use me. It's only the wastrels, or their mothers or fathers who bring their boys and husbands and cry, who try to use me, and I take 'em once or twice, but not oftener. When a man goes out of here cured, I know he is cured. I never want to see him again. I want him to go out in the world and stand up. I don't want him to come back here in six months sniveling to be put in shape again. He disgusts me. He makes me sick. I feel like ordering him off the place, and I do, and that's the end of him. Let him go and bamboozle somebody else. I've shown him all I know. There's no mystery. He can do as much for himself, once he's been here,

367

as I can. If he won't, well and good. And I'm saying one thing more: There's one man here to whom this particularly applies today. This is his last call. He's been here twice. When he goes out this time he can't come back. Now see if some of you can remember some of the things I've been telling you."

He subsided and opened his little pint of wine.

Another day while I was there he began as follows:

"If there's one class of men that needs to be improved in this country, it's lawyers. I don't know why it is, but there's something in the very nature of the work of a lawyer which appears to make him cynical and want to wear a know-it-all look. Most lawyers are little more than sharper crooks than the crooks they have to deal with. They're always trying to get in on some case or other where they have to outwit the law, save someone from getting what he justly deserves, and then they are supposed to be honest and high-minded! Think of it! To judge by some of the specimens I get up here" (and then some lawyer in the place would turn a shrewd inquiring glance in his direction or steadfastly gaze at his plate or out the window, while the others stared at him), "you would think they were the salt of the earth or that they were following a really noble profession or that they were above or better than other men in their abilities. Well, if being conniving and tricky are fine traits, I suppose they are, but personally I can't see it. Generally speaking, they're physically the poorest fish I get here. They're slow and meditative and sallow, mostly because they get too little exercise, I presume. And they're never direct and enthusiastic in an argument. A lawyer always wants to stick in an 'if' or a 'but,' to get around you in some way. He's never willing to answer you quickly or directly. I've watched 'em now for nearly fifteen years, and they're all more or less alike. They think they're very individual and different, but they're not. Most of them don't know nearly as much about life as a good, all-around business or society man" (this in the absence of any desire to discuss these two breeds for the time being). "For the life of me I could never see why a really attractive woman would ever want to marry a lawyer"—and so he would talk on, revealing one little unsatisfactory trait after another in connection with the tribe, sandpapering their raw places as it were, until you would about conclude, supposing you had never heard him talk

368

concerning any other profession, that lawyers were the most ignoble, the pettiest, the most inefficient physically and mentally, of all the men he had ever encountered; and in his noble savage state there would not be one to disagree with him, for he had such an animal, tiger-like mien that you had the feeling that instead of an argument you would get a physical rip which would leave you bleeding for days.

The next day, or a day or two or four or six later—according to his mood—it would be doctors or merchants or society men or politicians he would discourse about—and, kind heaven, what a drubbing they would get! He seemed always to be meditating on the vulnerable points of his victims, anxious (and yet presumably not) to show them what poor, fallible, shabby, petty and all but drooling creatures they were. Thus, in regard to merchants:

"The average man who has a little business of some kind, a factory or a wholesale or brokerage house or a hotel or a restaurant, usually has a distinctly middle-class mind." At this all the merchants and manufacturers were likely to give a very sharp ear. "As a rule, you'll find that they know just the one little line with which they're connected, and nothing more. One man knows all about cloaks and suits" (this may have been a slap at poor Itzky) "or he knows a little something about leather goods or shoes or lamps or furniture, and that's all he knows. If he's an American he'll buckle down to that little business and work night and day, sweat blood and make everyone else connected with him sweat it, underpay his employees, swindle his friends, half-starve himself and his family, in order to get a few thousand dollars and seem as good as someone else who has a few thousand. And yet he doesn't want to be different from—he wants to be just like—the other fellow. If someone in his line has a house up on the Hudson or on Riverside Drive, when he gets his money he wants to go there and live. If the fellow in his line, or some other that he knows something about, belongs to a certain club, he has to belong to it even if the club doesn't want him or he wouldn't look well in it. He wants to have the same tailor, the same grocer, smoke the same brand of cigars and go to the same summer resort as the other fellow. They even want to look alike. God! And then when they're just like everyone else, they think they're somebody. They haven't a single idea outside their line, and yet because they've made money they want to tell other people how to live and think. Imagine a rich butcher or cloak-maker, or anyone else, presuming to tell me how to think or live!"

He stared about him as though he saw many exemplifications of his picture present. And it was always interesting to see how those whom his description really did fit look as though he could not possibly be referring to them.

Of all types or professions that came here, I think he disliked doctors most. The reason was of course that the work they did or were about to do in the world bordered on that which he was trying to accomplish, and the chances were that they sniffed at or at least critically examined what he was doing with an eye to finding its weak spots. In many cases no doubt he fancied that they were there to study and copy his methods and ideas, without having the decency later on to attribute their knowledge to him. It was short shrift for any one of them with ideas or "notions" unfriendly to him advanced in his presence. For a little while during my stay there was a smooth-faced doctor, rather solid physically and decidedly self-opinionated mentally, who ate at the same small table as I and who was never tired of airing his views, medical and otherwise. He confided to me rather loftily that there was, to be sure, something to Muldoon's views and methods but that they were "over-emphasized here, over-emphasized." Still, one could over-emphasize the value of drugs too. As for himself he had decided to achieve a happy medium if possible, and for this reason (for one) he had come here to study Muldoon.

As for Muldoon, in spite of the young doctor's condescension and understanding, or perhaps better yet because of it, he thoroughly disliked, barely tolerated, him, and was never tired of commenting on little dancing medics with their "pill cases" and easily acquired book knowledge, boasting of their supposed learning "which somebody else paid for," as he once said—their fathers, of course. And when they were sick, some of them at least, they had to come out here to him, or they came to steal his theory and start a shabby grafting sanitarium of their own. He knew them.

One noon we were at lunch. Occasionally before seating

himself at his small central table he would walk or glance about and, having good eyes, would spy some little defect or delinquency somewhere and of course immediately act upon it. One of the rules of the repair shop was that you were to eat what was put before you, especially when it differed from what your table companion received. Thus a fat man at a table with a lean one might receive a small portion of lean meat, no potatoes and no bread or one little roll, whereas his lean acquaintance opposite would be receiving a large portion of fat meat, a baked or boiled potato, plenty of bread and butter, and possibly a side dish of some kind. Now it might well be, as indeed was often the case, that each would be dissatisfied with his apportionment and would attempt to change plates.

But this was the one thing that Muldoon would not endure. So upon one occasion, passing near the table at which sat myself and the above-mentioned doctor, table-mates for the time being, he noticed that he was not eating his carrots, a dish which has been especially prepared for him, I imagine—for if one unconsciously ignored certain things the first day or two of his stay, those very things would be all but rammed down his throat during the remainder of his stay; a thing concerning which one guest and another occasionally cautioned newcomers. However this may have been in this particular case, he noticed the uneaten carrots and, pausing a moment, observed:

"What's the matter? Aren't you eating your carrots?" We had almost finished eating.

"Who, me?" replied the medic, looking up. "Oh, no, I never eat carrots, you know. I don't like them."

"Oh, don't you?" said Muldoon sweetly. "You don't like them, and so you don't eat them! Well, suppose you eat them here. They may do you a little good just as a change."

"But I never eat carrots," retorted the medic tersely and with a slight show of resentment or opposition, scenting perhaps a new order.

"No, not outside perhaps, but here you do. You eat carrots here, see?"

"Yes, but why should I eat them if I don't like them? They don't agree with me. Must I eat something that doesn't agree with me just because it's a rule or to please you?"

"To please me, or the carrots, or any damned thing you please—but eat 'em."

The doctor subsided. For a day or two he went about commenting on what a farce the whole thing was, how ridiculous to make anyone eat what was not suited to him, but just the same while he was there he ate them.

As for myself, I was very fond of large boiled potatoes and substantial orders of fat and lean meat, and in consequence, having been so foolish as to show this preference, I received but the weakest, most contemptible and puling little spuds and pale orders of meat—with, it is true, plenty of other "side dishes"; whereas a later table-mate of mine, a distressed and neurasthenic society man, was receiving—I soon learned he especially abhorred them—potatoes as big as my two fists.

"Now look at that! Now look at that!" he often said peevishly and with a kind of sickly whine in his voice when he saw one being put before him. "He knows I don't like potatoes, and see what I get! And look at the little bit of a thing he gives you! It's a shame, the way he nags people, especially over this food question. I don't think there's a thing to it. I don't think eating a big potato does me a bit of good, or you the little one, and yet I have to eat the blank-blank things or get out. And I need to get on my feet just now."

"Well, cheer up," I said sympathetically and with an eye on the large potato perhaps. "He isn't always looking, and we can fix it. You mash up your big potato and put butter and salt on it, and I'll do the same with my little one. Then when he's not looking we'll shift."

"Oh, that's all right," he commented, "but we'd better look out. If he sees us he'll be as sore as the devil."

This system worked well enough for a time, and for days I was getting all the potato I wanted and congratulating myself on my skill, when one day as I was slyly forking potatoes out of his dish, moved helpfully in my direction, I saw Muldoon approaching and feared that our trick had been discovered. It had. Perhaps some snaky waitress had told on us, or he had seen us, even from his table.

"Now I know what's going on here at this table," he growled savagely, "and I want you two to cut it out. This big boob here" (he was referring to my esteemed self) "who hasn't strength of will or character enough to keep himself in good health and has to be brought up here by his brother, hasn't brains enough to see that when I plan a thing for his benefit it is for his benefit, and not mine. Like most of the other damned fools that come up here and waste their money and my time, he thinks I'm playing some cute game with him—tag or something that will let him show how much cuter he is than I am. And he's supposed to be a writer and have a little horse-sense! His brother claims it, anyhow. And as for this other simp here," and now he was addressing the assembled diners while nodding toward my friend, "it hasn't been three weeks since he was begging to know what I could do for him. And now look at him—entering into a petty little game of potato-cheating!

"I swear," he went on savagely, talking to the room in general, "sometimes I don't know what to do with such damned fools. The right thing would be to set these two, and about fifty others in this place, out on the main road with their trunks and let them go to hell. They don't deserve the attention of a conscientious man. I prohibit gambling—what happens? A lot of nincompoops and mental lightweights with more money than brains sneak off into a field of an afternoon on the excuse that they are going for a walk, and then sit down and lose or win a bucket of money just to show off what hells of fellows they are, what sports, what big 'I ams.' I prohibit cigarette-smoking, not because I think it's literally going to kill anybody but because I think it looks bad here, sets a bad example to a lot of young wasters who come here and who ought to be broken of the vice, and besides, because I don't like cigarette-smoking here—don't want it and won't have it. What happens? A lot of sissies and mamma's boys and pet heirs, whose fathers haven't got enough brains to cut 'em off and make 'em get out and work, come up here, sneak in cigarettes or get the servants to, and then hide out behind the barn or a tree down in the lot and sneak and smoke like a lot of cheap schoolboys. God, it makes me sick! What's the use of a man working out a fact during a lifetime and letting other people have the benefit of it—not because he needs their money, but that they need his help—if all the time he is going to have such cattle to deal with? Not one out of twenty or forty men that come here really wants me to help him or to help himself. What he wants is to have someone drive him in the way he ought to go, kick him into it, instead of his buckling down and helping himself. What's the good of bothering with such damned fools? A man ought to take the whole pack and run 'em off the place with a dog-whip." He waved his hand in the air. "It's sickening. It's impossible.

"As for you two," he added, turning to us, but suddenly stopped. "Hell, what's the use? Why should I bother with you? Do as you damned well please, and stay sick or die!"

He turned on his heel and walked out of the dining room, leaving us to sit there. I was so dumbfounded by the harangue our pseudo-cleverness had released that I could scarcely speak. My appetite was gone and I felt wretched. To think of having been the cause of this unnecessary tongue-lashing to the others! And I felt that we were, and justly, the target for their rather censorious eyes.

"My God!" moaned my companion most dolefully. "That's always the way with me. Nothing that I ever do comes out right. All my life I've been unlucky. My mother died when I was seven, and my father's never had any use for me. I started in three of four businesses four or five years ago, but none of them ever came out right. My yacht burned last summer, and I've had neurasthenia for two years." He catalogued a list of ills that would have done honor to Job himself, and he was worth nine millions, so I heard!

Two or three additional and amusing incidents, and I am done.

One of the most outré things in connection with our rides about the countryside was Muldoon's attitude toward life and the natives and passing strangers as representing life. Thus one day, as I recall very well, we were riding along a backwoods country road, very shadowy and branch-covered, a great company of us four abreast, when suddenly and after his very military fashion there came a "Halt! Right by fours! Right dress! Face!" and presently we were all lined up in a row facing a greensward which had suddenly been revealed to the left and on which, and before a small plumber's stove standing outside some gentleman's stable, were stretched a plumber and his helper. The former, a

374

man of perhaps thirty-five and the latter, a lad of, say, fourteen or fifteen, were both very grimy and dirty, but taking their ease in the morning sun, a little pot of lead on the stove being waited for, I presume, that it might boil.

Muldoon, leaving his place at the head of the column, returned to the center nearest the plumber and his helper and pointing at them and addressing us in a very clear voice, said:

"There you have it. There's American labor for you, at its best—union labor, the poor, downtrodden workingman. Look at him." We all looked. "This poor hard-working plumber here," and at that the latter stirred and sat up, scarcely even now grasping what it was all about, so suddenly had we descended upon him, "earns or demands sixty cents an hour, and this poor sweating little helper here has to have forty. They're working now. They're waiting for that little bit of lead to boil, at a dollar an hour between them. They can't do a thing, either of 'em, until it does, and lead has to be well done, you know, before it can be used.

"Well, now, these two here," he continued, suddenly shifting his tone from one of light sarcasm to a kind of savage contempt, "imagine they are getting along, making life a lot better for themselves, when they lie about this way and swindle another man out of his honest due in connection with the work he is paying for. He can't help himself. He can't know everything. If he did he'd probably find what's wrong in there and fix it himself in three minutes. But if he did that and the union heard of it they'd boycott him. They'd come around and blackmail him, blow up his barn, or make him pay for the work he did himself. I know 'em. I have to deal with 'em. They fix my pipes in the same way that these two are fixing his—lying on the grass at a dollar an hour. And they want five dollars a pound for every bit of lead they use. If they forget anything and have to go back to town for it, you pay for it, at a dollar an hour. They get on the job at nine and quit at four, in the country. If you say anything, they quit altogether—they're *union* laborers—and they won't let anyone else do it, either. Once they're on the job they have to rest every few minutes, like these two. Something has to boil, or they have to wait for something. Isn't it wonderful! Isn't it beautiful! And all of us of course are made free and equal! They're just as good as we are! If you work and make money and have any plumbing to do you have to support 'em—Right by fours! Guide right! Forward!" and off we trotted, breaking into a headlong gallop a little farther on as if he wished to outrun the mood which was holding him at the moment.

The plumber and his assistant, fully awake now to the import of what had occurred, stared after us. The journeyman plumber, who was short and fat, sat and blinked. At last he recovered his wits sufficiently to cry, "Aw, go to hell, you ———!" but by that time we were well along the road and I am not sure that Muldoon even heard.

Another day as we were riding along a road which led into a nearby city of, say, twenty thousand, we encountered a beer truck of great size and on its seat so large and ruddy and obese a German as one might go a long way and still not see. It was very hot. The German was drowsy and taking his time in the matter of driving. As we drew near, Muldoon suddenly called a halt and, lining us up as was his rule, called to the horses of the brewery wagon, who also obeyed his lusty "Whoa!" The driver, from his high perch above, stared down on us with mingled curiosity and wonder.

"Now, here's an illustration of what I mean," Muldoon began, apropos of nothing at all, "when I say that the word *man* ought to be modified or changed in some way so that when we use it we would mean something more definite than we mean now. That thing you see sitting up on that wagon seat there— call that a man? And then call me one? Or a man like Charles A. Dana? Or a man like General Grant? Hell! Look at him! Look at his shape! Look at that stomach! You think a thing like that— call it a man if you want to—has any brains or that he's really any better than a pig in a sty? If you turn a horse out to shift for himself he'll eat just enough to keep in condition; same way with a dog, a cat or a bird. But let one of these things, that some people call a *man,* come along, give him a job and enough money or a chance to stuff himself, and see what happens. A thing like that connects himself with one end of a beer hose and then he thinks he's all right. He gets enough guts to start a sausage factory, and then he blows up, I suppose, or rots. Think of it! And we call him a man—or some do!"

During this amazing and wholly unexpected harangue (I

376

never saw him stop anyone before), the heavy driver, who did not understand English very well, first gazed and then strained with his eyebrows, not being able to quite make out what it was all about. From the chuckling and laughter that finally set up in one place and another he began dimly to comprehend that he was being made fun of, used as an unsatisfactory jest of some kind. Finally his face clouded for a storm and his eyes blazed, the while his fat red cheeks grew redder. *"Donnervetter!"* he began gutturally to roar. *"Schweine Hunde! Hunds Knoche! Nach der Polizei soll man rufen!"*

I for one pulled my horse cautiously back, as he cracked a great whip, and, charging savagely through us, drove on. Muldoon, having made his unkind comments, gave orders for our orderly formation once more and calmly led us away.

Perhaps the most amusing phase of him was his opposition to and contempt for inefficiency of any kind. If he asked you to do anything, no matter what, and you didn't at once leap to the task ready and willing and able so to do, he scarcely had words enough with which to express himself. On one occasion, as I recall all too well, he took us for a drive in his tally-ho—one of two or three that he possessed—a great lumbering, highly lacquered, yellow-wheeled vehicle, to which he attached seven or eight or nine horses, I forget which. This tally-ho ride was a regular Sunday morning or afternoon affair unless it was raining, a call suddenly sounding from about the grounds somewhere at eleven or at two in the afternoon, "Tally-ho at eleven-thirty" (or two-thirty, as the case might be). "All aboard!" Gathering all the reins in his hands and perching himself in the high seat above, with perhaps one of his guests beside him, all the rest crowded willy-nilly on the seats within and on top, he would carry us off, careening about the countryside most madly, several of his hostlers acting as liveried footmen or outriders and one of them perched up behind on the little seat, the technical name of which I have forgotten, waving and blowing the long silver trumpet, the regulation blasts on which had to be exactly as made and provided for such occasions. Often, having been given no warning as to just when it was to be, there would be a mad scramble to get into our *de rigueur* Sunday clothes, for Muldoon would not endure any flaws in our appearance, and if we were not ready and waiting when one of his stablemen swung the vehicle up to the door at the appointed time he was absolutely furious.

On the particular occasion I have in mind we all clambered on in good time, all spick-and-span and in our very best, shaved powdered, hands appropriately gloved, our whiskers curled and parted, our shoes shined, our hats brushed; and up in front was Muldoon, gentleman de luxe for the occasion, his long-tailed whip looped exactly as it should be, no doubt, ready to be flicked out over the farthest horse's head, and up behind was the trumpeter— high hat, yellow-topped boots, a uniform of some grand color, I forget which.

But, as it turned out on this occasion, there had been a hitch at the last minute. The regular hostler or stableman who acted as footman extraordinary and trumpeter plenipotentiary, the one who could truly and ably blow this magnificent horn, was sick or his mother was dead. At any rate, there he wasn't. And in order not to irritate Muldoon, a second hostler had been dressed and given his seat and horn—only he couldn't blow it. As we began to clamber in I heard him asking, "Can any of you gentlemen blow the trumpet? Do any of you gentlemen know the regular trumpet call?"

No one responded, although there was much discussion in a low key. Some could, or thought they could, but hesitated to assume so frightful a risk. At the same time Muldoon, hearing the fuss and knowing perhaps that his substitute could not trumpet, turned grimly around and said, "Say, do you mean to say there isn't anyone back there who knows how to blow that thing? What's the matter with you, Caswell?" he called to one, and getting only mumbled explanations from that quarter, called to another, "How about you, Drewberry? Or you, Crashaw?"

All three apologized briskly. They were terrified by the mere thought of trying. Indeed no one seemed eager to assume the responsibility, until finally he became so threatening and assured us so volubly that unless some immediate and cheerful response were made he would never again waste one blank minute on a lot of blank-blank this and thats, that one youth, a rash young society somebody from Rochester, volunteered more or less feebly that he "thought" that "maybe he could manage it." He took a seat directly under the pompously placed trumpeter, and we were off.

"Heigh-ho!" Out the gate and down the road and up a nearby slope at a smart clip, all of us gazing cheerfully and possibly vainly about, for it was a bright day and a gay country. Now the trumpeter, as is provided for on all such occasions, lifted the trumpet to his lips and began on the grandiose "ta-ra-ta-ta," but to our grief and pain, although he got through fairly successfully on his first attempt, there was one place where there was a slight hitch, a "false crack," as someone rowdyishly remarked. Muldoon, although tucking up his lines and stiffening his back irritably at this flaw, said nothing. For after all, a poor trumpeter was better than none at all. A little later, however, the trumpeter having hesitated to begin again, he called back, "Well, what about the horn? What about the horn? Can't you do something with it? Have you quit for the day?"

Up went the horn once more, and a most noble and encouraging "Ta-ra-ta-ta" was begun, but just at the critical point, and when we were all most prayerfully hoping against hope, as it were, that this time he would round the dangerous curves of it gracefully and come to a grand finish, there was a most disconcerting and disheartening squeak. It was pathetic, ghastly. As one man we wilted. What would Muldoon say to that? We were not long in doubt. "Great Christ!" he shouted, looking back and showing a countenance so black that it was positively terrifying, "Who did that? Throw him off! What do you think— that I want the whole country to know I'm airing a lot of lunatics? Somebody who can blow that thing, take it and blow it, for God's sake! I'm not going to drive around here without a trumpeter!"

For a few moments there was more or less painful gabbling in all the rows, pathetic whisperings and "go ons" or eager urgings of one and another to sacrifice himself upon the altar of necessity, insistences by the ex-trumpeter that he had blown trumpets in his day as good as anyone—what the deuce had got into him anyhow? It must be the horn!

"Well," shouted Muldoon finally, as a stop-gap to all this, "isn't anyone going to blow that thing? Do you mean to tell me that I'm hauling all of you around, with not a man among you able to blow a dinky little horn? What's the use of my keeping a lot of fancy vehicles in my barn when all I have to deal with is a lot of shoe salesmen and floorwalkers? Hell! Any child can blow it. It's as easy as a fish-horn. If I hadn't these horses to attend to I'd blow it myself. Come on—come on! Kerrigan, what's the matter with you blowing it?"

"The truth is, Mr. Muldoon," explained Mr. Kerrigan, the very dapper and polite heir of a Philadelphia starch millionaire, "I haven't had any chance to practice with one of those for several years. I'll try it if you want me to, but I can't guarantee—"

"Try!" insisted Muldoon violently. "You can't do any worse than that other mutt, if you blow for a million years. Blow it! Blow it!"

Mr. Kerrigan turned back and being very cheerfully tendered the horn by the last failure, wetted and adjusted his lips, lifted it upward and backward—and—

It was pathetic. It was positively dreadful, the wheezing, grinding sounds that were emitted.

"God!" shouted Muldoon, pulling up the coach to a dead stop. "Stop that! Whoa! Whoa!!! Do you mean to say that that's the best you can do? Well, this finishes me! Whoa! What kind of a bunch of cattle have I got up here, anyhow? Whoa! And out in this country too where I'm known and where they know all about such things! God! Whoa! Here I spend thousands of dollars to get together an equipment that will make a pleasant afternoon for a crowd of gentlemen, and this is what I draw— hams! A lot of barflies who never saw a tally-ho! Well, I'm done! I'm through! I'll split the damned thing up for firewood before I ever take it out again! Get down! Get out, all of you! I'll not haul one of you back a step! Walk back or anywhere you please— to hell, for all I care! I'm through! Get out! I'm going to turn around and get back to the barn as quick as I can—up some alley if I can find one. To think of having such a bunch of hacks to deal with!"

Humbly and wearily we climbed down and, while he drove savagely on to some turning-place, stood about first in small groups, then by twos and threes began making our way—rather gingerly, I must confess, in our fine clothes—along the winding road back to the place on the hill. But such swearing! Such un-Sabbath-like comments! The number of times his sturdy Irish soul was wished into innermost and almost sacrosanct portions of Sheol! He was cursed from more angles and in more artistically

380

and architecturally nobly constructed phrases and even paragraphs than any human being that I have ever head of before or since, phrases so livid and glistening that they smoked.

Talk about the carved ivories of speech! The mosaics of verbal precious stones!

You should have heard us on our way back!

And still we stayed.

•   •   •

Some two years later I was passing this place in company with some friends, when I asked my host, who also knew of the place, to turn in. During my stay it had been the privilege and custom among those who knew much of this institution to drive through the grounds and past the very doors of the "repair shop," even to stop if Muldoon chanced to be visible and talking to or at least greeting him, in some cases. A custom of Muldoon's was, in the summer time, to have erected on the lawn a large green-and-white striped marquee tent, a very handsome thing indeed, in which was placed a field-officer's table and several camp chairs, and some books and papers. Here of a hot day, when he was not busy with us, he would sit and read. And when he was in here or somewhere about, a little pennant was run up, possibly as guide to visiting guests or friends. At any rate, it was the presence of this pennant which caused me to know that he was about and to wish that I might have a look at him once more, great lion that he was. As "guests," none of us were ever allowed to come within more than ten feet of it, let alone in it. As passing visitors, however, we might, and many did, stop, remind him that we had once been his humble slaves, and ask leave to congratulate him on his health and sturdy years. At such times, if the visitors looked interesting enough, or he remembered them well, he would deign to come to the tent-fly and, standing there à la Napoleon at Lodi or Grant in the Wilderness, be for the first time in his relations with them a bit civil.

Anyway, on this occasion, urged on by curiosity to see my liege once more and also to learn whether he would remember me at all, I had my present host roll his car up to the tent door, where Muldoon was reading. Feeling that by this venturesome deed I had "let myself in for it" and had to "make a showing," I climbed briskly out and, approaching, recalled myself to him. With a semi-wry expression, half smile, half contemptuous curl of the corners of his mouth, he recalled me and took my extended hand; then seeing that possibly my friends if not myself looked interesting, he arose and came to the door. I introduced them—one a naval officer of distinction, the other the owner of a great estate some miles farther on. For the first time in my relations with him I had an opportunity to note how grandly gracious he could be. He accepted my friends' congratulations as to the view with a princely nod and suggested that on other days it was even better. He was soon to be busy now or he would have someone show my friends through the shop. Some Saturday afternoon, if they would telephone or stop in passing, he would oblige.

I noted at once that he had not aged in the least. He was sixty-two or -three now and as vigorous and trim as ever. And now he treated me as courteously and formally as though he had never browbeaten me in the least. "Good heavens," I said, "how much better to be a visitor than a guest!" After a moment or two we offered many thanks and sped on, but not without many a backward glance on my part, for the place fascinated me. That simply furnished institution! That severe regimen! This latter-day Stoic and Spartan in his tent! And, above all things, and the most astounding to me, so little could one know him, the book he had been reading and which he had laid upon his little table as I entered—I could not help noting the title for he laid it back up, open face down—was Lecky's *History of European Morals*!

Now!

Well!

IN RETROSPECT

Two years after this visit, in a serious attempt to set down what I really did think of him, I arranged the following thoughts with which I closed my sketch then and which I now append for what they may be worth. They represented my best thought concerning him then:

"William Muldoon belongs to that class of society which the

preachers and the world's army of conventional merchants, lawyers, judges and reputable citizens generally are presumably, if one may judge by the moral and religious literature of the day, trying to reach and reform. Yet here at his sanitarium are gathered representatives of those same orders, the so-called better element. And here we see them suddenly dominated, mind and soul, by this being whom they, theoretically at least, look upon as a brand to be snatched from the burning.

"As the Church and society view Muldoon, so they view all life outside their own immediate circles. Muldoon is in fact a conspicuous figure among the semi-taboo. He has been referred to in many an argument and platform and pulpit and in the press as a type of man whose influence is supposed to be vitiating. Now a minister enters the sanitarium, broken down by his habits of life, and this same Muldoon is able to penetrate him, to see that his dogmatic and dictatorial mental habits are the cause of his ailment, and he has the moral courage to shock him, to drag him by the apparently brutal processes out of his rut. He reads the man accurately, he knows him better than he knows himself, and he effects a cure.

"This astonishing condition is certainly a new light for those seeking to labor among men. Those who are successful gamblers, pugilists, pickpockets, saloon-keepers, book-makers, jockeys and the like are so by reason of their intelligence, their innate mental acumen and perception. It is a fact that in the sporting world and among the unconventional men-about-town you will often find as good if not better judges of human nature than elsewhere. Contact with a rough-and-ready and all-too-revealing world teaches them much. The world's customary pretensions and delusions are in the main ripped away. They are bruised by rough facts. Often the men gathered in some such café and whom preachers and moralists are most ready to condemn have a clearer perception of preachers, church organizations and reformers and their relative importance in the multitudinous life of the world than the preachers, church congregations and reformers have of those in the café or the world outside to which they belong.

"This is why, in my humble judgment, the Church and those associated with its aims make no more progress than they do. While they are consciously eager to better the world, they are

383

so wrapped up in themselves and their theories, so hampered by their arbitrary and limited conceptions of good and evil, that the great majority of men move about them unseen, except in a faraway and superficial manner. Men are not influenced at arm's length. It would be interesting to know if some day a preacher or judge, who, offended by Mr. Muldoon's profanity and brutality, will be able to reach the gladiator and convert him to his views as readily as the gladiator is able to rid him of his ailment."

In justice to the preachers, moralists, et cetera, I should now like to add that it is probably not any of the virtues or perfections represented by a man like Muldoon with which they are quarreling, but the vices of many who are in no wise like him and do not stand for the things he stands for. At the same time, the so-called "sports" might well reply that it is not with any of the really admirable qualities of the "unco guid" that they quarrel, but their too narrow interpretations of virtue and duty and their groundless generalization as to types and classes.

Be it so.

Here is meat for a thousand controversies.

Bibliography

THE PRINCIPAL SOURCES OF INFORMATION about Dreiser used in the preparation of this edition are as follows:

Dreiser, Theodore. *An Amateur Laborer.* Ed. Richard W. Dowell et al. Philadelphia: University of Pennsylvania Press, 1983.

_____. *American Diaries 1902–1926.* Ed. Thomas P. Riggio et al. Philadelphia: University of Pennsylvania Press, 1982.

_____. *An American Tragedy.* New York: Boni and Liveright, 1925.

_____. *The Bulwark.* Garden City, New York: Doubleday, 1946.

_____. *Chains.* New York: Boni and Liveright, 1927.

_____. *Dawn.* New York: Horace Liveright, 1931.

_____. *The Financier.* New York: Harper and Brothers, 1912.

_____. *Free and Other Stories.* New York: Boni and Liveright, 1918.

_____. *A Gallery of Women.* New York: Horace Liveright, 1929.

_____. *The "Genius."* New York: John Lane Company, 1915.

_____. *Jennie Gerhardt.* New York: Harper and Brothers, 1911.

_____. *Newspaper Days.* Ed. T.D. Nostwich. Philadelphia: University of Pennsylvania Press, 1991.

_____. *Sister Carrie.* Ed. John C. Berkey et al. Philadelphia: University of Pennsylvania Press, 1981.

_____. *The Stoic.* Garden City, New York: Doubleday, 1947.

_____. *The Titan.* New York: John Lane, 1914.

_____. *Twelve Men.* New York: Boni and Liveright, 1919.

Griffen, Joseph. *The Small Canvas.* Rutherford, New Jersey: Fairleigh Dickinson University Press, 1985.

Lingeman, Richard. *Theodore Dreiser.* 2 vols. New York: G.P. Putnam's Sons, 1986 & 1990.

In addition to the *OED* 1st and 2nd editions, *Webster's Second* and *Third International* dictionaries, and the 1986 edition of the *Encyclopedia Americana,* information in the notes has been drawn from the following reference works:

Berrey, Lester V., and Melvin Van Den Berk. *The American Thesaurus of Slang*. 2nd ed. New York: Crowell, 1952.

Marks, Edward B. *They All Sang*. New York: Viking, 1934.

Partridge, Eric. *A Dictionary of Catch Phrases*. New York: Stein and Day, 1977.

Webster's Biographical Dictionary. Springfield, Massachusetts: G. & C. Merriam, 1972.

Wentworth, Harold, and Stuart Berg Flexner. *Dictionary of American Slang*. 2nd ed. New York: Crowell, 1975.

N̲otes̲

Rella

20   **Foreword**   Deeming this story to be too directly confessional, Dreiser created the "nominal subterfuge" of having it narrated by an imaginary deceased poet.

21   **Rella**   Dreiser originally intended to call his protagonist *Nadine,* and so titled his manuscript, but he changed his mind, crossed out that name and replaced it with a shorter one which in turn was crossed out and replaced with *Rella.* The second name, though now difficult to read, could be *Rose.* As Yoshinobu Hakutani has pointed out, Rella is almost certainly modeled on Rose White, the younger sister of Dreiser's first wife Sara Osborne White, whose nickname was Jug. ("Dreiser and Rose White," *Library Chronicle,* 44 [Spring 1979], 27–31.) Throughout the first typescript of this story, the narrator refers to himself as "Uncle Theo" and his wife is called "Mrs. D." or "Aunt J." The father of Sara and Rose was Archibald Herndon White, a well-to-do farmer living near the village of Danville, Missouri. Active in local politics, he had been elected county sheriff in 1885. He is the subject of Dreiser's "A True Patriarch," one of the sketches in *Twelve Men* (1919). Sara White is also the prototype of Angela Blue, the wife of Eugene Witla, protagonist of Dreiser's thinly disguised autobiographical novel *The "Genius"* (1915), which analyzes in great detail the incompatibility of Dreiser and Sara leading to the ultimate collapse of their marriage. Sara also appears as Marjorie Duer, the possessive wife of the short story "Married" (1917; republished in *Free and Other Stories,* 1918). Rose White figures in *The "Genius"* as Marietta Blue, Angela's

younger sister, and she is characterized briefly in Dreiser's autobiography *Newspaper Days* as lively, witty, and mildly flirtatious. Sara and Rose appear to have had a close, affectionate relationship. While Dreiser admits in *Newspaper Days* that he found her somewhat enticing, there is no evidence that she ever entertained more than a friendly or sisterly feeling for him.

(In view of the fact that for two other stories in this collection—"'Vanity, Vanity,' Saith the Preacher" and "Muldoon, the Solid Man"—the aliases Dreiser gave the protagonists are replaced with their true names, the question may arise as to why here *Rella* is not replaced with *Rose,* and similarly why in the third story *Reina* is not called *Myrtle.* Though both of these stories derive from the character and experience of actual people, they are still semi-fictional; they do not literally adhere to fact. Rella's story is not exactly Rose's, nor is Reina's that of Myrtle.)

22.9   thirty . . . married   Dreiser was born August 27, 1871. He and Sara White were married December 28, 1898.

22.21   derived society   That is, our American society derives its moral code from the Judaic-Christian traditions of European societies.

22.32   I had just had a play accepted   In his manuscript Dreiser originally wrote "a novel." His first novel *Sister Carrie* had been tentatively accepted for publication in June 1900. The following month he visited his wife's family in Missouri.

24.23   the region pictured   That is, in the opening paragraph of this story.

26.36   Keats, Shelley, Hardy, Omar   John Keats (1795–1821) and Percy Bysshe Shelley (1792–1822) were leading English poets of the Romantic school. (In the galley page proof of *A Gallery of Women* Dreiser substituted Shelley's name for that of his original choice, William Ernest Henley (1849–1903), an English writer now remembered chiefly for his poem "Invictus.") Thomas Hardy (1840–1928) was an English novelist and poet whose fiction Dreiser profoundly admired. Omar Khayyám was a Persian poet of the late 11th century whose well-known *Rubáiyát,* a series of meditations on the mysteries of life, was widely read in Dreiser's time in the translation made by the English poet Edward Fitzgerald (1809–1883).

27.37   Kentucky feudist   Dreiser probably has in mind the Hatfield and McCoy families, who lived in the mountainous border area of Kentucky and West Virginia, and whose notorious blood-feud was frequently featured in newspaper stories during the early decades of this century.

29.5   cribbed, cabined, confined!   Cf. "cabin'd, cribb'd, confin'd" in *Macbeth*, III.iv.23.

30.17   dibble   A pointed instrument used to make holes in the ground, especially for seeds or plants.

31.4   mumblety-peg   A game in which players try to flip or throw a knife from various positions so that that blade will stick into the ground, the loser of the game having to pull out with his teeth a peg driven into the ground.

38.24   chaffered   That is, the leaves of the corn plants made a pleasant rustle as they brushed against each other.

38.30   sworded   The leaves of the mature corn plant have a shape similar to sword blades.

39.3   Arcady   A region of simple pleasure, rustic innocence, and untroubled quiet. From *Arcadia,* a mountainous region in Greece, fabled for the contented life of its simple rustic inhabitants.

47.23   celebrated poisoning case then in the papers   Perhaps a reference to the circumstances in the murder of Avis Linnell by her sweetheart, the Reverend Clarance Richesen, whose arrest and trial were very much in the news in 1911–12—one of the several cases of murder that Dreiser seriously considered using as the basis of his novel *An American Tragedy.*

48.37   I was all . . . but physically   See Dreiser's *An Amateur Laborer* for details of the nervous breakdown he suffered in 1901–2 as a consequence of the failure of *Sister Carrie* to win critical or popular acceptance.

49.4   The unhappy . . . broken up.   Though never legally divorced Dreiser and Sara separated permanently in 1914.

49.10   and this before thirty.   According to a letter from Sara Dreiser in the Dreiser letter collection at the University of Pennsylvania, Rose White died in late March 1918.

49.11   "What is man . . . . continueth not."   *Psalms* 8.4 and *Job* 14.2.

Peter

51   Peter   His fuller name was Peter B. McCord. Dreiser incorporated several passages from this story into his autobiography *Newspaper Days,* where he gives additional information about his relationship with McCord in St. Louis.

51.18   I had . . . from Chicago   During the summer of 1892 Dreiser had worked as a cub reporter for the Chicago *Daily Globe* where he had shown sufficient promise to be offered a job by the more prestigious St. Louis *Globe-Democrat.*

52.31   bagnio   brothel

53.35   Tenderloin   A district devoted to vice from which corrupt policemen and politicians extort graft.

54.23   cuspidor   A bowl-shaped receptacle for spit, tobacco ash, etc.

55.16   Dick Wood   At this point in the copy-text Dreiser supplies just the initials D——— W———, a concealment that seems rather pointless in view of his references to *Dick* throughout the rest of the story. For historical accuracy the initials are here replaced with the name. Like McCord, Wood figures prominently in *Newspaper Days,* where Dreiser uses his full name.

55.33   "Quartier Latin"   The quarter of Paris on the south side of the Seine which is traditionally the home of students, artists, and bohemians.

56.2   "soldiers three"   A reference to the protagonists—privates in the British army in India—whose adventures are the subject of *Soldiers Three* (1888) by the English writer Rudyard Kipling (1865–1936).

56.8   Cruikshankian   Like the figures caricatured in the pictures of the English artist George Cruikshank (1792–1878), who illustrated the novels of Charles Dickens and other writers.

56.19   *rapprochements*   harmonious relationships

56.30   Rabelaisian   A reference to the broad, coarse humor that characterizes the work of the French writer François Rabelais (c. 1494–1553).

57.23   instanter   instantly

58.25   Maspero . . . Avebury!   Gaston Maspero (1846–1916) French Egyptologist and author of books on archaeology.

James Anthony Froude (1818–1894) English historian. Thomas Henry Huxley (1825–1895) English scientist and essayist who championed the evolutionary theory of Charles Darwin (1809–1882). Alfred Russel Wallace (1823–1913) English naturalist who formulated the theory of natural selection. Henry Creswicke Rawlinson (1810–1895) English Assyriologist *or* his brother George Rawlinson (1812–1902) Orientalist and professor of ancient history. Jean Froissart (1333?–1400) French historian. Henry Hallam (1777–1859) English historian. Hippolyte Taine (1828–1893) French philosopher, literary critic, and historian. Avebury, i.e., Sir John Lubbock (1834–1913), 1st Baron Avebury, writer of popularized studies of archaeology and entomology.

59.14   Zoroastrians   Followers of the 6th-century B.C. Persian religious prophet Zoroaster.

59.14   Parsees   Descendants of Zoroastrians who sought refuge outside Persia, principally in Bombay.

59.16   Sidon and Tyre   Important seaports of ancient Phoenicia.

60.3   puling   whining

60.20   Celestial   Chinese, from "Celestial Empire," the name of the former Chinese Empire.

60.26   the Six Companies   For a discussion of this organization of merchants in San Francisco's Chinatown see Herbert Asbury's *The Barbary Coast* (1933).

61.31   chinks   A derogatory American term for Chinese people.

62.4   recherché   studiedly refined or elegant

63.22   Mermod & Jacquard's   One of the leading St. Louis jewelry stores.

65.17   peradventure   by chance

65.26   badger game   Dreiser uses this term rather loosely in referring to Peter's practical joke. Strictly defined a "badger game" is an extortion scheme by which a man is lured into a compromising position by a woman.

66.32   the following winter   Dreiser left St. Louis to seek his fortune in the East in March 1894.

66.36   a paper . . . New York   From 1895 to 1897 Dreiser edited a music journal, *Ev'ry Month,* for his brother Paul's song-publishing house.

67.13   (*Wolf . . . -Dweller*)   This novel was published in 1908, shortly after McCord's death, by the B.W. Dodge Company, in which firm Dreiser owned a part interest. The copy-text gives the incorrect subtitle *the Autobiography of a Cave Dweller.*

67.26   the then dominant paper   That is, the *North American* for which McCord worked from 1898 to 1900.

69.24   *Thaïs . . . Vadis?*   These novels are all set in the ancient world and have vividly detailed scenes of luxuriously decadent life styles characterized by sexual revelry and violence. *Thaïs* (1890), set in Egypt, is by the French novelist Anatole France (1844–1924). *Salammbô* (1862), set in Carthage, is by the French novelist Gustave Flaubert (1821–1880). *Sónnica la Cortesana* (1901), set in Iberia, is by the Spanish novelist Vincente Blasco-Ibañez (1867–1928). *Quo Vadis?* (1896), set in Rome, is by the Polish novelist Henryk Sienkiewicz (1846–1916). Since the earliest translation of *Sónnica* into English was not published until 1912, it does not seem probable that McCord would have been familiar with it.

70.19   leave this to your Uncle Dudley   That is, "leave it to me," a widely used, early 20th-century American catch phrase of undetermined origin.

70.39   stein or a half-schoppen   That is, a mug or a half-pint.

71.15   Dutchy—you never saw the beat!   That is, "You never saw anyone more German than she." *Dutchy* is a mildly derogatory American slang designation.

72.27   netsukes   "A small object carved in wood or ivory or wrought in metal, pierced with holes, and used by the Japanese as a toggle to fasten a small pouch or purse to the kimono sash." *Webster's Third International*

72.27   inros   "A small closed receptacle or set of receptacles used by the Japanese to hold medicines, perfumes, etc., and carried at the girdle." *Webster's Second International*

72.35   the leading paper   The *Newark Evening News,* for which McCord worked from 1900 to 1908.

72.36 Tokaido   That is, "Eastern Sea Route," the scenery and stopping points along which were depicted in color prints by the painter Hiroshige (1797–1858). The copy-text incorrectly reads *forty views.*

72.37 Hokusai   (1760–1849) Important Japanese artist who specialized in wood engraving and the illustration of books.

72.37 Sesshiu   Presumably Dreiser is referring to the Japanese landscape artist Sesshu (1419–1506).

72.37 [Toba] Sojo   (1053–1114) Japanese satirical painter.

74.32 "rat's killer"   McCord's humorous mispronunciation of *ratskeller,* a restaurant or beer hall located in the cellar of a public building.

75.2 [Mark] Hanna   (1837–1904) American businessman and politician; chief advisor and campaign manager to William McKinley.

75.2 [Henry Huddleston] Rogers   (1840–1909) American financier and chief executive officer of John D. Rockefeller's Standard Oil Corporation.

75.2 [John Pierpont] Morgan   (1837–1913) The leading American banker and financier of his day.

75.2 [Robert Edwin] Peary   (1856–1920) American arctic explorer; presumed discoverer of the North Pole.

75.3 [Edward Henry] Harriman   (1848–1909) American railroad magnate.

75.19 Old "Doc" Cook   That is, Frederick Albert Cook (1865–1940) American physician and arctic explorer whose controversial claim to have discovered the North Pole in 1908 has been generally discredited.

75.23 Munchausen   That is, Baron Karl F. H. von Munchhausen (1720–1797), German soldier and raconteur whose name is now proverbial for the incredible and exaggerated tales of his adventures as narrated by Rudolf Erich Raspe (1737–94), German author and swindler.

75.24 [Lemuel] Gulliver   The protagonist of the satirical fantasy *Gulliver's Travels* (1726) by the English writer Jonathan Swift (1667–1745).

75.24 Marco Polo (1254?–1324) Venetian traveler, famed for his account of his travels to the Orient.

77.3 ghoula Apparently a Dreiser coinage meaning "ghoulish person." The word occurs also in *Newspaper Days* (p. 579 of the 1991 University of Pennsylvania Press edition).

78.7 Metropolitan Museum of Art The principal art museum in New York City.

79.33 This particular hoax Careful and extensive research has not yet uncovered any contemporary newspaper stories on this hoax. Robert Coltrane has, however, found a statement in the *Amusement News and Weekly Record* for April 6, 1907 affirming that McCord once engaged in the hunt for an imaginary "wild man or two down in the midst of Monmouth county."

80.4 Barnum . . . minute A reference to the saying "There's a sucker born every minute," attributed to the American impressario and showman Phineas T. Barnum (1810–1891).

83.24 Stevenson . . . Hyde The Scottish writer Robert Louis Stevenson (1850–1894) published his famous novel *Dr. Jekyll and Mr. Hyde* in 1886.

83.39 *outré* beyond the bounds of propriety.

85.21 "So it's all day with Philadelphia" A 19th-century American regional expression meaning, in this instance, that the German girl in Philadephia now had no chance to marry Peter.

88.3 Culmbacher More correctly *Kulmbacher*; a dark-brown Bavarian beer with a sweet malty taste, thought to be especially nutritious for mothers breast-feeding their babies.

88.5 'dichtig, wichtig' Apparently a phrase coined by McCord that means something like "strict."

88.32 Have a kid or two or three. Dreiser never had any children.

89.35 les onfong McCord's comic pronunciation of *les enfants*.

90.23 publishing house From 1907 to 1910 was chief editor of three magazines published by the Butterick Company.

93.20 pottered An incorrectly used word, although Dreiser's meaning is clear. More appropriate would be *fired*.

Reina

95   Reina   This tale is based on the life and character of Myrtle Patges, the sister of Helen Richardson, Dreiser's mistress (and subsequently his wife), an aspiring movie actress with whom he lived in southern California from 1919 to 1922. The actual counterparts of some of the episodes narrated here are recorded in Dreiser's *American Diaries 1902–1926*. Myrtle also seems partly to have been Dreiser's model for the avaricious and flirtatious Hortense Briggs in *An American Tragedy*. An earlier version of "Reina" that was published in the *Century Magazine* of September 1923 adheres somewhat more closely to actual circumstances than does the *Gallery of Women* version.

95.4   Dutch   George Patges, the father of both Helen and Myrtle, was Danish and is so described in the *Century* version of this story.

95.29 her stories   See Dreiser's *American Diaries 1902–1926*, pp. 337 and 387, for an inkling of the kind of stories Myrtle told.

96.3   Rhoda, the elder half-sister   Helen Richardson was Myrtle's full sister. The *Century* version identifies Rhoda as "the elder sister."

96.36 Sven   His real name was Grell.

98.14 Easterner from upper New York State   The *Century* version reads "a Southerner." Helen's estranged husband, Frank Richardson, was from Charleston, South Carolina.

98.33 *The Pot of Basil*   A painting that illustrates John Keats' poem "Isabella, or the Pot of Basil," made in 1849 by the English artist John Everett Millais (1829–1896).

98.39 Pantages   A leading movie and vaudeville theatre in Hollywood in the early 1920s.

100.12 The perils of Pauline   *The Perils of Pauline* (1914) was one of the earliest cliff-hanging movie serials. It featured the wild adventures and hairbreadth escapes of a young heroine played by the screen actress Pearl White.

101.4 *dolce far niente*   Pleasing inactivity. Italian for "It is sweet to do nothing."

101.26 "chick"   Reina's pronunciation of *chic*.

104.16 squeak   Slang for either "minor" or "close."

104.30 one of these for Sven   That is, Sven was going to have to rent one of these high-priced apartments.

107.12 victrola   The trade name for a phonograph; especially, when capitalized, one made by the Victor Talking Machine Company.

111.5 Delsarte   A system or method of using body movements to express emotional concepts; named after its originator François Delsarte (1811–1871).

114.19 turnout   That is, an automobile.

114.20 quarrels . . . Rhoda   Emended from the copy-text's misleading "adventures between her and Rhoda."

115.1 For one . . . an accident. See *American Diaries 1902–1926*, pp. 376, 380.

117.34 elevator starter   One who is posted in front of elevators to supervise the entry of passengers and to signal the operator when to close the door and start moving. See *American Diaries 1902–1926*, p. 383.

117.39 flapper   In 1920s slang, a highly unconventional young woman.

118.8 tin Lizzies   Cheap automobiles, especially Fords.

119.28 *The Way of All Flesh*   A posthumously published novel (1903) by the English writer Samuel Butler (1835–1902).

120.14 California top   A colored or fancy cloth automobile top having either a folding frame or a non-folding one with glass windows.

120.31 Francesca and Paolo   The story of the adulterous love affair of Francesca da Rimini and Paolo Malatesta is told in the fifth canto of Dante's *Inferno*.

120.33 Stygian   "infernal," "hellish" (derived from the mythological River Styx).

122.1 fulsomely   Dreiser uses this word in its obsolete sense of "copiously" or "abundantly."

122.5 the Selkirks   A mountain range.

122.16 candy girl   A slang term of approbation, meaning something like "star pupil."

123.19 Orpheum Circuit   A nationwide chain of vaudeville theatres.

"Vanity, Vanity," Saith the Preacher

127   Title "Vanity, . . . Preacher" *Eccles. 1.2*

127.3   [Joseph G.] Robin   Throughout the copy-text of this narrative, written and published when Robin and his chief adversary were still alive, Dreiser concealed their identities with the aliases "X———" and "Y———." Since both men and some other people who figure here have long been dead, no reason exists to hide their names when they are known.

127.7   Mr. Morgan . . . Mr. Brady   John Pierpont Morgan (1837–1913); August Belmont (1853–1924); Edward Henry Harriman (1848–1909); Russell Sage (1816–1906); John Warne ("Bet-a-Million") Gates (1855–1911); James Buchanan ("Diamond Jim") Brady (1856–1917). All were nationally famed financiers in turn-of-the-century New York.

127.12 *Frenzied Finance*   (1902) was written by stock-market speculator Thomas W. Lawson (1857–1925).

127.12 *Lawless Wealth*   (1908) was written by journalist, author, and socialist Charles Edward Russell (1860–1941).

127.14 Charles W[yman] Morse   (1856–1933) New York promoter and banker, sent to prison in 1910 for falsifying records and misapplying funds.
F[rederick] Augustus Heinze   (1869–1914) magnate, involved in extensive legal broils for control of copper interests.
E[dward] R[ussell] Thomas   (1874–1926) wealthy financier and sportsman; charged with, but not found guilty of illegal manipulation of insurance company funds in 1908.
David A. Sullivan   president of a Brooklyn bank wrecked in the 1907 panic; sent to prison for grand larceny in 1913.

128.21 man Robin.   At this point in the copy-text occurs the following sentence omitted from this edition: "I refuse to mention his name because he is still alive although no longer conspicuous, and anxious perhaps to avoid the uncomfortable glare of publicity when all the honors and comforts which made it endurable in the first place are absent."

128.29 'Icarus'   In writing this narrative Dreiser compiled a large file of notes and newspaper clippings about Robin, which is now in the Dreiser Collection at the University of Pennsylvania. One of the notes indicates that *The Flight of Icarus: An Idyll of Printing House Square* was published in 1898 by the F. Tennyson Neely Company. No book by Robin with this title is listed in the National Union Catalog however.

130.9   fidus Achates   That is, "faithful Achates," the proverbially loyal friend of Aeneas in Virgil's *Aeneid.*

130.24   frou frou   Fancy accessories and amenities.

130.37   Bacchus or Pan   In classical mythology Bacchus is the god of wine, and Pan is the half-man, half-goat god of forests, flocks, and shepherds who is associated with riotous festivities.

131.2   sideboard   A side table in a dining room on which food and drink are laid out for guests to help themselves.

132.23   But mine host, . . . attention.   Two critics note in this passage and elsewhere a marked resemblance between Robin and F. Scott Fitzgerald's Gatsby. See Maxwell Geismar's *Rebels and Ancestors* (1953) p. 342, and Eric Solomon's "A Source for Fitzgerald's *The Great Gatsby,*" *MLN* 73 (March 1958), 186–88.

133.4   his country house   Clippings in Dreiser's Robin file locate this house, called Driftwood, at Wading River, Long Island. Built of cement, it had twenty-five rooms and five baths, and it occupied a 110-acre tract two-thirds of a mile long on the Sound.

134.3   Can Grande   That is, Can Francesco della Scala (1291–1329), Italian nobleman of Verona, patron of the arts and of Dante during the latter's exile from Florence.

134.36   of sand . . . sand-binding grasses.   An emendation of the copy-text's incoherent "of sand held together in places in the form of hummocks and even concealing hills by sand-binding grasses."

135.23   [Adolphe J.T.] Monticelli   (1824–1886) French painter. [Antonio] Mancini (1852–1930) Italian painter.

138.6   one winter's day   The news of the collapse of Robin's financial empire was first reported in New York newspapers on 28 December 1910.

139.25   a bachelor sister   Dr. Louise G. Robinovitch or Rabinowitz was a practicing psychiatrist.

139.31 great lawyers   Robin was defended by William Travers Jerome (1859–1934), a celebrated New York trial lawyer and one-time district attorney.

143.8   Mr. August Belmont   In the copy-text Dreiser conceals Belmont's identity under the alias "Mr. Y———." Contemporary newsclippings in Dreiser's Robin file reveal his name however. One unidentified clipping, possibly of 30 December 1910, gives Belmont's warning to Robin in almost the same words Dreiser uses.

143.33 Western power deal   New York newspapers for 11 August 1905 reported that Robin had made $500,000 by signing over his control of the Niagara, Lockport, and Ontario Power Company to H. H. Westinghouse of the Westinghouse Company.

145.11 Max Donath   An undated clipping from the New York *World* in Dreiser's Robin file quotes this testimony as that of Donath. In the copy-text Dreiser used the alias Henry Dom.

146.16 I have . . . him since.   Actually Dreiser's *American Diaries* reveal a continuing relationship with Robin, who succeeded to a degree in rehabilitating himself after release from prison. He became associated with a New York law firm, and Dreiser consulted him about legal details in *An American Tragedy*. Under the pseudonym "Odin Gregory" he published two verse tragedies: *Caius Gracchus* (1920) with an introduction by Dreiser, and *Jesus: the Tragedy of Man* (1923).

Fulfilment

147   Title   A brief analysis of this story is in Joseph Griffin's *The Small Canvas: An Introduction to Dreiser's Short Stories* (1985), pp. 88–90.

147.12 forced . . . her   Emended from the copy-text's *forced or persuaded upon her*.

151.30 Lord Byron (1788–1824), [Percy Bysshe] Shelley (1792–1822), and [John] Keats (1795–1821) were leading poets of the Romantic period in English literature. [Franz] Liszt (1811–1886) was a celebrated Hungarian pianist and composer.

155.11 adream   Emended from the copy-text's *a—dream*, a misreading of Dreiser's typescript.

165.18 only the needs of   Emended from the copy-text's *only because of.*

Mathewson

167.5   *Globe-Democrat*   Dreiser began working for this paper in early November 1892.

167.19 Mr. Mitchell   A vivid portrait of Tobias Mitchell can be found in Dreiser's *Newspaper Days.*

167.20 St. Louis terminal accident   No newspaper story fitting this description and printed during Dreiser's stay in St. Louis has been identified.

168.1   [Hugh Keller] Hartung   The copy-text gives the name "Kitnong" for this person, but from the characterization of Hartung in *Newspaper Days* it is clear that Dreiser is thinking of him.

169.18 Rodenberger   Fuller characterization of this reporter is found in *Newspaper Days.*

170.14 [Thomas] De Quincey (1785–1859), the English essayist, and [Edgar Allan] Poe (1809–1849) were addicted respectively to opium and alcohol. [Daniel] Defoe (1660?–1731), the English novelist and pamphleteer, was, however, not addicted to any drugs.

171.39 whited sepulchres   That is, hypocrites. See *Matt.* 23.27.

172.4   *Globe* or *Republic*   No article on Zola appeared in either paper during Dreiser's stay in St. Louis.

172.5   Émile Zola   (1840–1902) Principal novelist of the French school of naturalistic fiction.

173.6   Rougon-Maquart . . . *Nana*   The twenty novels studying the members of the Rougon and Maquart families during the period of the Second Empire were published between 1871 and 1893. *L'Assommoir* appeared in 1877 and *Nana* in 1880. *Thérèse Raquin* (1867) is Zola's first naturalistic novel but is not part of the Rougon–Maquart series.

173.19 *Republic* (to . . . services)   Dreiser abruptly resigned from his job at the *Globe-Democrat* at the end of April 1893 and began working for the *Republic* some days later.

175.16 Chaplinesque   That is, in the manner of the pathetic little tramp character made world famous by the motion-picture actor Charles Chaplin (1889–1972).

176.1 "Ach, Himmel"   Oh, Heaven.

180.32 delicate but iron reserve   The cryptic reading *his delicate iron* occurs at this point in the typescript, p. 17, line 14; for this has been substituted a more meaningful phrase taken from p. 18, line 19, of the typescript.

182.1 [Charles] Baudelaire   (1821–1867) French poet whose famous collection of poems *Les Fleurs du Mal* appeared in 1857.

182.11 Anatole France (1844–1924), Pierre Loti (1850–1923), and [Guy] de Maupassant (1850–1893) were leading French writers of fiction.

183.28 chemisms   chemical activities

183.36 Sir William Hamilton   (1788–1856) Scottish philospher who published works on metaphysics and logic.

184.29 football . . . report   Dreiser wrote a short series of comic articles on a charity football game for the *Republic* in late December 1893.

184.30 a new girl   At this time Dreiser was courting Sara Osborne White who became his first wife.

184.34 spats   short gaiters worn over shoes to protect them from the spattering of mud and rain.

185.18 John Addington Symonds   (1840–1893) English poet, essayist, and literary historian, best known for his *Renaissance in Italy* (1875–1886).

185.19 [Abraham] Viktor Rydberg   (1828–1895) Swedish freethinker, poet, novelist, and crtic. "The Aphrodite of Melos" was written in 1874 and published in translation in *Roman Days,* an 1879 collection of his essays.

185.20 Voltaire's *Candide*   This well-known satiric novel by the famous eighteenth-century French writer appeared in 1759.

185.21 Blake's William Blake (1757–1827) English artist, poet, and mystic.

186.36 'Sound . . . nothing.' *Macbeth,* V.v.27.

189.17 The fall . . . St. Louis. Dreiser left to seek his fortune in the East in early March 1894.

189.26 Pittsburgh Dreiser worked for the *Pittsburgh Dispatch* from mid-May through most of November 1894.

The "Mercy" of God

191 A brief analysis of this story is in Joseph Griffin's *The Small Canvas,* pp. 91-93.

191.26 Keshub Chunder Sen (1838–1884), also known as Keshab Chandra Sen, Hindu social reformer, writer, and philosopher.

192.1 A friend . . . of Freud Dreiser clearly refers to his friend A[braham] A[rden] Brill (1874–1948), American psychiatrist who lectured at New York University 1914–1925 and is well known as a translator of Freud's works.

192.36 eminent physiologist Presumably Jacques Loeb (1859–1924), German-born physiologist who was a member of the Rockefeller Institute for Medical Research (1910–1924) and whose books, especially *The Mechanistic Conception of Life* (1912), exerted a profound influence on Dreiser's thought.

194.9 'I returned . . . them all.' *Eccle.* 9.11. Dreiser omits "nor yet riches to men of understanding," which occurs between "the wise" and "nor yet."

197.29 Vae Victis. "Woe to the conquered"; from Livy's history of Rome, *Ab Urbe condita,* V.48.

199.17 George Moore (1852–1933), Irish novelist whose work was heavily influenced by French realist writers.

199.17 [Feodor] Dostoyevsky (1821–1881), famed Russian novelist, perhaps best known for *Crime and Punishment* (1866) and *The Brothers Karamazov* (1880).

202.39 'fixy' fussy, particular, elegant

205.6   probity   Here the copy-text gives the word *polarity,* which has no relevance to the context. It seems clear that Dreiser intended something like *probity* to convey the idea of strict moral rectitude.

207.5   "red of beak and claw"   From *In Memoriam* (1850), 56.15, by the Engish poet Alfred, Lord Tennyson (1809–1892). The precise wording is "red in tooth and claw."

Ida Hauchawout

209.2   rural setting   Dreiser may have gathered the material for this narrative while staying at a friend's farmhouse near Westminster, Maryland, in June and July 1917.

214.9   unpivoted   lacking center, unstable

215.35 nibblish   hesitant

217.29 accouchement   period of confinement in childbirth

220.29 Karnak   The ruins of ancient Thebes in Egypt.
Acropolis   The ruins of ancient Athens, especially the Parthenon.
"Ode on a Grecian Urn"   One of the best-known poems of the English Romantic poet John Keats.

221.8   of the frame, it could not   Emended from the copy-text's *of the frame it held, it could not.*

221.23 face—the hand of the other arm holding Widdle's poem.   Emended from the copy-text's *face, the other, the hand of the same—Widdle's poem.*

Chains

231   This story, originally entitled "Love," is based upon personal experiences related to Dreiser by Louise Campbell, his sometime lover, long-time secretary and editor. See *American Diaries 1902–1926,* p. 232. A brief analysis of this story is in Joseph Griffin's *The Small Canvas,* pp. 77-81.

231.2   K———   Presumably to mask the identity of the prototypes of Garrison and Idelle, Dreiser resorts to using initials instead of city names, except for Pittsburgh. Given the source of this story we can speculate that *G*—— is Philadelphia (Louise Campbell's place of residence) and that *K*—— is probably Chicago. *E*—— would then likely be Ohio and its capital *Centerfield,* Columbus.

231.11 "thé dansant"   An informal dance held at teatime.

231.29 trig   trim, neat, spruce, smart

233.11 *"Yes, all . . . ticket!"*   Garrison addresses this remark to the railroad porter who is going to carry his bags on board the train.

241.8   thirty-four   The copy-text reads *twenty-four,* but other details in the story indicate that Garrison would have had to be at least ten years older at this point in his life.

242.11 a "blood"   A foppish man; short for "sporting blood."

244.22 How wonderful . . . . unconscious of them.   This passage, which occurs in Dreiser's typescript of "Chains" but not in the copy-text, is reprinted here because it provides more detailed characterization of Idelle. Perhaps it was omitted from the copy-text because Dreiser thought it betrayed too much of Louise Campbell's presumably confidential revelation to him. The typescript is in the Dreiser Collection at the University of Pennsylvania. This and subsequent passages from it, which are included for their added information about the main characters, are reprinted courtesy of the Van Pelt-Dietrich Library Center.

245.28 Pittsburgh   The copy-text here reads *B*——, but since Dreiser elsewhere identifies the locale in question as Pittsburgh, no purpose is served in concealing its identity at this point.

246.22 But somehow . . . . *the darkness!*   A passage from the typescript that was omitted from the copy-text.

248.12 return home, when . . . in Pittsburgh.   A passage from the typescript that was omitted from the copy-text.

250.3   evil pursuers . . . representatives generally.   A passage from the typescript that was omitted from the copy-text.

250.17 Coulstone   The copy-text reads *J*—— *C*——, but it is clear that the reference is to the previously mentioned Coulstone, and in the earliest published version of this story ("Love" in the New York *Tribune* of 18 May 1919) that name is used.

To prevent needless confusion, *Coulstone* replaces *J——C——* here and when it occurs later in the story on pages 251 and 252.

250.22   Coulstone had . . . on the scene.   A passage from the typescript that was omitted from the copy-text.

251.14   varietism   The practice of having sexual liaisons with a variety of lovers.

254.16   blank-blanked   Dreiser ordinarily did not use explicit epithets that genteel publishers and book reviewers in the early decades of this century would have deemed indecent or profane. Instead when writing his stories he customarily left empty spaces in his text or wrote words like *blank-blanked* instead of such commonplace oaths as *god-damned* and *son of a bitch.*

260.6   hubbies, "he . . . . years."   A passage from the typescript that was omitted from the copy-text.

261.16   collars   "Chains" takes place in the 1920s when men's dress shirts had detachable, replaceable collars.

The Second Choice

263   Dreiser based this story on his brief love affair of 1892 with Lois Zahn, a young Chicago department store clerk, the details of which are given in *Newspaper Days.* A brief analysis of "The Second Choice" is in Joseph Griffin's *The Small Canvas,* pp. 48-53.

275.9   retiring room   a dressing room

278.27   Dead Sea fruit   Something bitter or disappointing; a proverbial expression deriving ultimately from *Deut.* 32.32.

279.21   coal pockets   large storage bins of coal

282.27   fichu   A woman's light neck scarf or shawl of muslin or lace.

Sanctuary

283   A somewhat abridged version of this story was first published in *Smart Set* for October 1919, pp. 35-52. A brief analysis is in Joseph Griffin's *The Small Canvas,* pp.81-87.

285.18 growler   A pitcher, pail, or other container brought to a saloon by a customer for beer.

289.39 Wurra   A traditional Irish expression of woe.

297.8   Before this . . . suicide.   This sentence occurs in the *Smart Set* version but is omitted from the *Chains* copy-text. It is retained here because of the insight it gives into Mother Bertha's sympathy for Madeleine.

298.15 the peal of the Angelus   In Roman Catholic churches, a bell is rung at 6 a.m., noon, and 6 p.m. to indicate that it is time to recite the Angelus, a devotion in memory of the Annunication.

299.12 a machine   That is, an automobile

306.4   Fagins   Fagin, a character in Charles Dickens' novel *Oliver Twist* (1837–1838), trains young boys to be thieves and pickpockets.

310.21 twilled skirt   A skirt of material woven in the twill pattern.

Bridget Mullanphy

315.36 protectory   An institution for the care and protection of homeless or delinquent children.

316.36 vagrom   An archaic variant of *vagrant,* much favored by Dreiser in his writings.

317.37 the neo-impressionists of 1912   Originally Dreiser wrote *1917* in the page proof of *A Gallery of Women.* Perhaps he intended to refer to the famous Armory Show of 1913, an exhibition in New York City sponsored by the Association of American Painters and Sculptors which introduced various schools of modern painting to the American public.

319.23 roilin's   That is, the dregs or sediment.

320.19 Hogarthian   A reference to the sordid world depicted in some of the engravings of eighteenth-century London life by the Engish artist William Hogarth (1697–1764).

324.34 deserted . . . conditions   That is, they had deserted their place of employment.

325.3 Cornelia . . . returned fairly laden with spoils from   Emended from the copy-text's misleading *nieces were present, fairly laden with spoils.*

325.28 to "scab"   To cross union picket lines to take the place of a striking worker.

327.20 whisht ye!"   Hush!

328.10 fer one   Emended from the copy-text's *fer me,* a misreading of Dreiser's typescript.

337.14 Village   That is, Greenwich Village in lower Manhattan, the traditional locale of artists, writers, and bohemians in the early decades of the twentieth century. Dreiser lived there from 1914 to 1919.

Muldoon, the Solid Man

341   The subject of this narrative is William Muldoon (1845–1933), a champion wrestler and physical culturist who operated a sanatorium for debilitated men at Olympia, three miles north of White Plains, New York, beginning in 1900. Dreiser stayed at Olympia from April 21 to June 2, 1903. When he later came to describe Muldoon for his portrait gallery *Twelve Men,* he changed his name to *Culhane,* true to his customary practice of concealing the identities of persons still alive at the time he wrote about them. The sobriquet "the Solid Man," which was actually applied to the athlete, was derived from "Muldoon, the Solid Man," a popular song of the 1870s by Ned Harrigan, which was used in a humorous skit of the same title, also by Harrigan. *Solid* in the context of the song means more nearly *staunch, reliable,* or *unbreakable* than *physically strong.* Once William Muldoon had gained fame as a wrestler, he probably became quickly associated in the public mind with the song. Like many readers of *Twelve Men,* Muldoon, according to his biographer, recognized himself as the real subject of Dreiser's story (even though he had not actually read it), and he was not at all pleased with what he was told had been said there. (See Edward Van Every's *Muldoon the Solid Man of Sport,* 1929, pp. 265-66.) Though the portrait is not entirely flattering, Dreiser nevertheless had a sincere respect for Muldoon as an exponent of the philosophy of self-help, and the famous athlete appears to have long exerted an

407

influence on Dreiser, who as late at 1944 wrote of him as "a force which I . . . have felt throughout my life." Since Muldoon died long ago, no compelling reason exists to continue masking his identity. Throughout this text, therefore, the alias *Culhane* has been changed to the true name.

341.1   psychic depression . . . . sick spiritually   Dreiser's condition stemmed primarily from the disheartening circumstances attending the publication in 1900 of his first novel *Sister Carrie*. See *An Amateur Laborer*.

341.8   [Helena] Modjeska   (1840–1909) Polish-born dramatic actress who toured the American stage from 1877 on.

341.9   Before or . . . anyone.   Muldoon trained John L. Sullivan (1858–1918) for his championship bout with Jake Kilrain, fought on July 8, 1889.

341.12 Before that . . . to America   Edward Van Every states that Muldoon was born in the Genesee Valley district of New York state and that his father was a relatively well-educated Irish immigrant. (*Muldoon the Solid Man of Sport*, p. 13.)

341.13 Bowery   A section of lower Manhattan, known in the latter half of the nineteenth century for its cheap theatres and disreputable dance halls.

341.16 "short-change man"   A ticket-seller who short-changes customers.

342.18 my dear brother   Paul Dresser (1857–1906) Dreiser's eldest brother. (A comic actor, he changed his last name from *Dreiser* for stage effectiveness.) For a fuller account of the circumstances of Paul's sending Dreiser to Muldoon's sanatorium, see *An Amateur Laborer*.

343.18 medicine balls   Large, solid, heavy, leather-covered balls, thrown for exercise.

343.34 ostlers   Persons who take care of horses at an inn or similar institution.

344.4   *de rigueur*   That is, strictly required, as by etiquette, usage, or fashion.

344.6   Richelieu   (1585–1642) French cardinal and statesman; served as prime minister under Louis XIII.

344.6 Duc de Guise   A member of the powerful Guise family of the province of Lorraine that exercised great influence during the 16th and 17th centuries. It is not clear which particular individual, if any, Dreiser is referring to.

344.9 quirt   A riding whip consisting of a short, stout stock and a lash of braided leather.

345.23 feed his driver   tipped his driver

347.34 osseosity   boniness (apparently Dreiser's coinage)

347.35 Hoti-like   A reference to the familiar figure noted for his cheerful smile and protruding belly, one of the "Seven Gods of Luck" in Japanese mythology.

347.37 horn glasses   That is, horn-rimmed glasses.

347.37 pince-nezes   Glasses held on the face by a spring which pinches the nose.

348.4 lymphatic   In Dreiser's sense, *languid, passive,* and *lacking in mental and physical energy.*

348.19 whiskerando   A heavily whiskered man.

352.24 grave and reverend senior   See *Othello,* I.iii.76.

355.16 lobster . . . the way   Muldoon is alluding to *lobster* in its slang sense of *fool* or *dupe.*

361.25 "frog and switch" company   A company manufacturing parts for railroad junctions.

361.26 neurasthenia   functional nervous weakness

363.3 the Ten Thousand from Cunaxa   In his *Anabasis,* the Greek historian Xenophon chronicles the arduous retreat to the sea of Greek troops after the battle of Cunaxa (401 BC), a site near Babylon.

376.26 Charles A[nderson] Dana   (1819–1897) Owner and editor of the New York *Sun.*

377.8 "Donnervetter! . . . rufen!"   "By thunder! That pig of a dog! That dog's bone! Someone call the police!"

380.1 fish-horn   A cheap tin horn used primarily as a noise-maker on fishing boats or by sellers of fish.

380.39 Sheol   In Hebrew theology, the abode of the dead; less literally, hell.

381.31 Napoleon . . . Wilderness   Napoleon's troops defeated the Austrian forces at Lodi in Lombardy in northern Italy on May 10, 1796. Grant's Wilderness campaign of May–June 1864 was fought west of Fredericksburg, Virginia. Dreiser may have in mind a well-known Mathew Brady photograph of Grant standing before his tent. What picture of Napoleon he is referring to, if any, has not been determined.

382.27 *The History of European Morals from Augustus to Charlemagne*   by the Irish historian William Edward Hartpole Lecky (1838–1903) was first published in 1869.

384.15 "unco guid"   Dreiser probably takes this term from "Address to the Unco Guid, or the Rigidly Righteous" (1786), a famous poem of the Scottish poet Robert Burns (1759–1796).

Printed September 1992 in Santa Barbara &
Ann Arbor for the Black Sparrow Press by
Mackintosh Typography & Edwards Brothers Inc.
Text set in Sabon by Words Worth.
Design by Barbara Martin. This edition
is published in paper wrappers; there are
250 hardcover trade copies; & 126 numbered
deluxe copies have been handbound in
boards by Earle Gray.

Theodore Dreiser ca. 1915 (Photo by Marceau).

T. D. NOSTWICH is a Professor of English at Iowa State University. He is editor of *"Heard in the Corridors": Articles and Related Writings by Theodore Dreiser* (Iowa State University Press, 1988); *Theodore Dreiser Journalism, Volume I: Newspaper Writings, 1892–1895* (University of Pennsylvania Press, 1988); and *Newspaper Days* by Theodore Dreiser (University of Pennsylvania Press, 1991). *Fulfilment & Other Tales of Women & Men* is the first of a series of volumes by Dreiser that T. D. Nostwich will edit for Black Sparrow Press.